A DREAM OF TRUE TIME

A Dream of True Time

True Time Trilogy
Volume One

AVTAR SIMRIT

Apocalyptic Rhymes

Copyright © 2021 by Avtar Simrit

All rights reserved. No part of this book may be reproduced in any manner whatsoever without written permission except in the case of brief quotations embodied in critical articles and reviews.

First Printing, 2021

To Aleks, Elan, and Karan Prem;
my Violet Perfect, Perfect Forever,
and Perfect Spirit.

And

To Sherry;
without the Spiralverse using you
to find the unfinished manuscript,
these books may never have manifested.

CONTENTS

BOOK ONE
Through the Hollow

PART 1
Switchup

PART 2
The Soulmind

PART 3
The Realm of Infallibility

PART 4
Tripping Time

BOOK TWO
Wandering in a Dream

PART 5
Switchblade

PART 6
The Violet Perfect

PART 7
In Silence, In Pain

PART 8
The Perfect Forever

BOOK THREE
The Tethered Toys Come Out to Play

PART 9
Switchback

PART 10
Transcending the Schism of Duality

PART 11
GOD: Generator, Organizer, Destroyer-Deliverer

ABOUT THE AUTHOR
587

~ The Cats Of Ulthar ~

BY HP LOVECRAFT

It is said that in Ulthar, which lies beyond the river Skai, no man may kill a cat; and this I can verily believe as I gaze upon him who sitteth purring before the fire. For the cat is cryptic, and close to strange things which men cannot see. He is the soul of antique Aegyptus, and bearer of tales from forgotten cities in Meroe and Ophir. He is the kin of the jungle's lords, and heir to the secrets of hoary and sinister Africa. The Sphinx is his cousin, and he speaks her language; but he is more ancient than the Sphinx, and remembers that which she hath forgotten.

In Ulthar, before ever the burgesses forbade the killing of cats, there dwelt an old cotter and his wife who delighted to trap and slay the cats of their neighbors. Why they did this I know not; save that many hate the voice of the cat in the night, and take it ill that cats should run stealthily about yards and gardens at twilight. But whatever the reason, this old man and woman took pleasure in trapping and slaying every cat which came near to their hovel; and from some of the sounds heard after dark, many villagers fancied that the manner of slaying was exceedingly peculiar. But the villagers did not discuss such things with the old man and his wife; because of the habitual expression on the withered faces of the two, and because their cottage was so small and so darkly hidden under spreading oaks at the back of a neglected yard. In truth, much as the owners of cats hated these odd folk, they feared them more; and instead of berating them as brutal assassins, merely took care that no cherished pet or mouser should stray toward the remote hovel under the dark trees. When through some unavoidable oversight a cat was missed, and sounds heard after dark, the loser would lament impotently; or console himself by thanking Fate that it was not one of his children who had thus vanished. For the people of Ulthar were simple, and knew not whence it is all cats first came.

One day a caravan of strange wanderers from the South entered the narrow cobbled streets of Ulthar. Dark wanderers they were, and unlike the other roving folk who passed through the village twice every year. In the market-place they told fortunes for silver, and bought gay beads from the merchants. What was the land of these wanderers none could tell; but it was seen that they were given to strange prayers, and that they had painted on the sides of their wagons strange figures with human bodies and the heads of cats, hawks, rams and lions. And the leader of the caravan wore a headdress with two horns and a curious disk betwixt the horns.

On the third morning of the wanderers' stay in Ulthar, Menes could not find his kitten; and as he sobbed aloud in the market-place certain villagers told him of the old man and his wife, and of the sounds heard in the night. And when he heard these things his sobbing gave place to meditation, and finally to prayer. He stretched out his arms toward the sun and prayed in a tongue no villager could understand; though indeed the villagers did not try very hard to understand, since their attention was mostly taken up by the sky and the odd shapes the clouds were assuming. It was very peculiar, but as the little boy uttered his petition there seemed to form overhead the shadowy, nebulous figures of exotic things; of hybrid creatures crowned with horn-flanked disks. Nature is full of such illusions to impress the imaginative.

That night the wanderers left Ulthar, and were never seen again. And the householders were troubled when they noticed that in all the village there was not a cat to be found. From each hearth the familiar cat had vanished; cats large and small, black, grey, striped, yellow and white. Old Kranon, the burgomaster, swore that the dark fold had taken the cats away in revenge for the killing of Menes' kitten; and cursed the caravan and the little boy. But Nith, the lean notary, declared that the old cotter and his wife were more likely persons to suspect; for their hatred of cats was notorious and increasingly bold. Still, no one durst complain to the sinister couple; even when little Atal, the innkeeper's son, vowed that he had at twilight seen all the cats of Ulthar in that accursed yard under the trees, pacing very slowly and solemnly in a circle around the cottage, two abreast, as if in performance of some unheard-of rite of beasts. The villagers did not know how much to believe from so small a boy; and though they feared that the evil pair had charmed the cats to their death, they preferred not to chide the old cotter till they met him outside his dark and repellent yard.

So Ulthar went to sleep in vain anger; and when the people awakened at dawn—behold! every cat was back at his accustomed hearth! Large and small, black, grey, striped, yellow and white, none was missing. Very sleek and fat did the cats appear, and sonorous with purring content. The citizens talked with one another of the affair, and marveled not a little. Old Kranon again insisted that it was the dark fold who had taken them, since cats did not return alive from the cottage of the ancient man and his wife. But all agreed on one thing: that the refusal of all the cats to eat their portions of meat or drink their saucers of milk was exceedingly curious. And for two whole days the sleek, lazy cats of Ulthar would touch no food, but only doze by the fire or in the sun.

It was fully a week before the villagers noticed that no lights were appearing at dusk in the windows of the cottage under the trees. Then the lean Nith remarked that no one had seen the old man or his wife since the night the cats were away. In another week the burgomaster decided to overcome his fears and call at the strangely silent dwelling as a matter of duty, though in so doing he was careful to take with him Shang the blacksmith and Thul the cutter of stone as witnesses. And when they had broken down the frail door they found only this: two cleanly picked human skeletons on the earthen floor, and a number of singular beetles crawling in the shadowy corners.

There was subsequently much talk among the burgesses of Ulthar. Zath, the coroner, disputed at length with Nith, the lean notary; and Kranon and Shang and Thul were overwhelmed with questions. Even little Atal, the innkeeper's son, was closely questioned and given a sweetmeat as a reward. They talked of the old cotter and his wife, of the caravan of dark wanderers, of small Menes and his black kitten, of the prayer of Menes and of the sky during that prayer, of the doing of the cats on the night the caravan left, and of what was later found in the cottage under the dark trees in the repellent yard.

And in the end the burgesses passed that remarkable law which is told of by traders in Hatheg and discussed by travelers in Nir; namely, that in Ulthar no man may kill a cat.

"The thing about a story is that you dream it as you tell it, hoping that others might dream along with you, and in this way memory and imagination and language combine to make spirits in the head."

- Tim O'Brien, *The Things They Carried*

BOOK ONE

Through the Hollow

Life is a search for answers that never existed.
As humans it is only natural to look for
answers to these questions.
But as we search, we accumulate
more questions than when we started.
So we are plagued with thoughts;
thoughts that come from a mind
that can't comprehend them.

PART 1

Switchup

*Living and dying,
we feed the fire.*

- Clive Barker, *Sacrament*

Apart

The years of my existence
Have not yet been a hinderance
To my mind of chains and steel.
These sixteen years I've been
Out of luck sometimes
In years long since past,
But now in 2006
I break the walls down fast.
The risks are not less taken
But before I had been fakin'.
Time has lost
And love has died
And the ropes they have been tightened.

The blows
And shots
And stabs.
I've seen it all go down;
Till the Promise Land is coming
I'll still be down here drumming
On my gooey hyperconsciousness.

The things that I love most,
And the things that tear my soul
Will not be of consequence
When the world is void and bare.
I think the time has come
Where we have to breathe our last.
What, my man, will you do
When the beast has come to snatch?

- TERRY BROSWALD

SEPTEMBER

ONE

There is a difference between being sad and being scared. Some people who are sad cry themselves to sleep. But Terry was not sad; he was scared. During slumber, his mind harrowed itself. And in response, cried himself awake. He never told anyone about his dreams. His parents didn't even know because they never heard him crying. In truth he was ashamed; ashamed to be sixteen and having nightmares that scared him half to death. So he kept these experiences locked inside, intending that none of them escape or be discovered.

Other than these dreams, Terry led a pretty normal life. Normal kid: went to school, had a few friends and tried not to piss his parents off even if he didn't like them. But he wasn't happy no matter how much he tried to fake it. He needed a change; it was all too boring to him. Even though his dreams haunted him, he kind of looked forward to them, in a masochistic way, because it was a change from the mundane.

Terry knew that everything changed. Or, everything in *his* world changed. But in his mind, he had come to the conclusion that when someone wanted a change, there wasn't one; and when someone didn't, everything collapsed in differentness. So he was stuck; forever encapsulated in a world of predictability.

Terry just wanted release from his prison cell of mundanity. He paced the hallways of his school looking for loopholes in the invisible stratum of cliques. But for him, there seemed to be none; or none that he could readily identify if he saw it. He saw the hierarchy because he believed that that is how most people think, even though he didn't. And Terry, omnipotent being that he was, got the notion in his head that he was viewed as the lowest of the low; just another flea jumping around the hallways. But naturally, he did not like his position and it enraged him to no end that he could not find a solution to his tangled logic.

He observed and waited; watching the groupings of people oblivious to anyone other than the ones they had known since 5th grade. Terry had friends, but none that actually thought like he did. He couldn't shake off the idea that everything was pointless: his struggle, his pain, love, dreams, and a future in which he knows no one. So he watched the people he admired, and the girl he loved, from a distance. He must be content with that for now. But he wanted a change; to take some risks and have fun. He was optimistic that the time was near.

Terry knew that a person can never make a difference unless they take a risk and leap into a forbidden area. And at the moment, the forbidden area was a girl; a girl sitting right across from Terry. They talked avidly about something.

"It *is* hard to break into other groups once a person is cast," Terry said.

"No," Tracey protested. "It isn't hard at all."

"Bullshit. If I went to Joe over there right now and asked him if he wants to hang out this weekend, you know what he'd say? Huh? Huh? He'd look at me and say: *who the fuck are you?* My point made and you know it."

"No."

"Hah! Hey, if I asked you if you wanted to hang out, you'd say the same thing."

"No, I wouldn't say that. Hey, here's my number. Call me sometime."

Holy fuck, dude. Terry could not believe that he had a girl's number. It was about time, too. He couldn't understand how guys who are jerks could get girls but he couldn't. It was almost like he needed a guardian angel or something, to come and alter his reality.

Another thing that bugged him: time. It went entirely too fast for Terry. He seemed to always find that his chances became forever lost in the intricate fabric of the past. Funny idea: the Past. Is the Past actually a thing or is it an abstract idea? If the past can be named, then it must still exist, right? Since there is a word for 'the Past', then it must not have been purged. And if this is so, there must be a way to access it, regardless of the benefits it might bring. On the other hand, time might not contain anything except for the present. And in this latter mindset, Terry believed himself to be literally, utterly, and truly timefucked. These were just some of Terry's daily thoughts.

Sometimes he didn't even understand his own thoughts. But they burned him nonetheless. Sometimes he even thought that he was losing his mind. He considered himself in need of help, but found no one who could help in the way he thought he needed.

He knew, without a doubt, that his parents couldn't help him. His parents didn't understand. They didn't understand anything. And they certainly didn't understand him. They tried to get rid of him every chance they got. Because of this, Terry was constantly plagued with questions about his adequacy as a son.

He knew that he couldn't please them. In their eyes, since he was different, he wasn't worthy of them. Every time he was around them, he wanted to be instantly struck dead. It would be better than their unspoken waves of loathing.

Terry wandered down from his room into the Family Room where his mom sat in front of the box for eternity.

"I'm going out, Mom, okay?"

No reply. Not even an indication that she registered that he was alive.

So he just left. Hopped on his bike and pedaled away toward his dreams. He suddenly felt hot tears running down his face. He couldn't stop them, nor did he care. He was past the point of caring. Everything had gone to shit and he felt that just being himself had somehow fucked his whole world; bending its axis beyond all hope of repair. He suddenly felt like he was spiraling through the world that he didn't understand. And he knew that he never would. Everything was wrong. He was socially inadequate, he didn't meet his parents' standards, and all this happening while he was struggling with his grip on this world.

At that moment, his grip on the world was none too good. He wasn't really paying attention to his surroundings. He had surrendered to his tears and his haunted thoughts. He was just content to pedal into Oblivion.

He didn't realize that he was plummeting into a road that was swimming with fast-moving vehicles. In the flash of an instant before his ears were overwhelmed with noise and his head collided with a headlight and his body was sucked under, it seemed as if time stopped and he was granted one final thought. He remembered his many dreams where he watched himself dying. This was not one of those scenarios. But he felt that unconsciously he had made a decision.

Then impact...

TWO
FROM THE MIND OF TERRY BROSWALD:

It is dark and I am falling. I am falling with my stomach and eyes up toward the stars. I watch the heavenly bodies as gravity's clawed hand slowly draws me down. I close my eyes and lift my chin a little. I stretch this moment out to its max as I take in the night.

But the moment doesn't last for long because I notice that I am falling into a forest full of bare trees. Oh shit. I hope I don't get impaled by one. Oh, well. Whatever. I recline on the air and surrender myself to physics. Next thing I know, I am standing; standing in the middle of the wood in front of an entrance to a cave. What strikes me as odd is that the stars and moon lights the wood pretty well but none of that light penetrates into the cave at all. Sure, some of that light should have filtered into the cave, you know, maybe exposing about five feet into the tunnel. But it doesn't, flush with the edge of the entrance is darkness. It is like the dark is a liquid that entirely fills that space. I am half expecting the dark to spill out like milk. But no, it just stays there staring at me as if willing me to take a step into that abyss. I just stare back at its face, mulling over my options. I have a feeling that it's a forbidden area. A taboo zone. But it is calling me. I know what is in there is not for human senses. But, alas, my legs, acting on their own, carry me across the threshold to be consummated with the black.

I am not saying this to excuse myself of what I did; detach myself from the moment. No, I am simply stating what it feels like. I definitely made the choice, maybe not consciously, but the choice was mine nonetheless.

As I cross into the darkness, it feels like I am being swallowed by a giant fish. It feels like water is pushing me deeper into the cave. The empty darkness seems like water. I do not float to the top but I can feel currents flowing around me. Nothing so significant as to whisk me off my feet. Taking all this into account, I am surprised that I don't have any trouble breathing. The reason, I realize, is because I am *not* breathing. But there is no pain or lightheadedness so I merely dismiss this perception as I glide deeper into the cave. It does not matter that I cannot see anything, it is like I have been here before; enough times to know every rock, stalagmite, and stony orifice. So I go on, I don't know how long. In this cave, time means nothing. This is the second time I challenge time as an idea, not something you can actually measure. So I go on and I stop when stop comes. There is but one stop.

So I stop, not because I want to, just for the simple fact that it is. Stop is an order that the mind automatically obeys regardless of any other factors. So I accept this and stand here. This is my choice. To wallow in as I see fit.

The only thing that I can try to do now, in this black, is to try to perceive as much as is possible. Because that's what humans do, we try to perceive. The only sense which is of no use is my sight. So I utilize my other senses. Some perceptions are humanly impossible to comprehend. And when these things arise, we automatically dismiss it as fiction; as a trick of the mind. But we can't readily dismiss, or we shouldn't, because there are things in this world—and others—which cannot be justified in the human mind; but they exist nonetheless. What I am trying to say is that there are things we just have to accept because they are truth even if they defy explanation.

But the last two perceptions I am having now in this world are blatant as day and are by no means unidentifiable. First is the smell of brimstone, or what these days is more commonly known as sulfur; the second: something furry rubbing against my leg. Then it is over as it had begun: a flash of an instant, the toss of a rock.

THREE

Time had cracked and Terry awoke to find himself in a hospital bed. As he looked around it occurred to him that he was not in an emergency room because if he was, there would be medical personnel swarming around him. If he was dead, this would be a very strange afterlife: a hospital. He wondered if he was okay. He had some kind of IV in his arm and he had an oxygen reader attached to his index finger. He reached up and felt that he had bandages on his head. He must have injured his head pretty badly because it hurt just to the touch. He had bandages around his right ribs too. It hurt to breathe just slightly but nothing bad enough to constitute a punctured lung.

Just as he was getting his bearings and looking around the room, a very attractive young nurse came in and saw that Terry was awake. Terry was trying hard not to get a boner just from looking at her. He managed to mutter a small greeting but his jaw was a little sore.

"Oh, you're awake," the sexy nurse said as she entered the room. Terry had a better view of her now that she was entirely in the room. She had a perfect oval face that was complimented by gorgeous locks of straight black hair that was pulled back in a conservative ponytail. She had dazzling green eyes that seemed to pierce Terry to his core. He brought his gaze down from her full lips to her shapely body. Even through her loose nurse's shirt, Terry could see that she had lovely full breasts that he wouldn't mind getting his lips around. She had long legs. And that ass! Oh, yes! Terry was so horny he couldn't help staring at her.

"You know you are lucky to be alive," she said and waggled a finger at Terry. His heart fluttered a little. "You should thank whoever it was that brought you in. Well, it's too late now. They're probably long gone. We tried to contact your parents but couldn't get ahold of them. And someone higher up the ladder told me to keep it quiet that you are here." She threw up her hands. "And it is above my pay grade to ask questions... So, how are you feeling?"

"All right, I guess. What's wrong with me?"

"Well, you're lucky. You only suffered a minor concussion and two broken ribs. But, you're fortunate to be alive from the story I heard. You really should be more careful." She walked over to Terry and started fussing over him. Tucking him in and fluffing his pillows and checking all his vitals. "And," she added. "I'm sorry, but you are going to have to stay here for the next two days so we can keep an eye on you. You'll be good enough to go by then. I'll be looking after you. Just so you know. My name is Sylvia. If you need anything, just hit my call button. I'll be around." She left the room as gracefully as she entered, but this time Terry got to admire her backside as she walked out of the room.

Terry's heart skipped a beat—or maybe his dick skipped a beat. Sylvia... What an angel... He lost himself in his sexual fantasies that he knew would never come true, but he enjoyed them nonetheless. Two more days with Sylvia...

The first night was pretty uneventful except for the dream Terry had.

The dream:

Terry was standing in a snow-covered field. But he was not inside his body. The real Terry, the dreaming Terry, was just watching this over the shoulder of the dream-Terry. So, in the dream, Terry saw himself calling across the field toward something he could not readily make out. All he could tell about the thing he was calling to was that it was an animal and that it was small and black. Also, in the dream, he was crying, and as he called, the animal was steadily getting nearer.

Terry woke before he could get a good look at the creature.

He noticed that his throat was incredibly parched and his face was wet. He hurriedly wiped his eyes and pressed the call button. Sylvia entered soon after, more dazzling than ever. Her hips moved seductively as she walked.

"Yes?" she said.

"I was wondering if I could get some water, please." Terry said.

"Sure thing," she paused and looked down. "I'm glad to see you're doing better." Terry followed her gaze and to his horror he realized that he had an erection and that it was quite noticeable through his covers. Terry's face went beet red and he tried to subdue his manhood as best he could.

"Sorry," he said, looking away from her. She just giggled and left to get Terry's water.

Terry tried to squelch his manhood as best he could but to no avail. So he did the only thing that he could do: he gave himself release as fast as he could. And it was great. He bit his lip as to not cry out with the pleasure he was getting from picturing Sylvia. Then he wiped his hand onto his sheets where no one would notice. Just as he was doing that, Sylvia came back in with his water. She looked down at him and smiled. He smiled back, unsure of how to interpret her.

Sylvia had to lean over Terry's bed in order to set the glass of water on his bedside table. As she did so, Terry slowly leaned up and kissed Sylvia square on the mouth. She recoiled from his bed, but not too quickly.

"What are you doing?" she asked, looking not entirely disgusted.

"You're beautiful," Terry said. "And graceful."

"Well, thanks," she said. "But do you think that is entirely appropriate?"

"I guess not."

"How old are you?"

"Sixteen."

"Yeah," she said. "I'm 23, don't you think I'm a little old for you?"

"Love knows no age."

"Do you think in cliches or something? Even if life was as good as that, it wouldn't work out anyway."

"Why not?"

"I'm a lesbian," and with that, she walked out the door.

Fuck, Terry could have sworn that she was hitting on him. Maybe it was his wishful thinking. Of course she wasn't going to have sex with him. He was just a kid. And he was thinking like a kid. Why couldn't he just grow up? He felt terrible. *Huh, a lesbian nurse?*

She probably just felt that he was a pervert and just like every other kid. He couldn't have that. No fucking way. He pushed the call button about fifty times until Sylvia showed up again.

"What the hell do you want?" she asked as she entered the room. She crossed her arms over her chest, accentuating her breasts.

"I'm sorry," Terry said, like that was going to help at all.

"Woopdy-fucking-doo for you. What do you want me to do? Open my legs and fuck the shit out of you? I don't think so, dude... Maybe. But I don't even like men."

Was she hostile or what? Terry couldn't believe this, all over a little kiss. Maybe she liked Terry too and she was just reacting like this because she couldn't do the thing both of them wanted. Restraint is for the weak of heart and Terry couldn't stand it.

"Life is not a fantasy," Sylvia said and then she exited the way she had come: with grace and anger.

Terry could feel tears coming on and he couldn't stop them nor did he understand his reactions to certain things. He was a shit and he knew it. He also knew that she was right. Life was not a fantasy no matter how much people try to make it like that. Marriage, love, and those things all end up the same way: tragedy. Love ends in hate. Or maybe love and hate were really the same. Terry didn't know and he didn't really care at the moment. He just had to get the fuck out of there. He couldn't stand to be there one more second. You could cut him, castrate him, crucify him, anything; you couldn't make him stay. He tore off the oxygen reader. He tore, in a shower of blood, all the other tubes connected to him in various other places. Numbed by his mixed up emotions, he stood up to realize that he was naked as a whore just out of a session of passion. He found a pair of scrubs draped over a chair that he put on.

A spasm of pain pulsed between his injured chest and his injured head. He grasped his chest as he struggled to keep his balance. Terry didn't notice, but as he spasmed, his water glass shattered on the table behind him. Terry staggered and braced himself on the doorframe. "Shit."

The bright, white light of the hallway burned Terry's eyes. Both ways were the same: an empty hall lined with doors. He chose to go right because it looked like there was a stairwell at the end. So he staggered out into the hallway. He noticed that everything was deathly quiet. There was no one in the hall either. It was very strange, but it suited Terry perfect for his escape.

"Hey, you! Aren't you supposed to be in bed? Come back here!" A voice yelled from behind Terry. *Oh, fuck me!* Terry couldn't afford to look back, he just staggered as fast as he could to the stairwell. He heard the footsteps gaining on him from behind.

He finally made it to the stairwell and decided to look back. When he did, all he saw was an empty hallway. *That's funny. I could've sworn.* He just shook his head and turned to the stair steps.

Terry started walking down but was suddenly stopped when his face collided with a pair of voluptuous tits. And they could only belong to one person. And, yes, it was that one person: Sylvia. Terry slowly lifted his eyes and saw Sylvia's beautiful face frowning down at him.

As she looked down at him, she raised one eyebrow just slightly. "And just *what* are you doing?" she said.

"I... I, um..." Terry stuttered and then seemed to compose himself enough to find his voice. "I am taking my leave."

Sylvia seemed to find this very amusing. "You know that I could easily take you back by force." Terry highly doubted this but he made no attempt to correct her. "And why do you feel it is necessary for you to leave when you are not entirely well? Also, how do you know I will not change my mind?"

"You won't," he said, with truth laced between his teeth. He knew she would not surrender her passage to him. "Life is not a fantasy," Terry repeated her own words.

"But can we make it one? It is the choices we make that dictate our lives... Just so you know, I'm not mad at you anymore because I understand that you are just a boy. I am not going to stop you from leaving. So go and make your life sparkle." She placed her hands on Terry's shoulders and looked him square in the eyes. Then she continued up the stair steps with not as much as a backward glance.

Terry felt tears again. But he would not surrender to them this time. He knew that they had almost gotten him killed before, not that that was not his initial plan; but Sylvia had rekindled his hope that life could somehow become what you make it. So he decided to give it another try. He was glad he had met Sylvia; and because of the fact that she didn't have sex with him, he would remember her always.

So he ran. He ran like all hell, down the stairs back into the brilliance of existence. Maybe there was hope trapped somewhere deep in the darkness of his Pandora's Box. He just had to search a little harder.

Miraculously, he encountered zero resistance getting out of the hospital after that point. Terry stood inside the building, at the entrance, heaving. He blocked everything else out and focused on a single point in space straight ahead of him. He needed a reference point because everything seemed to be spinning again. Terry steadied the world and then stepped out as if experiencing everything for the first time.

It was raining. Terry stretched his arms out wide and turned his face to the sky and laughed. For no other reason than that he could feel. Maybe things weren't so bad.

His only problem was getting home from the hospital. Well, that wasn't the only problem that was racing through Terry's injured mind. What was he going to say to his parents? He didn't even know how long he was out. Maybe he had been in a coma for months and his parents had left him for dead. He didn't know.

Nothing could have prepared Terry for the sight that met him upon arriving home. He was definitely not ready to receive it for his reaction was not the best.

"Hello?" Terry called out as he entered his house.

No answer.

He went upstairs to the hallway outside his parents' room and he called again because their door was shut.

No answer.

They wouldn't be asleep since it was only 3 o'clock in the afternoon. So he opened the door a crack and what he saw hit him like a jackhammer between the shoulder blades. He saw his mother on the bed and his father on the floor. Both spread-eagled. Both naked. What was overwhelming was the stench and the amount of blood, mostly coming out of their genitalia. This was because his dad had been castrated and his mother had been spayed. His mother's ovaries were soaking on the bed. And his dad's testicles and penis had been severed and mutilated. Terry had not expected this and had a hard time taking it all in.

Then he blacked out.

FOUR

FROM THE MIND OF TERRY BROSWALD:

What the fuck is happening? Oh, fuck, man. Did I see what I think I saw? What the fuck is happening to me? This shit doesn't just happen to people.

I can't seem to move at all. I am lying in a dark room, or in a dark space void of anything. Except that there is light radiating off of my skin. What is this light? Most of the light is coming out of my chest and seems to wave like steam off of a coffee mug. What the fuck is wrong with me? Am I beginning to see things? Just like in the hospital? Oh, man, my head. Damn, man. My parents can't be dead. Maybe I am just dreaming.

"Oh, give me a fucking break," a voice speaks from the darkness.

"Who said that?" I say.

"You will know me soon enough. Just so you know, your little whinings don't mean shit. It's all real. And just because you're dreaming doesn't mean that it isn't real or true. It's just different. So wake up, I need to talk to you."

"But you're talking to me now," I say, puzzled.

The voice laughs, "You need me more than I thought."

FIVE

Terry woke up in his own bed. The day unfolded as any other day would except that he remembered what had happened, but he dismissed it as a dream. He didn't believe that it actually happened. He wasn't expecting anything to be different because the constricted mind that Terry had at the time automatically assumed that nothing would ever change; for the better, or for the worse.

He went to school just like on any other day; the school that kept his mind from expanding. Same old goddamn routine everyday. He'd go to school and he'd go to the same spot with the same friends every single day.

He went to a big high school. His school had about three-thousand people attending it and they rarely noticed when people were absent. He walked down the main hallway with its big windows looking out on the pond. *Same shit*, he thought.

So he went over to his group of friends that he knew. There was Rob and his *pursuit of Black*, as Terry liked to put it. There was Karl and his sunflower seed addiction. There was the modest Mexican Alex, as Stefano the Mafioso liked to put it very jokingly. And there was Mothman, as Terry liked to call him. They were all sitting and talking as they always did in their little corner by the conference room.

"Hey, look at your shirt," Rob pointed at Terry. "It's BLACK!"

Terry sat down. "Yeah, and so is my hair," he said.

"BLACK," Rob said, and started petting Terry's head.

"Get off!" Terry said and pushed Rob away. Rob laughed, showing his braces. Terry looked at Rob for a second. He was the epitome of nonghetto. He had fine blonde hair, and kind of a permanent stupid look on his face—not that he *was* stupid. But he *wore* ghetto clothes regardless of how stupid they looked on him. But, hey, that was his right.

"Ha, ha. BLACK..." Rob said. Terry just shook his head and turned to Karl who was Terry's best friend.

"What up, man?" Terry said, and slapped hands with Karl. Karl was tall, skinny, and an all-around good-looking guy. He had a gargantuan nose though. It went well with his face in spite of all the shit he took for it. He had really short brown hair too. His nose must not have been a total turn-off since he had a girlfriend.

"What up, Ter-man?" Mothman said with his hand outstretched. Terry slapped it. Mothman. Mothman was another story all himself. Terry and his friends all had a hunch that he was going to grow up and become a rapist. He wasn't a bad guy, he was just horny as hell—ALL THE TIME. Mothman had incredibly curly hair but he kept it short so it didn't get too out of hand. He wore glasses also; he kept saying that he was going to get contacts, but he hadn't yet. And when he stood up, he was over six feet tall.

Mothman jived to Korn with one headphone. The other headphone was in the possession of Alex who had another headphone from Karl's iPod. So Alex was listening to two things at the same time. Terry didn't know how Alex could do that without getting a headache. He was a short little man: about five-foot four-inches. He had short brown hair and brown eyes and he seemed to wear the same clothes a bunch of days in a row. He denied this though. Mothman also accused him of not taking showers.

Now, everyone has their quirks. And despite people's quirks, other people are still friends with them. Stefano was a prime case of this. He was racist, prejudiced, violent, and homophobic. But if a person didn't bring up topics of race and homosexuality, he was a pretty good guy. Terry just tried to get along but there was one thing he wouldn't do. Terry wouldn't compromise himself or his beliefs for anyone or anything, even if he was tormented because of it.

"Rob, would you go out with a Black girl?" Stefano asked.

"Yeah, Black chicks are hot," Rob replied.

"You fucking idiot. Don't go out with any niggers. They're not even people," this was Stefano's reply.

"Stefano, shut the hell up," Karl said. "You racist fuck!"

"Hey, I'm just saying they're still over there in Africa swinging from trees," Stefano said defensively.

"Your logic is so messed up," Terry said. "First of all, there are cities in South Africa. And secondly, they don't swing from trees." Just then the bell rang before Stefano could make a racist reply.

"Come on, Karl," Terry said. "We gotta get to Physics with Mr. Down Syndrome." Their teacher didn't really have Down Syndrome, but they thought it was an appropriate nickname for him nonetheless.

"Agghhhh," Karl groaned. "That class is so boring."

"Not to mention the teacher is an arrogant prick," Terry said as they walked toward the Physics room.

Some people think that what is on the inside of a person is what matters. Terry didn't really understand this because usually the only thing a person can know about another is their output. Unless you meet someone rare. You cannot go up to a person and say 'open sesame' and have some magic orifice open that can gain access to their soul. It just doesn't happen that way. So the statement is bullshit unless you possess the rare ability to see inside; and there is more than one way to do that.

This was especially true of Terry's Physics teacher whose name no longer exists in this world according to Terry's perception. Anyhow, Terry's teacher's output was everything that an acquaintance would label as 'nice guy' characteristics. But for Terry, that was secondary; what was primary was how he made Terry feel—*inside*. A person can always see inside *themselves* and that should matter to the individual because most wounds are not visible.

Everyone's perception is different. Everyone's perception is skewed in some way; some more than others. But all perceptions are true in the mind of the perceiver. And Terry's perception of his teacher was determined not just by his actions, but by how he made Terry feel. And, as previously stated, you can't see inside of others. *Wait*, Terry thought, *let me make that more clear.* You can't see inside a person *directly* but you can look inside *indirectly* through the only person you *can* look inside: yourself. If you are confused, I am sorry; Terry was still trying to explain this perception in his own mind. That was what he perceived.

After his teacher would talk to him, he would look inside himself and determine how he felt. He felt like he was shit, useless and discarded. He felt less than human, the lowliest, scum-sucking, pitiful fuck that deserved to always be in a dustpan. This guy restricted Terry emotionally and also Mr. Down Syndrome was just one of those people that rubbed Terry the wrong way; their souls clashed.

Terry looked at Down Syndrome's face and his arrogant smile. He was the model of a good-looking asshole. He had shortly cropped brown hair that he kept neat. He was average height, was a little overweight but he carried it well. He also had a permanent grin plastered to his face.

Since Terry could not tell Mr. Down to go fuck himself, he kept his mouth shut and his anger inside. And keeping emotions bottled up is not good for anything.

Terry wished that he lived in a world where it was not a crime to speak what he felt inside.

But he didn't.

He could only dream; because Utopia is different for everyone.

SIX

The next day; the day after the ordinary, was when Terry believed the real mindfuck began. Terry hadn't seen his parents the previous day but that was nothing out of the ordinary. So he thought nothing strange was going on. It was Saturday and he woke up in his room like he normally did.

Terry's bedroom was the bare minimum. If you were standing in the doorframe facing into the room, the head of the bed was against the middle of the left wall. At the foot of the bed was about a meter of walking space before you got to the dresser against the wall opposite the bed head. And on the wall opposite of the door was a little window that was about a meter and a half by a meter. The window was parallel to the bed and there was a little room in between for walking.

So it was the morning after the ordinary. Terry usually had his window shut most of the time, but on this particular morning, as he gained consciousness, he felt a breeze stroke his hair. He slowly opened his eyes. But with his vision still fuzzy from sleep, all he could make out at first glance was a black shape perched on the windowsill. He was so startled that he fell out of his bed on the side opposite the window.

As his eyes slowly brought the shape into focus, he realized that it was a cat; a cat sitting on his windowsill. The cat was completely black except for a patch of fur on its chest which appeared to be in the shape of a Japanese character.

The cat just swished his tail, looked down at Terry, and smiled. Terry did not know what to make of this. Then the cat laughed. A real laugh. He actually opened his mouth and let out a noise other than a meow. He shouldn't have been, but Terry was scared shitless.

"Is this a dream?" Terry said.

"Perhaps," was the cat's reply.

"Is it real?" Terry asked because he was unsure about the cat's answer to his previous question.

"It's your choice," the cat said. At the time, Terry just dismissed this statement because he couldn't comprehend it.

Terry was still curious so he inquired further. "What are you?"

"An October."

"October?"

The cat sighed, "Yes, there are a bunch of us. Only certain people get to see us though. Our job is to bring dreams to people. We don't really make the dreams, we just help unlock your unconscious and then it is *your* mind that makes you dream what you dream."

Terry didn't understand a word that the October said or he didn't want to; so he did what he usually did: he dismissed it. "I don't need you. And I don't need your stupid dreams. So fuck off!"

That seemed to get to the cat. His brow furrowed and he frowned. Then he said, "Hey man, you put your name on my list. I just happened to have some unfortunate cancellations and you were still left. I was skeptical, but now that I see you, I think you *do* need more than just my normal nightly attention."

"What?"

The cat was smiling again. He then stood up on all fours on the windowsill with graceful balance. Then he looked down at Terry almost with pity. And he would never forget what the cat said. So he just looked down at Terry with those big green eyes and he said, "What do you fear?"

Terry repeated his previous question.

The cat just kept on smiling as he bounded out of Terry's window and out of his world.

Terry yawned and stretched his arms above his head. *I've been having weird dreams lately*, he thought. Naturally he thought that these occurrences were dreams because they seemed illogical and he could not interpret them. But what if these occurrences were real? Was that what he was afraid of?

Terry left his bedroom and went into the hall. *What did he fear?* He turned to his right and the three other closed doors. *Terry*, he heard an announcer's voice in his head. *You have thirty seconds on the clock. Your fear, is it behind door A, B, or C?*

Terry had to find out. Where he was standing at the moment seemed to be real; and what he needed to find out was what was real. He stared at the door to his parents' room. *C'mon, Terry. Time doesn't wait.* He heard the cat's voice in his head. It was true. He must choose between living with the question and dying with the answer. And he wanted to know—even if it killed him.

Terry took a deep breath. And instead of turning the knob, he kicked the living shit out of that door. The door swung in violently exposing the already-known horror on the other side. But this time Terry didn't scream or black out. He took a couple of steady steps into the room to survey the carrion. He did not feel squeamish nor did disgust enter into his face. He just stared at his parents' naked, mutilated bodies and felt nothing at all for them. They brought it upon themselves.

Terry heard a faint meow and felt something rubbing against his leg. He looked down and saw the October, eyes closed, rubbing his head on the leg of Terry's pajama pants.

"All right, I give," Terry said. "This is real, and you're real. I accept it. Now what? Shower me with your wisdom, O mighty cat!"

The October bit Terry's foot and then he padded a little closer to the carcasses, swishing his tail as he went.

"You son of a bitch," Terry cursed under his breath.

The October sat down next to the father's castrated body and faced Terry with his eyes glittering and green.

"It seems we have not had a proper introduction," the cat said. "I'm Remius."

"And I'm—" Terry began.

"Terry. I know. I know more about you than you know about yourself. You have talents and gifts you could only before dream about; and with time, they would have been lost. You are extraordinary, but you need help."

Maybe he's *the one who can help me*, Terry thought hopefully. "But, what the hell is this?" Terry made a sweeping gesture over the bodies. "I mean, Jesus Fuck!"

"What? This is not what you wanted?" Remius looked very surprised. "It was your dream, wasn't it? To have your parents gone and off your back? Didn't really think it would happen, didja?"

Terry rubbed his eyes and tried to take it all in. Terry composed himself and then spoke. "Are you telling me," Terry began very slowly and softly. "That just because I had an overwhelming hatred toward my parents and—wait, how the *fuck* do *you* know what I want? I am not *that* fucking sick." Terry pointed at the apparent mutilations to his parents' tender parts. "I mean—*Jesus!*"

"You deny having these fantasies?" the cat inquired.

"You're a real bitch, you know that? Barging into *my* fucking house; messing with *my* mind; accusing *me* of being demented. Well, *you* can go *fuck* yourself. Get the hell out of *my* house, you sorry, creeping beast!"

Remius just sat there, swishing his tail. Then he smiled and let out a little *hmph* of amusement. "A little self-centered are we? Me, me, me, hmm? Well, anyway, that is not the real issue here is it? Do I think you're demented? No; not more than any other kid. And this," Remius swiveled his head toward the bodies. "This was not your fault." Terry breathed a sigh of relief at hearing this. "No. The real issue lay with them. Did they seem like exceptional people to you?"

"No."

"No. It was too late for them. They lost their way in this hollow world. They lost sight of what was really important. No, you did not do this. Oh, you see them this way because that is how you envisioned their deaths. But, I am sad to say, they did it to themselves. They drowned in a slough of their own making." Remius turned back to Terry. "But it is not too late for you, my boy. Like I said, you have gifts; and without my help, you would lose them and you would die. That is why you called me. And I am willing to give you a chance."

Terry was speechless and just stared at the cat in disbelief and confusion. All Terry could manage to get out of his mouth was: "H-h-hollow?"

"Um, yeah," Remius began to answer Terry's only half spoken question. "This is the Hollow Dimension. The Human World, to be more specific. You live in the between world. Meaning that it is between a bunch of other vastly different dimensions. It is called the Hollow Dimension because it is like all humans, in life, are just wandering around inside of a hollow log. Being born at one end and dying at the other. In between, most—if not all—are just lost. Some people don't admit that they are lost, but they are all searching for something they know not of. At least you, Terry, have admitted in your mind that you are lost. And you admit and accept that you are searching for something rich and meaningful. Maybe something beyond your world. And I say, congratulations, you have bridged the gap. Now I must go. We will talk more later. Ciao!" The cat bounded out of the room and disappeared, leaving Terry standing in silence looking after the cat's tail as he leaped out of the door.

When Terry turned around, the bodies were gone.

SEVEN
FROM THE MIND OF TERRY BROSWALD:

What am I to make of all this? All this shit is happening way too fast for me. This does not seem very reasonable to me. Shoving all this shit in my face so unexpectedly. I must be losing my mind.

That's it! I am leaving right this minute to get myself a psychologist. I don't want to become any more fucked up. I know of this good shrink up near the other high school. What was the dude's name? I think it is Tim. Tim Harold, I think it is.

My parents definitely won't need their car anymore so I might as well take advantage of that. As long as their deaths aren't one big hallucination I am fine, right? I'm not sure what is real anymore though. It fucking drives me crazy wondering if anything I perceive is real or not.

Fucking reality pisses me off. My fucking mind pisses me off. Why can't my mind just get off my back and not plague me with these kinds of thoughts that have no answer?

I definitely need a fucking shrink.

Now where are those damn keys? I look around for the car keys. Oh yeah, they are right over there on their night table. I grab them and am down the stairs in a flash of an instant.

Does this shit have something to do with me getting hit by a car? Am I dead or something? Jesus! So many goddamn questions I cannot answer. Maybe Tim can help me.

So I get in that cursed white minivan that my mother loved so dearly and I start the engine. Do I have my license? No. Fuck it! I can drive. I'll do what I want.

May god help me.

Not even He can stop me.

So I drive off to where I hope my mind can be healed if indeed it needs healing. Jesus, god, if not, I am seriously fucked because this cat makes no sense.

I drive on up the road and space out thinking about the worst case scenario: schizophrenia, paranoia, hallucination, hell I don't know what else. Just help me.

"I'll help you."

"HOLY PENIS!" I swerve like a drunk driver when I hear the voice from the passenger's seat of my car. After I steady myself, I look over and see that son of a bitch cat with that stupid grin on his face sitting in *my* car.

Then he starts laughing at me. "Holy penis. Ha, ha, that's one I've never heard before. You make that up, boy?"

Stop fucking calling me 'boy' you feline fucker. I can feel my rage surge up inside of me. I just wanna strangle his scrawny flea-infested neck. See if he's smiling then. Cheeky bastard.

"What the hell are you doing in my car?" I say to Remius.

"Saving you from a bad decision."

"What bad decision? I am getting help for myself because there is no rational explanation for this. There is no rational explanation for *you*!"

"Yes, but you said yourself—thought is more like it—that some things in this world and others are true even if they defy explanation and that we shouldn't dismiss them just because things don't make sense in your human mind. Did you not think these things?"

How the hell does he know what I think? This just makes me hate him more. That bastard, pointing out my hypocrisy. "Yes," I say. "But this is the human world and the human world makes sense. And other dimensions are other dimensions. One thing might be true in one dimension but not true in another dimension. Goes against this world's laws of physics. So do you understand why you cannot exist in this world? You might be real in my dreams but do you understand why you can't be real in this?'

"Sometimes dimensions overlap. Sometimes it is necessary for dimensions to overlap. Like this case. Sometimes the overlap can be catastrophic. Other times it is not. So do *you* see how this is infallibly real? You see me, I see you." Remius's form starts to fade a little bit. As he disappears all together, he leaves me with this: "This is all real."

Then he is gone.

This cat will not stop bugging me and will not stop messing with my mind. He says that I asked for him to help me but fuck, I don't want this shit. I don't need this shit. If there is a god up there, kill me now. Which I know that he will not kill me.

I was hopeful when I came out of that hospital. I am not sure now. I can't see that little white fairy at the bottom of the black box. It probably deserted me long ago. Oh, hey, I have arrived at the office building.

I drive into the parking lot and park. The building is about three stories tall. Brick building. There are stairs that lead up to the main entrance at the front. I climb those stairs and enter into the building. I chuckle as I lay eyes on the very bare ground floor. It is devoid of everything except for the elevator in front of me and the pharmacy to my left. And this pharmacy is shabby at best. I mean, they do have some good drinks, but nothing as good as Seven-Eleven.

I press the up button outside the elevator. I stand and wait, with my hands behind my back. I look up at the top of the elevator where the lit numbers are slowly decreasing until it gets to the ground floor. All right, good.

Then I take the first step toward recovery.

Think about what you are doing. You could jeopardize everything.

That damn cat just will not leave me alone. Even when I'm by myself! Maybe I'm hearing voices.

How am I jeopardizing everything? I say back, in my head.

Because you need to work on expanding your mind, not shrinking it. This man will do you no good. He will only make you deny what is real. The voice replies.

You are just a voice in my head. I say to it.

Whatever, dude. Do what you want. I'll talk to you later. Ciao and be careful. The mind is not something to be fucked around with.

I hear the voice dissipate and become nothing more than a ringing in my ears. Great, now I have tinnitus too. What more could be wrong with me?

I walk into the suite that supposedly contains Tim's office. It appears to be that everyone is in sessions or something. I sit down and wait to see who comes out first.

EIGHT

After his session with some stranger, Tim Harold walked out into the waiting room to discover a sixteen-year-old boy named Terry waiting for him.

"Do you need help with something?" he asked Terry.

Suddenly Terry got down on his knees in front of the psychiatrist and raised his hands up toward him.

"Yes," Terry said. "My sanity."

NINE

"So," Terry detected an irritated voice when he opened the door to his house after his encounter with the doctor.

"Huh?" Terry said.

Terry was in the entrance hallway of his house and he looked up at the stairs in front of him. At the top was Remius, looking down at Terry with disdain and frustration.

"So? What did the good doctor say? Did he completely suck out your soul yet? Because frankly, it wouldn't really bother me because you do not seem to be listening to anything I say. You may say that you are not ready for this shit now, but it's now—*or death*. Do you understand that? I haven't even explained much to you yet and you are all ready to think that you are insane. What is wrong with you? I am grieving that the Hollow world has gotten this bad."

Terry collapsed at the foot of the stair. When he lifted his head, there were tears in his eyes. Terry crawled over onto the couch in the living room. The cat followed.

Terry continued to weep, on the couch, with the cat beside him.

"I'm sorry," Terry managed between his tears. "I'm just so fucking scared, you know. This is so sudden. I just don't know how to handle all of this."

"That is why you called me," Remius said. "Don't worry, it will all be fine." This was the only time the cat ever lied to Terry, but it made him feel a little better. "So what did you tell him?"

"Nothing yet," Terry said. "He said to come back next Saturday for a session. I just need help. I am really confused." Terry wrapped his arms around Remius and laid down. Remius made no move to pull away. He stayed there for comfort as Terry drifted off into the Dreamsphere.

When Terry awoke, it was Sunday. The cat was gone and the phone was ringing. Terry picked it up.

"Hello?" Terry croaked. He was tired and his eyes were red-rimmed.

"Terry! What up, man?"

"Karl?"

"Yeah, dude. I got some cool shit to talk to you about. But we can't talk about it on the phone. Come over to my house, dude. Okay?"

"Okay, dude." Terry hung up the phone. He zombied into the kitchen to get some food and then he left for Karl's house.

As Terry rode his bike into Karl's driveway, he surmised that Karl's parents weren't home because there were no cars.

Terry let himself into Karl's house and found him in the basement smoking weed—by himself. Terry went down and took a couple to hits off of the joint.

"So, dude?" Terry said through the smoke. "What's this 'shit' you need to talk to me about?"

"RPG."

"What?"

"RPG."

"The fuck is that? Role Playing Game?" Terry said.

"No, you dumbass. It stands for Red Palm Gang. I'm starting a gang."

"Oh," Terry said.

"And," Karl continued. "All the other guys are already in. And, oh, here." Karl tossed Terry a heavy metal object.

Terry looked down and discovered that it was a beretta: black and sleek. "Oh, shit, dude, no. I can't take this."

"Trust me, keep it. You might need it sometime," Karl leaned back and took a huge drag off of the blunt contentedly.

Terry stuck the gun in his waistline.

"Now, Terry," Karl warned, "that shit's loaded. The safety's on now... but remember."

Terry would remember.

He would always remember.

PART 2

The Soulmind

*Memory, prophecy and fantasy—
the past, the future and
the dreaming moment between—
are all one country,
living one immortal day.*

To know that is Wisdom.

To use it is the Art.

- Clive Barker, *The Great and Secret Show*

TEN
FROM THE MIND OF TERRY BROSWALD:

I am not a piece of clay. I am not a piece of clay that is just gonna succumb to the pressure of whoever is on me at the moment. That is the problem with people that you think you know. It is enraging when people you know well think lower of you and think you are weaker than you actually are. I am not two-faced and I will never be two-faced. I will stand and wallow in my views steadfastly until they destroy me.

The problem arises when people *expect* you to be two-faced. To leave everything you hold dear inside and adopt their way of thinking. You know what I would say to those people? I would say: *go fuck yourself.* Even if you don't say that—even if you don't say anything—and you don't adopt their views, you get harsh and unreasonable punishment. You get loss of friends, spit in the face, and rejection. But I can handle that. I can handle that because I am doing what I believe is right and no one can persuade me from it.

Take, for example, my view about homosexuality. I have no problem with it and if people are that way—hey, more power to you. Unfortunately, not everyone shares my view. And some people are so against my view that they are pushed to the point of hate and violence.

It is the Day of Silence.

The Day of Violence.

Let me explain what the Day of Silence is. It is a day when all homosexual, bisexual, transgender, questioning, and their supporters stay silent for the whole day. It is a protest against the incessant shunning of queers and their allies. And because I am an ally, I am shunned. This world has donned the symbol of hate. The furrowed brow, the gaping yelling mouth, the punching fist, the slapping hand, spit.

This is my world. This is where I live and breathe. Hate is here; and hate breeds more hate, molding the people that have let themselves become clay. Their lives are shaped not by themselves at all, but by the anger they see around them and by hate speech.

I hate it. How ironic. I hate hate. But then I hate myself. How can I hate hate? Because this world is flawed and no one knows anything. And the thing I despise most, I do myself. How fucked up.

I sit in the little corner by the conference room where my friends and I usually meet before school. I am silent. I sit there and watch as Stefano, the first of my friends to show up, walks toward me with a scowl on his face.

"Are you being quiet for the queers today?" he says.

I nod.

"Don't," he says.

I just shrug.

"You fucking faggot," he says to me with all the fiery hate that he can muster. Then, this person—my friend—who I thought I knew, spits on me with his so-called righteous anger. "I hope you get a cock shoved up your ass!" He turns and starts to walk away.

I slowly get up and sneak up behind him. I slip my arm around his neck, get him in a choke hold, and take him down. He tries to scream but I am collapsing his windpipe as I force him to the ground.

I pin Stefano to the ground and have his wrists pinned too so he can't get me. I jab my knee right into his solar plexus and he screams with agony. Then I laugh. I pull out my pocket knife real fast and slice up Stefano's left arm enough that he can't use it in his favor. By now the floor under us is a pool of Stefano's warm blood. I love it and I just want to drink the blood.

Then I start raining down blow after blow to Stefano's face. I do this intentionally because he has braces. My plan is working. As I punch Stefano in the mouth, his braces are breaking and lodging in his gums and he is bleeding profusely from his mouth. He is sputtering and coughing because most of the blood is going down his throat and he is inhaling it. I laugh some more. Then I snap his neck and bathe in the blood.

My head jerks up and my eyes focus out of my trance. I see Stefano walking away. I will still stay steadfast to my beliefs. But I did not do any of that. I should have.

I guess I am weak.

ELEVEN

"Remius..." Terry said as he walked into the door of his house after the Day of Silence at school. "Are you here?"

"Yeah, I'm here." Remius was lying on the couch in the living room. He hopped down, yawned, and stretched like cats do. He walked over to Terry and rubbed against his legs purring.

"I appreciate your affection, man. I really do. But I really need to talk to you. Sit." Terry slumped down on the couch as Remius hopped up onto it.

"What's the problem?" Remius asked.

"You need to tell me exactly what the fuck is going on. And—and tell me exactly what all of this has to do with me because I am getting irritated that I am still in the dark about all this."

"Okay."

"And," Terry continued. "Some motherfucker—well, not just some motherfucker—my friend spit on me just because of my views about homosexuality. Now is that fair?"

"No," Remius agreed. "What did you do?"

"I should have killed him. I didn't though. But I still kept silent the whole day."

"Good boy, I'm proud of you," Remius said. "Don't compromise what you think is right."

"You know how everyone says that you should be yourself? Well, that's what I am doing. But it just seems to be ostracizing me. What should I do?"

"Well, that's tough. I think it is very important to be yourself, Terry. But you still have some friends that like you. Let that other guy fuck himself. He doesn't know shit. So keep doing what you think is right and eventually you will strike it up with someone." The cat smiled.

"That's all fine and good, dude, but I still don't understand why you are here or any of this other weird shit that is going on. Can you please—*please* explain this to me?"

"Like I said before, you called me, Terry."

"Yes, but not intentionally because I didn't even know who you were before you came sitting on my window. So how is that possible?"

"You have what is called a Soulmind," the cat continued. "Not everyone has one. That's why I said you have gifts and talents. But if I hadn't come, you would never have known that you had one, and it would have destroyed you because you would not know how to harness its power. So, to answer your question, Terry, it was your Soulmind that called me. Soulminds sometimes work on their own without the will of the person it's in."

"Soulmind?"

"Yeah."

"So how does it work?" Terry asked.

"Well, it gives different people different abilities. So, I am not exactly sure all that yours does. All I know for sure is that people with Soulminds have dimension abilities."

"Dimension abilities?" Terry said.

"Yes, dimension abilities. People with no Soulmind cannot survive in other Dimensions, but ones with one can. Like you. And I am sure you will have your share of dimension experiences."

"Oh, no, no, no, no, I ain't going to any other dimensions, I can hardly survive in my own. I don't think so." Terry seemed pretty sure he would not be experiencing any other dimensions.

"We'll see," the cat replied.

"I'm really confused," Terry said.

"I know," Remius responded. "But you will understand once you've experienced it. Perception serves for better learning."

"Do I have some type of destiny or something? You know, something I have to do?"

"Do you believe in predestination?" the cat asked.

"Do you?" Terry replied.

"No, it's bullshit," Remius said. "Because then nothing would matter. No matter what you choose to do, that was what was foretold for you to do. So if you believe that, it wouldn't make any difference what you do. But no, there is no destiny as you say. I do not know what is in store for you or what things you might have to do. I can just guide you."

"Okay, I understand. But what are all these dimensions that you are talking about?" Terry asked.

"Let's see if I can remember all of them. In order I think they are: Dreamsphere (where I am from), The Hollow Dimension (this world), Timestrus (Dimension of Reason), The Abyss of Ideas, Kingdom of the Stone Queen, Dementia, Dark Tethers, The Realm of Infallibility, and The Taboo Zone. We live in what is called the Fibonacci Spiralverse. In the inside of the spiral is the Dreamsphere, and you get to the others as you go out in the spiral. Sometimes the Dimensions overlap but that is very rare. And only people with a Soulmind can see the other Dimensions anyway."

"Oh," was all Terry could manage.

Remius laughed. "I know it's a lot of information to absorb right now. But you will understand all of it sooner or later. You are the Steward of Time after all."

"WHAT!!??!" Terry yelled, very surprised and confused.

"Just kidding," Remius said. "The most important thing is to keep your Soulmind under control. It likes to act on its own. The Soulmind is a different color depending on the person. But it is basically energy beams stretched between the soul and the mind. Your soul is near your solar plexus and your mind is in your brain, and as you know, the Soulmind is stretched between them. Sometimes you can even feel it in your chest."

"Do you have a Soulmind?" Terry asked.

"Me?" The cat laughed. "No, cats don't have Soulminds. Cats already have dimension abilities and we're also psychic so we don't need one."

"Oh," Terry said. "So that's why you knew so much about me."

"Yep."

"Oh, yeah, I keep forgetting to ask you," Terry said. "What does that symbol on your chest mean?"

"Oh, that? That is the Japanese character for *dream*."

"That's cool," Terry said.

"Yes," the cat agreed. "But there is one thing you have to remember and this is it: sometimes your life might seem like a dream, but as all dreams do, they come to an end. You must be prepared for the end, even at the beginning."

TWELVE
FROM THE MIND OF TERRY BROSWALD:

I have to start writing poetry. All that is happening to me is boggling my mind so I think it is important for me to have a way to get my feelings out even if they don't make sense at the moment. This is one I wrote just after the discussion with Remius. Make of it what you will.

> Snow is falling,
> Darkness is gathering
> In time and space between.
> My mind and vision a blur.
> Concept upon concept
> Spoon-fed to a mouth
> Which regurgitates every drop.
> The mind and soul connected
> Is daunting

As well as painful
To fathom.

It is hard
To be thrust into a world
Where in your own life,
You are the one making the least of the choices
That affects your death.

Beams of light
Stretched between mind and soul.
Knowing not the purpose,
Hinders the use
And to harness it,
Unthinkable.

THIRTEEN

Terry was tormented internally as he watched the beauty pass him. It was Kyleen, the girl that he had liked since eighth grade. He was a junior now. She was just perfect. So graceful. She had long, straight brown hair that swung seductively about her shoulders. She had brilliant, huge green eyes that could make any man crumble. She was about the same height as Terry. She had a small chest, but Terry liked that—better to have small and perfect breasts than huge and disgusting ones. She also looked like the athletic type; perfect figure. She was not too skinny and not too heavy. Perfect abs. Whoo man, and when she walked around in a skirt—damn! She was fine. And she was also one of the nicest girls that Terry knew. He would talk to her online occasionally but even that was torture because she didn't know how Terry felt about her.

She didn't know.

His love was not reciprocated.

He had also written a poem about her. It was a lovely and haunted poem. He knew that he could not give it to her because that is only something people that are going out do. So he had to sit and wait, stewing in his own shyness because she was so popular.

"Hey, there goes your girlfriend, Terry," Mothman said.

Terry had temporarily forgotten about all his friends that were sitting beside him, all in their usual spots before school. "Shut the fuck up!" Terry barked.

"Whoa, man, whoa. A little hostile there? Calm the fuck down, dude," Mothman said.

"I *will* get her to go out with me... One of these days," Terry said sadly.

"Yeah," Mothman laughed. "When time rewinds." Everyone laughed.

"Fuck you guys," Terry said, crossing his arms. "You wait and see. Before senior year, guys, mark my words." Another bout of laughter. "Suck my dick, guys. I ain't taking any shit from you. You watch."

"All right, all right," Stefano said between laughing attacks. "I bet you two hundred bucks that you won't get her. So, if you haven't gone out with her at all, okay, by graduation, you have to pay me two hundred dollars. Capisce?"

"You're on, fuck-face!" Terry stuck out his hand and shook Stefano's.

It seemed like all of the others wanted a piece of this. All the others except for Alex bet two hundred against Terry.

"Hey, guys, guys," Alex cut in. "Cut the guy a little slack. Don't you have any confidence in him? Here, dude," Alex turned to Terry. "I am going to bet one hundred dollars—*for* you."

Terry was astounded. He was overwhelmed with love for this little Mexican. "Thanks, dude." Terry hugged him.

"Get off me you gay fag," Alex sputtered, but he was smiling nonetheless.

"Rob," Terry said, "you better find yourself a black girl fast."

"What are you talking about," Rob said. "This is a fucking *Wonderbread* school. It's basically blinding me from all the white people. The only BLACK person here is the dude who works in the Xerox room."

"Yeah," Karl joked. "You can go fuck him on the copy machine."

They all laughed as the bell signaled the beginning of school and the ascent to Down Syndrome's class.

Karl and Terry ascended the stairs up to the physics room, griping about the teacher every step of the way. When they got there, Down Syndrome was standing at the door waiting to welcome all his lovely students into the room.

"Morning, gentlemen," Down said, patting Karl and Terry on the back as they entered the room.

Don't fucking touch me, you perverted bastard, Terry said to himself. He and Karl looked at each other and could read each other's disgust.

"Okay," Mr. Down said through his sickeningly fake smile. "We are doing a lab today. We are going to be using tennis balls to measure the height of the school. We're going to be going outside. Just don't lose any of the tennis balls."

All the kids grabbed a ball and a stopwatch and headed outside. Unfortunately, by the time Karl and Terry got up to the front of the class to get a watch, they were all gone. So, because of this, they were stuck waiting for Down to get another from his office while all the others went outside.

Down finally got one and so all three of them went out together. Begrudgingly for Terry and Karl.

"So, Terry," Down said. "I see you did the Day of Silence the other day."

"Yeah," Terry said. *This fucker has no respect for anything* were Terry's internal words.

"That's a very noble thing to do," Down said with a false sense of respect.

Yeah, bitch, too bad for you that pedophilia wasn't on the list of things being supported by it. This was what Terry wanted to say.

They got outside and kids were already taking their measurements. Terry and Karl went off to one side of the building and Down went to hit on the girls. *The sick bitch.*

"Karl," Terry said. "Look over there." Terry jerked his head toward Down and Karl followed the movement to see Down talking to Nikki with his hand on her shoulder. "Isn't he the lowest piece of scum you've ever seen?" Karl nodded in agreement. "He's married and look how the fuck he's acting. Don't you think he needs to be put in his place?"

"Definitely," Karl said.

"Well," Terry replied. "Watch this." Terry wasn't sure if he could do it but he decided to try it anyway.

Terry chucked the ball as hard as he could at an angle to the wall so that it would hopefully ricochet and hit Down. Terry's angle was miraculously correct and that ball shot off the wall so fast. It skimmed over Nikki's shoulder and hit Down square in the nose. Blood squirted freely as he put his hand over his nose.

"Who did that?" Down croaked through the blood.

Terry looked down and there was a ball in his right hand. He didn't know how it got there, but if he was accused, he would have an alibi because he *had* a ball and the one that hit Down was over by him. His ass was covered this time. Terry was overwhelmingly impressed with himself. *Maybe it's my Soulmind working*, Terry thought.

"How did you do that?" Karl whispered. "And where did you get that other ball? It just appeared in your hand."

Terry just stared into space and said, "I don't know, dude. I just don't know."

Terry didn't know if his Soulmind was working or what was going on with him, but he liked it whatever it was. Other than the pleasure Terry got from hurting Mr. Down Syndrome, he also got a kind of high after he had done it; a sort of lightness in his chest and head. He didn't know if he was tripping or what. All he knew was that he wanted more.

Terry was sitting in his Italian class just waiting for it to be over. It wasn't that he didn't like his Italian class, it was just that he wanted to talk to Tracey again and that was the class he had next.

"We are going to do a partner exercise," the teacher said. Terry groaned because he didn't have any friends in this class so he was always stuck with some ugly bitch. "So, get up and grab a partner."

Terry knew that he would be stuck with whoever wasn't chosen so he just sat in his seat awaiting the inevitable. So he put his head down on the desk and sighed.

"Do you have a partner?" a voice said beside Terry's desk.

Oh, Terry thought, *they can't be talking to me*. So he just kept his head down. The thing that told him that the voice wasn't for him was because it was a female voice.

"Hey, are you okay?" A finger poked Terry in the shoulder so he sat up and looked at who was bothering him. What he saw shocked him to the point of breathlessness. It was a beautiful girl—and she wanted to be *his* partner. He could not believe this.

She was a little taller than Terry but he could handle that. She had long black hair that was straight and stopped at the middle of her back. She had big gorgeous violet eyes and a pale face. She was wearing a tie-dye shirt that showed off her small budding breasts that Terry found irresistible. She was also wearing a long skirt that was mostly earthy brown but the bottom of it was white. Who was this girl, and why did she give a damn about Terry?

"Yeah, I'm okay," Terry said. "Sit down." Terry motioned to the desk beside him.

"I'm Jessica," she said. "What's your name?"

"Terry. Nice to meet you."

Jessica nodded her approval. Then they turned to listen to the teacher's instructions. They listened to the assignment that they had to do.

They finished with the task and had a little time to talk before class was over.

"Are you okay?" Jessica asked Terry again.

"Yes," Terry shot back, a little irritated. "What makes you think I'm not?"

"You look tired," she said. Terry didn't feel tired. "You need to do something with your hair." Terry felt indignant that she was insulting his hair. Who did she think she was? But he couldn't bring himself to say anything to offend her. "And you had your head down on your desk. You don't look well at all."

"Your point is? What do you want me to do?" Terry asked. This did not make any sense that this girl that he had never met before was now talking to him and pretending to be concerned about him.

"I think you should come to church with me on Sunday," she said.

"What? I'm sorry? I don't think I heard you correctly." Terry almost choked on his words. "You want me to go to church with you? This must be some trick."

"No trick," she said. "You look like a pretty nice guy. There is just some odd reason, don't ask me why, that I feel like I should get to know you. If you want to come to church with me, I'd like it if we could go to Starbucks or something so we could talk afterwards."

Terry didn't know why he did, but he said *yes*.

FOURTEEN
FROM THE MIND OF TERRY BROSWALD:

"Okay," I take a deep breath as I pace around my bedroom. Remius watches me from his perch atop my bed.

"What's the problem, homie?" The October asks.

"Seriously, dude, this is serious. Don't patronize me with your imitation of the way you think my friends talk. You don't have to do that. And I don't appreciate it if what you are doing is trying to make fun of me. THIS IS FUCKING SERIOUS, MAN!" I try not to get flustered but I can't help it. I can feel my face turning red.

I continue, "I don't know how well you can help me with this, man, but I desperately need someone's guidance. It feels like I'm drowning here." I keep pacing around the room.

"Well, you keep avoiding the issue. You are telling me that you need help but you aren't explaining to me what the problem is." Remius replies. I look over at his form as he sits on the bed. I try to read his eyes. They seem sympathetic and genuine enough.

"It's that girl Tracey," I say. "I told myself that I was going to talk to her today. But I couldn't get up enough courage to say a word to her. She was around her girlfriends giggling and... well, you know how it is." I sit down on my bed with my face in my hands.

"No," he says. "I really don't know how it is."

"It's totally fucked now, dude. Isn't it? I fucked it."

"No, you didn't fuck it just yet. You still got time. Even though it may be fleeting, you have a little time so you must make decisions regarding the present because you have no guarantee that you are going to be here tomorrow. So, this is what I say. Get your fucking cell phone and you call this girl, right now. You can't afford to wait. If you wait any longer, Timestrus is going to stick his penis in your ear and you don't want that to happen."

"Ew, that's disgusting," I say. I am puzzled. "Time has a penis?" I ask.

"Not time itself, Timestrus. He controls time. Now call before Timestrus can use your misfortune to fuel his sick sexual fantasies. Go!"

So I call. I pick up my cell and dial Tracey's cell number. It rings and rings and finally I get her voice mail. "Fuck," I curse under my breath.

"Hey, girlfriends, this is Tracey," the voice message says. "I'm probably, like, at the mall or something, and totally. Or I'm at the movies or the beach, or, like, someplace I can't get to my phone. Or maybe, like, I lost it. Okay, girlfriends, I'll, like, catch you later. Okay, bye." I hear the beep before you are supposed to leave a message. I just close the screen on my cell phone.

"She didn't answer," I say, devastated.

"Well, didn't you leave a message, you shitbrain? That's what you're supposed to do. You won't get anywhere if you don't try. And if you don't try, Timestrus will win. If you're not willing to try, don't complain to me. Go on, call her back."

I dial again. Same thing. It rings and rings and then I get the voice mail. But again, I shut my phone before I leave a message.

The cat stands up on the bed. "What is your problem, man?" I can't help staring at Remius's tail swishing back and forth, irritated with me. "What's so fucking hard about leaving a message for someone? Huh? Jesus, you are one of the toughest kids to help. If you want my help, you have got to do what I say. Damn!" His whiskers twitch as he is saying this.

"I'm sorry. Here, I'll send her a text message," I say, opening my phone again. I input her number so I can send a message to it.

This is what I write:

Tracey,
I tried to call you a couple times,
but I didn't get through to you.
I was wondering if you wanted to
hang out on Saturday or something.
You know, just talk or something.
I would just enjoy talking to you.
You contain stories that I cannot

go to the library to read.
- Terry

I send the message.

"What did you write?" Remius asks.

I tell him.

"Dude, no, no. What are you thinking writing: *you contain stories that I cannot go to the library to read?* That's gonna freak her out even more, man. You really don't know what you are doing, do you? Well, what's done is done."

"Yeah, I guess," I say. "I'll try to talk to her tomorrow."

"You fucking better, because I'm fixing to leave you as a lost cause. Go and cry to your shrink."

"No, don't do that," I plead. "I like you. Don't leave."

"I was only joking," he says.

"Now, tell me about time," I say.

"Timestrus? Well, Timestrus is a bitch is what he is," Remius says with disgust evident in his face.

"Well, that doesn't tell me much," I say.

"Yes, well, you know all this misfortune that you are having and your procrastinating because of your shyness?"

"Yeah."

"Well, Timestrus loves that. He loves that, as time moves forward, you and your chances are left behind and will never come again. That's what he loves. You see, he always remembers people's misfortunes on account of him. He feeds off people's sorrow. And then, the images of people's frustration and sorrow, he uses those to beat off. He gets aroused by your depression. The only way he can live, is by feeding himself negative energy that radiates off of humans."

"Jesus," I say. "That's some sick shit. So he just controls time? He is not time itself?"

"No, he isn't time itself, he just keeps it moving just a little faster than humans can keep up."

"Oh," I say. I know how that is. "So he knows the past and the future?"

"Oh, he knows the past very well. But he can't be certain of the future because it hasn't happened yet. He lives in a Dimension all his own."

"Have you been there?"

"Oh yes, and it was not a pleasant experience. It was total chaos. I was surrounded always by a green mist but as I looked closely, all the molecules of mist were made up of tiny numbers; ever-changing and ever-moving. Guhh." He shakes himself vigorously, as if to get the germs from that place out of his fur. "You must always be vigilant, during this time. You live in a perilous time, Terry. Not knowing at any second if a bomb could fall into your little existence. The wars in the Middle East could just as soon be swept into your life before you even know it. Be on your guard. Whoo, man, remember 9/11? Timestrus must have been having orgasms all day that day. What a bloodbath. Terrible. That's why I say you have to watch out. Decide for yourself what you believe is true. You are surrounded by hippies, liberals, terrorist sympathizers, and many others. If there was ever an appropriate time to predict the apocalypse, it is in these days."

"Do you think it is the apocalypse?" I ask him quizzically.

He sighs. "I don't know. No one knows. And it does us no good to sit and ponder when we should be out on the battlefield fighting. Everyday of your life is a battle. Well, you probably know that better than most. Don't let Time intimidate you. Always think of the now and make decisions regarding the now... well, within Reason."

"Okay," I say. "Back up for one second." I chuckle to myself, realizing what I just said. "I want to ask you a question about time."

"Shoot."

"Is time circular or linear?"

"It is most definitely linear. How many timelines have you seen? How many time-circles have you seen? Exactly. You don't need to go to the Dimension of Reason to figure that one out. If time was circular, it would just repeat itself and we probably wouldn't remember anything from the previous day. But the days and months and years are actually spread out in a line. And if you actually go to the Dimension of Reason, you will see that the numbers in the mist are aligned in lines and not circles. I hope that answers your question."

"That definitely answers my question." I am impressed with how detailed his explanation was. "So, what was before time?"

"Who knows?" Remius says. "We could sit and deliberate on it until our dying day and still it would do us no good because no one knows. We can only speculate. Some say God. Some say the universe was all there ever was and all there ever will be. Some choose to say fuck time. As for me, I speculate that it was some kind of super force; a higher power, god kind of thing. But I don't know. You can decide for yourself what you want to believe."

Hmm, I think, I will have to brood over that a while and then come to a conclusion. "Okay," I say. "Back to the now. If we are uncertain of anything at any given moment, isn't it total chaos?"

"Time is chaos, for those who know not how to use it. Time is chaos for those who dwell on it and don't build themselves in spite of Timestrus's fierce depravity. There is, uh, a verse in the Bible—by the way, I don't usually find scripture very helpful, but I think this verse is quite true. It is Psalm 90 verse 12 and it goes: 'teach us to number our days, that we may apply our hearts unto wisdom.' We never know what the number of our days is, but I think what it is saying is to number them just for the sake of living in the present. And the only thing we can do while we are swimming through the uncertainty is to gain wisdom and to make choices and to come to our own conclusions about things. And I think you are at least trying to gain wisdom as best you can. Well, you know, listening to me is always good. Everything that comes out of my mouth is wisdom—including hairballs! Ha, I wish. No, I'm good, but I'm not that good." He smiles and has that shimmer in his eye.

After Remius and I talked, in order to get out and process all of this information, I wrote a poem. This is what I wrote:

TIMEGASM

The dream
It is unfolding.
I have to start it now.
There is no time to waste,
Get it before it's gone,
Lost in a thought.
A memory
With denied access.
This instant
Will never come again.
Time is a sadistic
Forever.
Stroking itself
While others suffer
As it goes on

Leaving your chances behind
Charging you forcibly forward
While you are not ready
Going back is not an option.
Frozen in Time's memory
Forever used for it to get off.
Laughing and moving,
Constantly spanking you into submission
Like a disobedient lover.
Time penetrates and won't pull out.
Forever
Leaving its seed
In your mind.

FIFTEEN

"Hey, dude, dude." Karl was poking Terry who was staring into space. It was the beginning of another school day.

"What are you thinking about?" Karl asked.

"What do you think?" Terry said.

"Kyleen! Hey, hey!" Karl playfully nudged Terry's shoulder with his fist.

"Piss off! She'll never say yes to me. Only in my dreams." Terry put his head in his hands.

"Well, for a deep thinking guy like yourself," Karl said, "you sure have a lousy attitude. You're fucked if you do and fucked if you don't, right?"

"Yeah, dude," Terry said miserably. "This is fucked. I still have to ask her though."

There she went, down the hall. Terry followed her with his eyes but he didn't make a move.

"Dude," Karl said. "If you want things to change, it is *you* that has to do something."

It was the end of Italian and Terry was heading to English.

"Hey, Terry." He turned and found that Jessica was running to catch up with him. When she got to him she asked, "You still want to come to church with me on Sunday?" Her radiant violet eyes searched his face for any sign of apprehension. There wasn't any. The only thing she could see in his face was a kind of tired regret.

"Sure," Terry said. Then he smiled. "I'll need the company that day." And with that, he turned his back on her and disappeared.

Jessica found Terry confusing; a conundrum, even from the little contact she had with him. She wanted to solve him and share his dark secrets.

After English class was over, Terry stopped Tracey outside the room to talk to her.

"Hey, Tracey, can I talk to you?" Terry said as he approached her.

"Um, sure," she said, a little unsure if she wanted to talk to him or not.

"Do you want to hang out on Saturday? Or something?" Terry said.

"I can't," Tracey responded. She averted her eyes downward as not to have to look at Terry's face. "I, uh, have a boyfriend."

Terry slammed his hand against the wall and Tracey winced. "You failed to mention this to me when you gave me your number," Terry said, trying to keep his cool but not doing a very good job of it.

"I don't think you should call me anymore either." This time, as she spoke, she held his gaze without faltering. Terry licked his lips and looked up at the ceiling.

"Look," he said. "I just want to be friends. Y'know, talk and stuff."

"I can't," she said again.

Terry slammed his hand on the wall again. "Why the fuck not?!"

"Please," Tracey said, positioning her eyes toward the floor again. "You don't need to yell."

"I'm not fucking yelling!"

"No," Tracey said, shaking her head. She lifted her eyes to meet Terry's. There were tears in her eyes. "Don't do this. I just—" she started but then she just walked away leaving Terry to wallow in time and space that was full of shit.

Damnit, Terry thought, *she's such a bitch. She's just a cock-tease.* He hoped that Kyleen would be a better bet. So he waited for Kyleen after school to ask her to Homecoming. He was correct in his estimate on where to find her. He waited outside the spectator gym, going up and down on the sides of his feet nervously. He finally saw her and rushed over.

"Hey," Terry said smiling. "Can I talk to you for a sec?"

"Sure, but I got to be somewhere soon, so make it quick," she said.

"Well, I guess I'll get right to the point." Now Terry was unconsciously wringing his hands too. "Will you go to Homecoming with me?" He then laughed a little nervously.

"I can't," she said. "I'm already going with someone. I'm really sorry. You should have asked me sooner." She walked away leaving Terry with his eyes burning and his hair tingling.

"Penis!" Terry screamed as he walked into his house after school. "Cock-teasing bitch! I hope they all fucking die!"

"Whoa," Remius said. He was laying on the couch. "Slow down, and before you become homicidal, tell me what happened."

"I got fucking rejected by two fucking cunt-ass bitches!"

"Easy with the cunts and the bitches," Remius said, jumping off the couch and walking over to Terry.

Terry turned his face up to the ceiling and pumped his fist. "Fuck you, Timestrus. I'll fucking kill you! You might have won this time, but I swear to fucking God..."

"Right on," Remius said with a tilt of his head. "Ha, ha. Spoken like a true psychopath."

"What the fuck do you mean by that?" Terry asked incredulously.

"Nothing, all I'm saying is that you need to get your girls straightened out."

"Well," Terry said, flopping down on the couch. "There is this one girl who still seems to be interested in me but I'm not sure if her agenda is just to get me saved by fucking Jesus Christ."

"Do we wish to go back in time?" Remius asked.

"Huh?"

"Do you wish to go and take it all back?"

"No," Terry said. "It hasn't gotten that bad yet. I'll stay in the present thank you."

"Whatever works," the October said.

"Am I going crazy?" Terry asked with dread in his eyes.

"What does that word mean?" the cat asked.

"Y'know like when people do or say fucked up shit."

"Fucked up shit?"

"Yeah."

"I don't think you know what the word crazy means. I like the word *fanatical*. But that's just me. Anyway, I have some things I'd like to show you."

"Okay."

"Take a drive with me into the city. And, believe me, we'll see some crazy shit."

SIXTEEN

It was the end of the rejection day at school and everyone was packing up to go home. Rob was no exception. He was fumbling with his locker looking for the stuff he needed to take home. When he felt like he had everything, he decided to take a quick bathroom break before he rode his bike home. He walked into the bathroom which was deserted because most people had gone home already.

Rob took a piss in the urinal and then went to wash his hands. He looked down into the sink as he did so. When he looked up into the mirror, he was startled to find a dark figure in the mirror that was standing behind him. *BLACK*, Rob thought. Rightly so because this person's clothes were *all* black.

Rob turned to face this thing. He could not make out if it was a man or a woman because they were entirely covered in a black robe. The only body part Rob could see was the person's hands sticking out of the top layer of the cloak. This person's head was almost entirely encircled with black cloth. The only part that didn't have cloth covering it was the eyes which were hidden by dark glasses. Moving down over the abdomen was like a black poncho made out of cloth instead of plastic. And then a black skirt that touched the floor.

Rob looked up and smiled his moronic smile. Then the figure removed their glasses revealing eyes like Rob had never seen. The eyes had no irises that Rob could identify. It was just an enlarged pupil that seemed to drill into the deepest parts of his soul. Then the figure removed their hood. In doing this, they exposed a head that was completely bald and devoid of eyebrows as well.

Still Rob could not tell if this was a man or a woman. The figure then removed their entire cloak revealing that, in fact, it was a woman.

Rob stared at this woman. Underneath her cloak, she wore a skin-tight black leotard. The leotard was all one piece except it had a zipper that curved from where the woman's pubic hair would be and under toward her ass.

Rob wanted this woman—at any price. And how could he resist? She had black on, didn't she? And he was a sucker for black.

"Come," she spoke, and her voice was like a petal falling onto still water. Rob came, called by his mistress. Rob considered himself lucky this day.

She grabbed Rob's wrist. To the touch, Rob noticed, she was cold like a corpse. But he didn't care. He knew what he wanted. His fantasies were becoming a reality.

She guided his hand to unzip her and then floated his fingers over her sex. She let his hand go and Rob knew what to do. He was getting hard as he pleasured this woman. She moaned and Rob could feel her lubricant slippery on his hands. He took his fingers away and licked them. She must have liked that because she laughed. Then Rob resumed fingering her again.

But suddenly she pulled his hand away and zipped herself back up. "Don't worry," she hissed. "You will most definitely get more later. If—and only if—you help me."

"What do you need me to do?" Rob asked.

"I am weak in this world and you can help me to get strong. I cannot survive under the sun, that is why I have to wear all of these black clothes. Can you take me to your house?"

"What?" Rob said. "No, my parents will definitely see you."

"No, they won't. Trust me on this. They can't see me."

"Really?"

"Yes, I know what I am talking about. I will explain everything after I am in a good place where I can gain my Hollow strength."

How could Rob say no to this woman? She was the only one who had ever surrendered their pleasure to him. So he agreed.

Rob rode home, on his bike, with the woman riding on his pegs.

Rob didn't really understand what was going on but he didn't like to ask questions. He left the understanding for others who were smarter than him. He just concerned himself with the little pleasures of life. And one of his principle pleasures was anything that was black. He didn't know why and he didn't feel like exploring it.

SEVENTEEN
FROM THE MIND OF TERRY BROSWALD:

My Happy Thoughts

One hand is on the 16,

The other on the nine.
Everything I want
That couldn't be mine.
Been searching for the right line.
It's all in my mind.
The flowing hair,
The haunting, enchanting smile
Of one flaunting, daunting,
And unattainable.
The fall of the outstretched hand
Creates unknown wind through her hair.
Distantly I see that face, beautiful
And fair.
The goal and target
In this
Is known
And is wanted.
Trying to reach through the black veil
That malignantly covers my face.
The crash and crack of bone
As my hand smashes into
The brick barrier.
To break it down
Is possible
If I persevere
And the motivation holds.

The skull crack and shatter of glass.
Frustration is an impenetrable cloak
That I wear always.
To look down at the maze,
Is to see my path.

I can't find my way.
The mouth of the mountain
Cries with shrill laughter
At my trouble.
What is there to lose?
She slips from my grasp;
Swimming in the ever-growing
Dark gap.
Between me and my door
Is a crimson battlefield.
There is a battle to end all things.
I see my reflection in the green
Pool of vomit.
My past, present, and strife
The black whips of life
Grow as dreadlocks
Out of beauty's head.

Trapped in a group because of overrated stereotypes.
To break the cycle.
To take a stand.
To put your manhood out
Just to get your sac brutally sliced
With a jagged female snake-tongue.
Hissing and bile-spitting cock-teasing demons.
The succubus.
Your status is predetermined
And judged
By the sunken eye-masks of the blind light-eaters.
My label is not known but is there.
The busy knife-plunge to the heart
Leaves me wallowing in blood,

Vomit.
Two balls roll down the hall to be trampled.
Mucus and cum and vomit
Spewed out of one source
The human soul.
Acts and personality void
In the eyes of the Judges.
Have a heart,
We're all people.

EIGHTEEN

Rob and the woman went into Rob's house and the woman followed Rob into the kitchen where his mom was.

"Hey, Mom, I'm home," he said as he walked through the kitchen toward the stairs.

"Okay, honey, come down for dinner in an hour," she called after him as he and the woman went up the stairs toward Rob's bedroom. As the woman had said, Rob's mother did not notice her at all.

They got to Rob's room and it was small. There were posters of rappers all over his walls, not to mention a huge Tupac poster on the back of his door. His bed was shoved in the corner of the room and across from it was a waist-high desk that had his old crappy Windows 95 perched on it. And there was a beanbag chair over by Rob's bed.

"Nice," the woman said, taking off her sunglasses and removing her cloak. She draped them over Rob's computer monitor and went to sit down in the beanbag chair.

"All right," Rob said. "First of all, what's your name?"

"It's Maya," she said with a wave of her hand.

"Maya," Rob rolled the name over on his tongue. "How come my mother couldn't see you?" he asked.

Maya shrugged, "They do not have the eyes to see. They are not as talented as you." Maya stretched her hands out, beckoning for Rob to come and sit with her. He did so, walking over to her and sitting down on her lap.

"I need you to make me strong," she said. "And the way I can do that is by human contact with you and I need to eat food from this world. Will you do these things for me?"

"Mmm-hmm," Rob started kissing Maya's neck and collarbone. She closed her eyes and sucked in his energy. This was what she wanted. This was the human contact that she craved because getting strong entailed leeching energy. And he was giving it to her free of charge.

Maya was still cold but Rob didn't care; he wasn't picky. He would take what he could get. Maya touched the bulge that was the crotch of his pants. Rob moaned and then kissed Maya on the lips gently. Her lips felt like her voice—a petal falling on still water. He drank it in and his tongue wandered into the vicinity of her mouth and she returned the affection. Each moment Maya felt her strength gaining. Soon she would be able to attack the certain Soulmind that she wanted in her power. But not quite yet. She was not nearly strong enough. She needed more contact.

Maya unzipped Rob and took his member in her hand.

Rob broke his own rule and asked, "Why did you come?"

"There is someone I need."

"Who?"

"Someone by the name of Terry Broswald."

"Oh, that guy? He's nothing special. Don't waste your time with him. I know that guy."

"You do, do you?" she said. "Well, I need him. Will you agree to help me get him?" She stroked his cock as she said this.

"Uhh," Rob moaned. "Most certainly. Whatever you want, my mistress."

"Excellent," she said and unzipped herself as well.

Rob knew what was coming and he couldn't wait. He never had any patience and this moment was no exception to that rule. He wanted to be inside of her more than anything. And if that required him to turn one of his friends over to her, then so be it. He didn't care. He would do whatever she wanted, whenever she wanted. She was his mistress now.

Rob was content with what little information he had about her. If other people wanted to know about her—fine. That was their beef. But he knew what he wanted. All that he wanted. Rob's world was confined to his hormones and his blackness. No one understood Rob's obsession with black and he never explained it to anyone. All his friends accepted it as an idiosyncrasy.

Maybe understanding was closer than he realized. He would soon be thrust into a world where understanding was mandatory. If he liked it or not would not be an issue. He would just have new knowledge. Then he pushed into her.

NINETEEN

"You think you know crazy?" Remius asked. "You ain't seen nothing yet."

Terry got into the driver's seat of his car and Remius crawled into shotgun.

"There are some things that you are going to see today that you will wish you hadn't seen," the cat continued. "And there will be things that you will wish you hadn't heard. But you need to know how some people in this world are. Fanaticism is something that comes differently depending on the person. There is a rich world of freaks out there. Oh, they are freaks in the public's eye, but I will reveal to you what they do not know. Drive on my dear boy, the city waits."

Terry backed out of his garage and headed for Chicago.

"Here! Park in the parking lot of that Burger King," Remius said when they made it into the city. "No one will care."

Terry did so and then they got out.

"Jesus," Terry exclaimed. "This place is fucking filthy. Look at all the garbage and shit."

"Well," Remius said. "You ain't seen the human shit yet."

"Doesn't Chicago mean, like, smelly onions or something?" Terry asked.

"Something like that... Look over there."

Terry looked. There was a park on the other side of the street and it was deserted except for one man. This man was filthy too. He had a long beard and long hair that didn't look like it had been washed in years. He had on a long green coat and a ripped up pair of jeans. He was running around in circles and lashing and punching out at the air. He was also saying something that was indistinguishable to Terry.

"What's he doing?" Terry asked.

"He's fighting demons," Remius answered. "Because that's what he sees."

"He's one crazy fuck," Terry said.

"Well," Remius said. "He's just doing what the rest of us are doing—reacting to his perceptions. His perceptions may be different than the rest of us though. Does that make him crazy? How do you know that you aren't hallucinating right now? You don't."

"But he's *fanatical!*" Terry yelled.

"You think about it. I'm not saying anything either way. You have to determine this on your own. I can just show you. You see that guy over there on the bench?"

"Yes."

"We're gonna go talk to him."

"Oh, no," Terry said. "I ain't getting near no hobos."

"Oh, come on!" Remius walked over toward the bench where the man sat and Terry had no choice but to follow. The man was weeping with his head in his hands. This man looked exactly like the first man.

"Elvis stole my face," the man sobbed. "He's still alive, I know it. He's gonna come back and get me. Ahhh." The man continued weeping.

"You didn't try to stop him?" Remius asked the man.

"Oh, I tried. But then he called Chuck Norris down upon me. And Chuck held me down while Elvis peeled off my face. And then they flew away into the sky leaving me down here, faceless and kicked aside." He wept all the louder.

Terry and Remius decided to leave the man then.

"How could he see you?" Terry asked.

"Believe you me," Remius said. "That man has a Soulmind. It just destroyed him for he knew not how to use it."

"Shit, man, I don't want to become that way," Terry said, full of horror.

"*You* won't. You got me now."

Something in an alley caught Terry's eye. He turned and saw that it was another hobo; and he was masturbating.

"What about that guy?" Terry asked, pointing with his thumb.

"Oh, don't worry about him. He just has nothing better to do."

Then they came upon a man that was standing in front of a train station spouting off at the mouth.

"I am Jesus," the man said. "You bow down and repent before me and I will give you the honor of licking my giant cock. The angels in heaven and the demons in hell know me and fear me. So you must fear me. Fear me! Or burn in eternal hellfire."

The man continued his tirade. Terry stared in awe and disgust at this man who seemed to be spouting what he believed to be true. But how could it be true? And if it wasn't true, then this man was crazy, right?

"If you do not lick me, then when you have to stand before my father in heaven, he will damn you to an eternity of eternal ass ramming. Ha! How do you like that?"

"Okay," Terry said to Remius. "Let's leave now."

"All right. I will not inflict upon you anymore brain scrambling information. You have enough to sort out as it is. Let's go back to the car."

They headed back to the car. When they got to the parking lot, there was a man standing on the roof of the Burger King.

"Oh, no," Terry groaned. "What is this wacko doing?"

"Watch," Remius said and they both tilted their heads up toward the man on the roof.

The man was swatting at his face and screaming: "Bats! Bats! They're all around me! Fuck, it's that dragon again. Get him away from me! The shadows move and I know not from where it comes. Gahh, ahh, ahh!" The man wept into his hands.

"I don't know where I am," the man screamed as he continued his monologue. "Help! These figments are real!" Then he hurled himself from the roof—dove was more like it. Remius and Terry anticipated the skull crack even before it happened. They winced in unison when it did.

"Shit, dude, did you see that guy?" Terry made a gesture toward the body.

"Oh, I saw it all right. Get in the car."

They got in. Then Remius spoke.

"You saw these men and how they were. But, they were all acting on their perceptions and the truth as they knew it. Just like us all. I am not going to tell you what to think. You have to come to a conclusion yourself. Just think about it. What is true? And what is real?"

PART 3

The Realm of Infallibility

"The pagan will be sanctified, the tragic becomes laughable; great lovers will stoop to sentiment, and demons dwindle to clockwork toys. Nothing is fixed. In and out the shuttle goes, fact and fiction, mind and matter woven into patterns that may have only this in common: that hidden among them is a filigree that will with time become a world."
- Clive Barker, Weaveworld

"For if after they have escaped the pollutions of the world through the knowledge of the lord and saviour Jesus Christ, they are again entangled therein, and overcome, the latter end is worse with them than the beginning. For it had been better for them not to have known the way of righteousness, than, after they have known it, to turn from the holy commandment delivered unto them."
- II Peter 2:20-21 (KJV)

OCTOBER

ONE
FROM THE MIND OF TERRY BROSWALD:

What *is* proof? What *is* evidence? Is it just what people choose to see? The convenience is that they use it to back up their hypothesis. But couldn't someone else use that same evidence to prove what they believe? So which is true? What you *choose* to see. Could *both* hypotheses be true? Or is everything not as it appears? A cruel trick by God to make us confused? What is this God? Does the proof point to God or man? Or both? And people just choose the one they want to see. Embrace one and dismiss the other. But that sluffs off the truth as a lie and the lie as truth. Could they both be true and a lie at the same time? The uncertainty is what rules this world. How can we entirely rule out what someone sees just because *we* can't see it? What constitutes reality? Is it the eyes? Because people see many things. Some people see things that others might not be able to see. Does that mean that what they see is not reality? How could *that* be true? Just because someone can't see what I am seeing does that make me crazy?

Everyone survives the best they can or they just give up and surrender themselves to what they see. They let their perceptions rule them instead of ruling their perceptions. That is where it gets dangerous. It is just when they start acting *different* from the rest of the world that people look at them funny. Then people tell them to get psychoanalyzed. Or get their head checked. Just because someone cannot see stars on a cloudy night, does that mean that the stars are not real? We just can't see them. We cannot trust our eyes all the time. They can play tricks on us. That is why we have to be masters of our perceptions and not the other way around. When people don't realize that they still have power, they lose it and what they see takes over. But does that mean that they are crazy? Does that mean that what they see is unreality? I don't think that it is fair to say that. We say something is real because we can see it and taste it and touch it. That's what is real, right?

Remius told me about the Realm of Dementia. People in our world view them as crazy. But for them what they see is real. They can smell it and taste it and touch it. And above all, they can see it. Can we deny this? I don't think so. So, if we view their perceptions as crazy, can we trust our senses at all?

At school, these thoughts would condemn me to the realm of the weird. Because most kids don't think at all. Then they frown on people who put even the littlest amount of thought into this world. The 'normal' kids swallow everything that they are fed and automatically accept it as truth without even testing it out for themselves. And they think *I'm* weird. This whole fucking system is screwed up. It's like we're being indoctrinated with garbage that we just have to accept with the absence of thought. And when someone actually does try to understand something, they are told not to ask questions... I hate school.

No one is infallible. Especially when it comes to their faith and doctrines. Most people who go to my school say that they are Christians, but they usually can't tell you anything about the Bible or the Christian faith. On the other hand, the people who aren't Christians don't know what they believe either. They either say that they don't believe in anything—which is bullshit—or they just shrug off a crappy answer. It is the same with beliefs about origins. Kids who say they believe in evolution don't know anything about it and kids who believe in Creation really don't know anything about that either.

We know nothing. I know nothing. It scares the shit out of me that I am on a planet that is spinning through the void that I know nothing about. We can never have infinite knowledge. Only God has infinite knowledge and I don't know when I'll get to meet him. So all I can do while I'm alive is search for meaning in this dark and bitter world.

TWO

It was Saturday and also Terry's first session with Dr. Tim Harold. Remius was not too thrilled about the prospect of Terry sharing all of his thoughts with this guy.

"Just tell him that you don't need him anymore," Remius said as Terry was walking out the door.

"I can't do that," Terry said and looked down at Remius who had his tail all puffed out and swishing.

"All right, then I'm coming with you."

"Fine, Jesus, let's go then," Terry said and they both walked out and got in the car.

"I'm driving," Terry announced.

"I wasn't offering," was Remius's retort.

"Bastard cat," Terry muttered as he got in the van.

Terry shot out of the garage and down the road like a demon with Jesus on his tail. He sped on toward the Constrictor.

"You can still back out of this, y'know," the October said, narrowing his eyes at Terry.

"Jeez, will you shut the fuck up for one minute?" Terry gripped the wheel tighter. "I made up my mind, okay? I am not saying that I'm going to believe everything this guy says, I just want someone's opinion. That's all. What harm could it do?"

"I'll tell you what harm it could do. He could make you stop believing and dreaming. And when people stop dreaming—y'know, dreaming is the essence of the Soulmind—and if you stop dreaming, you deny your Soulmind. Then it consumes you."

"That is the exact reason why I'm going. What you said just made no sense to me. Nothing makes any sense."

"Terry, in Time, in Time, in Timestrus you'll know."

Terry ignored the stupid cat and drove on.

"Okay, Terry," Tim said. Terry was in the psych room with Tim and Remius. And Remius was not too happy. "What do you like to do?"

"Don't tell him anything that would be bad for us," Remius warned.

Terry ignored him. Obviously Tim couldn't see Remius and that was both good and bad. It was good because Terry would not have to explain a talking cat. It was bad because Terry didn't know if the reason that the doctor couldn't see him was because the cat was not real or just because he didn't have a Soulmind.

"I like hanging out with my friends. And I'm addicted to music," Terry said hesitantly.

"That's one of the only addictions that may be counted as good. What kind of music do you like?"

"All kinds," Terry answered. "But I despise Country. I like 3 Doors Down a lot. I also like making playlists that are unique."

"That's good."

"This is all right now," Remius said. "But I swear to God, Terry, you better pray that he doesn't ask about your parents."

Terry glanced at Remius out of the corner of his eye but held his tongue and his hand. He was close to crushing the cat's baseball-sized head if he didn't shut up.

"So how's school?" Tim asked.

"Boring."

"How so?"

"It's fucking predictable."

"Well, yeah, school is a routine. And routines are always the same."

"Routines can change. I just have to destroy the conventions first."

"That went pretty well today, Terry. Nothing too serious. Basically bullshit," Remius said on the drive home.

"Yeah, he didn't ask about my parents," Terry said, puzzled. "I thought for sure he was going to. Why do you think he didn't?"

"Because you didn't want him to." Remius's eyes flashed.

"I don't understand."

"It was your Soulmind, okay," Remius said as if he was talking to a child.

"So, are you saying that I can control people with my Soulmind?" Terry asked, obviously disbelieving.

"To a certain extent," Remius said. "But don't abuse it."

"I'll try my best." With that Terry drove into his garage.

***

Meanwhile, at Rob's house, he had basically become a slave to Maya and her black presence. He had been feeding her and housing her for a few days now and did everything she told him to do. He was officially pussy whipped.

"Is there anything else I can get for you, your Blackness?" Rob asked, bowing to Maya who was lounging in the beanbag chair near Rob's bed. She was in her black leotard and her robes were still draped over Rob's shitty computer.

"Sit down, cutie," Maya said, flashing a white smile. Rob sat down on his bed. He was wearing a grin also; the only differences were that Rob's was a metallic smile and it was the smile of ignorance.

Maya leaned her elbows on her knees and looked Rob in the eyes. She was definitely stronger. Her appearance was mostly unchanged, except for her eyes. Her already oversized pupils had grown. Now her entire eyeball was black. Both eyes.

"I can give you anything you want, just name it. What is it you want?" Maya spoke softly and with her face only three inches away from Rob's face.

"Anything?"

"Anything and everything."

"Can you make me BLACK?" Rob asked hopefully.

"Anything you want."

Rob laughed, the laugh of someone who fails to foresee.

"But not yet," Maya said. "Not until I have what I came for. I want his soul."

"But—" Rob started but was cut off.

"Shh, shh!" Maya put her hand up to silence him. She was looking off to one side as if listening. "What was that?"

"What?"

"That noise."

Their attention was now focused on Rob's desk that contained his computer. There was a white dove perched on top of Maya's robes and Rob's computer. When Maya laid eyes on it, she scrambled to get to the place in Rob's room farthest away from the interloping bird, hissing as she went. She continued hissing for another minute. The bird just sat there. When Maya realized that the bird was not going anywhere, she stopped hissing.

Suddenly the dove flew up into the air but only for a second because it shifted shapes as soon as it was airborne. In place of the dove now was a woman standing there. This woman did not look solid and was semi-translucent. She was a black woman. She had white dreadlocks and was wearing white robes. Then she spoke.

"Maya, we're watching your every move. Mind your boundaries." As soon as the woman was there, she had disappeared. The apparition was swept away as if tossed aside by the wind.

Maya was huddled in the corner cringing and shaking.

THREE

"Shit, dude, I'm fucking nervous as hell." Terry paced his bedroom floor. It was Sunday. Terry's date day.

Remius was on his usual perch on the bed. "Don't be," he said. "Just relax."

"Easy for you to say, you're just a frickin' feline. You don't have these types of problems."

"Just don't worry about it," Remius grinned a fang-filled smile.

"What the fuck am I supposed to do? Not give a fuck?"

"Just be yourself and she'll fall right into your hands... Oh, and by the way, I'm coming with you."

"No, no, no! Absolutely not! You always fuck shit up!" Terry was determined not to let Remius come with him.

"No, I don't. Hey, she won't even be able to see me. And if she can, I'll get the hell up out of there fast, kay?"

"Fine, bitch. Let's go."

They got in the car.

"You better not fuck this up for me, man," Terry repeated, making sure Remius understood.

"Don't worry," Remius said. "Chicks love cats."

"I thought you said she wouldn't be able to see you!"

"Oh, yeah, right, right..."

They sat in the car outside of Jessica's house. Each second that ticked by escalated the tension that was running through Terry.

"Shit," Terry was freaking out. "I don't know if I can do this."

"Don't be such a pussy."

The next thing Terry knew, he was standing in front of the door to Jessica's house. Terry stared at his hands. The door swung open unexpectedly as Terry turned around. His face collided with the edge of the door and he felt hot blood seeping out of his nostrils—

He opened his eyes and realized he was standing with his back toward the closed door. He saw Remius smiling from his perch atop the car. Terry shook his head violently and felt his dry nose. Then Terry turned his face to the still-shut door.

Terry reached his hand out, hesitated, then rung the doorbell. There was a moment in which he stood silently, then the door opened *inward*. Terry did not realize the discrepancy between the door of the Real and the door of the Mind. He just watched as Jessica poked her white face out into the sun.

"Hold on a sec," Jessica said. She started to turn back into her house, then stopped. She stared straight ahead past Terry. "Wait," she started. "Terry... There's a cat sitting on top of your car."

"Huh?" Terry turned around but Remius was already gone. "Where?"

"Nevermind," she said, turning back into her house. She closed the door of the Real and then returned about two minutes later.

"Ready to go?" Terry said.

"Yeah, let's walk. It's not far."

They walked in awkward silence for about five minutes. Then Terry finally broke it.

"So... are your parents going to be there?"

"No," Jessica replied. "They're out of town."

"Oh," Terry said. They continued to walk in silence. It was at this time that Terry observed what Jessica was wearing. She was wearing a shiny dark purple dress with black shoes. Terry thought that purple looked good on her. She also carried a black King James Bible. *What the fuck did I get myself into?* Terry asked himself. He normally didn't like religious chicks but there was something different about Jessica. Whatever it was, Terry couldn't place it at the moment.

They kept walking in silence until Jessica stopped in front of a large brick building.

"Well, this is it," Jessica declared. Terry looked up; it looked like a church. The roof was pointed and there were stained glass windows with images of the crucifixion. Terry shrugged and followed Jessica into the building.

As they walked into the building, Terry saw a slightly overweight man in a suit greeting people going into the main sanctuary. The man noticed Jessica and immediately started walking over toward her with his arms outstretched.

"Jessica Thorn," the man said happily as he embraced her. "How are you?"

"Fine," she said, and kissed him on both cheeks. The man held Jessica out at arms length to have a look at her.

"How are your folks doing?" the man asked.

"Oh, they're fine." As Jessica was saying this, the man finally noticed Terry standing quietly to one side.

"And who's this young man?" The man eyed Terry a bit. That made Terry slightly uncomfortable. Jessica walked behind Terry, grabbed his arms, and pushed him forward. "This is my friend Terry," Jessica said. "Terry, this is Brother Evan. He's the pastor here."

"Nice to meet you," Terry said. They shook hands. A little shock went up Terry's arm as they did. Evan didn't seem to notice.

Evan smiled. "Likewise," he said. "I'd better go get ready. Nice talking to you two." With that, Brother Evan walked off.

"Isn't he a nice man?" Jessica said, smiling. "He's a friend of my family too." Jessica grabbed Terry's hand and dragged him toward the sanctuary. Terry went along passively. He didn't notice, but he was bleeding under his fingernails.

Jessica successfully dragged Terry to a pew and sat down. Terry was present throughout the whole sermon but heard none of it because for most of it he was carrying on a mental conversation with Remius. What was weird about it though was that while Terry talked with Remius, he was in his head. *They* were in his head. Not just in it, *present* in it. Let me put it this way, Remius and Terry carried out their conversation sitting in two wooden chairs in a bare, dark attic—in Terry's mind. Well, anyway, this is what they said.

"I thought you said that she wouldn't be able to see you," Terry said.

"How the fuck was I supposed to know?" Remius blurted out. "I'm not omnipotent you know!" Remius was clearly pissed—maybe at Terry, maybe at himself.

"Whatever," was Terry's response.

"Listen to me, Terry," Remius suddenly got serious. "Don't get too involved with this girl, Terry, she's got a Soulmind. Well, I'll explain more later. But when two Soulminds become romantically involved, it usually doesn't turn out well."

It was Terry's turn to go spastic. "What the fuck does *that* mean?" He jumped up out of his attic chair with his fists clenched. "What the fuck, man! The first girl I might have a chance with you take away from me? I'll do what I want! Fuck you!"

"All I'm saying is don't bang her," Remius said.

"You cunt rag!" Terry screamed. He grabbed Remius by the neck and shook him. It didn't faze the cat, he just bit Terry's hand. That shook Terry from the attic.

He was suddenly back, staring at the preacher. Terry did not want to listen to what he had to say though. As Terry thought that, Evan started to speed up as if someone had hit fast-forward on his personal remote control. Terry had sped up time. But this was a mortal sin.

"Stop!" Remius invaded Terry's head again. "Dude, don't fuck with Time."

Just like that, everything went back to normal speed. "Timestrus gets pissed when someone other than him can control time," Remius warned.

"Thanks for warning me," Terry said. Just at that moment, Terry noticed something he hadn't noticed before. It was a giant cross just to the right of the pulpit. He stared at it for a while then realized that everyone was getting up to leave.

"C'mon," Jessica motioned for Terry to get up. "Let's go to Starbucks."

FOUR
FROM THE MIND OF TERRY BROSWALD:

In my world,
Sleep doth come but once a year.
I do sleep but once a day.
But that sleep,
Haunted and Hellish.
Ripped by dreams of
Death and Rape.
Protection does not come
In this barren wilderness.
My own mind betrays me.
And finds new ways to hurt me.

But soon.
When Time is gone and dead,
Sleep will come,
With broad white Wings.
That one single day.

And I will Sleep.
Like every night
Except,
This time,
The wing will be my
Protector.

FIVE

"We're gonna get caught," Jessica tried to sound scared but was laughing nonetheless.

"No, we won't," Terry said.

It was Monday and twenty minutes before school was supposed to start. Terry and Jessica were sneaking into the vacant auditorium.

"C'mon, c'mon," Terry was basically dragging Jessica down the aisle toward the stage. They were both laughing and enjoying themselves. Terry told Jessica to sit in the front row and that he was going to perform for her. Terry scrambled onto the stage, almost slipping off as he did so. Jessica laughed. When Terry got onto the stage, he looked down at Jessica, who was still laughing. Boy, was she cute. Her long, smooth hair, dark as the mouth of hell. Her skin so pale, so fair. And those eyes—penetrating, like a cat's. He couldn't even believe she was real.

He paced the stage, thinking of something to perform. And then the right passage finally came to him. He turned to his audience, and acted.

"She should have died hereafter," he began, quoting Shakespeare's *Macbeth*. "There would have been time for such a word. Tomorrow and Tomorrow and Tomorrow creeps in this petty pace from day to day to the last syllable of recorded time, and all our yesterdays have lighted fools the way to dusty death. Out, out, brief candle! Life is but a walking shadow, a poor player that struts and frets his hour upon the stage and then is heard no more. It is a tale told by an idiot, full of sound and fury, signifying nothing." Terry gave a little bow with his head.

Jessica began to applaud. "Thank you," he said, bowing more. "Enjoy it. Because from this life I am untimely ripped."

By this time Jessica was climbing up onto the stage herself. She immediately started running around the stage. She stopped, lifted her hand in the air, and danced to some imagined chorus. Terry couldn't help but be enthralled as she spun.

Suddenly she halted and pointed at something in the audience. "Look," she said.

As Terry focused, trying to see what she was pointing at, he was totally caught off guard when she tackled him to the stage floor.

Jessica looked down into Terry's eyes. Terry swam in her's. She smiled and then spoke.

"What is your fascination with the macabre?"

Terry didn't answer, he just started to bring his face closer to hers—then the bell rang.

They bolted to their feet.

"Fuck," Terry said. "We're late now."

They gave each other one final look and then darted in separate directions.

The day passed as it always had but Terry was just in a better mood than usual. He was in his own little world. Terry's last class had just ended and he realized he needed to take a massive piss, so he headed for the bathroom. He did what he needed to and then went to wash his hands in the sink that was stationed in front of the stalls.

He looked up into the mirror and saw that Rob was standing next to him. Terry didn't get a chance to say anything because Rob backhanded him in the face. Terry fell back, through the stall door. The only thing that Terry saw before the black was a flash of cat's eyes as his head busted open on the porcelain bowl.

Then Black... and Rob had sent him there.

Rob walked triumphantly out of the room where he had just stunningly taken Terry to the ground where Rob preceded to leave him bleeding from his head. Rob felt very pleased with himself and knew that Maya would be pleased with him too.

Rob arrived back at his house chanting "black man in the copy room" to himself. He took off his shoes and went upstairs to his room. When Rob opened the door, Maya immediately jumped up from her seat with an eager expression on her face. She was no longer bald. As she got stronger, her long straight black hair had grown back.

"So, did you get him?" Maya asked expectantly.

"Who?" Rob said, puzzled.

"Terry, you numbskull!" Maya smacked Rob on the head.

"Oh," Rob said as if a very important realization had enlightened him. "I laid his ass low! It was real gangster." Rob gave a little laugh.

"Oh, my God!" Maya turned away from Rob shaking her head. "You are such a dumb piece of shit. You were supposed to bring him back to me."

"Bring back?... To you?" Rob said stupidly. He put a finger up to his chin as if thinking. "Ahhh..."

Maya whirled around and kneed Rob squarely in the balls. There was a sharp intake of breath then he was on the floor—eyes shut, teeth clenched, holding his wounded manhood. Maya sat down in her beanbag chair, ran her fingers through her hair, and sighed. Rob came out of his initial shock in about a minute and went over and sat in front of Maya on the floor. She looked down at him.

"Maybe I should get someone smarter than you," she said.

"Rob? Not smart? What?"

Maya shook her head. "This would all be over if I could just do it by myself." She clenched her fists in frustration.

"Why can't you?" Rob asked.

"Do you remember the dove?" Maya said.

"Black woman?"

"Yeah," Maya continued. "That's Rahjiah. She's from the Dimension the Stone Queen rules. Rahjiah is in the Order of the Transcendent. This Order has thirteen members who can travel to any Dimensions at will. They are in charge of keeping order and separation between all Dimensions. So, I'm not allowed to hurt anyone from this hollow realm where everyone's life is spent oblivious to how spiritual the world is. Humans are just walking clutter, not needed. And Rahjiah knows that I am after Terry so I cannot be seen trying to capture him."

"So what are we gonna do?"

"I'll tell you what we are going to do..."

* * *

When Terry came to, it was ten o'clock and no one was around. He was surprised no one had moved him or woken him up. He felt the back of his head and there was dried blood, but the gash didn't seem too serious. He grabbed his books and headed for the exit.

He found himself in front of the Gatorade machine near the spec gym. Terry put two dollars in and pressed the button for Lemon-Lime. Nothing came out. Terry just stood there for a second.

Then he kicked the side of the machine.

Nothing.

He was pissed now.

Terry screamed and became a bareknuckle boxer on that vending machine's ass.

Niente.

"Fuck on a flagpole," Terry said between pants. His eyes drifted onto his Algebra Two book lying on the floor.

Terry picked it up.

Raised it above his head,

Then he chucked that shit with such a cry that it could have been his Gatorade Jihad.

That book went straight through the top of the flimsy plastic front. It made a hole about two feet in diameter.

Terry looked through the hole and all that he could see was darkness. It was odd but Terry had no trouble peeling off the rest of the plastic.

He stepped inside.

The plastic seemed to regenerate itself behind him. But it lacked substance; Terry could move through it freely but decided to move into the black passage.

Terry did not know what it was about darkness that just called out to him. He gave in to it every time.

His eyes were getting used to the darkness and could see that there were brick walls on either side of him. They were covered with graffiti. They were mostly of deformed clocks and weird phrases like: 'The Tethered Toys' and 'Infinite Connection Time.' Terry had no clue what any of this meant.

Then he came to a two-way fork. He turned toward the left. Terry was suddenly grabbed from behind and enveloped by what seemed to be a large blanket, but then he realized they were great black wings. Terry's arms and legs were paralyzed beneath the wings. Terry could tell the wing was attached to some human-like creature because it had its hands on Terry's shoulders. Terry could also feel its body pressed against his back. The creature brought its face up beside Terry and began to lick his face. Terry closed his eyes and cringed as the thing made out with Terry's neck and collarbone.

Terry felt utterly naked.

And he was.

Then the creature spoke. It's voice was smooth, neither deep nor high and Terry didn't know if this thing was male or female. He would know soon.

"You fuck with Time," it hissed. "Time will fuck with you."

Terry tried to scream as something long and slimy penetrated him. With horror Terry realized what it was when it started thrusting in and out. Terry tried to scream again. He couldn't make a sound. The creature laughed and continued thrusting and licking.

Terry was helpless. He could do nothing as his manhood was violated. Terry was appalled when he realized that he himself was getting a hard-on. He was cumming too. *Goddamn it*, Terry thought. He closed his eyes. The final stab of pain was when the *monster* came. Terry could feel its fluid pulsating through his body.

Then he passed out.

When Terry woke up, it was only ten minutes later. He was sprawled naked in front of the vending machine and bleeding from his nether regions.

Terry ran the fuck home—crying and exposed.

When Terry reached his house, the only thing he could see was a blinding white light. He smashed the door open and fell in a heap to the floor sobbing. Remius was instantly at his side but said nothing. Terry then stumbled to his feet and went into the living room. With a cry of anguish, he clutched the TV and hurled it to the floor where it shattered into sharp shards. Terry vomited violently onto the remains of the TV and then dropped his naked body on the couch.

"FUCK! WHAT THE FUCK?! AGGHHH!" Terry got up just as fast as he had sat down. He crossed into the kitchen adjacent to the living room. Remius just observed Terry's pain. Terry went to a drawer and opened it, revealing an assortment of meat cleavers and butcher knives. Terry pulled out the longest and sharpest-looking one. Terry gritted his teeth as salty water still poured out of his eyes. He placed the blade lightly vertically with the veins in his wrist and prepared to slice.

Remius jumped up on the kitchen counter beside Terry and said, "Do you really want to cut yourself, you fucking emo bitch?"

How the fuck can he make light of this? Terry asked himself. "Fuck. You..." Terry said slowly. "Look at me! You fucking pussy-cat bitch! I'M BLEEDING FROM MY FUCKING ASS! Can you not see this? Fuck Time and fuck this place." He made a motion as if he was going to start cutting.

"I am fully aware of what has transpired and what has been done to you. It could have been much worse."

Terry rolled his eyes.

"Let me finish," Remius continued. "You are alive, are you not?"

Terry nodded.

"Okay, be thankful of that. Now, let's just sit down and talk about this, there are things you still don't fully understand."

Terry narrowed his eyes and threw his knife forcibly to the floor. They went and sat down on the couch.

"Now," Remius said in a more caring tone. "What happened?"

"Time," Terry started slowly. "...raped...me."

"Now repeat that."

"Time...raped...me."

"Now, we want to rationalize this in the mind, okay," Remius said slowly. "What does time consist of?"

"Numbers, uh, it's just an idea, basically."

"Exactly," Remius said with a smile in his eye. "People made up the concept of time. This is an infallible fact. However, we gave him life and he has gotten out of anyone's control. However, he is still just an idea. The reason that he still exists is because so many people have him in their mind. They are willingly fucked by him, every fucking day of their pathetic little lives. See, time is really just an absurd little kid trying to maintain everyone's attention and just gets pissed off when someone does not bow to his every command. Do you see?"

Terry had a puzzled expression which suddenly exploded into a laugh and a smile. "That's absurd," he said. "It makes sense though. Now that you put it that way."

"When you try to rationalize, you come up with the absurd. And that is what is supposed to happen. Is Time infallible? Does he know everything? No. What is really contained in the pages of the infallible, and what is contained within the pages of the ludicrous? You are beginning to distinguish between the two. This is good. But look at it this way, you may have an advantage over Timestrus now."

"Why?"

"Because you have some of his fluid inside of you."

"How would that make any difference?"

"Your Soulmind can figure out what he is made of," Remius explained. "Which tells his weaknesses, and the things the Soulmind tells are infallible." Remius winked at Terry.

Terry was beginning to see the brighter side of this situation and not just to dwell on the brutal crime that was committed against him. Remius was insanely good at making the situation seem better than it actually was. He could spin anything. He would not lie, but he was an expert at persuasion.

SIX

The rest of Terry's week went by as it usually did except for one little oddity.

Terry was in his math class on Monday and the teacher asked the students to open their textbooks. As Terry opened his Algebra 2 textbook, he noticed that the insides of all the pages had been cut out forming a hidden compartment. The weirdest part was what was hidden in this compartment. It looked to Terry like the handle of a machete. He quickly shut the book and shoved it into his backpack.

When Terry went home that day, he took the handle out and the pages regenerated before his eyes. Terry was puzzled but he just pocketed the hilt.

Saturday. Terry's second session with Dr. Tim. He continued to not tell the doctor too much. Terry simply bullshitted for an hour.

Sunday. Church. Misery. Jessica. Beauty. Terry was sitting beside Jessica in the church, not listening to what the pastor was saying. Terry was contemplating the meaning of the machete hilt but coming up with nothing. Terry suddenly snapped out of his trance and began to hear the pastor's words fully and clearly.

"For if after they have escaped the pollutions of the world through the knowledge of the lord and saviour Jesus Christ," Brother Evan continued, "they are again entangled therein, and overcome, the latter end is worse with them than the beginning. For it had been better for them not to have known the way of righteousness, than, after they have known it, to turn from the holy commandment delivered unto them."

What's he saying? Terry wondered. *Is he saying that since I have come to church and listened and not believed, that it is worse for me now because of it?* That really pissed Terry off a lot. He did not like this guy anymore. Saying that it would be worse for him than the beginning. How could things get any worse? What's worse than being raped by Time? This guy did not know shit about suffering. But he would soon.

SEVEN

FROM THE MIND OF TERRY BROSWALD:

I am dreaming. I know I am dreaming. I am standing in the middle of a deserted street. It is pitch dark and yet I can still see. I know that this is a dream because there are no buildings in sight, just the street in front of me and behind me, and grass on both sides of the street as far as I can see. I look down at my hand. I am clutching that machete handle. What the hell? It is just a fucking handle. I have no use for that shit. I chuck it into the grass.

I feel like there is something I must do. Something I must accomplish. Someone I must teach. But I cannot do this task alone. I shut my eyes and mentally summon Karl to my side. When I open my eyes he is there, beside me, holding a beretta. He nods to me. I grab his hand and we close our eyes tight. I can feel white light spiraling around us as I will our bodies to instantly switch locations. I feel that the spirals have dissipated and we open our eyes. I let go of Karl's hand. We are staring at the church. Jessica's church. Brother Evan's church. My church...

"Are you ready to do this shit?" I ask Karl.

"Fuck yeah, dude! Red Palm, bitch!" He flashes our sign then we start walking toward the building.

We find Evan praying in front of the cross by the altar.

"Lucifer is here," I say. He turns around and smiles at me. "Wipe that smile off your face, old man." I walk over and backhand him across the face. He turns to face me again, smiles, then turns the other cheek. I gladly accept and backhand him again. Blood comes freely from the corners of Evan's smiling mouth.

"Stop smiling!" I scream as I kick him in the face. He instantly falls and is splayed on his back at the foot of the cross. I stand over him. "You are the cross, bitch, literally and metaphorically. What are you going to do? Repent?" I squat down and look into his face. "What is it going to be then, eh? Your choice."

"Jesus loves you," Evan manages to choke out.

"Yeah, yeah, yeah, and everyone else thinks I'm an asshole, right? What do you think?" I poke his nose with my finger. All this time Karl is just watching, waiting for my command, whatever it may be.

"Am I a sinner?" I say.

"We have all sinned and come short of the glory of God," he quotes.

I kick him in the side of the head. "Stop quoting verses," I say matter-of-factly. "Now let's talk about that little verse you were saying this morning. Oh, what was it? You think that since I know the 'Word' and turn away then my punishment will be worse than if I had never have known the 'Way?' Is this correct?"

"It would be better for them not to have known," he coughs. I forcefully straddle Evan's stomach and grab his collar and pull his face up to mine and give him a little verse of my own.

"It would have been better to have known the way of Darkness and to embrace it, then after having seen it, turned back and blinded yourself with the light." When I say the word 'light' a burning spear of white light shoots out of my chest and into the eyes of the pastor. He shields his burning eyes with his hands. The light fades and I get off of his pathetic little being. "Karl," I say. "Make sure he doesn't go anywhere. I'll be right back." He nods and I walk over to one of the pews where I have dream-spawned four railroad spikes and some rope. I take these items and dump them beside the altar.

Then I look down. What the fuck? The hilt of the machete is sticking out of my solar plexus. I grip the handle and rip it out of my chest. It is not just a hilt any longer. There is a blade. But it's weird. The blade is made out of that light. My Soulmind light. Burning threads are lacing all around the blade like it is on fire. I stare in awe at this weapon that has come from my being.

I stick my right arm out at a ninety degree angle and point the blade down, then drop to my knees. In doing this, it imbeds the blade up to the hilt in Evan's stomach. He screams with pain and blood shoots from his mouth. As Evan chokes on his own blood and coughs, I rip the blade brutally from his intestinal area. Evan cringes as I do so.

Evan tries to speak. "It would have been better—COFF—for them not to have known."

"What was that?" I say as I thrust my hand into the hole that I have made in Evan's belly. Aren't dreams great? Anyway, I tear some of his intestines out of the hole as he screams and writhes in pain. He gushes blood profusely, which I am covered in now. I stand up and start taking off my clothes. Don't worry, I'm not going to rape him. I'm not that fucking sick. I take off all my clothes and just stand there, naked, covered with blood. I look down at Evan as he bleeds and clutches his midsection.

"Karl," I say. "Beat this guy while I get the cross down." Karl straddles Evan's stomach like I had been doing and starts beating him in the face with his beretta. I pull the huge cross down and lay it flat on the altar. I smile to myself.

I pull Karl off of Evan and tell him that that's enough. I grab Evan's collar and say, "You love God?" Evan nods. "Well, you're gonna meet him. And you're gonna die like him. Karl, bring me those railroad spikes." I lay Evan on top of the cross with his arms out. Karl hands me the spikes. All this time Evan is trying to say that stupid verse through all the blood in his mouth.

I take one of the spikes and place the point in the palm of Evan's hand and use the hilt of my machete to pound it down into his tender flesh. He tries to scream but it seems more like a gurgle due to all of the blood in his mouth and throat. Blood gushes out of the hole I have made in his palm. Just like Jesus, he will bleed. He should feel honored. "You want to be crucified upside down?" I ask him. He can't answer because his teeth are broken, he is drowning in his own blood, and he's almost unconscious. "I take that as a no." I pierce the other hand and then tie his arms to the cross with the rope so his hands don't rip. Speaking of rip—I rip all his clothes off. Jesus died naked and so will Evan.

I nail his feet down and then me and Karl hoist the cross back into place. Hell yeah, now it is a real crucifixion. "Give me your gun," I tell Karl, and he does. I aim the gun at Evan's kneecap and shoot both knees out. This makes him sink down even more which hinders his breath even more. I hand the gun back to Karl and thank him. "Go tag Red Palm Gang all over. I'll watch this holy man die slowly." Karl goes to mark our new territory.

I watch as Evan has increasing trouble inflating his chest. Since he is upright, his intestines are starting to fall out of his stomach and they are hanging down in front of his genitals. After a while Evan's head flops to his chest and he stops moving. By this time Karl is back. "You know how it is in dreams," I say to Karl. "People don't die as easily. So we have to make sure." I take out my machete and stab Evan under his ribs. Blood spurts and I am satisfied with my work. I thank Karl for helping me in accomplishing this task, even though it was just a dream fantasy.

I piss on the foot of the cross. "That's my burden, bitch. You can have it. It has been weighing me down all night." We turn and walk out the door—Karl like a gangsta and me like a blood-drenched rapist.

Then I wake up.

EIGHT

When Terry got to his usual spot before school on Monday morning, he found Jessica there, crying. She stood up, hugged Terry, and continued to cry on him. Terry put his arms around her and asked what was wrong.

"It's Brother Evan," she managed to choked through her tears. "He's dead!" More sobs.

Oh shit, Terry thought.

"He was crucified on the cross in the church," she sobbed.

Oh damn, Terry said to himself. *What have I done? This wasn't supposed to happen.*

"Isn't it awful?" Jessica said, clutching Terry's chest.

"Yeah... awful." *I don't want to be a murderer!*

When Jessica went off to her class, instead of going to class, Terry decided to ditch school and go find Remius. Terry found him watching TV at the house. When Terry got there, he picked up a hammer that was laying on the counter in the kitchen and hurled it at the TV. The hammer lodged in the TV, breaking the screen in half.

"What the fuck!" Terry screamed.

Remius jumped off the couch and walked over to Terry. "Oh, shit," Remius said. "What happened?"

"You don't know?" Terry said. "It happened in dreamworld or whatever. I thought you knew everything."

"First of all, I don't know everything," Remius continued. "And second of all, Octobers are not allowed to see human dreams, we just help you unlock them. I made one for a person once and I was punished for that. Anyway, I'll tell you about that later. What happened?"

"I killed someone."

"Shit, dude, are you sure?"

"What the fuck do you mean, am I sure? Of course I'm sure. I thought it was only a dream." Terry flopped down on the couch and Remius did the same. Terry ran his hand through his hair and weighed his frustration. "Why the hell is this happening to me? I thought it wasn't real." Terry put his face in his hands.

"Remember when I said," Remius reminded Terry, "that just because it is a dream does not mean that it is not real or true."

"Ah, shit."

"Yeah. But don't worry. No one will find out that it was you."

"I don't care about that," Terry confessed. "I only *thought* about killing people before, I never thought I would really do it. I don't want to be a murderer. I did not want to kill someone for real—make it infallible. Shit. Why do I always manage to screw up someone's life? I don't want to cause anymore hardship."

"You can't take it back now, it's too late."

"Wait, are you saying that it was possible to take something back? In time?"

"Yeah, but it is extremely risky and difficult. Most people do not have the ability to do it. The window of opportunity to do it is only seconds after the deed took place. After that, it is lost to history. The risky part is that Timestrus gets even more pissed off at you. I would be careful. You probably can't do it anyway, but don't even try to reverse time even if you thought you could. Timestrus is not one to forgive. And he can kill."

That night Terry laid awake in his bed thinking about Jessica. "I'm so sorry," he said, starting to cry. "I didn't mean to hurt you." Terry found his mind drifting back to their first date, after the church service. In the Starbucks, where it all began...

"What do you want?" Terry asked Jessica as they stood in the line to get coffee.

"Uhhh," she put her finger to her lip, trying to decide. "How about a green tea latte?"

"Sounds good," Terry said. He ordered the green tea latte for Jessica and a Java Chip Frappuccino for himself, then they sat down at the table by the window.

"So," Jessica said, taking a sip of her latte. "What do you do?"

"What do you mean?" Terry asked.

She paused, staring into Terry's eyes. "Did anyone ever tell you," she began, "that your eyes are like clocks?"

"What?"

She seemed to snap out of her trance. "Oh, uh, I mean, uh, what do you like to do?"

"Oh, I don't know. I like acting." Terry shrugged.

Jessica nodded. She stirred her coffee absentmindedly with her wooden stir stick. "So," she said again. "What did you think of Brother Evan and my church?"

"Oh," Terry said, self-consciously. "Um, I thought Brother Evan seemed like a nice guy and it was a nice and warm, welcoming church."

Jessica smiled. "I'm glad."

"What do you do, then?" Terry asked.

"I don't know." Jessica stared down into her coffee, lost in thought. "Searching," she said after a while. Her eyes darted up to see Terry's reaction to this.

Terry perked up at this. "Really?" He said. "Me too. Aren't we all?"

"No," she said, looking down again. "Not everyone."

"What are you searching for?" Terry asked, interested.

"Truth."

"Truth," Terry repeated. "The ultimate search."

"Do you ever get this feeling that you are just helpless," Jessica seemed desperate now, and scared. "And alone?"

Terry just looked into her eyes for a time, contemplating this girl. She was complicated. But she seemed to be looking for the same things that he was: truth and meaning. Did she want something from him? Did she think that she would find answers in him? Because Terry knew that he had no answers to give her. He felt just as helpless and alone as she did.

"I'm sorry. I..." She broke her eye contact with Terry and looked around nervously.

"No," Terry said, grabbing her hands over the table. "I do." He looked into her eyes and there was a moment when they felt completely connected, as if their thoughts were synced together through a complicated network of emotion. "This world is complicated. And it is all we can do to try to find these things out. Is there a God? Why are we here? All of these questions we ask. We cannot answer these questions on our own. We can look on our own, but I don't think it is possible to succeed being totally alone."

"Yes, we need others to share the pain." Jessica turned her head to the side, not looking at Terry. A tear escaped from the corner of her left eye. "I'm sorry," she said. "I did not mean to burden you with all my philosophical bullshit from the start. I do not know what came over me."

"Don't be sorry," Terry had said, as he wiped a tear from her eye. "These things are normal."

Jessica smiled at him. "There is just something about you, that makes me feel like I can tell you anything. I know that we have only just met. I don't know. It's weird."

"I know," Terry said softly. "I needed someone. And you needed someone. Some things cannot be rationally explained in the human mind." Terry leaned over and kissed Jessica on the forehead. "Life is like a frontier. And we have to explore it, or we will die, squandering time away. We are given time to search, not to be idle."

And that was how it began.

Terry was still lying in his bed, awake, crying quietly. "I think I love you," he whispered in the dark.

PART 4

Tripping Time

*"To every hour, its mystery.
At dawn, the riddles of life and light.
At noon, the conundrums of solidity.
At three, in the hum and heat of the day,
a phantom moon, already high.
At dusk, memory.
And at midnight?
Oh, then the enigma of time itself;
of a day that will never come again
passing into history while we sleep."*

- Clive Barker, *Sacrament*

NINE

"Dreams, Time, Truth. Are these three related?" Terry was sitting on his bed with his eyes up toward the ceiling in contemplation. Remius was on his usual perch on the window sill, looking out.

"One of the Holy Trinities," Remius said after a while. "Like time, space, and matter... a trinity of trinities. Time consists of past, present, and future. Space consists of length, width, and height. Matter is solid, liquid, and gas... Funny how these things work..." Remius trailed off again, looking at the sky.

"Yeah, but what do Time, dreams, and truth have in common? Why are they a Holy Trinity?" Terry asked again.

Remius sighed. "Okay, Time cannot affect dreams. Truth affects dreams. Truth also affects Time, but nothing can affect truth. Think of it as a kind of check and balance thing... You don't get it." Remius sighed again. "I am not a Spirit Being who can describe things infallibly. I am just an October, just doing my job."

"You don't want to be with me, do you?" Terry said.

"That's not true," Remius responded. "I have come to care about you a lot. So much so that I want to protect you." They did not say anything for a while. Remius broke the silence by saying: "You know, I wasn't always an October."

"What?" Terry exclaimed.

"Yeah," Remius began. "When I was a kitten. I belonged to this little boy who traveled with a caravan. Our caravan stopped in the town or Ulthar. There was one October who was in the town when we came. He told me of wondrous dreams and Meddia, the cave between the Hollow and the Dreamsphere where all the Octobers ultimately go out from and return to once our work is done. He told me that I was called to become an October. He was sent to fetch me. It had to be in Ulthar because it was prophesied in Meddia that I would have some task in Ulthar. So the caravan left and I stayed.

"It turned out that a couple in the town got sick pleasure from trapping and dissecting cats alive. It seemed I did have a task to complete in Ulthar. I aided in the killing of the couple. And after that remarkable day when the cats were triumphant was when they passed the law that in Ulthar no man may kill a cat. When mine and the October's task was done, I went with him to Meddia."

"Wow, that is a pretty awesome story," Terry said.

"Yeah, well that story got me in trouble once."

"When?" Terry asked, intrigued.

"It was the only time I ever broke an October law. You see, Octobers are forbidden to create dreams. But, I wanted more than anything for someone to know the story. So, one night, I created a person's dream. It was a guy named Lovecraft. I remember it clearly. I breathed the story into the man's unconscious head. And he wrote it down for the world to see. I still think it was worth it. So people would know the story of what happened in Ulthar. I was strictly punished when Sul found out. I was forbade from my work for seven years and I couldn't drink from Vivere during that time either."

"Who's Sul?" Terry wondered aloud.

"He's the dragon who governs us. He lives in Meddia and looks after us all," said Remius.

"I see. And what's Vivere?"

"That is the stream that flows through our cave. I cannot tell you anymore about that though," Remius stared out the window.

Terry sank back into his bed and closed his eyes.

* * *

"I am Arash fucking Khan! That's right, bitches. Arash Khan... I just transferred yesterday." Terry was sitting at his lounge table at school with Karl and his other buddies. This new guy—Arash Khan—sat down next to Terry. Terry gave Karl a weird look.

"Guys, guys," Arash said. "You know that Public Works building across from the Mitsubishi dealer? Well, they always have that huge pile of salt for the roads in that building, you know. Why would they need fences and barbed wire and security guards around that building if there is just salt in there? I don't think it's salt that is in there—it's crystal meth!" He looked at them with a smug smile on his face and nodded. Karl and Terry looked at each other. Arash stuck his hand out at Terry. "Hey, I'm Arash Khan." Terry shook it.

TEN

"So, why are you really here?" Dr. Tim asked that Saturday. Terry had been rambling on for about forty-five minutes about movies and books. Terry stopped mid-sentence and looked at Tim. He stood up and walked over to Tim's chair.

"Because I don't want to be who I am."

Terry walked out of the building. He got into his car and popped in his mix CD he made the day earlier and turned on *Twisted Transistor* by Korn.

"Because the music do / And then it's reaching / Inside you, forever preaching / Fuck you, too / Your scream's a whisper..."

Terry drove over to Golf Mill, the nearest mall. He was feeling generous and wanted to buy something nice for Jessica—they had a date that night. Terry wandered around the mall for a while contemplating what gift would truly compliment her. He absentmindedly passed a little stand where someone was selling necklaces. He stopped and backed up to look at the necklaces. His eyes fell on a thin silver chain on which dangled a small, plain silver cross. The cross was only a little thicker than paper. Delicate jewelry for a delicate girl, Terry thought. He bought the necklace and left. No one except for the man who sold him the cross noticed his presence.

A few hours after Terry was at the mall, he drove over to pick Jessica up for their date.

"I got something for you," Terry said when Jessica got into the car. Her eyes brightened and she smiled.

"What is it?" she said. Terry handed her a small box which she took out of his hands tenderly. She opened it, and when she saw the cross, she smiled at Terry and kissed him. She took it out of the box and put it around her neck. "I love it. It's perfect," she said. "Thank you so much... So where are we going?"

"That, my pretty thing, is a surprise."

As they drove, Jessica got more and more excited about this surprise date. When Terry finally pulled off the road, it was at the Allstate Arena.

"Oooh," Jessica cooed. "Are we going to see a concert?"

"Yep."

"Who?"

"Korn."

"No way! I love Korn!" She couldn't contain her excitement, and hugged Terry.

"Easy, you're gonna make me crash," Terry said as he pulled into a parking space.

Their seats were only a few rows back and they could see everything. The concert was great. They knew most of the songs and sang along. One song was Terry's favorite. "This is my favorite song," Terry said.

"Which one is it?" Jessica asked.

"*Alone I Break*." Terry sang it out with emotion:

"... Now I see the times they change
Leaving doesn't seem so strange
I am hoping I can find / Where to leave my hurt behind
All the shit I seem to take
All alone I seem to break
I have lived the best I can
Does this make me not a man..."

Terry was so enthralled in the music that he was oblivious to what was happening to him.

"Terry?" Jessica said, a little frightened. "What the hell is that?"

Terry looked down and saw the white spiral of light spinning out of his chest, threads of light dancing to the music. Terry looked back up at Jessica.

"Shit..." he said.

ELEVEN

Terry told Jessica to come over to his house that Sunday because he wanted to explain everything to her when she was rested and in a safe environment. Jessica was a little weirded out at the concert, but Terry was able to calm his Soulmind back into his body pretty quickly even though no one except for Jessica could have seen it anyway. She asked Terry if he had slipped any acid into her drink. Terry told her he had not. But that was the response Terry was expecting to get.

Terry's doorbell rang and he knew that it was Jessica coming to see him. He got up off of his couch—where he had been sitting with Remius—to answer the door. He opened the door to reveal a confused Jessica waiting for some explanation for these weird visions that she thought she saw.

"You must trust me a lot to be willing to come to my house after seeing light coming out of my chest," Terry said as he led Jessica into the living room where Remius was waiting patiently. Jessica sat on the couch next to the cat and Terry pulled a chair up so he could look Jessica in the eyes while he was talking to her.

"So," Jessica initiated. "Did I see what I think I saw? Light does not just come out in threads from people's chests—or am I missing something?"

"No, no, you aren't missing anything. I have something special. A gift." Terry took Jessica's hand and stared into her violet eyes. "I have been wanting to tell you for a long time. But I was not strong enough to do so. I still don't fully understand it. Jessica, I have a Soulmind."

There was a pause then Jessica said, "What?" She abruptly stood up and began to walk toward the door.

"It's true," Remius finally decided to speak. Jessica froze for a second and then slowly turned around to face the couch again.

She opened her mouth and pointed at the cat. "Holy shit," she said. "Did that cat just talk?"

"Yes, I did," Remius said. "You want to know about the Soulmind, eh? Then sit down, missy, and let the cat have a word..."

It goes without saying that Jessica was a little weirded out. She even pondered the possibility that she was loosing her mind—talking to cats and all. But she gave Terry the benefit of the doubt and decided to believe him. Jessica was now aware of the possibility that she had a Soulmind herself, but she didn't want to think about that. She must have liked Terry very much because she decided that she was not going to let this new information affect their relationship.

The next day at school, Terry was talking to Karl at free period.

"Yo, Karl," Terry said. Karl looked up from the homework he was doing. "Did you ever have a dream about killing a pastor on a cross? Ya know, recently?"

"What are you on? Crack?" Karl looked at Terry like he was crazy.

"Forget it." Terry glanced over and noticed Arash coming his way. "What up, Arash? Come sit with us, dude."

Arash sat down and pounded fists with Terry and Karl. He had an incredibly excited expression on his face. "Guys, guys," Arash started blathering right off the bat. "You remember the Public Works building I was telling you about?" Terry nodded. "Like I said, that salt that is not really salt—crystal meth. You follow me? Okay, I know for a fact that that shit is crystal meth because they unload that shit in armored trucks. Why would they need armored trucks to transport salt? Huh? They wouldn't. I'm gonna get to the bottom of this, guys. This is pissing me off. We are going to break into that building, guys."

There was a silence for a couple seconds until Terry burst out laughing. "You're fucking crazy, man. Are you serious?"

"Absolutely. Next week, we're hittin' that shit."

"Why are you so interested in this?" Karl asked.

"Why? Why? You're asking *me* why? Is that it? Well, I have not seen one person go in or out of that building, only trucks and—"

"People drive those trucks, dude," Terry interrupted.

"Let me finish, goddamn! Okay, I know people drive those trucks, man, but I have not seen anyone come out of there on foot or walk around that place. I want to find out who is running that place. That's one reason. And I want to see what is in the actual building. Okay?"

"So basically you just want to know about this place to fulfill your sick curiosity, is that it?" Terry concluded.

"Basically."

"You up for this shit, Karl?" Terry asked. "We could get all of RPG into this."

"I'm in," Karl said.

"What's RPG?" Arash asked.

"I'll explain later," Karl said. "So how are we gonna do this?"

"I was thinking we could go next Saturday. We'll have to have some ski masks and gloves and shit, you know. The whole shabangabang."

Terry laughed at that. "Did you just say shabangabang, dude? No, no."

"What?"

Terry just laughed.

"Okay, I gotta go," Arash said. "But think about that, we are definitely doing that next week. See ya." Arash got up and went on his way.

"What do you think about that?" Terry asked Karl.

"That guy is losing his mind. But it can't hurt though. We won't get caught. And I'm kind of curious about that place myself. And if that shit is really crystal meth, maybe we could get some so we could sell it."

"Yeah," Terry agreed.

"Hey, baby." Terry felt a pair of hands squeezing his shoulders. He looked up and was staring into Jessica's smiling face. "Hey, baby," she said again as she sat down beside him.

"What are you doing here?" Terry asked.

"Oh, I ditched Driver's Ed to come and see you guys. Hey, Karl." Jessica tried to hug Karl across the table but it didn't work so well, so she just sat back down, brushing crumbs off of her jacket.

"Oh, Jessica," Terry said. "You want to got to Homecoming with me on Saturday?"

"Sure," she said. "Are you still gonna see Dr. Tim in the morning?"

"Fuck that guy."

TWELVE

The day of the dance finally arrived and Terry was trying to make himself perfect and presentable. He had looked forward to this day all week and wanted to make sure that everything was in place and nothing was amiss. It was 6:45 pm, just forty-five minutes before the dance. Terry had donned his gray striped suit, combed his hair, and was ready to pick Jessica up. He had the corsage bracelet—what was he missing? Terry ran back up to his room to acquire what he had forgotten.

* * *

"What do you say to giving a little visit to Terry while he's at the dance?" Maya said to Rob. They were both in their usual spots in Rob's room.

"What about Rahjiah?" Rob still did not understand all of the information about the Order of the Transcendent, but he knew that his woman—Rahjiah—was watching Maya closely.

"As long as I don't touch the human, I'm in the clear. You'll be the one touching him. And that does not attract the attention of the Transcendent. Do you understand?"

"Yeah," Rob said. "When are we gonna go?"

"Have you ever traveled by Matter-Relocation?"

* * *

Terry crawled into his van to go pick up Jessica. He was shaking from nervousness. He did not know why, but he was filled with self-doubt. *Does she really like me? Is she gonna stand me up? Do I look okay?* Terry tried to shrug off these thoughts and started the engine. He zoomed off down the road, his head filled with pleasant thoughts of Jessica. He had a feeling this would be a good night.

He pulled up at the Thorns' driveway ten minutes later. Trying to maintain his cool, Terry approached the door. An image of the door swinging into his face flashed in his mind. He shook the image from his head and knocked. The door was answered by a somewhat burly man. Terry assumed that this man was Jessica's father, whom he had not had the pleasure of meeting before this moment. The man was about Terry's height, but a hundred pounds overweight. The man had thinning gray hair and a five o'clock shadow. Terry introduced himself.

"Come on in, sit down. Jessica will be down in a few minutes," said Mr. Thorn.

* * *

"Matter-Relo-what?"

"Matter-Relocation," Maya continued. "People from the Dark Tethers have the power to manipulate matter." Maya held out her hand, palm up. Black energy immediately started to dance up from Maya's palm. To Rob it looked like threads of black light growing out of her hand. "As I was saying. I control the Ropes of Dark." The black light waves left Maya's hand and hovered in the air, growing into black ropes with dark steam wafting continuously off of it. "This dark energy is part of my being so I control it. The ropes have to envelope the person fully and then I tell it where to send you. I can also do it to myself. So are you ready?"

"Uhhh..."

* * *

Terry was on the couch in the Thorns' living room across from Mr. Thorn. There was a very awkward silence as well as a feeling that Mr. Thorn was analyzing Terry.

"So, have you found another church to go to?" Terry broke the silence.

"No, not yet. My wife is out church-hunting tonight. Just horrible what happened to Brother Evan. Who could do that? They haven't even caught the murderer yet."

"I hope the detectives stumble upon a lead in the near future."

"Are you a Christian?" Mr. Thorn asked, very seriously.

"No, I'm not—but I respect every person's different religious beliefs." Just at that moment, Jessica came down the stairs wearing a tight, sleeveless purple dress that went down to her ankles. "You look marvelous," Terry said appreciatively.

"Thanks," Jessica said. She looked at her father.

"Come home straight after the dance, Jessica. I have to talk to you." Mr. Thorn said, pointing a finger at Jessica.

"But, Da—" she started.

"Don't argue with me. Just do it." He turned and walked out of the room.

Jessica turned to Terry and grabbed his hand. "Let's go," she said. As they left the house, Terry noticed a photograph hanging by the stairs. It was a family photo. Of Jessica and her parents. They looked so happy in that picture. With that image in his head, Terry was swept out of the door by a maiden in a violet dress.

When they were by the car, Terry gave Jessica her corsage bracelet. He slid it onto her wrist and then they embraced each other. Jessica put her hands on the sides of Terry's face. "Your eyes are clocks," she said.

"Shhh," Terry put a finger to Jessica's lips. "Don't talk about time." Terry dropped his finger, leaned in, and kissed her. In that moment it was just them. The world did not exist. Time did not exist. Nothing mattered except for the moment. But it was only a moment in *time*.

They got into the car. Terry held Jessica's hand as they drove to the dance. "I see you're wearing your cross. It looks good," he said.

"I know. The beauty comes from the significance."

Terry and Jessica arrived at the school where over two hundred students were outside waiting to be let in. They parked and joined the crowd.

"I got the tickets," Terry said. He flashed the tickets to Jessica.

"Cool," she said. "You're gonna dance, right? Because I really want you to."

"I'll dance."

"Y'know, it would be funny if Remius showed up with some female cat. They could have some feline fun." She grinded up against Terry.

"Haha, yeah, he's sleeping at my house. He also has a wife though, you know."

"Where? In dreamland?" She rolled her eyes.

"Forget it. They're going in. Let's go."

* * *

"Matter manipulation is really quite simple, but I guess the human mind is simpler because you people don't have the faintest clue how it works. Otherwise, teleporters would have been invented long ago. Okay, let's do it. Are you ready? It might hurt a little bit the first time you do it but you will be fine. Okay?"

"Uhh, I guess," Rob said hesitantly. "Let's get this over with. Where am I going to end up?"

Maya closed her eyes. She opened them and said, "The V-wing hall... I think that's what it said. It's a hall with a bunch of lockers."

"Okay. I'm ready." Rob went rigid anticipating the worst. Maya swept her hand across Rob's body and the rope followed. She spiraled her hand around his body, starting with his ankles. The rope began to wrap around Rob's legs as a Boa constrictor would around its victim. "Oh, God!" Rob cried out.

"Stay still," Maya hissed. The rope enveloped his entire body. It looked as if he was cocooned in thick black spider string with black steam wafting off of his entire being. "Okay, this is the part that may hurt." Maya snapped her fingers once and immediately Rob felt like his bones were being crushed. He tried to scream out but his mouth was covered with black rope. The darkness increased and swirled around Rob. Rob felt his ribs collapsing inward and piercing his heart. His eyes were exploding and legs were being shattered. He just knew it. Maya snapped her fingers one final time. There was an explosion of blinding light around Rob followed by the black steam shooting out from the center. Then it shrank into nothing.

Just as Rob was about to pass out from the pain, the agony subsided, everything stopped and he was in darkness.

***

"Are you having fun?" Terry yelled over the music. They were dancing like wild animals and rocking out to the music.

"Yeah," Jessica screamed to be heard. "It's great. I'm glad you're dancing."

Terry spotted Karl running over to them with a pretty girl in tow. She was a tall girl but not as tall as Karl. She had long blonde hair and fierce green eyes. She was also wearing a green dress that matched those eyes.

"Hey, guys," Karl said, greeting his friends. "I want you to meet Kelly." They all said *hi*. "I just met her. So we are gonna dance over here by you guys." They returned to the mass of dancing bodies.

"Oh yeah, this is a great song," Terry said. "Perfect."

"What is it?" Jessica asked.

"It's called *Missing Time* by MDFMK." And so it went. Terry sang the verses as he grinded with Jessica.

"Black is everything /
Pull me right out of reality /
The emptiness that's me /
Black is everything /
Put me right out of my misery /
Do what you want to me..."

Rob opened his eyes and realized the pain had subsided and he was in the V-wing hallway next to all the student lockers. He looked around and presently Maya materialized from a black mass of energy beside him.

"Are you ready to get this guy?" Maya asked Rob.

"Sure thing!"

"Life outside goes on /
My world is crashing inside out /
I'm gently hacking off the hinges /

Erase the space, erase the memory /
Missing time /
What I don't know will never hurt me /
Missing time /
Cannot forget, cannot remember /
Missing time /
Disinformation is forever /
Missing time..."

"This song is awesome," Karl yelled to Terry.
"I know," Terry yelled back. "This is a great dancing song."

"Black is everything /
Got the answer right in front of me /
It's everything I see /
Time outside moves on /
The world I know is crumbling down /
Clinging to a lost sensation..."

"Aren't you gonna get hurt just wearing that leotard?" Rob asked.
"It's night time," Maya said. "And I'm a lot stronger now than I once was."
They entered the gym where everyone was dancing.

"Erase the space, erase the memory /
Missing time /
What I don't know will never hurt me /
Missing time /
Cannot forget, cannot remember /
Missing time /

Disinformation is forever /
Missing time..."

"I think I see Rob," Karl said to Terry. "I'm gonna go talk to him." Karl left to go talk to Rob. Terry couldn't see him because his back was turned toward Maya and Rob. However, Jessica spotted them before they were about five yards away.

"Terry! Terry!" Jessica stopped dancing.

"What is it?" Terry asked.

"There's some chick in a really tight black leotard with Rob and she's has completely black eyes! They're coming this way. What should we do?" Jessica sounded panicky.

Terry turned and got a glimpse of Maya, Rob, and Karl. Karl could not see Maya—that was obvious now. "That woman doesn't look like she came here to dance. Let's get out of here." Terry grabbed Jessica's arm and started to lead her toward the door.

"Where the fuck is he going?" Karl asked, directing the question at Rob.

"Follow him!" Maya and Rob started running after them.

"Hey, what's your rush?" Karl stood still and looked around for his date. When he couldn't see her, he shrugged his shoulders and ran after Rob.

Terry and Jessica ran out of the gym's double doors that led out to the football field. It was deserted. The night was clear and the moon lighted the football field with an eerie glow. Terry continued to drag Jessica toward the field.

"Hey, can we slow down? You're hurting my arm," Jessica said, wincing.

They stopped so Jessica could rest for a bit.

"Hey, shithead!"

Terry looked over and saw Rob, Maya, and Karl standing right outside the gym doors.

"Why you calling him a shithead, Rob?" Karl asked.

"Shut the fuck up! This is none of your business." Rob punched Karl in the stomach and ran toward Terry. Maya just stayed at the edge of the football field close to the door they came out of and watched what unfolded.

"It is my fucking business. He's my friend, you asshole!" Karl ran after Rob.

"Let's just run," Jessica whispered to Terry as she clung onto his shirt.

"Here," Terry said to her. "Take my car keys and get out of here." Terry looked up just in time to see Karl tackle Rob to the ground. "Go on. I'll handle this." Jessica took Terry's keys and left without question.

Karl and Rob were rolling and wrestling on the ground, swinging viciously at each other's face. Karl got a couple good shots and Rob was bleeding from his split lips. Karl had a bloody nose.

"You motherfucker!" Karl screamed. "What the fuck do you think you're doing?" Karl decked Rob in the face again.

Rob was on his back with Karl on top of him. He kicked Karl off of him, and now Karl was on his back as well. Rob quickly got over top of Karl and pulled his fist back to punch. Then Rob heard a click by the back of his head and felt something hard and metal against his skull.

"Don't fucking move," Terry said to Rob.

"Terry, calm down," Karl said. "Don't do anything rash. Now, just put that thing away." Terry's hand was shaking and he was close to tears.

"Now, Terry—" Rob started.

"Fuck you!" Terry screamed, exploding in a torrent of anger. "What the fuck are you doing with someone from another Dimension? Would you betray your own friend, you sick bastard?"

Rob didn't have time to answer because Terry pulled the trigger. As if in slow motion, Terry saw the bullet enter Rob's skull and explode out the other side, squirting blood and bits of brain onto Karl's face. Terry silently screamed "NO!" as he saw the bullet keep going and penetrate Karl's skull with the same explosion of blood and brains. It was all over before Karl or Rob knew what happened.

Rob's dead body flopped on top of Karl's and laid still.

"FUUUUUCKKK!" Terry screamed and threw the gun down. He sank to his knees and started to cry. He cried until he felt his eyes burning and opened them to see a spiral of light coming out of his chest. The light pulled him to his feet and then it pulled him into the air, his feet dangling five inches above the ground. The light shot out of his Soulmind and circled him in a storm of light and energy. He closed his eyes and surrendered to the power within him.

He opened his eyes. The light was swirling around Terry and the two dead bodies now. That was all he could see. The gun shot up from the ground and, as if a video tape was being rewound, it went into Terry's hand and his arm outstretched toward the bodies. Terry could not believe what he was seeing. The bullet that had penetrated Karl's head just a minute ago was going backwards out of where it had entered. This all seemed in slow motion to Terry. The bullet retracted from Karl's head and the pieces of Karl's skull were sucked back into place as the bullet zoomed up and into Rob's head again. The pieces of brain were going back into Rob's head as the bullet finally exited backwards out of the back of Rob's head and slid back into the barrel of the gun. The whole incident was being extracted from history as well as everyone's memory except for Terry's. It was like it never happened.

The light dissipated and Terry was standing with the barrel of his gun pointed at Rob's living brain. Terry realized he had given himself a second chance and whacked Rob over the head with the butt of the gun. His unconscious body fell onto Karl who pushed it off of him.

"What the fuck was that all about?" Karl asked.

There was a thunder clap and Terry looked up to see the sky being filled with black clouds. Soon the moon was covered and everything was pitch black. There was another crack of thunder and a bolt of lighting instantaneously struck a spot not ten yards away from where they were standing. Terry heard a honk and turned around to see his van in the parking lot some distance away.

"Let's get out of here," Terry said. They ran for the car.

Terry opened the driver's side door and told Jessica he wanted to drive. She got into the back with Karl. Remius was in the passenger's seat. Terry got in and started driving.

"Where did you come from?" Terry asked Remius.

"After Jessica left you she came right to your house to get me. She told me everything that was going on. You see those black clouds and lightning? You really pissed Timestrus off this time."

"How?"

"What do you mean, how?" Remius replied. "You just fucking reversed Time. Only he gets to do that. You got to control your Soulmind... And try not to shoot your friends either."

"I can go back in Time?" Terry asked. "That's what that was?"

"Yeah, I told you that you had a gift. Time control and shit. Remember the fucking church where you sped up time? Well, this is just the clock hand that broke Timestrus's spine. Figuratively speaking." Remius said.

"So what do we have to do?" Terry asked.

"Timestrus wants to kill you now."

"Shit."

"Yeah. The only place you are going to have a chance of fighting him off is in the Dreamsphere. So we're gonna have to go there."

"How?"

"We got to go to Arkansas. That's where the cave of Meddia is," Remius said.

"That's over fucking twelve hours from here!" Jessica exclaimed.

"Okay," Karl said, finally. "Who the fuck are you talking to?"

"Uhhh," Terry fumbled for the words. "I'll explain it to you once we get going. Are you willing to go with us?"

"This is fucking insane. You guys are insane. Whatever. I'll go. But there better be a good explanation," Karl conceded.

"Won't Timestrus be here before we get to Meddia?" Terry asked Remius.

"No, it takes Timestrus a while to travel between Dimensions because the Order of the Transcendent will try to prevent him. But he'll elude them," Remius said.

"Well, you got to tell me who that woman in black was," Terry said.

"I will," Remius replied. "Start driving."

* * *

Rob woke ten minutes later with a terrible headache. Maya was standing over him but not helping at all. She had an amused look on her face.

"Shit," Rob said, touching his bleeding skull. He took his hand away and looked at the blood.

"Oh, suck it up," Maya smacked Rob hard on the back of the head.

"Ow! You bitch!" Rob cried out.

"Well, you should have done better," Maya said. She grabbed Rob by the collar and screamed in his face. "You fucking let him get away! Now you *will* do better! You know what, your little friend just fucked with Time again. That's why there are all these clouds and lighting. And they're going to Meddia!"

"What the fuck's Meddia?" Rob asked.

"Somewhere I can't go!" Maya screamed. "Now you have to go get him. And don't fuck it up this time, okay?"

"How am I gonna get there?"

"I am going to send you onto the top of their van. And you are gonna hold on for your life. When they get to Meddia, find a way to lay him unconscious, then tie him up. I will find you."

"Tie him up with what?" Rob asked.

"I trust that you'll figure that out when the time comes." Rob saw the black steam coming out of Maya's palms and knew that the pain was inevitable.

* * *

Terry was driving with an embankment just to his right that stopped at the road. It was very unsettling to Terry for some reason. He kept dashing his eyes over to the hill expecting it to come alive or something. Suddenly a car came hurtling down that embankment and solidly struck the side of Terry's van. He hardly had time to react before his car was rolling out of control. Glass shattered all around them. Everything was spinning out of control! In a death spiral and—

"Terry... Terry... TERRY!" It was Jessica's voice screaming at him. "You're fucking driving. Watch the goddamn road! Don't space out!"

Terry snapped out of his trance just in time to swerve away from an oncoming bus.

"You scared me, man," Remius said. Terry was breathing quite heavily now. There was no glass and no blood. He shot a glance to the right—there was no embankment to be seen. Terry shook his head and fixed his eyes on the road.

"So... Hmmm," Terry cleared his throat. He noticed Karl had fallen asleep in the back of the van. "Soooooooo... What the fuck just happened back there at the school?"

"Okay," Remius started. "In technical terms, you were Tripping Time."

"Tripping Time?"

"That is what it is called when someone other than Timestrus himself reverses Time and takes back something that was supposed to be already written in Time's memory. And that is what you did. You have a remarkable power. But using it will always piss off someone. Now Timestrus wants to kill you. You are going to have to fight him one way or another. And you will have a better chance to defeat him if you are in Dreamsphere than if you were in the Hollow Dimension."

"Why is that?" Terry asked.

"Because," Remius answered. "It is a dream. And Time cannot affect dreams. You can still be killed in a dream. But some things are different or more suited to you because it will be your dream."

"Okay. And who was that woman in black?"

"I think that is a woman named Maya who hails from the Dimension of the Dark Tethers. She's very dangerous, watch out for her. I don't know why the Transcendent don't have a noose around her neck yet. Anyway, I don't know the exact reasons for why she wants you, but it seems like your friend is working for her. Watch out for him too."

Rob's pain subsided and he found himself crouched on the roof of Terry's van. He grabbed onto the rack that was on the roof. He braced himself for a long drive.

"Can't I just speed up time so we can get to Meddia faster?" Terry asked.

"Do you really want to piss Timestrus off more than you already have?" Remius twitched his whiskers.

"Good point. Do we have time to stop and get something to ea—"

"No!" Remius cut Terry off. "Just keep on driving. Look, we're already crossing the border into Arkansas." Terry saw that Remius was right.

"How the fuck?"

"Think about it," Remius continued. "The mind is a powerful thing independent of the soul also. You don't have to physically speed up time with your Soulmind to get what you want. The concept of Time is all in the mind. Look, they're sleeping in the back. They're doing the same thing. You know how it is when you fall asleep and then the next second you are awake ten hours later? You're just doing the same thing while you're awake. And that is not physically speeding up time because it is just a perception of the mind. It is not really going faster, your mind is just tricked into thinking that it is."

Terry nodded and kept driving. This was good information for him to have. You could speed up time with the mind, but you can't reverse time with the mind.

"It's True Time," Remius said.

"What?" Terry asked.

"True Time. It is the time that is in your mind. Your own time. The time you give life. Timestrus has no control over True Time. Only the person who knows that there is such a thing as True Time. Your mind is a clock you set the hands on. And it is infallible. You see, the truth has been rejected all these years, so the lie is being accepted as truth. They have believed Timestrus's lie. He has life because people have surrendered their minds to him. He makes them reject the truth of the mind and spoon feeds them bullshit so he can be in control. But now you know what is True."

"Okay, you're going to have to direct me from here," Terry said, looking at the road.

"Yeah. Take a left here and..."

Remius directed Terry for a while. There were many dirt roads and side streets they had to drive through. The sky was still black with clouds and there were claps of thunder and lightning every couple minutes.

"Okay, take a left here, right now," Remius commanded.

Terry looked around, it was pitch dark and there were trees on either side of the car. "But it's all woods," Terry said.

"Exactly, numbnuts. You don't think that the cave would be right in the middle of the road, didja?" Remius laughed.

"Oh, no. Duh." Terry jerked the wheel hard to the left and penetrated the dark trees. "How am I gonna avoid the trees?" Terry asked.

"Don't worry. You won't crash into any of them." Remarkably, Remius was right. Terry managed to dodge every tree. He wasn't really trying to avoid them, he just kinda did.

"What's that? Up ahead." Terry asked. He slowed the car down.

"That's the cave," Remius said. "Stop the car."

Terry stopped the car with a jolt and Karl and Jessica woke up out of their True Time slumber.

"Are we here?" Jessica asked groggily. She yawned and rubbed her eyes. Then she pointed out of the windshield. "Is that the cave? It's so dark. I can barely make out an outline of a giant hole in the side of that massive rock."

"Yeah, that's it," Remius assured them.

"Is that the cave that was in my dream?" Terry said.

"It was," Remius responded. "Let's go then."

Terry turned around in his seat. "Karl, can you stay here and guard the car? We'll be back soon."

"Sure, man. I'll just listen to some Project Pat or something. You guys go on. Good luck with whatever crazy shit you guys are doing. I don't really want to know. I probably wouldn't understand it anyway. Go on. Get out of here."

"Thanks, dude," Terry said. He opened his door and hopped out. Remius was on the ground beside him before he was even out of the car. Jessica got out, said good-bye to Karl and took her place by Terry's side. Rob watched silently, unseen, from the roof of the van.

The three walked up toward the cave. They stopped when they got to the mouth of it. Remius stopped them before they could enter.

"Okay," Remius began saying. "You need to know one thing. The first half of the cave is meant as a test for any wandering Soulmind who happens to wander into the cave. It is designed to see if the person entering is worthy to see the Dreamsphere. If you get through the first half, you will find solace in the dwelling of the Octobers. I will be waiting. I have no doubt you will do fine. Just remember this: it is what you choose to see." Then Remius disappeared into the cave. Jessica exchanged a glance with Terry, shrugged her shoulders, and walked into the black. Terry followed in after her.

After the three were out of sight, Rob jumped down from the roof and ran after them. Karl spotted Rob as he hit the ground beside the car, but he could do nothing. All opportunity was lost as Rob dashed into the darkness.

BOOK TWO

Wandering in a Dream

*"For once there was an unknown land,
full of strange flowers and subtle perfumes,
a land of which it is joy of all joys to dream,
a land where all things are perfect and poisonous."*

- Velvet Goldmine

PART 5

Switchblade

*"I'll be back baby /
I just gotta beat this clock /
Fuck this clock"*

- Marshal Mathers, *Rabbit Run*

THIRTEEN
FROM THE MIND OF ROBERT BLACKGUARD:

Black. Everything around me is black. What have I gotten myself into? I walk forward, deeper into he blackness. I can feel the black as if it is water all around me. Oh, shit. How the fuck am I gonna find Terry in this blackness? I can't even see my dick to jack off. Fuck this shit. I walk forward, hesitating a bit. I put out my hands to see if I can feel a wall to follow, but something hits me in the head and I fall to the ground. All of a sudden I am surrounded by gigantic flood lights blinding me. What the fuck is this? All I hear is a voice saying something that I cannot understand in an announcer's voice. I stand up and realize, after I get my vision back, that I am standing on a basketball court across from—no way!—Michael Jordan! And the fucking basketball is dribbling beneath *my* hand. Oh, hell no! I can't beat Michael Jordan. I suck at basketball. I start dribbling toward the net, literally shitting in my pants because I am so close to an important black man. Oh, shit, my shit is leaking out of my shorts all over the court.

Before I know it, Jordan grabs the ball away from me. He bites down hard on the ball, and it bursts into razor-sharp glass fragments which slice through my arms. Now I am bleeding all over the court as well as shitting all over the court. Jordan walks up to me and puts his hand on my forehead.

"Sleep," he says. I close my eyes and fall backwards through Time. After a few moments, I open my eyes and all I see is black. I am floating in midair on my back. I am swaying up and down a little bit. I start seeing some light. But wait, the light is coming from me. It's as if there is shiny dust wafting off of my entire body. What the fuck is this? As soon as I think this, my body snaps in half violently. An indescribable pain shoots up my spine. I scream and watch as my entrails and my body fall to the cave floor. I lay on the floor, just a top half, helplessly whimpering for my mother. Whimpering for God to look down on me. As I look toward my steaming intestines, I see Terry rising from the carnage. He stands above me. He offers his hand to my helpless self. I gladly take his hand. As he pulls me up from the rubble, my body grows beneath me and I stand on my own—on new legs. We look at each other.

"I thought we were friends," Terry says to me.
"Are we? Are acquaintances considered friends?"
"Should betrayal be excusable?"
"Should death become a necessity to get what you want?"
"Take me or leave me."
"I will."
"I offer you my hand, my friendship," Terry reaches his hand out.
"What's in it for me?"
"Does everything always have to have a payoff?"
"Yes."
"I can see what you want through your blue eyes."
"Can you now?"
"Time stops here and I can make you do what I want."
"No."
"Is it easier to be friends, or enemies? Is it easier to betray, or stand up for?"

"What does it cost? What do I gain?"

"My trust. My friendship. My loyalty. My brotherhood. Everything a man would want."

I laugh. "Do I want that?"

Terry laughs back at me, mirroring. "Deep down, I think you do, my brother. Deep down." He taps my chest then forcefully thrusts his hand deep into my chest. I just watch as he rips out my heart. I see it beat and bleed in his palm. "You don't think I know what you want? You long for the blackness, don't you? The black, the darkness. The solitude. The nothingness. No one to bother you. You know me. Know me, brother." He crushes my heart. I gasp and fall through the sun.

I'm burning! I'm fucking burning! Fuck! Wait. Shit. I fall into a pool of cool water. I swim to the bank and collapse, coughing. What the fuck? I see the light of day. I roll over and hit something long and slender. I sit up to see what it is. It's a bow. I see no arrows though. I stand up and pick up the bow and sling it over my shoulder. I walk out toward the light. I finally break free of the cave's grip and look back. What? I can't believe what I am seeing. It's my body. My body is laying just inside the cave. It seems as if my body is sleeping inside the cave, but I am also awake and conscious outside the cave. I shrug, turn around, and walk on to find my brother.

FOURTEEN
FROM THE MIND OF JESSICA THORN:

"Terry! Terry!" I scream out for Terry in the darkness. My yell reverberates off of the wall and all I can hear is my own voice. I pull out my cell phone and flip it open to see if I can use the light from it to see where I am going. I scream as I see that the floor is covered with centipedes. I try to avoid them but it is no use because they cover as far as I can see and the pile easily reaches to my ankles. A small rock falls and hits my hand. My cell drops into the floor of insects. Now I am in complete darkness again. It is eerily silent. I don't hear the sound of water or even of the bugs under me.

Suddenly I am being pulled down into the mass of bugs below me. I try to scream but no sound escapes my lips. I am ripped down into the mosh pit of insects. I am pulled through so that I am completely surrounded on all sides by them. I try to breathe but the centipedes start crawling into my lungs. Before I black out, I see an explosion of purple light before my eyes.

I wake up with a gasp. Tears are running down my face. I look up and realize that I am in Terry's arms. It is still dark but I can see him because a light is radiating off of his body. He doesn't say anything but just starts to take off my clothes. He rips my top down violently and starts sucking on my breasts. I moan. No, no, I just know there's something wrong here. He detaches his lips from my nipples and pulls up the bottom of my dress to reveal my black panties. Instead of pulling them down, he uses his teeth to rip them off. This is just getting too weird. But I don't stop him. He pulls his penis out which is already hard as a rock. He strokes himself a couple times just to make sure he is fully erect.

"Put me in, bitch," he says. I am startled by his forcefulness but I do what I am told. He thrusts violently in. "You like that shit, bitch?" Even though he is treating me like shit, I can't help but enjoy it. I close my eyes and lay back. I scream with pleasure from what seems like an everlasting orgasm. It is so intense that I think possibly I am going to die. It feels as if he is stabbing me with his cock, but in a pleasurable way. I don't know, it's hard to describe. He lets out a yell as I feel his fluid shoot into me. Even though he is done, my orgasm does not subside. I look down and notice that seeping out of my vagina is not only semen but blood also. I scream but my scream is stifled when Terry grabs my throat and squeezes.

"Shut the fuck up, bitch!" He yells, then he slaps me in the face and I start crying. He bends down and starts kissing my neck. Or that's what it feels like until I feel his teeth ripping into my flesh. He starts ripping parts of my neck off with his teeth. All I can do is lay there with him inside me and bleeding away my womanhood.

No, no, wait. There's something wrong here. It's what I *choose to see*, isn't it? Is this what I have chosen to see? No, no. This is wrong. Terry sits up to look at my face. Blood and neck parts are dripping from his mouth. NO! Purple light starts to emanate out of my vagina and move up Terry's penis and encompass his whole body. He puts his hands up in front of his face and screams. His body starts steaming with purple smoke. He lets out one final scream as his body dissipates in a purple explosion. I just lay there panting—virginal and perfect.

I stand up and pull my top back up and the bottom of my dress back down. I am in complete blackness again. I suddenly hear my dad's voice all around me.

"Jessica, Jessica," he says. "Baby, you don't need to hurt anymore. Daddy's here. No one's gonna hurt my baby girl. Follow my voice, honey. Follow my voice."

I start walking forward slowly. My foot taps something on the ground. I bend down to pick it up. There are two of them. They feel like handles of some kind. Sword handles or something. But there are no blades attached to them. I drop them back to the ground because they are completely useless to me. I hear my father's voice again and slowly follow it.

"Jessica... You don't have to worry anymore. You don't have to cry anymore."

"Daddy?"

I start to sob as I follow his loving voice. I stop when I feel my foot fall into what seems like a cave lake or stream. I take a step back.

"Daddy, there is water." At this moment I feel really small. I see myself as a six-year-old girl sitting on my daddy's knee. He is telling me a ghost story. I remember I was crying and he was telling me that everything would be all right. That it was just a story.

"Don't worry, my sweet."

Suddenly I see a light being produced from the other side of the lake. The light is coming off of my dad's body. He walks down toward the water's edge.

"Be careful, Daddy. Watch out for the black water."

"Shh..."

He puts his foot on the water and just for a second I think that he is going to sink and drown. But I see him bring his other foot in front of the other and walk on water!

"Wait for me, honey. I can save you," my father tells me. I wait on the bank, helpless as a little girl, as he walks on the water over toward me. He walks up the bank and takes me in his arms. I start bawling my eyes out and I stretch my arms around him. He kisses the top of my head. He pushes me slowly to arms length away. He has his hands on my shoulders and he looks deep into my eyes.

"Jessica, baby, you need to come home. I am worried about you."

"But, Daddy," I sob. "Terry needs my help. He cannot overcome this force without me. Let me help him."

"No! I forbid you from associating with this pagan. You are my daughter and therefore you do what I command!"

I break away from his grip, suddenly angry. "No! Fuck you!" I scream at him. "I can choose who I want to associate with and who I want to date. I'm sick of you always controlling me." Suddenly I transform from a six-year-old to a mature girl of seventeen. "I'm not your little girl anymore, Dad!" I am furious now. I see purple light emanating from my chest in a spiral. Purple steam is tantalizing from my solar plexus. I look down and see the two sword hilts poking out of my chest. I can see now that they are katana hilts. I grab one with each hand and approach my father.

"I am not your property," I say. I rip the blades out of my chest in opposite directions, slicing my father's neck as they leave my being. He stares at me for one second before his head falls off and his body collapses to the ground. I look at my blades and realize that the blades are not made out of steel, but out of some energy. I assume that this purple energy is my Soulmind. Purple steam threads and wafts off of the light blades. I drop both of them suddenly into the water. I fall to the ground and black out.

I wake up to a cat licking my face. I sit up and see about twenty or so cats huddling around me. The one that was just licking my face is Remius.

"Congratulations," Remius says. "You have made it to the realm of the Octobers. Lie back down. Terry will be here soon."

FIFTEEN
FROM THE MIND OF TERRY BROSWALD:

I've been here before—in my dreams. My fucked up dreams that consist of sulfur fumes and weird creatures. I have no way to discern which way is up or down. I am swaying from side to side. I cannot keep my balance and I feel as if I am about to fall to my almost certain death. I steady myself as to not fall and break my face on the rock, but it does not matter because the rock crumbles beneath me and I fall into the pit that I feared would come.

This unexpected fall has put me in a shocked state and I feel oddly relaxed as I fall because I know that this cave is just a dream in my warped head. A kind of nightmare that I enjoy. Once I realize this, I hit the ground hard on my back. The wind is knocked out of me but it doesn't matter because I don't need to breathe. I could breathe my own blood and I would not die in this cave because it is of my own making. I lay there for a while, staring up into the blackness, just thinking about what kind of shit I could think up next. What is my deepest desire?

I can think of but one thing: Jessica. The moment I think her up, she is standing over me radiating purple light off of her entire body. I am not sure if this apparition is friendly or homicidal. What intentions does it have?

"Why have you come?" I ask.

"Because you summoned me," she says.

"This cave works to my command, eh?"

"To that extent, yes. You can *do what thou wilt* with me."

"Anything I wish?"

"Anything you can dream of."

"I dream you to take off your clothes."

She strips off her purple dress and stands naked in front of me. Her naked body is perfect in every way. Everything that I like and everything I imagined a woman to be, she is. Her small perky breasts were exactly what my heart-lust desires. Her flat, tight abs are just what I want to slide my hands over. And that shaved pussy—I want to be inside of her. Since this is a dream, I can do what I want, when I want, right?

She lays herself down and I get on top of her. My clothes are already off because I just wish them to be. This is my cave, and I make it do as I wish. I penetrate my subject and she moans with pleasure. I don't know what has come over me. I have this strange sensation that I am not myself. That something has come over me and is making me act and think in a way that I do not normally. But how am I *not* myself? I don't know. More aggressive or something. I keep thrusting away. It feels so good. Even though I am not ejaculating, it feels like I am having an everlasting orgasm. I feel like killing someone at this very moment. I do not know why but there is some sort of demon inside of me that has come into me from the darkness. I know that I should stop and not go on with this aggression and anger even though it seems like it's just a dream.

As soon as that thought crosses my mind, Jessica has vampire fangs and is ripping into the flesh of my neck. I do not stop her. I do not cry out. I just sit there and let her gnaw away at my flesh. I feel as if I need to be eaten away. I need to be eradicated from this world. Not even the dream world needs me. I always manage to fuck shit up and piss people off. I think everyone would be better off if I am killed by a vampire ho.

She continues to suck my blood and make out with my neck. I know that her eyes have turned completely white because she is no longer Jessica. She is solely a part of me—a part of my mind. I spawned her and I might as well let my imagination take me over. I let it always take me over anyway. Is anything real anymore or is it all just my imagination? These things that I see, are they real? Is this even real? This whole ordeal. Timestrus. Jessica. Rob. That woman in the black leotard. Is it just my imagination? Is Jessica just a figment of my imagination created to make myself feel better about my life? Someone to talk to and share my pain? Are my parents still alive and I just choose to ignore their existence?

"NO!"

I scream in the blackness because all of these thoughts haunt me all my days and there are no answers that exist for me so I must guess for myself what is real and what I need to accept. I let my scream die down and I close my eyes and let my head fall back. I can feel that the vampire Jessica has chewed through my entire neck and I just accept it and let go. I lean back and my head rolls to the ground.

I feel the silence and I hear the blackness. Time does not matter here. If I stay here forever, in this dream-like stasis, I don't have to face my fear which is Timestrus. I can just stay. Just stay. In the time with no Time. It all makes sense here. And it all falls apart here. And it all comes together here. And the fur is always here. In the darkness of a dream. In the darkness of my dream I can know that I can make it all end. If I want it to. I can make it all end. If it gets too bad. And if the horrible things turn out to be real, I can always fall back into the comfort of a dream. Dreams always forgive. Dreams always understand if you have sick fantasies. Dreams don't judge. Dreams don't criticize. Dreams don't fucking kill you if you don't do everything exactly right.

So I sit here. Or lay here. Just a head. With my fragmented thoughts. Because I am fucked up beyond belief and can't form any coherent thoughts since Time has stopped and I have to create some new worlds and new scenarios. And I can't do that without making everything go to shit and hell and have everything completely screwed up. Because I am. I am completely screwed up. This Time. This Time. This Time nothing will happen because it is what I choose. Everything is what I choose because it is my life and I write it the way I want and I know that I cannot always fix the things and the people I want to fix, but I will always know that here—here it is always what I choose to see. Because I make the rules in this place.

I am standing in the middle of a pool of blood. I am knee deep in the shit. I try to wade to the shore but I can't see anything. I just see red in all directions. I can't decide whether to change what is going on or not because I want to see how this plays out.

A figure rises from the pool about six feet in front of me. I squint my eyes to see if I can make out who it is. It seems to be my father. I try to cry out but no sound escapes my lips. I try to run to him but I cannot move in this red lake. I can just think. But all in vain. He just stands there looking at me. He is completely naked and has blood dripping all down his body. I cannot tell if the blood is from his body or from the pool. I finally find my voice after a couple of vain attempts.

"Dad! Dad! I'm sorry! I didn't mean to kill you!" My eyes begin to tear up and I use my hand to wipe it away but it comes back red. I yell out and beckon for my dad to come to me.

"Dad! I didn't mean to hurt you! I—it wasn't my fault, I just... I..." And suddenly I can't contain my feelings any longer and my lungs burst with the truth. "I couldn't take you anymore! Okay? I just couldn't! I hated you! I hated you!" He starts walking toward me. "NO! Stay away from me! You fucking piece of shit!"

I start to break down and cry. I can't control myself. It is like my emotions have rebelled against my mind. Then I hear my voice speak on its own without me knowing what I am going to say. Is this the truth? How do I know what is true?

"Dad, I'm sorry. I love you! I really do! I know you tried to do your best and you were just looking out for my best interests. But sometimes I thought I knew better than you. Teenagers do that sometimes. You know? Sometimes I wanted you dead. Sometimes I wanted to stab your bitch ass to death." I laugh. "But this... I never imagined that this is what I would imagine. You, dead Dad, with your dick severed and destroyed—your manhood spread for all to see like butter on rye toast. I can't say that I understand all that I imagine, but I do know that I want to harness it—and use it!"

I just stand there, staring at the image of my father—naked and exposed again. The mind is an interesting thing. The subconscious may show you what you truly want, but can we work against it? Can we rise above our primal instincts and become better than the animals? Sometimes not. I continue to stand there, soaking in the blood. I just stare and wonder how much longer this hallucination will last until my mind sends me into another nightmarish loop of my own making.

But he finally speaks.
And I finally know.
And everything finally rings true.
With one word.
All of the nonsense becomes powerless.
My dad opens his mouth and utters just one word:
"Catch!"

And I catch the thought and go spinning through the darkness. I don't know if it is the darkness of space or the darkness of the cave. All I know is it is the darkness of my mind. I know my mind is dark. But I also know that Jessica can shed some light on my darkness. Or I hope that she can shed some light on my darkness. This thing that's inside me. This thing that feeds and grows on the darkness—is it of my own making? Can I harness it? Can

I think something and make it happen? This cave is a complete mindfuck. These thoughts confuse me and I don't even know if any of them make sense, but I am certain that someone can find meaning in everything. Even if something may seem to be nonsense, it can be caught and used for enlightenment.

I am straddling a giant crack in the cave floor and do not know if I am going to live to fight Timestrus. And if I do live, I do not know if I will be sane enough to do it. I am feeling pretty crazy right now and don't know if there is any point to this trip or not or even if this Timestrus is real or just a figment of my imagination. I can't determine if cats can talk or if spirals can come out of people's chests. But I do know that we were put here. And we need to accomplish something in our lives. And I don't want my life to be a waste. So I must do everything in my power to get out of this cave of my mind and find what is real and what is true and what Time that truth is in and if the dream is true. Because it is important to have a dream. And if we have a dream, it is our duty to make it come true. Nothing will happen until we try something.

My brain seems to be overloaded. What did Remius say? *It is what you choose to see?* Well, what about *what I choose to think?* Is this what I choose to think? Because this seems more like a thinking trip than a hallucination trip. Anyway, my crotch is really hurting me because I am straddling this big crack and do not know what is below me. But I give in and fall. I just fall. I close my eyes and don't think of a single thing. I clear my mind of every unwanted thought and just feel the wind rushing past and blowing my hair up as I fall. But all of my bliss of nothing is shattered as I feel something sharp penetrate my ass. It feels like a spike and it is being driven through my body and up through the top of my head. There is no pain and I feel no blood seeping out of my body. I just feel peace. It is peace I feel. Is this what it feels like to die? Is my spirit being ripped away from my body? No thoughts. No images. No screams. No sexuality. I am just here—in the moment. For the first time I am completely and utterly in one place. My spirit, my body, my soul, and my mind are one and united in unison. But what about my Soulmind? Is it joined in this holy matrimony of my being? I don't see it and it is not spiraling violently out of my body as I would have expected it to.

I forcibly try to break my mind away from the bond and call forth my soul to join it, but to no avail. All I can do is hover here, suspended in midair with a wooden spike shoved through my body. But wait... This is what I choose to see. Isn't it? So, why this? Why this way? Why is my subconscious putting me through this?

But the spike is not really a spike. It is a living breathing creature. I just have to figure out what it is. I can feel the spike breathe inside me and expand and shrink as it takes in breath. I suddenly come to a realization that breaks me from the prison of the mind—the spike is me! The spike is my being as well. As I think this thought, I fall to the ground and see a shining figure walking towards me. It is myself. My mirror reflection.

"Very well," my other self says to me. "You are able to distinguish your true self from your dream self. I am very impressed."

I am still puzzled as I sit on the ground where I have fallen.

"Come," he says and extends his hand to me. "Take my hand." He reaches his hand out and I take it. He pulls me to my feet and looks me in the eye. "You are my guardian. The guardian of your dreams. Harness them, and make them come true." He leans forward and kisses me on the mouth. As he does so, his form vanishes and becomes, once again, part of myself. I know now that my dreams can sometimes seem grand and unrealistic, but there is a big difference between what is real and what is true.

I suddenly feel like I have gotten punched in the face and I black out for a second but open my eyes to realize I am lying on my back on the cave floor. I look up and see a familiar furry face and then hear the familiar voice the belongs to that face.

"Did you have a good trip?"

SIXTEEN

"Is this Meddia?" Terry asked as he sat up and looked around.

"Yeah," Remius replied. "This is where the Octobers reside." Terry stood up. The cave was lit, but not by sunlight or conventional lights. The light was coming off of the rocks. There was a strange luminescence oozing off of every rock.

"Terry!" Terry looked up and just had a second to brace himself before Jessica wrapped him up in a hug. In a second, Jessica and Terry were on the ground and covered with twenty cats. Terry laughed and they kissed. The Octobers meowed their approval.

Jessica pulled Terry to his feet and said, "Come on, you gotta taste this water." She dragged him through a narrow passage and down a small mudslide and stopped at a small stream.

"It's really cold," Jessica said.

Terry looked at the stream.

"Vivere." Terry turned around and saw Remius sitting on top of the little mudslide. "It is refreshment. It contains all the nutrients you need. It will revive you and will make sure you are not deficient in any essential vitamins and minerals. I don't know why all those people in your world call those soft drinks 'refreshments' when they can't refresh you. *This* is a refreshment. Drink it."

Terry looked at the water and debated whether or not he should trust it. Remius had never led him wrong before. And besides, he was going to need all of the strength he could get for his fight with Timestrus. Terry crouched down on all fours like a cat and put his lips to the cool stream. He took a long drink. The water was sweet and seemed to course through his veins. All traces of tiredness left him, his vision seemed to sharpen, and his muscles seemed just a little tighter. Terry stood up and looked back at Remius and smiled.

"That was the best water I have ever tasted," Terry said surprised.

"One sip will do it, but too much could be bad," Remius said.

"Really? I don't see how it could be," Terry said questioningly.

"Yeah, well, I wouldn't abuse it," was what Remius said as he turned and walked back through the passage.

Terry turned back, sat down on the rocks, and looked out over the water. He sighed. Jessica sat down beside him and put her arm around his shoulders.

"What's wrong?" she said.

"What the fuck do you think?" Terry snapped and pushed her arm off of his shoulders.

She stood up. "I was just trying to be a little fucking sympathetic, all right?" She rolled her eyes and followed Remius.

Terry tossed a couple rocks out over the Vivere.

Jessica ran back into the room where they had woken up and mingled with the cats. She would cradle the kittens in her arms as if they were her own children. She was a little annoyed by being pushed away by Terry. She just wanted to comfort him.

Remius could tell what was on her mind without her even having to say anything.

"Terry just needs some time alone to think. He's worried about this fight and himself in general. Just give him some space."

"I know," Jessica said. "I just want to be able to help him."

"I know you do, but sometimes people are meant to find themselves on their own."

When Terry first got to the Vivere, it looked just like a little brook, about a foot deep and just a few yards across. But as he had been throwing stones into it, it began to widen and deepen into a massive channel. He wasn't sure if he should be scared or not. He just kept tossing stones and thinking. He suddenly stopped though because his nose wrinkled to a familiar smell—sulfur.

What the hell is that? Terry wondered. He looked up over the water and suddenly saw something break through. He stood up with fright and stumbled backwards, almost falling over his own feet. Two green, scaly ears broke the surface. Then he saw that it was attached to a reptilian head. Terry gave a muffled cry as he recognized the shape as that of a dinosaur. Or a dragon. Then it opened its mouth and spoke.

"Fear me not," it said. "I mean you no harm."

"What are you?" Terry stuttered a little as he said this.

"You have dreamt me, haven't you?"

"I have. So?"

"My name is Sul. I am a Siddiariat, or you would know me as a dragon."

"Are you gonna roast me?" Terry asked.

"No. No, I am not going to roast you. I rule the Octobers."

"You tell them what to do?"

"Yes." Terry sighed and knew that he was a good creature if he ruled the Octobers.

"What do you want?" Terry asked.

"To talk with you."

"About what?"

"Timestrus and your fight," Sul said.

"What do you know about it?" Terry asked. He asked just purely out of curiosity, not out of hostility.

"You will do fine, I know it. You are the Steward of Time after all."

"What? Why do people keep saying that to me? I thought that was a joke," Terry remembered Remius saying those words to him, but then he said he was just joking.

"Remius doesn't know," Sul said. "But he suspects. But I know. The prophecies come to me in my dreams."

Terry stepped forward a little. "You can see the future?" Terry asked excitedly.

"No, I see what may come to pass. But Timestrus is a tyrant and must be stopped. There needs to be someone benevolent that controls time. I believe that person is you. You must rid him of the thing he uses to inflict pain on people."

"Why do I have to be the Steward? Why can't it be you? I don't want this responsibility."

"It needs to be someone with character, and someone with power."

"Well, that definitely rules me out."

"You have better character than you give yourself credit for." Terry laughed. "I think you will do fine. But you must blaze your own path toward victory."

Terry's eyes suddenly went wide as he remembered something.

"What is it?" the dragon asked.

"I just remembered," Terry said, a little sadly. "It's my birthday."

SEVENTEEN

Sul disappeared and Terry made his way up the muddy slope to be reunited with Remius and Jessica. He squeezed through the narrow passage and saw Jessica playing with all the cats.

Jessica looked up and said, "How you doing?"

"I'm all right. Still a little scared, but that water strengthened me a little."

"You talked to Sul," Remius said decisively. Jessica looked questioningly at Terry.

"Yeah, I did," he said. "He made me a little more confident." Terry smiled and kneeled down to pet one of the kittens. "But I still don't know what to do." Terry stroked the back of a little black kitten as it closed its eyes and purred under his hand.

"You have the power, remember that," Remius said. "I have faith in you. I just want you to know that."

"Thanks, I appreciate that," Terry said, but he shook his head. "I don't think I'm any match for a strong rapist demon that's bent on filleting my ass."

"I have faith in you too," Jessica said. She looked over at Terry but made no move to go to him. She wanted to give him his space.

"You shouldn't wait too long to go out there though," Remius said.

Terry laughed. "It's all about Timing, isn't it? Always about Time?"

Remius didn't laugh. "I'll show you the way out into Dreamsphere." Remius turned and started walking down a dark passage. Terry and Jessica looked at each other and then followed. The passage that Remius was leading them down was pitch black and they could not see a thing. However, they could sense where Remius was walking so they had no trouble following him toward the outside. They knew that they were getting closer to the outside because they had to shield their eyes from an intense white light that was coming from ahead of them.

"We are almost there," Remius said. Terry and Jessica had to close their eyes against the light because they feared that they would be blinded. They couldn't see, but this time it wasn't from the darkness. They stopped because Remius sent a telepathic message to both Terry and Jessica that they were about to cross the threshold.

"Okay," Remius said. "When I start walking through the Hetag, the gate to Dreamsphere, just keep going. It will feel as if you are being pushed back and being burned. The heat will be unbearable, but just keep pushing through." Then Remius walked through.

Terry walked into the light and Jessica followed. Terry couldn't see anything but he gritted his teeth against the intense pain. It felt like there were flames lapping at his skin and a thousand blowtorches were melting the flesh off his skull. But just as the pain got to the point of excruciating, Terry fell forward and a wash of cool air bathed his skin. He stood up and looked back at where he had come from. There was the mouth of the cave. He could see three bodies lying inside the cave: his body, Jessica's, and Remius's. It was as if they were in REM sleep.

"What?" Terry turned to Remius who was sitting in front of him. He pointed his thumb back toward the cave.

"We are resting," was all that Remius said.

"Wow," Jessica exclaimed. Terry turned and she was standing beside him, wide eyed and looking around. "What a beautiful beach." She ran off a little ways. Terry was puzzled because all he could see around him was a dead forest and crisp leaves underfoot.

"No," Terry said. "It's a forest."

Jessica turned to look at him. "It's a beach," she said. "Look at the pretty water." She pointed to a pile of fallen leaves.

"It is both," Remius said. "I see it as a lush grassland that blows in the wind. We all see what we wish, as in a dream. This is our own personal dream landscape."

"Oh," Terry said, and looked around at all the dead trees.

Rob saw the land as a mire, a black swamp infested with parasites. That was how betrayers found themselves, mired in their own sludge. As he trudged through the filth, he heard voices. He listened as he pulled leeches off of his neck. He was a little angry at the landscape he found himself in. He blamed Maya and cursed her a thousand times.

"That fucking bitch," he said under his breath.

"Is there anything I should be doing right now?" It was Terry's voice. Rob tried to listen but stay as quiet as possible. He wanted to figure out where the voices were coming from.

"No," Remius said. "Just wait."

"When's he gonna come?" Terry asked.

"I expect we'll know," was Remius's reply.

Rob was scared. He didn't know who this Timestrus was. He didn't know what they were talking about, but he didn't want to have anything to do with it.

"I can't do this," Terry said. "I wanna go back. I can't fight this demon, are you crazy?" Terry paced back and forth with nervousness. Jessica and Remius tried to calm him down by giving him words of encouragement. But all words were extinguished as the sky became covered with clouds and the wind started to pick up. It was cold and dark now and all of them watched the sky as bolts of lightning coursed the clouds horizontally.

"Shit," Terry said.

All previously viewed dream landscapes disappeared as Timestrus's desolate plane of sadness filled everyone's view. Suddenly they were standing in a barren plain. The ground was dry and cracked underneath them and the dust was being kicked up by the churning wind. There were also rocks and cliffs on all sides of them. Remius stood on Terry's left and Jessica stood at his right as they watched the sky in horror. Rob stood up because he had nothing left to hide behind. He watched the sky with fright, he couldn't move. The others didn't notice him because they were too busy watching out for Timestrus.

The clouds parted in a spiral of electricity and they knew what was coming. There was a roar that almost ruptured their eardrums. And then Timestrus shot down through the tunnel of electrified clouds and cracked the ground as his knee and one fist collided with the ground. They all stared. Rob pissed his pants from fear.

Timestrus kneeled in the dirt and rested on his fist in front of him. His head was down but his black wings were spread out fully on either side of his shoulders. His wingspan was about twelve feet altogether. As he stood up, no one could say anything. His height was about seven feet and his skin was completely black. He was as skinny as an anorexic, but built like a boxer. He had no ears, no nose, and no hair. He opened his eyes and stared straight at Terry with those completely white orbs in his head. Timestrus didn't have to say anything. Terry knew he had to fight.

As soon as their eyes met, Terry's machete handle shot from his chest and he ripped it out violently. Timestrus gave a shrill yell. And before anyone could stop him, Terry screamed and charged straight for the black demon. Even as fast as Terry was, Timestrus was faster. Terry slashed his blade toward Timestrus. In response, Timestrus just moved his bony hand up and grabbed the blade. It cut his hand open but didn't seem to produce any pain. Terry's eyes widened in panic as he saw the blade come to a halt in midair. He stared at the green blood that dripped from Timestrus's hand. Time slowed to a slow-motion camera as Terry looked into that vacant, black face. Timestrus cocked his head and smiled, exposing rows of pointed canine-like teeth. Terry knew it was over.

Almost in the same moment that Timestrus grabbed Terry by the throat and lifted him into the air, Remius leaped onto Timestrus's back and scratched around his head, aiming for his eyes. Timestrus gave a shrill cry and dropped Terry to the ground. He coughed blood into his hand as Jessica ran over to help him. They watched as Timestrus struggled with Remius who was madly trying to claw out his eyes. Timestrus managed to rip a paw from his right eye, but Remius raked a claw across his left eyeball causing it to burst and gush green pus. Timestrus screamed again but managed to rip Remius off of his head by the tail and hurl him through the air. He fell in a heap, motionless.

"You fucker!" Jessica screamed. She was already up, katanas out, ready to fight. Timestrus was temporarily occupied trying to regain his composure after his eye had been gouged. She started to move towards the wounded demon but Terry stopped her.

"I'll handle him," Terry said.

"But you're hurt."

"I'm fine. Go see if Remius is okay."

She hesitated, but then ran over to Remius's body. Terry stumbled to his feet and raised his sword as he saw that Timestrus was looking at him with his single eye. He smiled his razor teeth and motioned for Terry to come. Terry ran and made like he was going to slash for the face, and as Timestrus grabbed for Terry, Terry ducked down and slashed a gash across Timestrus's shin. He wasn't expecting that. But as the green bile pulsated out of the cut, Timestrus knew he was bigger and stronger than Terry, by far. Terry didn't know what to do, he'd never fought before, so he slashed upward, toward his hanging black genitals, but Timestrus was too fast. Terry's wrist was wrenched back by a huge hand. As he pulled Terry off the ground, Timestrus leaned into his face and licked his long tongue around Terry's lips and then forced his tongue into his mouth. Terry tried to bite it off but it was too thick and strong. Timestrus pulled out suddenly.

"How does it feel to know you are about to die?" Timestrus said. Terry spat in his face. "Not a good move. Now I must have more pleasure before you die."

Oh shit, Terry thought. Timestrus pinned Terry to the ground, stomach down. He leaned his face down beside Terry's and said, "I'm gonna fuck you again."

Timestrus ripped Terry's pants off, exposing his white ass cheeks. Terry tried to squeeze his anus shut as tight as he could. He didn't want this again.

"What the fuck are you doing?!?!" It was Jessica's voice. Terry looked over and saw her standing beside Remius who had stood back up. He looked a little dazed but okay. "Don't you touch him!" She started running back towards them. Timestrus didn't seem to care that she was running toward him with two long Soulmind blades out because he just looked back down and started to put himself between Terry's cheeks.

"NO!" Terry screamed. But there was nothing he could do.

In a flash Jessica was there, screaming and crying. She was behind Timestrus, violently hacking at his wings and back with her katanas. The demon seemed to like it because he was laughing. His skin was incredibly tough, like thick leather. She cut and cut and cut and only small gashes appeared that would bleed for a moment or two then heal.

"Terry, Terry..." Jessica cried. After a few minutes of spastically cutting and thrashing and trying to get Timestrus off of him, she collapsed in a heap exhausted. "I'm sorry," she whispered.

All this time Rob was just watching. He couldn't take his eyes off it, but he couldn't bring himself to do anything because he was too scared.

Timestrus thrusted in and out, but that didn't seem to be satisfying him, so he decided to have a little fun with Terry's arm. The demon grabbed his left arm and pulled. Terry screamed at the top of his lungs. Timestrus had just popped his arm out of the socket and was wiggling it around and laughing. Terry began to cry as he closed his eyes tightly. He didn't know what to do anymore. Timestrus then made a little cut with his finger nail in the skin near the rotator cuff. Then he ripped. He just ripped. The only one who screamed this time was Jessica, she covered her face with her hands. She couldn't watch as Terry's arm was forcibly torn from his body. Blood gushed from the shoulder where the limb used to be. Terry didn't really feel it. His mind wouldn't let him. He had given up and all he could see behind his eyelids were stars.

Suddenly Terry heard a yell escape Timestrus's lips. He felt the monster pull out of him. Terry couldn't see since his face was pressed against the ground. Jessica was startled when the arrow flew past her head and slid straight into the side of Timestrus's neck. As Timestrus stumbled up and away a little bit, Jessica rushed over to pull Terry away. He yelled as she dragged him across the ground.

"I'm sorry," she said.

"I know—ahh—it's just my fucking arm," he grabbed the bloody spot where his arm used to be. They looked up just in time to see a second arrow fly right into Timestrus's right temple. He stood up and howled toward the dark, cloudy sky. Timestrus ripped the arrow from his neck and then snapped the other off at the point it started to go into his skull. Green blood covered the side of his face and down the right side of his body.

Terry looked up and saw Rob walking toward him, arrow strung, raised, and pointed at Timestrus.

"You all right, Terry?" Rob asked. "I couldn't just stand there and let him fuck you to death. I couldn't live with myself. You're my friend, man." He looked over his shoulder and smiled at Terry.

Timestrus ran straight for them and Rob loosed another arrow—right into the demon's other eye! He yelled, ripped the arrow out, and held his bleeding eye socket. Even blinded, Timestrus had a good sense of where things were. He knew where Terry was. Rob stood between them.

"Don't fucking touch him," Rob said with a tone of authority. Timestrus rushed at them. Rob threw his bow down, raised his arms in one second, and black ropes of energy shot out of his sleeves. These ropes wrapped themselves tightly around Timestrus's wrists and pushed him away. They were stronger than him. Rob's black Soulmind started to spiral out of his chest. Rob gritted his teeth and strained to keep Timestrus at a distance with his ropes.

"Terry!" Rob shouted. "TERRY! GET RID OF HIS PLEASURE!"

Terry knew what to do. He ignored the pain in the stump of his arm and grabbed his machete. Rob spread his legs out and Terry scooted under them. Timestrus let out a yell when he realized what was happening. Terry stood up bolt-fast, raised his machete, and cut down. He cut down through shaft, tissue, and scrotum. A fountain of green blood sprayed Terry's face and he passed out instantly. Timestrus's black member fell to the ground and squirmed around like a worm as it died. The hideous demon yelled again and ripped his arms up, pulling Rob off the ground with the energy ropes. Timestrus threw his arms forward causing the ropes to snap and Rob to go flying some distance through the air.

Jessica didn't know what to do. She just stared. Terry laid in front of her, unconscious in a puddle of Timestrus's blood. Remius was too hurt to move. Rob also laid unconscious where he had fallen. Jessica looked up at Timestrus who was clutching the area where his cock used to be, empty eye sockets dark and vacant. A tornado of dust and white light started to swirl around Timestrus as his body lifted up toward the clouds. As he was ascending into those gray bodies, Jessica remembered looking over at Rob's body and seeing his Soulmind light wrapping up his entire body. However, it wasn't black anymore—it had turned electric blue. When she turned back, Timestrus was gone. Looking down, she saw the black severed penis of the sadistic demon limp and dead on the ground.

Then she blacked out.

EIGHTEEN

"Up!"

The voice was distant but slowly became clearer as Terry regained consciousness.

"I said up, you fucker!" There was a sharp slap to the side of Terry's face. At that he decided to abandon the idea of sleep and to awaken to whomever was violating his personal space.

Terry opened his eyes and Rob's white face slowly came into focus. He was laying on the ground that was now covered with colorful leaves yet again. His eyes wandered up to meet the forms of skeletal trees above him. Terry wondered if anything had ever happened. He felt his arms and both of them were intact. Terry breathed a sigh of relief and sat up. Rob was kneeling beside him.

Terry rubbed the side of his head. "What the fuck?" He yawned.

"I was wondering when you were gonna wake up," Rob said.

Terry looked at him. "Weren't you, like, against me a while ago?"

"Umm, about that…" Rob smiled sheepishly and shrugged his shoulders. "Friends are sometimes more important than pussy." Rob gave a thumbs up sign. "Even though I already got the pussy." He laughed.

Terry rolled his eyes. "You're something else, Rob. Where is everybody?"

"Umm, well, Remius is back in the cave and he brought you water earlier that healed your arm. And Jessica's over in that direction." Rob pointed in some general direction of the forest.

"Okay," Terry said.

"So, I'm gonna go back and hang out with Rem, okay."

"Yeah, sure. I'm gonna go find Jessica."

Rob stood up and walked back toward the cave. When he was out of sight Terry stood up and stretched. The air felt crisp and refreshing, just like the leaves under his feet. He looked in the direction that Rob had indicated Jessica was. There didn't seem to be much more than trees. Terry shrugged and started walking.

It was the strangest thing, Terry thought. With each step he took, the forest felt like it was getting colder. However, the cold was oddly pleasurable. He could see his breath now and white flakes had started to fall all around him. Terry stopped and looked up at the sky. The snow was falling from a cloudless sky. The sky was perfect blue and the snow sparkled as it wafted to the ground. Terry filled his lungs with the refreshing air and soaked in the white purity.

The chill of the snow seemed to be washing this world clean of the residue Timestrus had left. Terry felt at ease. And he smiled and filled his lungs again. He noticed a cave off in the near distance.

"Same cave? But I thought..." Terry mumbled and pointed in the opposite direction. He shrugged and walked toward the cave anyway.

As he got closer, he noticed that it was definitely different from the cave he had come out of. He could see a little into the cave and it looked white and crystal-like. There were ice shards poking around the edges of the entrance. Terry stepped into the cave.

"Jessica?" He called out. He could see his breath as he spoke. The frost chilled him and tantalized him at the same time. He had stepped into what seemed like an ice kingdom, a cave covered in shiny crystals. Terry walked over to the wall and ran his hand down the sharp peaks. This was pleasure. This was where he wanted to be. Where it was cold, and his soul could be clean. So he walked in deeper.

There was a bend in the tunnel up ahead and it looked dark around the corner. Terry hesitated, but decided to go into the black. As he rounded the corner into the darkness, something grabbed his shirt, he was pulled off balance and fell to the ground. At the moment when he landed on top of Jessica on the cave floor a blast of light illuminated the cave in radiant rainbow shimmers. Terry looked down into Jessica's violet eyes and then up at the ice.

"Wow," was the only thing he could utter at the moment. Jessica was naked under him. She kissed him. She didn't have to say anything. Their souls and minds were connected. Terry rolled off of her and they both laid on the sheet of ice below them and looked up at the shards above them.

Terry shifted to his side to look at Jessica. "Beautiful," he said.

Jessica smiled and got on top of Terry. As she straddled his pelvis she began to take his shirt off. Neither of them spoke, they instinctively knew what the other one wanted. Once Jessica had Terry's shirt off, she scooted her body down until she was kneeling between his legs. She slowly unzipped his pants. She ran her hand over his cock through his boxers, which was already beginning to get hard. Terry had let his guard down since the pace was slow and relaxed. Suddenly Jessica shattered the ease of it by ripping the pants off his body. She grabbed his boxers and tore them off ravenously. Terry didn't have time to react because Jessica immediately started to go down on him.

Terry just ran with it. He could not deny that he was enjoying this. She pulled her mouth off of his cock and moved her body on top and began to ride him. Terry closed his eyes and moaned. Jessica moved her body up and down on his hard cock. He opened his eyes and looked up at her. She was incredible. She swayed her body on top of him, her mouth half hanging open, an unheard moan between her lips. She slid her hands down her body as the pleasure began to build between them.

Techno music shook the cave and strobe lights began to be produced from the crystals around them. Lasers of every color weaved and shot all around them. As Jessica's head tilted back and she began to moan, purple light began to spiral out of her chest. It threaded out of her solar plexus and started to rope around her body as she continued to move up and down.

Terry looked down at his own chest and white light was spiraling out of him also. The strobes made everything have a kind of stop-motion quality, which heightened the intensity of everything. It filled his head and the only thing he could think about was what they were sharing as the beats pounded in his ears.

Jessica moved her body down to meet Terry's. She laid on top of him, still making love. Their energies met as her breasts met Terry's chest. They both gasped as the purple and white light braided themselves together into one. Their Soulminds intertwined and began to wrap both of their beings in a purple and white spiral. Is this what it felt like to become one with another person?

As they continued to make love, they were pulled up off of the ice and were suspended in air by their shared energies. Their souls connected, one mind, one body. Their Soulminds knew what they both needed and made it happen. The spirals flipped them as the strobes accentuated their sex. Terry was now on top of Jessica. He thrusted deep inside her being. Her head tilted back as she screamed with pleasure. The purple light was wafting out of her vagina as well. Terry knew that they were becoming one being in spirit as well as in body. Nothing else mattered. The ice melted away and everything around them speeded up and died and was reborn all in a second as their rapture became the greatest part of their mind. What mattered was the connection.

And with this thought, they both came together, with a scream and a realization. Their eyes shot open as the energy that surrounded them exploded in a radiant spike ball of furious pleasure. And as quickly as it had begun—

They laid on the ice looking up at the shimmering crystals.

There was no strobe, to techno beats, but as they looked at each other, their Soulminds were connected in a braided rope. Forever one.

As quickly as their realization had come, it had erased as they came. They still felt the pangs of something great. They knew they were at the pinnacle. But even when the bravest of souls reach the top of the iceberg, they must slide back down the slippery slope eventually.

Their eyes knew all. And they stared into the depths of each other's soul.

Terry and Jessica joined the rest some time later back in Meddia and they decided it was time to dive back into the Hollow world once more. Terry knew that he would be back. He was connected to this place as well now. They all were.

Remius and Rob walked out into the light into the human world again. Terry looked back at Jessica. She looked uncertain.

"What's wrong?" Terry asked.

"What if I'm pregnant?" Jessica whispered.

Terry laughed and held out his hand to her. She grabbed it.

"Don't worry," he said. "It was just a dream."

PART 6

The Violet Perfect

*"To be a boy is to be a fool.
And being a fool is pure bliss."*

- Hajime Ueda, FLCL vol. 1

NINETEEN

Terry and Jessica walked out of the cave entrance hand in hand. Rob and Remius were walking toward the car where Karl was dozing off slightly. Rob crawled into the back seat with Karl. Terry got into the driver's seat, Jessica beside him. Remius jumped up onto Jessica's lap.

Karl slowly opened his eyes to see Rob sitting next to him. He was a little startled. "Is he supposed to be here?" Karl asked. "Need I remind you, Terry, he tried to kill you."

"I never tried to kill him," Rob said.

"Relax," Terry said, turning on the engine. "He's one of us now."

Terry gasped as everything came flooding into his eyes. Snow, trees, Time, false epiphanies. Everything came rushing at him like a torrential storm. He couldn't breathe. He could see Jessica out of the corner of his eye saying something, but he couldn't hear any words. His ears were flooding with the sound of rushing currents. Then, just as everything became overwhelming and he felt as if he was going to pass out, his head broke the film of his awakened consciousness. He pushed through it and suddenly—

He was back in his own bed, sitting up in the dark, sweat pouring from his brow. Terry began to slow his breathing down.

Remius was curled up at the end of the bed—curled up and sleeping. Terry began to get up out of his bed. The cat opened one eye to look at him.

"Everyone's safe," Remius assured him.

"What did I do?"

"You just Accelerated, again, without meaning to. You need to work on your control."

"Okay," Terry said as he walked toward the bathroom.

"They're all in their beds," the cat purred. "Safely dreaming."

Terry stared at himself in the mirror. He didn't really know who he was anymore. He didn't recognize the person he saw in the reflection. It wasn't him. It was some supernatural being that had powers that he did not understand. So how could he use himself in a greater way if he couldn't even control his own abilities?

A tall black figure appeared behind Terry in his reflection. Terry didn't say anything, he just eyed Timestrus on the other side. The tall demon walked up behind Terry and slipped a clawed hand around Terry's chin. Timestrus's black tongue slid out and over the side of Terry's face.

"Oh, my boy. My sweet innocent boy," the angel of darkness hissed. "You think you can figure this out? You think you can discover who you are in this incarnation? But you can't. You are going to die. And only then will you know. But by then, it will be hopeless for the human race."

Timestrus's tall figure faded away out of the reflection after these words, leaving Terry staring at the stranger he saw before him.

NOVEMBER

ONE

"Bam, boom, bang! You, you, you, and you!" It was Arash Khan running up to Terry's lunch table that Friday.

Rob, Terry, Jessica, and Karl just stared at Arash like he was a lunatic.

"What was that?" Terry asked.

"C'mon, don't tell me you forgot," Arash looked at them, begging for a tinge of recollection. He got none. "Aww, you guys are useless." He sat down next to Terry. "Public Works building, you guys, come on!"

"Oh yeah, your crazy ass idea that there's crystal meth in there, right?" Rob said.

"And not just that," Arash said, lowering his voice a bit and leaning into the table. "Secret cults." He looked at everyone. "Yeah?"

Nobody said anything to him, they just looked at each other.

"Where do you get this information from?" Karl asked.

"That is irrelevant," Arash dismissed Karl's question with a wave of the hand. "What matters is we are going to bust open whatever shady deeds are happening in that building. No, no, I'm not nuts. Just hear me out. We have, what? Five people including me, right? So we can make Karl the lookout and if anything goes wrong or he sees someone go in while we're in there, he'll call one of us so we're not taken off guard."

"Why am I always stuck being the lookout?" Karl whined.

"Okay, forget it," Arash said, getting up to leave.

"No, wait," Terry said, stopping Arash from leaving. "I'm in."

"What?" Jessica blurted out.

"Yeah, I want to know what's going on in there too. I don't want to wonder about it forever like Arash has been. I want to find the truth."

"Oh," Jessica said. "Then I'm going too."

Karl and Rob reluctantly agreed to go as well.

"So, we all agree to go at sunset?" Arash asked them.

"I think that would be best," Terry agreed.

"Then it's a date." Arash tipped an invisible hat toward his friends at the table and then walked off.

The sun was setting on another dreary day of nothingness, but Terry knew that he was about to step into chaos a degree he had never experienced. He was standing with Jessica, Rob, and Arash outside the tall metal fence that blocked off the Public Works building from the sidewalk in front of it. The building was made of concrete and was about five stories tall. It looked like a prison and had small square windows that could not be seen through. There was a small cement circle driveway in front of the building where trucks and whatnot would come to drop goods off.

"Where the fuck is Karl?" Arash asked to no one in particular. "Shoulda been here by now."

Just then Karl ran up to them, out of breath.

"Sorry I'm late," he said.

"Well, if you're gonna be late to help us out, next time just stay home and jerk off," Terry said. Karl just stared at him.

The gate was made up of eight foot tall iron bars, but there was no barbed wire at the top. Terry started to climb up the fence. When he got to the top, he jumped down onto the cement on the other side. The others followed.

"Karl, stay here by the gate. If you see anything suspicious, call my phone, okay?" Terry patted Karl's shoulder through the bars of the fence.

"Sure."

The four of them circled to the back of the building to find the back door into the stairwell. They found it. It was a heavy metal door with a rectangular glass window with wires through it. They could see a stairwell just inside the door.

"Shit," Arash said. "How are we gonna open this thing?"

Terry whispered something into Rob's ear and then took Arash aside to distract him while Rob destroyed the doorknob. As Rob lifted his hand toward the knob, thin black ropes shot out from inside his sleeves and wrapped around the knob and inside the lock. They twisted and fought with the metal violently until it snapped off loudly, sending metal shards in all directions.

"Let's go," Rob said. Jessica and Rob quickly stepped through the door followed by Arash and Terry. They started to climb the dank, dark staircase quickly. With each step they took, purple fog seemed to thicken around them until it was hard for them to see anything at all. By this point Terry was holding Arash's hand and Rob was holding Jessica's. They coughed and sputtered trying not to slip onto a hard landing.

Encompassed by foggy splinters in their minds, it was hard to tell or determine Time in any rational fashion. They knew they had been climbing, but inhaling this intoxicating gas was making them feel rubbery in mind and in soul. In this state they weren't really surprised when they stopped and realized they had reached the end of the stair steps, but there were none left to descend. They had disappeared. And what was left? A stone wall. Stone walls surrounded them on all four sides. They still could not see because they were surrounded densely by the purple fog.

As they blindly groped around, the fog slowly sank down around their ankles, revealing the blank, hard walls. But the ceiling was high—or they thought it was high. They couldn't see it, it was so far above them, it was lost in shadows. However, they could see each other, but were puzzled as to where the light was coming from.

Terry cried out as he felt something snake around his wrist. They all looked up toward the invisible ceiling. Purple ropes of energy shot down like whips from above and curled around their wrists as if they were constricting snakes.

"What the hell is this!" Arash screamed as he tried to break free.

The ropes started to pull back up into the ceiling, lifting them off the ground by their wrists.

Arash was panicking, he couldn't wrap his mind around this. He was screaming at the top of his lungs and thrashed around.

"Calm down, Arash!" Terry yelled. "It'll be fine. Don't fight it!"

Arash's eyes shot open and clouded over. His mouth hung open as his head dropped. He had passed out. The ropes stopped pulling upward and they just swung against the walls. Rob was looking up and around, but all he could see were shadows above and floor below.

"What now?" Rob said.

Terry stared as shiny glitter oozed from the wall behind Arash's limp body. It started swirling around him and pulling his body back toward the wall. As his back touched the hard surface, it became a living liquid swallowing him whole. The yellow drywall gushed and slid around Arash's face, mummifying him in glitter and yellow ooze. In a moment he had disappeared completely into the wall.

Rob stared beside him at the spot where his friend used to be. Then he was dropped. The ropes released him and he fell. He fell two hundred feet onto the hard ground below. As Rob's shoes connected with the ground, his knees locked and then snapped, pulling his legs into two pieces. The skin on his lower legs split as the bone was violently exposed to the air. He had no time to scream as the floor opened like a great mouth, revealing what looked like a giant garbage disposal. A deafening whirring sound reached Terry and Jessica's ears as they were sprayed with bone and body matter. Rob's ribs were split open to reveal his still beating heart for a minute before it was ground up beyond recognition.

The whirring stopped and the human garbage disposal retracted into the floor leaving behind Rob's blood still dripping from the walls. Jessica vomited and it splashed into the red as it hit the floor below.

"Oh, god." She closed her eyes.

Nothingness filled Terry's mind. And with that thought, they were pulled up into the darkness.

TWO

FROM THE MIND OF TERRY BROSWALD:

By this point, I have dismissed all my preconceived ideas about how I thought the world was supposed to work. In reality, that isn't reality. I have come to realize that. And because of this fact, it seems completely normal that I am standing in complete darkness and yet I can see an illuminated figure in front of me.

Speckles of what I have come to see and it is beautiful. A small naked girl-child stands before my naked eyes. Her skin is white and glistens in the darkness of this recess of what does not belong here. She carries the head of my girlfriend Jessica. The naked nymph looks up at me but does not smile. She drops the head onto the invisible floor.

"I am what you want," it speaks to me. "She is what you got. Your prisons rot, and hell is hot."

I look at this misplaced, forgotten, and under-appreciated munchkin before me. "Where are your parents, little one?" I say to it.

"You are," she says. "Slide the watch in front of your eyes. Shh! Do not speak of this, it is forever. Timepiece now, see not, because I have not lied to the deceiver."

I walk toward her but she backs away as if frightened.

"You only deceive yourself. Trip you on the reeds of desire and you will fall into the light ropes of cotton." She puts her finger up to her lips. "But I can keep a secret. Time doesn't forget."

She spreads her legs and the pretty crease of her vagina closes up like an invisible zipper leaving flawless smooth skin, forever virginal.

Now that she has a permanent chastity belt, she walks toward me with a spring in her step. She stops in front of me and makes a 'come here' motion with her finger. I bend down to look into her eyes.

"Be aware of yourself," she says. "Because sooner or later you will crack."

She taps me on the spot between my eyebrows. It leaves a little dent and tiny cracks start to spiderweb my forehead. I grab my head as flakes of skull start falling off.

Walls grow around me, wooden slats coming up like teeth. The girl disappears and I am left in what looks like a small bare room with wooden walls and floor. Jessica lays beside me. I can see that the walls are covered with gibberish about the end of the world and repenting. I shake Jessica and she wakes up.

There is one door in front of us that is a little cracked. I walk up to it and motion for Jessica to follow. She does. We walk out of the room into a narrow hall. There are two holding cells on each side of the hall, one man in each. As we pass by them, Jessica holding on to me, the men look startled. They jump up from their cots and rush to their bars. They both say the same three words right after each other.

"The Violet Perfect."

"What are they talking about?" Jessica whispers to me.

"I dunno," I say. "Ignore them."

One man shoves his hand through the bars, trying to grab Jessica. "Save us, Violet," he pleads.

Suddenly two women rush at us from the shadows in front of us. They both are wearing white robes. One woman is black with white dreadlocks, and the other is white with black hair that reaches down to her ankles.

They pull us through a darkened doorway, through a brighter bleak hallway with gray concrete walls, and into a huge room. The women throw us into the room and we trip down onto our knees. I look up to behold the vastness of this space. The room reminds me of a huge ballroom in an old mansion. The floor is black and white checkered marble, and there is a giant chandelier hanging from the ceiling that seems miles above us. There are no windows. And the middle of the room is a vast round table. There are eleven women sitting around the table, with two seats empty that I assume belong to the women that are escorting us. Thirteen women in all. They watch us. I suddenly feel a warm substance slip around my neck and tighten. My head pulls up and I look at Jessica. Her eyes are clenched closed as a shining yellow energy rope tightens around her throat. The black woman is holding the other end of the rope like a leash—she also has her foot on Jessica's back.

A woman from the table stands up and looks our way. Her blue hair is puffed out like lion's mane. "Your crimes are many, and strictly linear," she says. "You are also denied access to this space, making you in violation of the Ordinance."

I don't say anything.

The woman with the blue hair walks around the table and approaches me.

"We have enough of our own problems keeping the balance without you and your little cat friend meddling into the spirals of what you do not understand." She kneels down in front of me and proceeds to pry my jaws open. She pushes her right hand into my mouth and pulls it out slowly, pulling my essence with it. When her fingers come out of my mouth, a thin stream of white light is pulled out from my throat. She places the fragment of my Soulmind into a thin glass cylinder that she has pulled out of her robe. I gag as she seals the cylinder and the reflection of my Soulmind light dances in the corners of her eyes.

"Learn your world." The woman then stands up and takes Jessica's leash out of the black woman's hand. She stamps down on Jessica's back with her foot, making her collapse to the floor. Blood pours from Jessica's nose as her face hits the checkered ground.

The lion woman with the blue hair pulls out another cylinder from her other pocket and sets it on the ground. Then she flips Jessica roughly over onto her back. As she rips Jessica's shirt open, I can see a small purple spiral begin to form between Jessica's breasts.

"Don't you fucking touch her!" I scream, not even totally convincing myself of my harshness. The woman just smiles and waves her hand over Jessica's Soulmind. Suddenly the purple energy lunges up and engulfs the lion woman's face, taking her off guard. But as soon as that happens, her hand shoots out for the glass cylinder. The Soulmind energy is more attracted to the box, and it leaves the woman's face and is sucked into the glass. After a bit of energy is trapped within the container, Jessica's Soulmind is sucked back into her body and disappears.

Jessica just lays there, half conscious, with her small chest exposed to the cold air. I should feel outraged, but I feel like I'm slowly becoming numb to anything that happens to myself or the people around me. It can be called cold-hearted, but being forced into a world that I do not understand has made the walls grow slowly and I don't seem to mind the way that the mind bleeds to accommodate the cynical, brutal world that only I perceive. Forgive only the ones who wish to be forgiven.

"He doesn't understand what we are trying to protect him from," the lion woman says to the black one. "Give him a dose of Dark Tethers so he knows that his world needs us to protect it."

Metal shackles are clamped on each of my ankles and I am hoisted into the air. Pulled up into the infinite ceiling. I feel the blood rush to my brain as

THREE

Nonetheless, everything was abstract as Rob awoke from his painful silence. He still felt as if his limbs were severed from his torso, but upon awakening he found that he was attached. He was imprisoned within the Specific Cage from which he could not pronounce correctly. Arash was beside him, but he was not conscious. This cage was not tall enough for them to stand up, but it was long and wide enough for them to sit and lay. Their cage was in the middle of the wooden floor of the room. And the walls seemed to be wood with apocalyptic graffiti covering them. There was no Door.

"Arash," Rob whispered, shaking his companion slightly. Arash just groaned and rolled over.

Rob sighed and looked up to see a figure standing above their cage. It was the black woman. The one who Rob had seen shift-shapes from a dove in his bedroom. However, now she wore a white blindfold, and she had no mouth, just smooth skin where it should have been. The woman reached through the bars and grabbed Rob firmly by the front of his shirt. She pulled him through the bars into the space room. She pulled him through solid matter and his body was still in one piece.

She held Rob's throat and pushed him against one of the wooden walls. Rob did not struggle or protest, he didn't see any need to. He became a submissive. Again. But this time it was to his greatest desire. His desire for the darkness made flesh. She kissed him with her nullified mouth. Stripping his clothes off, he became a child. Once blameless and yet completely shamed. He was small, with a tiny manhood. But this was not to be worried about since the woman could not see through her forever blindness. All she could see was into the dark. All she did was feel down Rob's six-year-old body and start to stroke his penis. Rob closed his eyes and acted like a child. He squirmed a bit, biting his lip, but he was slowly getting an erection.

Then she spoke without speaking. Bending down to Rob's ear she said, "In the Treehouse with many bottles."

"Why hasn't this ended yet?" It was Arash's voice. Rob's head jerked over to look at his friend, and he became his normal age again. The woman vanished as only a fantasy can. And Rob was happy to know that this time he was in the Treehouse Mind and not the Treehouse Real.

"Yeah?" Rob said, looking at Arash who was still in the cage.

"What the fuck happened?"

"Ummm. About that..."

"This can't be real," Arash put his arm over his face.

Suddenly a burst of wind shook the room and Jessica was standing in front of them, elevated on a wooden crate. She didn't say anything, she just raised her arms, revealing bat-like wings hanging below each one. Another burst of wind knocked Rob back against the wall. As he struggled to get back up, a thick stream of purple energy shot out of Jessica's solar plexus toward Arash. The stream snaked through the bars and entered Arash's chest, making him convulse. He screamed as a spiral of yellow light was pulled out of him. It began to braid through the purple as if it was making love to the other energy source. Then the explosion happened. It broke forth from Arash's ribcage, vaporized the cage's bars, and blew through Jessica, making her explode in a mess from heaven that hung from every wall. Ending the blast was a huge chunk of wall being blown out into whatever was beyond this Treehouse.

It died and Arash's newly discovered Soulmind shriveled back into his chest. Rob couldn't really think of anything to say. It was dark on the other side of the hole in the wall, but Rob knew they had to find a way out of this spiritual meth lab. He walked up to the hole and looked back at Arash who was laying on the floor in a semi-shocked state.

"Are you ready to go?" Rob asked.

Arash struggled to his knees, then vomited.

FOUR

FROM THE MIND OF TERRY BROSWALD:

my body sinks into the glass floor. I look around me and there is nothing. Is this Dark Tethers? It seems as if I am inside a glitch in some video game—some hidden interior that was never supposed to be explored. From my waist down I am trapped inside the blue transparent glass that seems to be the ground. Above me is completely white. And as far as I can see, all around me is just an expanse of glass floor. I try to push my hands down on the glass and dislodge myself. I don't have any luck whatsoever.

I sigh. I'm not really surprised anymore at any of this. These new abstract worlds that I have recently come to explore have now become as mundane as my old life. I'm not sure which one I prefer. The adventure has already begun to dull me. I don't even know if it is possible for me to die. I might welcome it if it came.

Spiraling out of my chest is my Soulmind coming to my aid. The machete hilt pops out and I grab it with my right hand. Ripping it out, I look at the white light blade. Then I slice—severing my torso from my legs. I swipe it from my right hip through to my left hip. And I am free. Bleeding, but free. I throw the blade from me as I fall forward and begin to crawl on my elbows. I scooch along, not knowing in which direction I should be going. Suddenly I am picked up and slung over someone's shoulders.

It is the black woman from the Order. The one with the white dreadlocks. I wrap my arms around her neck and hang onto her like a living backpack.

"Sorry for the brutality before," she says. "That's Leeah's style. I'm Rahjiah. Leeah wants me to show you the Dark Tethers so you know what we are up against at the moment. Maya, who is from this world, is still loose in the Hollow Dimension and still may be capable of destroying a great portion of your world. So, needless to say, we have a lot to deal with without you making things harder for us. But you seem to be the one she's after, so you should know what kind of power is looking for you. Don't worry, nothing will harm you here as long as you're with me."

I nod.

"We will observe, but not participate," Rahjiah says.

The smoke in front of us clears and I stare at the little girl I had seen earlier. She is standing in front of me—but it isn't me. It's a reflection of me. And I am restrained by black ropes around my wrists. Tethers. I keep running at the little girl, but the ropes pull me back and I can't reach her. My mouth is snapping open and closed like a rabid dog. I am salivating. But she remains a foot in front of me. And suddenly the ropes snap down, brutally ripping my arms off. The breaking sounds like celery stalks being broken. I see myself stand there for a second, with blood gushing from my open wounds. Then he lunges for the child, tackling her and bearing his teeth. Then he sinks them in.

I close my eyes, not wanting to watch. Then the girl speaks. I listen but do not open my eyes.

"I love all your porno beats, Mr. Muffin Man. But the time has come for me to swim, and Dormy knows how Dina sings. For great are things to come in fact. Everything in tact, is now. But all come round and Time be gone and Time be on. From time to time the creatures tick, and from below come Trick, Tock, and Tick."

"Make it stop!" I scream.

Then there is silence.

I open my eyes finally and see we are in a different area. We are in the hospital. The one I woke up in after my accident. We're in the hallway outside the room they put me in. The light from the fluorescents is almost blinding.

"Look familiar?" Rahjiah asks.

I watch as my reflection self comes running out of the room looking for the stairs. He spots it and stumble runs toward them.

"You heard something, didn't you?" Rahjiah says.

I hear footsteps and look down the hall away from my reflection. There is a male nurse coming toward him.

"Shit, there was someone!" I say.

"Shh."

I look. My reflection has stopped, but hasn't turned around to look yet. I turn and watch as the nurse crosses in front of the hospital room door where my reflection was moments ago. As he does so, black ropes of energy shoot out of the door from inside and wrap around the man's wrists and ankles. My mouth hangs agape as he is dragged into the room. And when my reflection turns around, there is not a person to be seen. He walks on toward the stairs. The scene evaporates and we are back on the blue glass.

Rahjiah doesn't say anything. She doesn't need to. Connections are made from new perceptions in our minds, whether real or hallucinated. They become real to us as we come to our own conclusions through the way we connect every detail in our own small worlds. Making them become bigger as the mysteries only grow larger.

"And here," Rahjiah says as another image of destruction comes into view a little bit in front of us. It is Chicago. And it is on fire.

Every building is ablaze under a cloud-darkened sky forever. Under the light of the fires, men rape women and children—as well as other men. Women beat their children. Children enjoy it. They are all in a trance-like state, hateful, and overcome with selfishness.

"Why are they doing this?" I ask.

"Because they've given in to what keeps them in bondage. And in doing so, it has made them free."

I don't understand, but I don't ask any more questions. "That's sick..." I mumble.

Rahjiah chuckles. I don't know why.

"What's so funny?" I ask her.

I look up to the top of the John Hancock building and see my reflection again. I am taken aback, but then I look harder. He is standing on the edge of the building looking down at what he has created. His arms are stretched out toward the heavens. And he is struck by dry lighting again and again and again. The electricity fails to kill and succeeds to stimulate. He is absorbing the energy of the lightning directly into his Soulmind.

I don't want to believe it; and just before I ask for it to stop, I see a female form walk up behind my reflection and put her hands on my shoulders. It's Maya.

The figures then disappear like smoke and Rahjiah speaks again. "But all this could be prevented."

"I will prevent it," I say indignant.

"Not by you. Watch."

I look again. The buildings have ceased to burn, they are charred and destroyed, but still standing. The people have ceased to be violent and they have gathered in Daley Plaza. Next to the Picasso statue is an excessively raised platform that towers above the people that stand around it. The sky is still dark and overcast. Rain has started to fall. On top of the platform stands Jessica. I look closer. She is standing in the same position that my reflection was on top of the John Hancock. She wears a long white robe and looks like Jesus would have after his resurrection. Her whole form glows with a purple aura. She has restored order to the city, and the world. Then she speaks to the crowd.

"Do not seek destruction, seek creation."

Charismatic I did not think she was. Savior of the world, she did not have it in her. I don't think she even has the capacity of saving herself from herself—much less the world from its own destructive nature. All of these visions may be the morbid thing that the Order would wish for me to believe were real, but if I know one thing it's that I have power beyond anyone's comprehension. It's the way that I choose to use it that will determine the fate of the world. I know that I can destroy, create, kill, or bring to life. I am that master. And I am the Steward of Time. To all the world, they will know my name soon. Some will cower before me. But the choice is to be a peacemaker or a great destroyer. I have the capability.

"No, you don't," Rahjiah says as she grabs my wrist and whips me off of her back toward the floor. As my head hits the glass, it changes into a concrete sidewalk. I am on my side and I look up. The gate to the Public Works building looms over me. I hold my head and cough blood onto the dirty ground.

FIVE

Rob grabbed Arash's hand and pulled him through the throbbing hole in the wall. They fell into the darkness as the orifice closed behind them. The room they found themselves in smelled cold and was too dark for them to see anything. Rob looked over at Arash.

"You were the one who wanted to come here," Rob said.

Arash didn't say anything. Rob wanted to be able to see where he was headed in this unfamiliar space, so he exploded his Soulmind into blue light in front of himself. It shot out of him like a giant lightning bottle rocket in all directions and illuminated their surroundings somewhat. They were standing at the edge of a concrete path, cracked off and leading into the abyss. And from the edge of this crevasse, to Rob it looked like space. Pitch black outer space. Suddenly stars began to appear in the blackness. Rob turned back around to look at the room where they had come from but it was gone. They stood on a floating piece of concrete in deep space.

A staircase appeared before them, a glass staircase leading up toward the stars. Rob started to climb.

"What's this? The stairway to heaven?" Arash said. Rob ignored him and kept walking up into the black. But then he suddenly stopped and turned back to Arash who was still standing on the platform below.

"We're trapped in here," Rob said. "Stuck. Way too long."

"Yes..." Arash hesitated. "How do we escape?"

"I don't know if I believe in God, but whoever is god of this place, I'm in their hands." Rob jumped up into the air and brought both his feet down hard on the glass, shattering it. Rob went straight through it, cutting up his body as he began to fall. "Goodbye," he whispered to Arash as he fell out of sight. When will it end?

But he stopped. He just stopped. Rob was standing straight up in the black expanse, unable to see anything other than the shine of stars an eternal distance away. Rob sighed.

"FUCK YOU! FUCK YOU! FUCK YOU! Why won't you let me leave? I just want to go!"

Rob didn't know if he was expecting a response, but he got one nonetheless. "You came here of your own volition," the Black said.

"Did I? Or was it you? You're making me more like Terry! He's my friend, but I'm not like him. We're different! I have my own needs!"

"I won't let you leave because you haven't learned what you need to learn yet."

"And what do I need to learn?"

"To move on."

"Aren't I supposed to figure out for myself what I need to learn? You're not even giving me my own voice anymore. You stole it! I need my Black back!" Rob screamed.

"You're talking to the Black. You are in the Black. Aren't you happy?"

Rob didn't say anything for a moment. Then finally: "No."

"Well, even though the Order of the Transcendent have headquarters in this building, this is still my domain. You're still a slave. And you're still hers. Learn your world."

Suddenly the figure of Maya was illuminated in front of Rob. She lunged forward, wrapped her arms around Rob and pulled him into the darkness.

Arash sat at the dining room table. It was an incredibly long table; wooden, with clawed feet. He sat at the head, an empty plate in front of him. Rahjiah was sitting at the other head of the table. They were in the giant ballroom, but they were alone. Completely alone. Rahjiah looked at Arash from her side of the table.

"Well, come on, eat up. It's not every day that someone gets invited to a Transcendental dinner," Rahjiah said.

Arash looked down at his plate which had food on it now. A nice juicy steak sat on his plate. By this point Arash's body was still functioning, but his brain had completely shut down—almost completely. All of this had completely shaken his complacent world off of it's rusted hinges, broken them, snapped them, and had not yet spit them out yet. Arash cut into his steak. Yellow egg yolk mixed with blood oozed from the meat. As he cut more into it, a dead chicken fetus plopped out of the meat onto his plate. Arash slowly put his silverware down and looked at Rahjiah. Suddenly she stood up out of her seat.

"Enough with the formalities," she said as the other twelve members of the Order appeared around Arash's seat and grabbed his arms and legs. They picked him up and forced him to lay down on the table. Four women held his arms and legs down so he couldn't struggle. Rahjiah crawled onto the table and got on top of Arash. She ripped his shirt off and then plunged her hand into his solar plexus. Arash screamed in pain. As Rahjiah twisted and pried and pulled, a light started to emanate from Arash. A yellow light spiraling from his chest.

Rahjiah seemed pleased and ripped her hand out of Arash's body. "Very good," she said as she pulled a silk scarf from her pocket. Wrapping it around Arash's neck, she smiled. "He is to be trained." Then she choked him until his body matched his brain.

SIX

Jessica stood on the edge of destruction and was doing nothing to help. She knew that her powers were great, but she chose to be a passive observer. And in turn she was part of the problem. She stood on the chaotic streets of Chicago. Screaming pedestrians ran around her, some on fire. They were all in some sort of pain. Some were vandalizing, stealing, and raping. Daley Plaza was on fire and the Loop was now Layer Zero of Hell. That was how Jessica saw it at that moment.

There was no hope left for humanity, so why bother to help? Terry was on top of the John Hancock building raining down fire from an electric sky. This was all too predictable, too cliche. That's why Jessica just sighed and walked down the middle of the carnage, separate from it. As she walked down the middle of Clark Street, a figure appeared walking toward her from the middle of the burning buildings. It was Rahjiah.

They met each other in the midst, and they saw one another for what they both were: Spirits within a domain that had rejected them. Inside a Dimension where they didn't belong. It was spitting them out and then killing them. Rahjiah leaned in toward Jessica and kissed her softly on the mouth. Rahjiah took Jessica and led her toward an apartment building. They walked between the Hollow people who seemed to be oblivious to their presence. Entering through the front door, Jessica felt a familiar but somewhat disconcerting air about the dwelling. It was her psyche as she had lived for so long and how she saw herself as separate from her body. Into the small apartment they quested.

Rahjiah turned to Jessica as they stood in the living room of the apartment. It was small and had a tiny kitchen. All there was was a couch and a busted TV where they were standing. A closed door led into the bedroom.

"I shall be your guide," Rahjiah said. "You are the Violet Perfect. Never forget this as it is the only thing that will save you from Oblivion."

"But why won't I help the world? I know desperately that I am capable!"

"The world has betrayed you. And you cannot help something that has rejected you. And the absence of God that you feel in the world and your family re-instills your pessimism."

Jessica touched her breast. Her Soulmind was spiraling out of her chest, but weakly. "I'm weak."

"No you're not. This has not come to pass yet, and it is just a vision—not a fact. Your life is something that you create yourself. No one can show you what you are going to do. But here, this is what I see in your Soul."

Rahjiah opened the door to the bedroom and walked in. Jessica followed after her. What she saw made her stomach surge up into her throat. It was her own body sprawled out naked on the disheveled bed. She had been brutally raped and murdered. Her blood soaked the white sheets. It looked like blood had been pouring out of her vagina as well as the giant gash across her throat. But the most interesting thing to note was that Jessica's body looked like it had been pregnant.

Jessica couldn't look anymore. She turned around and walked out of the room. She stopped in the middle of the living room for a second and put both of her hands over her face. Then she ran out of the apartment into the middle of the street. She looked around her at all the fucking people. The lowlifes, the rapists, the murderers—everyone that was scum. They burned and screamed and died around her. Suddenly she screamed at the sky with a cry like that of a mother wolf who has lost her cubs. As she screamed, the pavement around her began cracking in a spiral pattern as if her body was pushing down into the ground making a crater. Then her violet Soulmind exploded out of her entire body, ripping through people and buildings alike. It was as if her own body was a detonated bomb, and she had just exploded. The whole city was ripped to shreds and nothing was left alive.

Jessica's Soulmind shrank back into her body. Then she collapsed onto the ground, dead. Rain started to patter on her pale face. Rahjiah was standing over her now. She held out her hand over Jessica's face and dropped a few rose petals onto her. Then she spoke softly to Jessica's lifeless being.

"But you don't have to listen to me. These are my visions, and I am only your dream. Sleep, sweet Violet. You'll save the world in time."

SEVEN

Nothing was ever the same, as things always are in a world of inertia. Terry woke up, as if out of a reality dream, and he was looking up into Karl's worried face. Terry blinked and looked around groggily at his own belongings. He was on the couch in his own house. Karl seemed to be tending to him from a chair in front of the couch. Terry scanned as far as he could see for Remius. The cat wasn't anywhere to be seen.

Terry grabbed his head. "What in the fuck?" He clenched his eyes shut against the pain. "I feel like I've been hit in the head with a sledgehammer."

"Well, you did puke and pass out," Karl said.

"Ah, yeah. Right." Terry looked around for a second. "Is everyone else okay?"

Karl looked sheepish as he shrugged his shoulders. "You're the only one who came out."

Terry fell back onto the couch. "How long did you wait for them until you brought me back here?"

"About an hour," Karl said. He leaned in closer to Terry. "What the fuck happened in there?"

Terry let out a long stream of air and then looked over at Karl again. "I really don't know. It's all fuzzy, like a dream a few minutes after you wake up."

"Fuck, man." Karl looked like he was about to freak out, but he had to forcibly hold himself back. "Should we call the cops?"

"No. There's nothing we can do. All we can do is wait and see if they turn up." Terry shrugged.

Karl stared at Terry as if he were an alien. "How can you be so fucking cool about this? Aren't you scared at all? Or worried that we're going to be in deep shit? And I mean deep!"

"If we are, there's nothing we can do about it."

Karl stood up and looked down at Terry. "I need to go, it's almost six in the morning. Are you going to be okay?" Terry nodded. "Let me feel your face. I don't want to leave you alone if you're really sick or something." Karl leaned down to feel the side of Terry's face. As he did so, Terry slowly leaned up and kissed Karl on the lips. Karl pulled back fast and stared at Terry for just a second before the rage entered into his face like a speeding train enters a tunnel of madness. Without warning Karl punched Terry in the face. Terry's hands shot up to his face as Karl began to walk away.

Before Karl reached the door, he stopped and turned halfway around to say one word. "Faggot." Then he left.

Terry leaned on his elbow and spit blood onto the floor. "Fuck." He briefly looked at the door where Karl just exited. Then he got up off the couch, a bit wobbly still.

"Remiuuuuuuuuus!" Terry yelled. "Are you here?" Terry looked in the kitchen and the bathroom for Remius. When he was thoroughly convinced that the cat was nowhere on the ground level of the house, he climbed the stairs and checked all the rooms upstairs.

Calling Remius's name still, Terry searched every corner to no avail. His companion had abandoned the house. Terry was suddenly overwhelmed with despair. His vision distorted by tears, he stumbled into his bedroom. Seeing the world only through the mist of pain, tears, and rejection resulted in Terry filtering the world as if he were in an infinite pit of sinking dirt.

And as he tried to climb out, he only accomplished filling in his own grave.

He collapsed on the floor beside his bed. Groping around, Terry closed his fingers around a black permanent marker. As he sobbed, he made three dots on his throat in the shape of a triangle, the tip pointing up to his chin.

"Jessica... Jessica..." Terry cried to the expanse. He dropped the marker and sank into himself. Making no attempt to suppress his anguish, Terry let out the most painful scream that filled every corner of his house, but didn't leak out to the ears of the dreamers of the world.

Suddenly each dot on Terry's throat started to emit bright white light, as if there was a light source trapped in his neck and he had poked holes in his flesh with a needle. Each dot detached itself from his body. Terry looked at the three points of a triangle shining in space about four feet in front of him. From each point, lines of bluish-gold fire began to join the points of the triangle together into one figure. And then the portal opened into the infinite, revealing Jessica in her bedroom. Terry watched the triangle as if it was a screen into another universe. It linked his room to her room.

Terry scooted closer to the gateway. As he was doing that, Jessica was sitting on the floor leaning against her bed. She was crying. It was only then that Terry realized she was holding a razor blade in her right hand.

"No!" Terry blurted out. He suddenly tried to break through the gateway into Jessica's world. He touched the middle of the triangle with the tips of the fingers of his right hand. The image started to ripple like a vertical pond. And as the ripples got more violent, it started to release a current of electricity into Terry's arm. He cried out as he was forced to withdraw his hand. All he could do was watch as Death took hold of Love.

Slowly Jessica placed the razor vertically over her left wrist. Then she cut. She cut her soul, her mind, her heart, her Perfect. What leaked out was not blood, it was Soul. Purple smoke began to ooze and billow out of her cut, pouring onto the floor instead of floating. Jessica's mouth hung open as her eyelids fluttered shut. Her head tilted back against the bed. It looked as if she was going to pass out. Terry felt sick. His Soulmind was being torn out of him violently and taking every ounce of his strength with it. He didn't know how to help this girl, he was useless in his longing, in his emptiness.

Suddenly Jessica's door was flung open and her father stood there, silhouetted against the bright hallway. Her eyes flew open and looked terrified as her dad stared at her with rage in his face. Jessica hugged her dripping wrist to her breasts.

Her father didn't say anything, he didn't have to. He lunged into the room and grabbed Jessica's right wrist and wrenched her to her feet, almost dislocating her shoulder. She let out a small yell which she stifled when her father shot her a look. He dragged her out of the door and down the stairs. The triangle followed like a camera.

Her father pulled her into the kitchen where there was a pot on the stove that was boiling water. Jessica looked at it with fear and uncertainty. Mr. Thorn grabbed the pot off the stove with one hand, his other grabbed the back of Jessica's neck. He pushed her forcibly over to the sink where he proceeded to hold her bleeding wrist, palm up, over the sink. Then he poured. He poured the boiling water onto his daughter's vulnerable wrist. She shrieked and tried to pull away but he was too strong. He emptied the entire pot onto her arm. Jessica was sobbing now. Terry was crying also.

Jessica's father grabbed a roll of duct tape off of the kitchen counter. He proceeded to tape his daughter's gashed wrist shut by spiraling the tape around her whole forearm. After he was done, he threw the tape down and dragged Jessica back up the stairs and threw her into her bedroom. Slamming the door, he left her in the dark.

Jessica screamed to the emptiness. Terry screamed to the emptiness. They let loose every demon that was ever trapped inside, letting them mingle and make love in the space between consciousness. Jessica's head suddenly turned and looked in Terry's direction as if seeing him through the gateway. She stood up and approached him and then stopped. Holding out her arms like a cross, Jessica's violet aura began to shine in the dark room. Her clothes and hair were blown by an invisible wind as the area of her ribs between her breasts opened up revealing her Perfect heart. She put both her hands on either side of her heart and offered it to Terry.

He accepted and the image shattered and exploded into his imagination, filling the room with a glow that was oddly warm. But the cold wind quickly swam into his world again, reminding him of the absence of a black furry creature.

EIGHT
FROM THE MIND OF TERRY BROSWALD:

Triangulate my throat
And slit a hole so deep that I would never be able to climb back out.
Stabbing at the trachea with giant knitting needles,
I slip back into the mucus.
To finally become Seven, I need to reach the knowledge suspended in the

splintered air behind the throat.
Body is a prison for the soul.
We are hollow, trapped, and dead
Inside our blood vessels.
You are a wheel postponed indefinitely
And I am your flat.
Come and fill me to tipping.
But then I fall into the Spindle Trap.
Forever being carried on a cloud of spider tongues.
And forever impaled on woven cotton.
I prick my finger,
It has just begun.
Inject your arm down my oiled throat as I beg you
To save me.
Everything is illuminated
And I asphyxiate on your loveliness.
Seduction isn't what it seems
And premonition may be wrong
But I know for a fact,
Parting ways always leads to strawberry paragons.

NINE

Terry awoke the next morning to violent currents of electricity coursing through his throat. He could not speak or make any noise through his mouth. He was rigid like a log floating in a swamp, being torn apart with lightning. He felt his pulse inside and outside, and his neck beat like his heart. When it finally subsided, the air in front of Terry's face became a haze of purple smoke. Inside of that cloud was an image—a vision. A vision of a girl he once knew but had since lost sight of. As Terry reached his hand out to brush the smoke, his vision of Jessica had become a hopeless wash of greys and blacks. The purple fog had now become black mist as he watched Jessica leave her house through her front door. Were those tears in her eyes?

As if he was being struck by lightning again, Terry finally realized what Jessica was about to do. His soul went cold and he couldn't breathe. As he gasped for air, the black mist swirled into nothingness and escaped into his nostrils. The action dormant is an action lost. Terry could only breathe again once he was in motion. He had to go to her. All that was left to do was run. To meet her on the bridge that fell into traffic below. Terry couldn't let her do what he had done. To him, at that very moment, it seemed so long ago that he had been dead. He was living now, but not fully. Something had remained dead inside himself and Jessica was taking it with her.

Leaving his domain and hastily closing his front door behind him, Terry dove into the world. His destination was the bridge over the freeway—the one where people decided to paint the road with their colors. The rainbow of human combustion. We always decide to spread our substance on the world. Terry did not have the help of Remius this time, he had to do everything himself. His legs burned and pumped oxygen deprived blood into his system as he ran for what seemed like an infinite stretch of burning desert.

When he reached the bridge, sucking in corrupted air, he saw Jessica. Her back was facing him and she gazed sadly over the edge down toward the blazing noise of machines. Terry took a couple steps toward her. She turned slowly to meet his gaze. There were tears in her eyes.

Terry grasped the air with his hands, looking for words but finding there none. His mouth opened and closed soundlessly.

His eyes were desperate but sunken into himself. She didn't have anything left to give him. So she shook her head.

"I have to go," she said simply.

As Terry watched, she began to glow—that violet glow that used to energize him so now made him apprehensive. She now wished to erase herself from this world. The spiral or purple began to emerge from between her breasts, and it all began to envelope her. She was surrounding herself with Soulmind fire, lapping up the air of Time. Terry didn't want this. He ran to her and speared his hand into her spiral, digging around for her heart. His hand disappeared into her solar plexus as he tried desperately to keep her in this world. Jessica's body was starting to become translucent.

"Don't fight me, Terry. I am not your enemy."

Terry screamed as tears streamed down his face. "I can't let you leave me!" Jessica's purple Soulmind was now wrapping itself around Terry's arm and creeping toward his shoulder.

"You're selfish," Jessica said quietly. "You always were."

"Oh, God... You fucking bitch..." Terry sobbed uncontrollably.

"You have to let me go."

"I won't!"

"You must."

"You haven't put me back together yet. Fucking please..." He begged her like a child begs his mother for a piece of candy.

Jessica's body began to flicker now like a lonely film projector.

"Close your eyes, Terry." Terry did. Jessica lifted her finger up and touched the middle of the triangle that was still on his throat. A picture began to appear on his deranged eyelids. It was in Jessica's house. Terry saw the stairs that led up to Jessica's bedroom. Lining the wall going up the stairs were photographs of her family. The three of them in their family portrait all seemed to find painted pastel smiles that dissolved once the film had been exposed.

As Terry looked, he realized what Jessica was doing. She was completely erasing herself, as well as her memory, from the Hollow World. Her small form, between stagnant parents, was beginning to disappear. She was leaving, leaving her parents behind, alone, without a memory of their daughter.

Terry opened his eyes slowly. Jessica's violet eyes burned as she unblinkingly gazed into his hollows. "Now do you understand?" She asked.

Instead of answering, Terry slowly retracted his hand from Jessica's chest. Energy clung to his arm for a second and then began to fall off like slimy tentacles. Jessica was leaving him. She was leaving this world behind to start a new life in the expanse of the Spiralverse. Perhaps they would meet again on some distant planet in the future, or perhaps the past.

Jessica spoke one final time before she eradicated herself into the infinite. As she unclasped the cross necklace from off of her neck she uttered these words, "Stop believing the lies."

Then she became the sparkle dust of space, shattering her form into shiny purple. As she was blown away into the clouds, along with the memory, her necklace fell to the ground handless.

Terry had become completely empty. He had heard her words, but he was too stubborn to really give them weight. Anger was his ally now that he was alone. He burned with it. Terry bent down and picked up the necklace; it was all he had left now. And as he squeezed it into his palm, drops of blood sizzled to the pavement and became dust.

PART 7

In Silence, In Pain

*"I remember your eyes: fifty attack dogs
on a single leash, how I once held that
soft audience of your hand. I've been
ignored by prettier women than you, but
none who carried the heavy
Pitchers of Silence
so far, without spilling a drop."*
- Jeffrey McDaniel

TEN

No matter how hard he tried, Terry couldn't get used to the sudden absence of Jessica. She had become part of his heart, he loved her, but now he felt like his heart had been ripped in two. He was reminded of when he was in the hospital after his accident on the bicycle. It seemed so long ago to him now. So much had happened between then and when Jessica erased herself from the Hollow Dimension. The pain in Terry's chest was so intense, it was like nothing he had ever felt before, so much that he even made a name for it: *Chest Death*. Chest Death is the most intense pain in the Universe because it is emotional pain that has breached the threshold and become physical pain. He felt like someone had taken a giant hook and gored his chest and punctured his still beating heart.

The first Sunday after Jessica disappeared, Terry found himself driving over to her house, with hope beyond hope that she might still be there and everything that preceded was all just a sadistic dream. He parked his van across the street from the house his lover had used to live in. Terry pounded on the steering wheel as tears welled up in the corners of his eyes and started to fall through the air like liquid diamonds.

"Why?" Terry whispered under his breath. "Why did you have to fucking leave me?" He gritted his teeth against the Chest Death and his fists were clenched so tight that his hands were turning red. Terry glared at the house through a blur of tears. He was seething with sadness and rage that threatened to bubble to the surface in not so productive ways. The wind blew through the Thorns's porch, scattering a few leaves from the ground. Through the mixture of the wind and tears, Terry almost thought he saw Jessica's form appear there in front of the door, waving at him. When he blinked it was gone. "Bitch... I really loved you."

"You have some serious abandonment issues."

Terry jumped, startled by a voice from the back seat that he wasn't expecting. It was Remius, of course. He yawned and licked his paw, then continued. "You should get some professional help for that."

Terry turned around in the driver's seat and stared at Remius, his mouth hanging open. "Well, look who decided to show up." Terry said sarcastically. He instinctively, unconsciously touched the cross around his neck to comfort himself.

Remius jumped down from the back seat, stretched, and then hopped up onto the passenger seat next to Terry. "You know," Remius began. "If something is going to be your downfall, it's gonna be your anger and rage, and the sadness which is the foundation of that. I'm afraid you have some serious psychological issues." Remius gave Terry a very wide cat grin.

"Are you fucking for real right now?" Terry spat. "You aren't supposed to say that shit to me. Especially not now. I'm vulnerable. The love of my life just erased herself from the fucking world. Don't you have any compassion?"

"That's something you should talk to your psychologist about, don't you think? Are you still seeing that guy—what's his name—Dr. Tim?" Remius asked.

Terry blinked at the cat, dumbfounded. "Seriously? I stopped seeing that guy a while ago. And YOU were the one who didn't want me to see him in the first place, you whisker-faced cunt. Now you change your tune?"

"Nah," Remius conceded. "I was just fucking with you. Jeez, you're fucking dense, aren't you? That was just a little joke. *I* thought it was funny... Anyway, in all seriousness, you think that Jessica was the love of your life? You're so young. Don't get the one-itis, thinking that there's only one girl out there for you. Hell, there could even be three."

"What?" Terry said, only half paying attention. He was still looking over at the porch of the Thorn house, hoping Jessica might decide to materialize back there from wherever she was. "Where did she go?" Terry asked. The question wasn't really directed at anyone or anything, just spoken to the air.

"I'm sorry, Terry. I don't know. I wish I had some answers for you, but I don't. I can only tell you what I know." Remius's tone softened and there was genuine compassion in his voice. He knew when to quell the jokes.

"It's okay," Terry said. "I just need some time to grieve, I guess. It almost feels like someone I was very close to just died. I don't know..."

"Terry, snap out of it!" Remius said in a firm tone. If he had had thumbs, he would have snapped to get Terry out of his melancholy trance. Remius continued, "Lest we forget that there are other things we still need to worry about. I know Jessica had become your world and you wanted to keep her close to your heart, but there are immediate threats now—in this world—that we're gonna have to deal with. Maya isn't going to give up, you know that. And the Order of the Transcendent, they're watching us and I don't know what their agenda is—which worries me. And your friend Rob, I hope you know that even though he helped you in Dreamsphere, we still don't know if he can be trusted."

"Speaking of Rob," Terry said thoughtfully. "Where the fuck is that motherfucker? Karl and I never saw him after we went to that Public Works building. Speaking of which, we never saw Arash come back out either."

Remius shook his head. "That worries me. A person with a powerful Soulmind will have many enemies. People of a lower vibration that want to crush your light. They don't want you to shine. But what they don't know is that you're gonna get brighter, and brighter, and brighter."

Remius could see the overwhelm take hold of Terry and register on his face. He looked totally exhausted. "I'm so fucking tired, Remius. Let's go home." Terry said as he put the key in and started the ignition.

ELEVEN

Rob awoke to find himself alone in the Specific Cage again, but he was not in that same wooden room he was before. This time his surroundings were very strange and surreal, nothing really looked solid. There were a lot of thin shadows and gray masses moving around above him. The ground that his cage rested on was completely black—it looked like shiny obsidian. He tried to squint into the horizon to see something—anything at all. There was nothing in front of him except gray haze. Rob felt like he was in the unrendered graphics of a yet-to-be-created video game. He started to panic and all manner of thoughts and scenarios ran through his mind: *Am I dead? Is this hell? Can I get out of this cage like I did last time? What the fuck has been going on lately? Am I going insane?*

Then he heard something. Rob crawled to the front of the cage and peered out, his hands grasping the bars. As the sound got louder, Rob identified it as footsteps. Slowly coming into focus out of the haze stepped a figure that he immediately recognized. There was the tight black leotard, the long straight black hair, and eyes that were bottomless wells of darkness. It was Maya, and she was carrying a long cattle prod in her right hand.

"Let's get one thing straight," Maya said as she reached the cage. "Your loyalty is to me and me alone." Rob didn't say anything so Maya stuck the cattle prod through the bars and shocked him in the side of the ribs. Yelling in pain, Rob scooted farther toward the back of his cell. "You work for me, Robert," she continued. "As far as you're concerned, you have no friends."

"What are you going to do with me?" Rob asked.

"I haven't decided yet. But I know now that you can't be trusted to complete the mission and deliver Terry to me. Now I'm forced to find someone else who will complete this task with obedience."

Rob stared at Maya, his captor. "So you're not going to let me go, are you?"

"Not just yet," Maya replied. "You must be made to suffer for your crimes. Besides, I like seeing you in that cage. You look so helpless and cute." Just for fun she shocked him again. Rob screamed and tried to make himself small.

"Terry will come and rescue me! And he'll kill you!" Rob said, he was angry now.

Maya laughed. "No one gives a fuck about you. Besides, they all probably think you just got killed in the Public Works building. No one knows where you are or how to get to this part of the Dark Tethers. We shared energy so now I own you." She smiled menacingly.

Rob grimaced and felt his stomach sink at the prospect that he would be trapped in the Specific Cage forever.

"Hey," Maya poked Rob until he looked at her again. "Say *specific*." Rob rolled his eyes and kept silent. "Say it. Say *specific* or I'll shock you again." Maya waved the cattle prod in front of his face.

Rob slowly opened his mouth and tried to pronounce the word. "S-s-s... pacific."

"Nope!" Maya jabbed the cattle prod into Rob's chest and unleashed the current. Rob screamed and begged for mercy. "You should have pronounced it right," Maya laughed in his face. "You're so fucking useless you can't even pronounce the word *specific*. It comes out like you're talking about the Pacific Ocean. That's why you're in this fucking thing!" She shook the cage hard and Rob rattled around inside.

"You're such a psycho cunt!" Rob screamed at her. She stopped and gave him the harshest look that could have killed a cat in mid-prance.

"What did you call me, you worthless piece of shit!" Maya shook the cage again. "You're lucky I don't just kill you now. No matter though. You can rot in here."

Without another word, Maya walked off and disappeared into the haze. Rob was left to contemplate his pronunciation, desperate and alone.

Maya had a new plan, and a new accomplice in mind. Actually it was accomplices—there were three of them. These three individuals had been the orchestrators of many of the destructive movements in the Hollow Dimension: Hitler and the Holocaust, the assassination of JFK, World War One, September 11th—and the list goes on. Unfortunately for Maya, they were currently imprisoned in the Dark Tethers's Cube Containment Facility—which was also known as Astral Prison. This cube had no doors in and no doors out. For Maya this was just a speed bump, not a road block.

As Maya dematerialized and rematerialized through the many layers of her domain, she got closer and closer to the Cube. As she went down the layers, the atmosphere got denser and denser. Maya could feel the weight threatening to crush her body; luckily she was from this world and knew how to manipulate her physicality through her own mind and energy. She stopped for a second in an area where solid black and grey clouds were surrounding her. She made a fist and raised her index and middle finger. Raising the two fingers up to her forehead, she began to chant.

"Oh gods of darkness and bondage, grant me passage through the solidity of material reality. Though I am pushed from above, below, left, and right, I am never crushed nor defeated. I call to the ropes of my ancestors. Pull me through into the underground. I surrender, yet I remain steadfast. The black is mine and I am the black!"

Maya's corporeal form flickered like a bad TV and then was pulled through the ground into the most hidden recess of Dark Tethers.

Maya stood in a new space, and as the black mist cleared in front of her, there stood the immense Containment Cube. It was made of flawless obsidian and on the front face, stretching from the ground all the way to the top of the cube, was a white Mercury symbol. Maya closed her eyes and brought the two fingers back to her forehead. As she concentrated, she began to levitate into the air and came to a hover at the middle of the Mercury symbol. Her hair blew in the wind energy which she was creating. At the same time the symbol began shining with a brilliant white light, Maya began to glow golden around her whole body. A beam of energy suddenly shot out of the midpoint of the symbol directly into her heart. Maya's physicality immediately evaporated and became a pure light body. She was drawn into the beam of light as it pulled her through the obsidian and into the Cube.

Once inside, she regained her physical form. Inside the Cube was like a labyrinth. Maya was in a narrow hallway, walls on either side of her, and the passage stretched in front of her farther than she could see. There were no traditional prison cells in the Cube, they were all completely sealed for the purpose of keeping the entities inside and any entities out that may try to break them free. Luckily she knew more about the facility than most. That was how she knew how to get in and that the three she was looking for were kept captive in the geometric center of the Cube since they were the most dangerous individuals kept there.

"Fuck this place," Maya said under her breath. "Good thing I know the cheat codes." She turned to the wall to her right and punched in the access code on the invisible keypad that was there. The spaces she touched on the wall lit up orange.

"Passcode accepted," a robotic voice said, echoing off the walls.

"Of course it is, you automated piece of shit," Maya mocked the disembodied voice. She waited and watched as the wall in front of her opened up a circle a foot in diameter. A transparent crystal ball rolled out and hovered in the air in front of Maya. There was a miniature version of the Cube rotating inside the sphere. As she swiped her fingers around the sphere in different patterns, she could explore the interior of the Containment Cube like a holographic map. Maya navigated to the centermost chamber. She could see it visually now within the sphere. It was a small room with three sarcophagi made of amethyst. Maya closed her eyes again and held her hands on either side of the crystal ball. As she concentrated, her palms began to glow red. The air around the sphere began to wave with the heat. Suddenly the hallway around her melted away and the central chamber began to take shape. When the room around her and the three amethyst sarcophagi became completely solid, Maya opened her eyes again.

Each sarcophagus in front of her had a name carved into it. The first was Trick. The second was Tock. The third was Tick. These were the three entities who would now help her capture Terry's Soulmind: Trick, Tock, and Tick.

Maya held out her hands, palms up. Now her black ropes began to dance up from the middle of her hands. When they were large enough, they detached from her body and began to constrict around each crystal containment unit. The black ropes squeezed with an infinite amount of pressure. The amethyst began to crack, and as fractures appeared in each, Trick, Tock, and Tick opened their eyes.

The amethyst shattered into a billion fragments and a flash of an instant later the three were standing in front of Maya. Trick was a very large man. He was about six feet tall and built like a wrestler. Trick wore white sweat pants but was shirtless; his muscles rippled and bulged from being contained for so long. Across his stomach was tattooed the word *penetration*. "Oh yeah!" Trick growled. "I'm ready to fuck shit up! Let's go!"

Tock was shorter than Trick by about half a foot. He was super skinny like an anorexic heroin junky. He was also shirtless and wore black shorts. His whole body was covered in tattoos, even his face. He also had long stringy hair. "Let's torture them till they shit themselves!" Tock's voice was shrill and he laughed hysterically.

Tick was the fat one. He was the only one wearing a shirt. His clothes were jeans and a stained white tee-shirt. Tick was bald also and had a crazy look in his eye. He licked his lips and said, "I hope we get to wipe out some entire races this time!"

Maya smiled and was pleased that she had been able to perform a jailbreak so easily. "Boys, boys," she said. "I have freed you to put your mark on the world again. Now let's get the hell out of here. I have a new mission for you."

TWELVE

Terry returned to school out of habit—or it could have been out of boredom and loneliness. Of course he had Remius to keep him company at home, but the cat couldn't provide him the human contact he craved. When he got to school, Terry went to the normal spot he and his friends hung out at until the bell rang. It was apparent that his group of friends had grown very small. The only two people of Terry's crew whom he found sitting by the conference room were Mothman and Alex. Karl wasn't anywhere to be seen. Terry wasn't very surprised by this; he had pretty much burned that bridge completely.

Mothman and Alex were sharing earbuds and Mothman was air-drumming on his legs. They greeted Terry as he approached.

"What's going on, motherfucker?" Mothman said as he high-fived with Terry. "Where the hell have you been? It seems like forever since we've seen you!"

Terry shrugged and sat down next to Mothman. "I've been around," he replied. "I don't even know why I bother to come to school anymore."

Mothman studied Terry out of the corner of his eye. "You seem different, man," Mothman said. "I don't know what it is... And seriously—where the FUCK is everybody? I mean, I haven't seen black man Rob for at least a week. And Karl seems to be avoiding us like the plague. We almost even got into a fight the other day... Did you do something to him?"

"Ummm..." Terry said, remembering when he kissed Karl and the punch that came after. "I might have."

They fell silent for a moment and just watched the boys and girls walking in an endless flow through the halls. The students all went to and fro, back and forth to the same rooms every day. "Why do we even come here?" Terry asked, more rhetorically than anything.

Mothman snorted. "Because we have to. Believe me if I wasn't forced to go here by my parents, I'd be the first one to be fucking outtie this bitch." Mothman looked over at Alex who was just bobbing to the music, in his own little world.

Terry smacked Mothman's leg. "Hey, man," Terry began. "You should just start coming over to my house after school. We'll hang out and do some fun shit. Try to forget about this mundane school bullshit. This place doesn't help us learn and think critically, it's just conditioning us to be good little mind slaves to put into society's robot boxes."

Mothman raised one eyebrow. "Okay, dude, whatever you say. I'm always ditching the assemblies after school anyway. That shit's so fucking gay... Hey, you still trying to go after Kyleen? I don't know if that bet is still on since everybody is fucking ditching us. Stefano doesn't even talk to us at all anymore either."

"I don't know," Terry said after a long pause. "I'm not really going after her as the *target*, but if she's attracted to my energy,

I'll let her come to me. I'm the prize, and I don't know if she even deserves me."

Mothman burst out laughing. "That's the excuse you're gonna come up with because she's out of your league? Making yourself sound all smart and like a diamond in the rough? You do seem to have changed though—more confident."

"Fuck me, I don't even want to go to class today," Terry whined. "I'm gonna have to go to Mr. Down Syndrome's class and face Karl."

"What did you do to him?" Mothman asked.

"I kinda, like, tried to make out with him," Terry answered reluctantly.

Mothman couldn't contain himself and erupted into hysterical laughter. "He's so fucking homophobic. What did he do?"

"He punched me in the face."

"Just for one kiss?" Mothman shook his head. "I wouldn't have hit you, I would have put my tongue in your mouth." Mothman winked at Terry who just gave him a weird look in return.

The bell rang for first period. "Oh, shit, we're gonna be late," Alex said as he ripped the earbud from his ear and sped off down the hallway.

"See you later?" Terry said. Mothman nodded. They gave each other a fist bump and went their separate ways.

Terry climbed the stairs toward Mr. Down Syndrome's class, the dread building with every step he took. When he got to the Physics room, most of the students were already there. Mr. Down was standing behind his desk at the front talking to a female student, his hand on her arm. Terry shook his head; Mr. Down was already up to his old perverted tricks. Karl was there, seated a few rows back. He glared as Terry entered the room.

With a deep swallow and knots in his stomach, Terry sat in the desk next to Karl. Obviously this was an unwanted move.

"Don't sit next to me," Karl hissed at Terry out of the side of his mouth.

"I can sit wherever I want," Terry replied confidently.

"Don't fucking sit next to me, you gay faggot!" Karl was more adamant this time, spitting insults through a harsh whisper.

"Don't call me that," Terry said, a little louder than he should have. "You're a fucking faggot, Karl!"

Karl snorted. "You're the faggot!" He shot back.

"Fudge-packing big-nosed faggot!" Terry traded insult for insult.

"Get the fuck away from me," Karl hissed under his breath and punched Terry in the arm.

"YOU FUCKER!" Terry yelled this time and the entire class's heads turned as Terry kicked the leg of Karl's desk.

Mr. Down didn't see Karl punch Terry, but he looked up after Terry yelled and kicked Karl's desk, which made a loud scraping noise on the floor.

"Uh-hmm!" Mr. Down cleared his throat and an angry dissatisfied expression entered his face. He must have been pissed that his perving had been interrupted. "Terry! How good of you to join us after so long of an absence." The sarcasm dripped from his voice. "Now," Mr. Down continued. "Now that you have joined us, you may leave us. For disrupting the class, you can go sit out in the hall until I say you can come back in and join us—if I'm nice enough to let you back in."

Terry shot daggers from his eyes at Karl who almost couldn't contain his laughter. Mr. Down gave Terry the stare down until he got up from his desk and walked toward the door in shame and degradation. Terry wanted so badly to make a comment to Mr. Down Syndrome which would cut him down and crush his arrogance, but he bit his tongue. The whole class laughed at Terry as he left the room.

Terry sat down in the desk that was outside the door which was designated for 'bad' students. Tears began to well up in his eyes and rain down onto the surface of the desk. The depression took hold of Terry and enveloped him in a tight dark blanket. Why had he even bothered to come back to school just to experience this abuse?

Terry went home right after school, forgetting that he had agreed to meet Mothman to hang out. As he came in the side door, Terry contemplated whether he would ever go back to high school again. After all that he had seen and experienced, what was the point of falling back into that mundane existence? Terry looked around the house for Remius, but the cat's presence seemed to be gone for the moment.

The doorbell rang and without any hurry, Terry walked over to see who it was. Mothman stood outside the door waiting to see if his friend was home. Terry opened the door and invited Mothman to come inside. "Mothman!" Terry said with a smile. "Sorry I forgot to meet you after school to walk over here. I had a lot on my mind. School was worse than usual today."

Terry closed and locked the door behind them and they strolled into the living room. "It's okay," Mothman said. "Good thing you live right next to the high school." Mothman glanced around and noted how quiet the house was. "Your parents aren't home?"

"Nah," Terry answered. "They're out doing whatever it is they do." How could Terry explain to Mothman that his parents were gone for good? He decided just to leave it at that for now.

"Good!" Mothman said as he took his backpack off and flopped down on the couch. "Cause I brought some weed!"

"Of course you did. Is it that dank dank?" It had been a while since Terry had smoked any weed.

"Only the best! It's that purple kush." Mothman pulled out a ziplock baggie of nugs and a glass pipe that was red, green, and gold with a picture of Bob Marley on the bowl piece. Terry sat down next to Mothman as he packed a nugget of weed into the bowl.

"You know what, Mothman?" Terry said. Mothman looked over as he took a fat rip off the pipe. "I'm thinking of just dropping out of school."

Mothman held the hit in his lungs and passed the pipe to Terry. "Really?" Mothman asked as he exhaled the smoke. "I don't want to go anymore either. But I don't know if my parents would let me do that. They're strict like that. And I don't think I could tough out the monotony without you."

Terry took a big hit and passed the pipe back to Mothman. "This is just a thought," Terry said after a pause. "You could come live with me here. We'd have a blast."

"Fuck yeah, dude! I'd love to do that. Have to figure out how I could get away with that shit. What about your parents?" Mothman asked; he passed the pipe after he took another huge hit.

Terry took the pipe from Mothman's hand. "Let's just say for now that they aren't an issue."

Mothman looked quizzically at Terry. "There *is* something different about you. I can't place it."

"That's like the third or fourth time that you've said that today. What's so different about me?" Terry asked.

"It's, like, your energy or something. Like you've learned a lot and become more solid in yourself." Mothman squeezed Terry's thigh as if to see if he was really there.

"Well," Terry said. "I don't necessarily feel more solid. I don't know what I feel..."

Mothman's eyes were red as the devil's dick now and he put the pipe and weed back in his backpack. He turned to Terry who was feeling quite stoned as well. "Umm..." Mothman hesitated for a second. "Terry... can I kiss you?"

Terry's eyes widened; that wasn't what he was expecting. He moved back on the couch instinctively and wasn't sure at first how to react. Finally Terry said, "O-okay..."

Mothman leaned forward jerkily and planted a kiss full-force on Terry's mouth. Terry fell back onto the couch and Mothman crawled on top of him. Mothman's lips parted and he shoved his tongue deep into Terry's mouth. It was so forceful that Terry almost gagged and couldn't get a breath. Mothman must have wanted to do this for a long time, and he was so enthusiastic that he was practically about to swallow Terry's whole head. They licked each other's tongues and swapped saliva.

After a minute Terry pushed Mothman off of him and gasped for breath. "Easy, easy!" Terry said, winded.

"Sorry," Mothman said, his hand was groping Terry's crotch now. Mothman could feel Terry's cock getting hard as he unzipped and began to peel his pants off. Terry was fully erect by the time Mothman had pulled his boxers off too. "Damn! Did your dick get bigger?"

Terry shrugged as Mothman stroked him and then dropped his head to suck him off. As Mothman licked and sucked his friend's cock, Terry threw his shirt off too—now he was completely naked. He moaned and breathed heavily as Mothman's head bobbed up and down. Mothman stopped for a second and smiled up at Terry who was red in the face and had an o-shaped mouth. Mothman began to strip off his clothes till he was completely naked as well. "Don't stop," Terry said and put his hand on top of Mothman's head as he resumed the blow job.

Mothman was hard now too and stroked himself as he licked the tip of Terry's penis. "I want to fuck you," Mothman said. "I'm gonna fill you like a Thanksgiving turkey on Christmas!"

Terry wasn't quite against the idea, but he was nervous about it. Mothman's cock was on the larger side—and thick. Mothman slid a finger into Terry's anus and began to finger him. Terry closed his eyes and leaned his head back. "Oh my fucking god, that feels so fucking good! Okay, we can try. I'll let you try to fuck me. But if it hurts then I'm done."

"Do you have a condom?" Mothman asked.

Terry thought about this. "No, I don't think so," he replied.

"Hmm," Mothman's creative brain was working overtime. "How about, do you have Saran Wrap and a rubber band?"

Terry laughed. "Seriously?" Mothman was dead serious. "Fuck it," Terry said. "I'm up for whatever."

"Good," Mothman said. "Go grab it and meet me upstairs in your bathroom." Mothman got up off the couch and Terry smacked his ass as he went by.

Still at full salute, Terry grabbed the Saran Wrap and a rubber band and took them upstairs. Mothman was in the bathroom stroking himself. "Never tell me that I'm not experimental," Terry said as he handed Mothman the stuff.

"Oh, I can never say that you don't try new things," Mothman said, ripping off a piece of plastic wrap big enough to put around his huge cock. He wrapped it and secured the rubber band at the base of his penis. "You got lube?"

"No. If I didn't have a condom, you think I got lube?" Terry said.

Mothman looked over at the sink and saw a bar of soap. "No matter, I can improvise," Mothman said as he grabbed the soap and ran it under water, lathering it up on his hand. He rubbed the foamy soap over the Saran Wrap around his dick. "Now bend over! You are about to be filled by my majestic cock!" Mothman said with a grin.

Terry got on all fours and spread his ass cheeks for entrance. Mothman dropped to his knees and rubbed the tip of his cock against Terry's asshole, which puckered and quivered. He moaned as Mothman prepared to penetrate. Terry's anus began to stretch as Mothman began to push his thick tip in.

"Oh, fuck, oh, fuck..." Terry gasped as he felt his sensitive asshole being stretched. Suddenly Mothman let out a moan as the whole tip of his cock popped inside. Terry lurched forward as the pain registered. "Oh shit, oh fuck. No, no, no, no. That's it!" He reached behind him and pushed Mothman away. Terry's asshole clenched shut, but felt rubbed raw from the Saran Wrap. "Maybe next time," Terry said. "You gotta ease me into it with your monster cock... Just go to my room. I'll be there in a second."

After Mothman left the bathroom, Terry wiped himself with some toilet paper. There was a little spot of blood on the paper when he took his hand away to look at it. Terry threw it in the toilet and flushed it away.

Terry walked naked into his bedroom where Mothman was already laying on the bed with his eyes closed, about to take a nap. The Saran Wrap and rubber band had been discarded onto the floor. Terry crawled into bed behind Mothman and snuggled up against his naked body. They both fell asleep in each other's arms.

THIRTEEN

Rob was still trapped in the Specific Cage, however, he was slowly becoming more calm about it. He still had the desire to escape, but he wasn't panicking. If he was able to get out one time already, he could get out again, right? Rob knew that even if he got out of the cage, he still would have to figure a way out of Dark Tethers altogether and get back to the Hollow Dimension. He tried to shake the second thought from his mind and just focus on the task at hand—escaping from the cage.

As Rob became more and more calm, his breathing slowed and the electric blue energy of his Soulmind began pulsing out of his solar plexus. He had never prayed or meditated a day in his entire life, but now as his awareness seemed to be growing past the bars of the cage, the impulse emerged organically from within him. Rob closed his eyes and placed his palms together in prayer pose. As he did so, the blue energy of his Soulmind began to braid out farther and envelope his body in a fluorescent aura.

"Oh, whatever god or spirit is within me," Rob prayed. "I pray for power and assistance in my time of weakness. If I cannot rely on my own abilities to escape from this cage, please come to my aid."

Rob's aura began to pulse and get brighter, a more vivid blue. The energy of the light began to seep into his skin and take hold of his physical body. Slowly the solidity of Rob's body began to dissolve. He opened his eyes and looked at his hands, which were now translucent. "No fucking way!" Rob said, turning his hands over in front of his bewildered eyes. He reached his arm out and it went right through the solid bars of the cage.

Still in dumbfounded disbelief, Rob stood up and his head and upper torso went right through the top of the cage. Then he just walked out of it and he was free. Once Rob was outside the Specific Cage, his solidity returned to him and his Soulmind retracted into his body. He looked at his hand and squeezed it into a fist to feel himself again.

Slowly Rob walked into the gray mist ahead of him. After only a few steps in, he could no longer see the cage he had escaped from. The gray fog was so dense that Rob became disoriented very quickly. The fear began to take hold of him again, so he began to run. Not sure what direction he was going or where it would lead him, Rob just hoped he would end up somewhere or find something that wasn't just gray masses.

As he ran, a different shape and color began to appear in the distance. It began as a black dot, and as Rob got closer it became larger and clearer. He could feel that it was a human form. Rob slowed down and approached the being which he now could see was a man with pitch black skin. This man was the same height as Rob and had the same blonde hair that Rob did.

"Hey!" Rob said as a greeting, stopping several feet from the black figure.

"Hey!" The figure said back.

"Are you real?" Rob asked nervously.

"As real as you are," the being replied.

Rob took a couple slow steps forward. "Who are you?" He asked.

"I am you. The beingness that resides deep within your heart."

"What?"

"Your true identity. Your silent emptiness, your spaciousness. The quiet awareness you feel in the beautiful moments of life."

Rob didn't say anything at first. He came closer and studied the black face, looking deep into the eyes and then down at its penis which was the same size and shape as Rob's. "So, the inner me is BLACK?" Rob chuckled at this.

"Do not get hung up on color. This will hinder you from connecting with me, your spacious awareness," the reflection replied.

"You keep saying *my awareness*," Rob continued. "I don't understand what you mean."

"When you're aware of your mind and your thoughts, try to bring your awareness from that down into the space of your heart and you will feel me as a vast peace and spaciousness. Only then can you become still enough to operate from there."

"Can you help me get out of here? Back to my own world?" Rob asked desperately.

"Is that of immediate concern to you at this moment as we are having this conversation?" The being asked.

Rob thought about this then shook his head. "I guess not." Rob sighed and let all the tension in his muscles go and a deep relaxation took over his body.

The black reflection of Rob continued speaking. "Just for now don't think about escaping Dark Tethers and getting back to the Hollow Dimension. Just be within your heart and be quietly aware of what is immediately around you in this present. No one is trying to hurt you and no one is after you."

Suddenly there was something inexplicable that shifted within Rob. His breathing slowed and his awareness dropped from his overactive mind into his heart and body. There was at once a quieting of thoughts—he wasn't frantic to be away from this place, the sense of urgency just evaporated. Then Rob began just to experience the fog of gray clouds moving lazily around him, and this being in front of him that didn't seem to be a person at all but just a pure presence with no self and no constructed identity.

"Holy shit," Rob said. "I've never felt like this before."

"Radical, isn't it?" The being replied. "But this is the real you. It has always been inside you deep within. The pure essence of a being can become polluted and cluttered with so much garbage that they start thinking that they are the garbage instead of this peaceful space."

"Will this help me to be able to function in this strange new reality I've recently found myself in?" Rob asked.

"You will find that this is the reality that has always been. You just weren't yourself."

Rob smiled and felt an overwhelming sense of peace. "Can I be this all the time?"

"Sometimes you will forget and slip away into thoughts again and all the drama that creates. All you need to do is remember that those things are not you. This is your natural state." As the black Rob said this, his form shone with a brilliant white light. Then at once that light became a ball the size of a fist and entered back into Rob's heart.

Within that silence was a final whisper: "Be still and understand."

FOURTEEN

FROM THE MIND OF TERRY BROSWALD:

I need some pussy. I need to get some fucking pussy in the worst way. Getting Mothman's dick just didn't cut it for me. Remius is sleeping curled up on my bed and I'm sitting at my desk in front of my computer trying to figure out what the best website would be to meet girls. *Fuck it*, I say to myself and pull up Google in my browser. I type this in: *Facebook for fetish people.*

I scan through the results that come up. There is one that pops out at me—fetlife—and I click on that one. The whole site seems pretty user-friendly, so I set up a profile where I can specify all my fetishes and what I'm looking for. I upload some naked photos of myself and then log off for now. No matter how much I try to distract myself from thoughts of Jessica, I just can't seem to. She must be out there somewhere. And if she is, I could bring her back, right?

Suddenly I'm seized by an idea. I grab a black sharpie from off of my desk and draw three dots on my throat to form a triangle like I had before. If it worked once, it could work again. Almost immediately light begins to emit from each of the dots. The dots of light detach from my throat and form the triangular screen in front of me.

"Show me where Jessica is..." I beg. I pray.

At first blue and white light starts to flicker inside and I hold my breath waiting for a picture to form. Then the light turns into static like on a bad TV screen and my heart sinks. I sigh and shut it off, retracting the dots of light back into my throat.

I look over to the bed and notice that Remius has one eye open. "What?" I say and throw the sharpie across the room. As I flop back down into my desk chair, Remius yawns and stretches as he wakes up.

"What are you doing?" Remius asks.

"I was trying to see if the throat triangle would show me where Jessica is," I grumble as I slump down in the chair.

Remius jumps down from the bed and walks toward me. "Did you ever stop to think that maybe she doesn't want to be found?" Remius says, twitching his whiskers.

"No, not really..." I say after a while as I chew on a fingernail and stare off into space.

"Yes, Terry, you know that. You just don't care." Remius says to me and he speaks the truth. I do know that the reason Jessica erased herself from the Hollow Dimension is because she didn't want to be connected to this story anymore. I can't blame her. Sometimes I too want to escape into another Dimension and start a whole new life as someone else.

I hear the doorbell ring downstairs. As I go down the stairs to see who it is, I notice that Remius doesn't follow behind me. Getting to the door, I almost know it's Mothman before I see him out of the window. And I open the door to let him in. As Mothman enters the house, he grabs me by the back of the head and kisses me on the mouth.

"School just get out?" I ask after the kiss.

"Yeah," Mothman says with a sigh and throws his backpack down on the floor as if relieving himself of a burden that had been weighing him down his whole life. He strokes my chest and walks into the living room which seems to be our hang out spot. "I was thinking about you all day," Mothman continues. "Your lips, your hard cock, and your cute little bubble butt."

I blush as I follow him into the living room. "Thanks," I say. "Flattery will get you everywhere in life."

"Will it get your cock into my ass?" Mothman asks and smiles at me.

"What?"

"I was thinking about that all fucking day," Mothman replies. I can see that he is getting horny already. "Oh my god! It made me so fucking horny thinking about riding your cock."

I don't say anything, but to be honest, the thought does start the juices flowing in my nether regions. "Hmm," I say after a second. "That idea doesn't sound entirely unpleasant. In fact, it gets me kinda hot."

"Oh, great!" Mothman lets out a sigh of relief and pulls me toward him, initiating foreplay. We kiss, and grind, and hump, and stroke, and lick. The two of us become a mass of tongues and fingers and breath.

My head begins to spin with all of the feel-good chemicals that the brain releases during intimacy. Before I know it, we are undressing each other in the most sensual way—not violent and not aggressive. We stand before each other naked—and strangely, I feel love. We embrace, skin on skin. I feel Mothman's heartbeat and I feel my own. I am not sure how long we remain in this embrace of bliss, it is like time completely stops and we melt into one beingness.

I lay down on the rug. Mothman looks down at me and smiles. I feel his lust but also his tenderness. My penis is hard and I feel pre-cum at the tip. Mothman straddles me and guides me inside himself. He gasps as I slide deep inside him. I close my eyes, bite my lip, tilt my head back, and moan. And we go slow. Mothman moves his body up and down as I stroke his hard cock. The intensity and pleasure builds. The air around us becomes charged with electromagnetic energy converging in one huge field of orgasmic light.

I know Mothman can't see it, but my Soulmind starts to braid out of my solar plexus and wraps like a DNA strand around Mothman's body as he rides me. I feel myself building to an orgasmic peak and I can feel Mothman building to one as well.

"Oh my god, Terry. Oh… fuck…" Mothman moans. His eyes are closed and he is totally melted in the moment. I spit on my hand and continue to stroke his cock. I can feel its warmth and pulse in my palm. We are both on the verge of explosion.

"Oh yeah, Mothman…" I let out a loud moan of pleasure. "Fuck me…"

Mothman opens his eyes and looks into my flushed face—his eyes are deep wells. "I want you to cum inside me. I want to feel it."

"Are you sure?" I ask.

"Yes," he says sincerely. "Fucking cum in my ass!"

As he says this I feel like I'm about to burst. And then it happens. With a loud yell, I ejaculate deep inside Mothman's being. And as I cum, he yells too and orgasms, ejaculating onto my cheek and into my open mouth. At the peak of my orgasm, I see my Soulmind light burst out the top of Mothman's head and then fan out into a shimmering halo. I swallow Mothman's semen as he collapses onto me, utterly spent. My Soulmind light dissipates and returns to my body.

We aren't in a hurry to detach from each other. I just remain inside Mothman and we kiss for a while, enjoying the afterglow. Finally when we do separate, we lay there on the rug holding hands and staring up at the ceiling.

"Wow," Mothman says as if coming back from a very far away place. "That was... I can't even describe how that was. I've never experienced anything like that before. There are no words. It goes way beyond mere sexual satisfaction."

I lay there in silence just enjoying the moment. We are there in that meditative state for I don't even know how long—it could have been minutes, it could have been hours.

"You're a good friend, Terry..." Mothman's voice shakes me from my meditation and I turn my head to look at him. He's been staring at me with an admiring smile on his face. Slowly Mothman gets up and begins to dress again.

"Where are you going?" I ask.

"I have to get home today. I can't stay over like I did last time. My parents yelled at me." Mothman says, sadness in his voice. I know he doesn't want to leave, he wants to stay with me. And—to be honest—I want him to stay too.

I stand up too but remain naked. Mothman grabs his backpack and with a sad face he kisses me as I see him out. "Come over tomorrow?" I ask.

"I'd like that," Mothman replies. "I'll see what I can get away with as far as my parents are concerned."

We kiss again and I close the door behind Mothman as he walks down the porch stairs and toward the sidewalk. I turn around from the door and walk back upstairs to my room. Remius is snoozing on the bed. He opens his eyes as I enter the room.

"Hey, you," he says. "I think you got some notification on your computer. Email or something."

"Oh yeah?" I turn and go over to my Apple computer. Sure enough there is an email notification from fetlife—that fetish site I just joined. I have a new message. It's from a girl! And her name is Eden.

FIFTEEN

Maya and her three co-conspirators made their way back up through the levels of Dark Tethers toward where the veil between that realm and the Hollow Dimension was thinnest. The area in which they stopped looked to be some kind of ghost village. There were several 'houses' on either side of the path. These houses looked like they had been converted into dwellings from small barns. Bluish-grey translucent human-shaped figures floated back and forth on either side of them.

"What fresh hell is this?" Tock asked as he swatted at one of the ghostly figures. His hand went right though the spirit, leaving him with a chill that ran through his whole body.

"These are the people who were ripped untimely from the Hollow Dimension," Maya replied. "But instead of ascending to higher spiritual planes, they descended to the least dense level of Dark Tethers. Now they have the potential to either descend to denser levels, or ascend back and try to reach higher… If they could ever figure out how to do it. Wait!" Maya raised her hand and the three stopped abruptly behind her. She sniffed the air. "I thought I smelled a human." Maya shook her head as if clearing the dust from between her ears. "It can't be…" She whispered under her breath.

"What is it?" Trick asked.

Maya shook her head. "Forget it. Here." She extended her index finger and began to slice with her fingernail through the fabric of the Dimension. A window slowly began to open up. What could be seen on the other side was Daley Plaza in downtown Chicago. The Picasso sculpture was clearly visible through the inter-dimensional window. Maya nodded at Trick, Tock, Tick, and all four of them silently left their Dimension and entered the Human World.

Maya didn't even bother to close the window behind her after they crossed over. She wasn't an entity who was known for overlooking details like that, so this may have been intentional on her part. Leaving a window open between the Dark Tethers and the Hollow Dimension could prove to be very dangerous. Several of the ghost-like beings floated over toward the rift and observed it for a moment, trying to assess what it could be. After a minute, they began floating through the window out of their dense Dimension and into the Hollow to enact whatever mischief was dormant in their non-corporeal forms.

Rob just stood there with his eyes closed after his other self re-entered his heart in a sphere of light. Holding his hands over his chest where the light had gone in, Rob silently asked his heart for guidance to lead him out of the Dark Tethers and back to his own world. He felt confident that his intuition would guide him and that the love from the heart would never steer him wrong. After several minutes of sinking deeper and deeper into the heart space there was an unmistakable pull on Rob's body in the direction to his right. He knew without a doubt that that was the direction that would lead him out of this insane Dimension. And as Rob began to walk the direction his heart was leading him, a distinct odor entered his nostrils.

"That's weird," he said to himself. Rob stiffed the air again. It was definitely Maya. He'd know that scent anywhere. The odor of her body made Rob slightly aroused, even though she'd been his lover, his tormentor, and his captor. The feeling was strange in a Stockholm Syndrome type of way. He shook off the thought of fucking her again and continued toward freedom, determined not to get distracted from the guidance of the heart.

After an amount of indiscernible time through dense clouds and over shiny grey and black ground, Rob reached the ghostly village where Maya had opened the window into his own world. As he caught sight of Daley Plaza through the window, Rob picked up his pace, excited to be out of this cursed realm. Then Rob stopped suddenly as he began to notice the ghost figures floating around him and all flowing in a stream through the inter-dimensional window. As the ghosts continued to float through him, Rob felt his body go frigid as they touched him. Terror gripped him as the culmination of all the suffering and anguish of the past lives of these ghosts entered into his magnetic field.

"This can't be good," Rob said as he pushed his way through and jumped through the window amidst the river of ghosts. He was in front of the Picasso sculpture, and no one walking through Daley Plaza seemed to notice that he had just appeared from nowhere. As Rob looked back at the window, ghosts continued to pour out of the rift and float away into all parts of the city. Desperately he tried to pinch the window shut so that the breach between the Hollow Dimension and Dark Tethers would be sealed and no more Shadow Beings could escape. But every time Rob tried to close the window back together, it would just fall open again. "Fuck it," Rob said as he finally gave up trying.

As the ghosts unceasingly continued to infest downtown Chicago, Rob left the scene and made his way to the Blue Line train so he could finally make his way back home to the suburb where he lived. As he sat on the train, Rob chewed on his fingernail, worrying about the shadowy ghost figures he had seen, and also about what his parents would say when he arrived home. He himself didn't even know how long he had been gone. All he knew was that he had to find Terry but also avoid Maya wherever she might be.

Terry sat on his couch reading a book on Sexual Magic. Remius was curled beside him, purring softly. As he read, Terry petted the cat tenderly. There was suddenly a loud knocking at his front door and then the doorbell ringing. Someone outside was yelling his name as Terry put his book down and got up off the couch. Remius stretched his paws out as he yawned, curling his tongue.

It was Mothman at the door. He looked frantic, worried, and very pale. Terry opened the door for his friend. "Terry, I think I'm going completely crazy, bro! And I didn't even drop any fucking acid!"

It took Terry a second to register what was happening and what Mothman was talking about. He looked down at Mothman's chest and could visibly see a spiral of orange light energy spiraling from his solar plexus.

Terry put his hand up over his mouth and his eyes grew wide. "Oh... fuck..."

SIXTEEN

Rob was about two blocks away from his house when he started to rethink his plan of returning home. If Maya had decided to come after him again, that surely would be the first place she would be waiting for him. He was definitely afraid of what she might do to him, or put him back in the cage in the Dark Tethers. *Fuck that*, Rob said to himself. Life had gotten way more complicated than he had ever expected. What was this tapestry of Never Never Wonderland that he now found himself in? And how was he to navigate its unpredictable waters?

Rob decided that the best course of action was to seek refuge with Terry. He was the one who started all of this, and Rob knew that Maya wasn't allowed to go near him directly. Abruptly changing course, Rob found a side street that his house wasn't on and quickly made his way to Terry's house near the high school.

Terry and Mothman were sitting next to each other on the couch in the living room. Mothman stared at Remius—who he was only now seeing for the first time—who was staring back at him from his seat on the rug.

Mothman's mouth hung open and he struggled to put a sentence together. "So, um... You live with a cat that can talk?" Mothman pointed at Remius who smiled a whiskery grin. "Terry, you didn't slip me some acid as a joke, did you?"

Remius laughed. "Seriously, Terry? This is the goofball you've been fucking?"

"Seriously, Remius, you're such a dick!" Terry said as he chucked a throw pillow at the cat. Remius moved his head to the side as the pillow missed him by a hair.

"This is what happens when someone with a connected Soulmind has sex with someone who isn't awake like that. It activates them," the cat continued.

"Activates them? What the fuck does that mean?" Mothman was getting agitated again, his newly activated Soulmind spiraling out of his chest in orange tendrils.

"Oh fuck, oh fuck! I get it," Terry exclaimed, wagging his finger at Mothman.

"What? What?" Mothman sputtered. "Spit it out, goddamnit!"

"The power and energy of my Soulmind energy, coupled with the orgasm penetrating though our bodies, must be enough to link up the soul and mind of the unawakened human," Terry replied.

"You catch on quick," Remius confirmed, his whiskers twitching on the sides of his cheeky smile.

Mothman's mouth was still hanging open in disbelief. He couldn't think of anything to say, he was still in shock from his sudden activation.

"So that must be the fastest way to activate someone's Soulmind—through sex," Terry continued, his train of thought running fast across his cerebral rails. "So many people are still asleep, Soulmind disconnected, offline. We could facilitate a global awakening through sex! We could—"

"Whoa! Whoa! Put on the brakes there, buddy!" Remius jumped up on the couch next to Terry, swishing his tail like a live antenna. "This is why I didn't want to tell you about this. It could be dangerous, even fatal for some people if they are activated too late in life. That's why we Octobers mostly come to the aid of humans who's Soulminds were already naturally awake from birth. If someone with a natural Soulmind activates another person, then it's usually their responsibility to mentor that person whom they've awakened. This is called Transmission. Now that you've used yours sexual energy to activate Mothman, he's ultimately your disciple now. I'll be here to guide you both. I'm primarily here for Terry," Remius continued, addressing both boys now. "A Master can only teach you so much, and then you must leave to become the Master yourself."

Suddenly the doorbell rang. Mothman was deep in thought, and the ring startled him out of his trance. Terry's and Remius's heads swiveled toward the front door. They exchanged glances. "Who could that be?" Terry asked. If cats could shrug, Remius would have shrugged in that moment. Terry got up and went to the door to see who it was. "Holy shit!" Terry yelled back toward the couch. "It's Rob!"

Terry unlocked the door and let Rob inside. He looked like he had been through a ringer. Nobody except Maya had seen him since he disappeared in the Public Works Building. "I almost thought you died or something," Terry said as they walked back into the living room. Rob's face changed to an expression of surprise as he saw Mothman sitting there with a spiral of orange light coming out of his solar plexus.

Rob stopped and pointed at Mothman. "He's one of us now?"

"Yeah," Terry said. "He's part of the Soulmind Squad now."

Rob turned to Terry and raised an eyebrow. "How the fuck did that happen?"

Terry chuckled. "That's a long story... Come, sit." Terry flopped back down on the couch next to Remius and Rob sat down on the floor with his back against the couch. It felt so good to sit down, Rob suddenly felt the exhaustion take over his body like a wave of heavy lead. He closed his eyes and blew out a long exhale. Terry patted his shoulder. "You can stay here as long as you like, Rob," Terry offered. "Rest. Relax. Hide out from that crazy bitch."

"Thanks, brother," Rob said. The relief was so palpable he could almost grasp it with his hand.

"It's actually really good to see you alive," Terry reassured Rob. "I can't even imagine what you've been through... Well, I could if I tried. I went through some intense crazy shit with Jessica in that building myself."

"Yeah..." Rob began. He coughed a few times and Terry got up to get him a glass of water. "At first it was me and Arash, we had to break out of this weird cage... And then there was this glass staircase... blackness of space... I don't know, it's all kind of a blur to me now." Terry handed Rob the water. He chugged it gratefully. "Thanks... And then suddenly Maya was there somehow. She was able to pull me from wherever I was to her realm of the Dark Tethers. She kept me in a cage there too... and tortured me. I finally managed to escape and follow her scent to a window that had been ripped between that world and downtown Chicago." Rob took another drink of water. He decided not to mention the ghost specters that had—and probably still were flooding into Chicago from that dark place.

Mothman coughed very awkwardly and they all turned to look at him. They all had almost forgotten he was sitting there. "I don't know what the fuck y'all are talking about, seriously. I need to, like, sleep this off for now." Mothman said, rubbing his temples as if he had just developed a serious migraine. "Terry, can I go upstairs and lay down in your room? You guys can stay down here and chat if you want. I'm overloaded."

"Uh, yeah sure. Make yourself at home." Terry gestured with his hand toward the stairs and up toward his room. Mothman took his leave to get some rest.

"You know, it's actually a really good thing that you all are here together right now," Remius interjected. "I have a feeling you're going to need each other more than ever now."

Terry sighed. "Yeah, you're right Remius." He put his hands on Rob's shoulders again and squeezed them lightly, lovingly. "It's been pretty lonely here since Jessica left."

Rob looked up at Terry with a confused, quizzical expression on his face. Then he asked, "Who's Jessica?"

PART 8

The Perfect Forever

"Power exchange in Tantric and/or erotic context means power sharing, not power taken by force. If you choose to surrender some of your power to someone else for a ritual or scene, you are loaning a portion of your personal power to your partner for a specific period of time. To do that, you must be able to access and own your own power. Powerless people can't give what they don't have."

- Barbara Carrellas, *Urban Tantra*

DECEMBER

ONE

Jessica Thorn found herself in a beautiful Redwood Forest. She didn't know what Dimension she was in or even what time period this could be. When she had 'traveled' out of her world, she hadn't any particular destination in mind. Looking down at herself, Jessica realized she wasn't even wearing the same clothes as she had been when she departed. Now she was wearing an outfit that looked like something a peasant girl from the medieval times would wear. "What the fuck? Where the fuck am I now?" Jessica said aloud to herself.

Suddenly there was a thundering sound like the pounding of hooves some distance away in the forest. Jessica jumped out of alarm and the unexpectedness of the noise. She stumbled and almost fell flat on her face. When she regained her balance, Jessica began to run in the direction away from the commotion she was hearing some distance away. As she gained ground between herself and the sound of horses galloping, she couldn't help her mind from going to extreme scenarios of where she had transported herself to. *Is this the real Middle Earth?* Jessica's mind spun like a lawn gnome that had been given ten hits of LSD. *Are there psychotic vampire elves after me on horseback?*

After a few minutes of sprinting like a criminal running from the police, Jessica became extremely winded and started to wheeze and breathe heavily, sucking air at a rapid pace yet not feeling like the oxygen was making its way to her muscles. Her legs burned as if the lactic acid had become hydrochloric acid, but she dared not slow her pace. Meeting the unknown on horses was more terrifying to her than running blindly deeper into the forest.

When she finally tripped, falling down, her body splayed out on the ground, she was almost delirious with fear, confusion, and exhaustion. Where Jessica fell was a small clearing in the dense wood. The trees around this area were in what appeared to be a perfect circle. The ground was carpeted with lush green grass and some scattered leaves, which was drastically different from the hard earth that was the floor of the rest of the forest. She laid there with her face in the grass, panting with difficulty to catch her own breath.

"Greetings there, miss! I've been waiting here fer ya. Knew you'd be here right about this time too." It was a man's voice, speaking with an Irish accent. Jessica heard the voice while her face was still in the grass. Struggling, she jerked her head up to see who the voice belonged to. There, a few feet away from where she had fallen, was a man sitting on a large log. He was wearing a white tunic and white linen pants. His reddish-brown hair fell all the way to his lower back, and his beard was so long it reached his navel. The man smiled down at Jessica as he whittled a foot-long stick with a small knife. "I'm Jay," the man said. "It's good to see you made it here in one piece, Jessica."

Jessica was still quite frightened and disoriented, but she managed to get up on all fours and started backing away, not sure whether this man could be trusted.

"Don't be a-feared," Jay continued. "We've been expecting you. Me and my partner Magda. She's back in the cottage over yonder fixin' supper for all of us right now. You must be hungry after your Travels." Jay returned the knife to its sheath on his hip and he twirled the stick he'd been carving through his fingers.

Jessica stopped her retreat and eyed this new man suspiciously. She had finally caught her breath and wasn't relishing the thought of having to run away again. "H-how do you know my name?" She asked hesitantly.

Jay chuckled as if he had a special secret between just him and the Universe. "Magda and I, we be folks of Magick. We saw you in a vision several days ago, told that you would come to this very spot, and that we were to assist you." He paused as if in thought. "You're very special, you see."

Jessica swallowed hard and tried to determine whether she was dead, hallucinating, or dreaming. Coming up with no solid answer, she decided to just trust as much as was possible for her in this situation. "How am I special? I'm not special. I wanted to leave everything and be nothing, not even myself anymore. But now I'm somewhere else, but I'm still me..." She sat back on the ground and hugged her knees into her chest.

"That's a beautiful thing that you're still you," Jay reassured her as he stood up off of the log. He extended his hand to help her up. "You are the Violet Perfect, after all." He smiled again behind his wild beard and mustache. Jessica grabbed his hand and allowed Jay to pull her to her feet. He put his arm around her shoulders to comfort her and they began walking in the direction of where he indicated the cottage was.

"What is this business about the Violet Perfect?" Jessica mumbled this almost inaudibly, the tiredness suddenly threatening to take her over. "That's the second time I've heard that..."

"Magda and me can explain some things to you. Shine light on some things you might be confused about. People could always use a Shaman in their lives to shed light on all the mysterious bits they don't understand, am I right?" Jay chuckled again. "However, the mystery can never be solved. It's not meant to be. Life is a mystery to be lived, not a puzzle to be solved." Jessica felt a pang of dizziness and her knees began to give out under her. Luckily Jay caught her and was strong enough to carry her in his arms. "Whoa there, little missy. Wouldn't want you dying on us before we had a chance to teach you the Craft."

Jessica looked up into Jay's crystal-clear blue eyes and tried to say something. Before she could move her tongue to ask any more questions, she had fallen into unconsciousness.

Some time later Jessica awoke on a cot that had straw instead of a mattress. She was covered by a thin wool blanket. As Jessica blinked the sleep out of her eyes, she looked around and took in her surroundings. The interior of the cottage reminded her of pictures she'd seen of medieval Irish peasant houses. The walls were stone, but above her were wood beams. The ground floor was one large room. Opposite of where Jessica awoke on the cot was a stone fireplace which was also used to cook. There was a large caldron hanging above the fire, steaming and smelling of potatoes. There was also a table set up with some ceramic plates and cups. Jay and Magda were sitting across from each other at the table speaking in hushed whispers to each other.

Jessica also noticed that one wall was a large bookshelf with ancient-looking books. There were also assorted stones, crystals, herbs, and a skull on the shelves. When she looked back at the table, Magda and Jay were staring at her. Jessica yawned very loudly and stretched her arms over her head. "Welcome back to the land of the living," Jay said to Jessica and then took a drink of whatever was in his ceramic mug. Magda smiled but didn't say anything. She was a real redhead. Although she could have been maybe in her sixties or seventies—it was hard for Jessica to tell—she had a young air about her, but also the energy of ancient wisdom, someone who is intimately familiar with all of life's complexities. Magda was wearing a dress similar to the one Jessica had found herself wearing, earthen colors and natural fabric.

"Come," Magda said finally. She spoke with an Irish accent as well. Motioning with her arm, she encouraged Jessica to come join them at the table. "Here, sweetheart. I made potato stew. You must be starving, poor dear. You've been through so much. Almost too much to ask of a girl so young." She looked at Jay when she said that last part, compassion in her dark eyes.

Jessica got up and slowly made her way over to the table where the only two people she knew from this new world were sitting, waiting to feed her and take care of her like loving parents. She sat down in the chair next to Jay as Magda got up to fill a bowl with hot stew. "Thank you so much," Jessica said as Magda placed the steaming bowl in front of her and handed her a wooden spoon. "Again, tell me how you two knew I was coming?" She continued, blowing on the stew in her spoon to cool it down before putting it to her lips.

Jay turned toward Jessica to explain in more detail. "We both practice Magick and sometimes will be shown prophetic visions. You see, dear, Magda is an Earth Witch and I am a Celestial Wizard. We make a perfect partnership, a balance of all the elements. But you, Jessica, you're already a Perfect."

"Yeah, you said that before," Jessica responded, not sure if any of this new information was shedding light on her confusion. "What does that mean?" She took another sip of stew. "This is really yummy, by the way. Thank you."

Magda smiled and then answered the question. "A Perfect is a being who has perfect balance within themselves of the celestial and the terrestrial. You naturally transcend the polarity already. Given the proper training, you can master *all* the Elements—all of the Elements of Earth and Space that we both have mastery over. You have the ability to master the Craft and benefit from what both of us can teach you."

Jessica put her spoon down next to her bowl and swallowed hard. Nervously she managed to piece her question together. "Craft?" She asked, shifting her gaze back and forth between the two of them. "As in *witch*craft?"

"Of course, dear," Magda answered softly. "You didn't think we were talking about *arts* and crafts, did you?"

Jessica coughed lightly and looked down into her bowl sheepishly. "Uhhh... But I'm a Christian." She said this so softly that it was almost inaudible.

Jay laughed and shook his head. "Well, you know, that won't do at all."

Jessica unconsciously brought her right hand up to her neck to touch the cross that usually hung there, but was surprised to feel its absence. She swallowed hard again and managed to look up at Magda, who was smiling, looking at Jessica with so much love and compassion in her eyes that Jessica just naturally relaxed. Magda reached over and put her warm palm on Jessica's left hand which was still resting on the table. "Oh, honey," Magda said comfortingly and reassuringly. "You're not a Christian."

"I'm not?"

"No," Magda replied. "You're a witch."

Jessica's mouth hung open in disbelief. "I... but... how... why?" She stammered, but couldn't seem to get out anything coherent.

"Do you have an affinity for the natural world?" Magda asked.

Jessica was silent for a moment. "Yes," she said.

"And a love for the stars and planets?" Jay asked.

"Yes, I do actually."

"And you have a Soulmind," Magda continued. "That gives you trans-dimensional powers. You only think you're a Christian because you were conditioned to think so from birth. You never questioned it. But... you're a witch. Welcome to the party." Jay and Magda both smiled and chuckled, happy to welcome Jessica into their coven of two—hoping to now make it three.

"Am I gonna go to hell for this?" Jessica whispered. "Or worse—burned at the stake?"

Jay and Magda exchanged glances and then burst out laughing as if this was all some hilarious joke. "No, of course not," Jay said authoritatively. "That's all Christian Catholic propaganda. Witches and wizards are not evil. Sometimes Magick practitioners choose to take actions that harm other people—they have the free will to do that—but that's not us. We don't enact curses or things of that sort. No, we're more the type that just like helping people, communing with the natural world, and using the elements of earth and heaven to expand consciousness."

"Huh..." Jessica thought about what was just said. "That doesn't sound that bad actually."

"It's not bad at all," Jay agreed.

"Hey, what were those noises I was hearing earlier? The ones I was running away from when I ran into you, Jay?" Jessica asked.

"What? You mean the hunting party?" Jay said, stroking his beard. "Men from the village come riding on horseback to hunt in the forest sometimes. But they can't pass the magical circle where you found me. We put a spell on that area, you see."

"Okay..." Jessica looked off in the distance for a moment as if deep in thought. "And where are we exactly? This is still Earth? The Hollow Dimension?"

"I knew you were going to ask that," Magda said. "We're in Pangea. This is actually an overtone of the Hollow Dimension—a place outside of time, magical. It's also been called the Otherworld. Sometimes shamans come here for their journeys—and sometimes they stay."

"Pangea?" Jessica said skeptically. "Like the huge continent made up of all the other continents?" Jay and Magda nodded their heads. "This just gets better and better... Next I suppose you're going to tell me that the Earth is flat!"

Magda and Jay shared another look between each other, but neither confirmed nor denied what Jessica had said. Suddenly Jessica grabbed the mug that was in front of Jay and took a huge swig of whatever was in it. The liquid was sweet and bitter, and she could taste the alcohol. Slamming the mug back down on the table, Jessica took a deep breath, the liquid wet on her lips.

"What is this stuff?" Jessica asked.

Jay laughed again and smacked her festively on the back. "I take it that was your first taste of the mead?" He said.

Jessica coughed lightly. "Fuck yeah! Let me have one. I need it right about now."

They all laughed heartily. The fire blazed under the caldron full of stew, casting shadows and warmth on the three witches come together in this new Otherworld.

TWO
FROM THE MIND OF TERRY BROSWALD:

It's snowing. As I stare out my kitchen window into the backyard that is currently being blanketed by whiteness, I think about Jessica and how it's going to be another cold winter in Chicago. It always is. Mothman and Rob decided to go to school today; for what reason I can't even fathom. I mean, I tried to talk them out of it but it was no use—at least for now. They'll stop once the conditioning of *having* to go really falls away, and it will, especially since their Soulmind's are active. With them off at the high school—which is really a nice way to say *prison*—I'm here alone with Remius sleeping on the couch. It's nice, he's comforting, but isn't he supposed to be teaching me more about using my Soulmind; being my guide into the unknown? I don't know. I shrug and wonder if maybe Remius is waiting for *me* to do something. Are we just waiting around for Maya to strike again? Or what the fuck are we supposed to be doing?

I pull out my cell phone from my pocket and scroll through the text messages. Eden—the girl who I met on fetlife—and I have been texting back and forth for the past couple days. She really likes my pictures that I put up on my profile. She likes young feminine guys. I guess I am kind of girly in a way. And I do enjoy wearing women's clothes and dresses now and then. Earlier today she sent me a text that reads: *When can I see you?* I replied: *How about next week?* To which Eden responded just a few minutes ago saying: *I can't wait that long to fuck you!*

Damn, this girl really wants it. And I want to give it to her! Oh, yeah, I can almost already feel that wet pussy tight around my hard cock. My face gets hot and flushes red just thinking about it. I have browsed through her photos also and she is so fucking hot! She has long hair dyed pink, which is a good contrast to her bright blue eyes. She's also thin and has cute small titties that get me hard. And when I see her shaved pussy in some of those pictures, I totally want to suck on her clit for hours. So I open up a reply message and write: *How about meeting up today?*

What is the probability that this girl already has an active Soulmind? I think that the possibility of that is pretty slim. When I make love with her I'll have to be ready for the aftermath of having activated her. Nervously I glance over at Remius who still seems to be in his slumber on the couch. Hopefully I can get out of here before he wakes up; there's a good chance he might try to stop me since he did say that it could be potentially dangerous to sexually activate people who aren't ready to be awakened. My phone dings and I look at the reply: *Let's do it! Meet me at my place*—and she gives the address of her apartment in Wicker Park. I know exactly where that is; off the Damen stop on the blue line train. But I don't need to take the train, I've got the van. As quietly as I can, without waking up Remius, I grab my keys and slip out the front door undetected.

As I fire up the van, I slide the *Heavy Metal 2000* soundtrack into the CD player. That's some of my favorite music to rock out to when I'm driving. Just to put me in the mood, I cruise to the song *Psychosexy* by Sinisstar.

"*Psychosexy*
New world
Talking revolution
Psycho
Freakshow
Sexy
Everyone's invited"

When I find a parking space near Eden's apartment, I'm nervous. Why am I nervous? I hope she likes me in person and isn't disappointed, having some idea of me from what she saw in my pictures. Get it together, Terry. Women don't like men who lack confidence. She's fucking gorgeous and hot and sexy. Is that why I feel intimidated? I don't need to be. Okay, positive self-talk. I am sexy, I am gorgeous, it's her who's lucky to be with me. I'm confident and secure in myself. As I say this to myself, I look down and realize my Soulmind has become active. It's lighting up all of my chakras—especially my navel chakra. And suddenly I feel a wave of relaxation and renewed confidence wash over me. I close my eyes and focus on my third chakra, charging it up with Soulmind power. My whole aura lights up for a few moments. I open my eyes and the light of my spiritual energy returns to the inside of my body. I take a deep breath and get out of the car.

As I approach the door, I make sure that my hair is at least decently in place. What the fuck am I wearing? I didn't even think about it. I look down at myself; jeans and a Billy Idol t-shirt. Shrugging, I guess I'm presentable. Almost before I have a chance to knock on the door, it opens. And then there's Eden in front of me—in the flesh. She's just as gorgeous as in her pictures, even in the dress she wears that's barely a long t-shirt with Jim Morrison's face on it. Eden smiles at me, I blush, and before I know it she grabs my cheeks and kisses me hard on the lips. I close my eyes and her tongue finds its way into my mouth; my tongue meets the challenge to play with hers. Then she pulls me into the apartment and shuts the door behind us.

"I've been waiting for you, cutie. You're even prettier in person," Eden giggles.

"That was some greeting," I say. "If that's any indication, we're gonna get along great." At this point I take in my surroundings. We're in the small living room, it looks like. The floors are hardwood and light streams in through the windows that look out on the street in front. There's a red leather couch and a TV. There's someone on the couch playing a video game on Playstation—*Kingdom Hearts* it looks like. The person playing the game is a cute transvestite. Not some macho fat guy with a beard wearing a dress; no, this boy is very feminine, slim, with long black hair wearing dark makeup around his eyes. The dress he wears is long, silky, and blue.

"Terry, this is Kat. Kat, this is Terry," Eden introduces us.

"Nice to meet you," Kat says without looking away from the video game.

"Kat's part of our polyamorous family. He's pretty much gay so we never have full-on sex. We play with each other and sometimes I suck him off and he goes down on me. We have fun. Like I said, I like girly guys... Like you." Eden smiles seductively, looking deep into my eyes. "Maybe sometime we'll bring him into our play," she says as she turns and continues toward the other room. "Come along."

The next main room I can see is the kitchen, and between the living room and kitchen is a hallway with three doors off of it. "I like your place," I say.

"This is our kitchen," Eden continues with the tour. "Out that sliding glass door is the backyard and how we get to the basement—the basement is the dungeon where we have fun. And down that hallway are the two bedrooms and bathroom." Still smiling, she eyes me up and down.

"What?" I say.

Eden grabs me by the waist and pulls my body into hers. I can feel my dick pressing against the area between her legs. "You're so fucking cute!" She pushes my shaggy hair out of my face and tucks it behind my left ear, then she kisses me again. This time longer. Our lips and tongues dance together as if performing a tantric tango. My hands slide around Eden's slim waist and down to her ass. It's a nice firm bubble butt. I squeeze both ass cheeks and feel myself getting hard in my pants. Still squeezing her ass with my left hand, I bring my right hand around to her front and between her legs. She grabs my hand to stop me. "All in good time. I haven't even shown you the dungeon yet." She whispers this to me seductively. Eden kisses me again and bites my lip playfully. I taste blood in my mouth. "Do you like that?" She asks me.

"Yeah," I assure her as I enjoy the taste of blood on my tongue.

"Good. You're a submissive, aren't you? I can tell."

I nod in affirmation.

"Good, cause I'm a dominant. We're gonna have lots of fun... Flogging. Blood play. Role-playing. Bondage."

Eden turns around to face the sliding glass door and I spank her on her tight sexy ass. She moans softly and smiles back at me. "You like *that*?" I ask.

"I love that! Come, I'll show you the basement and we can play and fuck." Grabbing my hand, she leads me through the sliding glass door. The backyard is small, but nice and green; the grass well kept up with. We go down another small set of stairs to the basement door and she takes me inside.

The light is low and inviting; like in a club or a pool hall. Strings of lights along the corners of the ceiling add to the ambience. The large part of the room when we first walk in is taken up by a table as long as a person's body. It looks like a pool table, but it isn't. There are wrist and ankle restraints attached to each corner of the table. On the far side of the room is a bar area with a couple couches against the walls on either side of it. The room is carpeted in red shag. And between the area where the table is and the bar area is a suspension harness used for bondage play. On the walls are paintings and drawings of red tantra—gods and goddesses in intimate embrace.

"You like what you see?" Eden asks.

"I fucking love it!" I respond enthusiastically. "This is so amazing. It's like something out of a dream... I really love the art on the walls too."

"I had a feeling you would. My landlord is into BDSM also. He set this all up and is nice enough to let us use it."

"That's so awesome! I'm excited for all the things we can do down here!"

Eden giggles. "You know you're very cute, don't you?"

I shrug sheepishly.

"You see that door right there?" She points to a door off to the left of the bondage table. "That's the master bedroom where a lot of magic happens. Go in there, get naked, and lay in the bed. I'm gonna grab something and I'll meet you in there."

She smacks my ass like I did to her earlier. I go into the room as Eden goes over to the area behind the bar to get whatever she has in mind. Most of the room is taken up by a massive bed. It's heart-shaped with a black headboard. The sheets are red and shiny; the pillows are red and pink. The bedroom has the same low light as the rest of the basement. The walls in this bedroom are also lined with framed artwork—what looks like drawings from the *Kama Sutra*. This is definitely meant to be. Tantra, spirituality, sexuality—my Soulmind is attracting the experiences that challenge me and help me expand my awareness.

I strip off my jeans, boxers, and t-shirt. When I'm completely naked I lay down on top of the silky red sheets. They are soft and feel sensual against my skin. I look around at the drawings on the walls and touch my soft penis between my legs, feeling the blood start to fill the tissues there. Eden enters the room holding a long wooden rod. It reminds me of a magic wand for some reason—but thinner. She swings her hip seductively to one side and smacks the rod into the palm of her left hand. As I continue to touch myself, I watch her watching me. She likes what she sees in her bed waiting for her.

"Have you ever been caned?" Eden asks, raising her eyebrows.

"No, but that sounds hot." I bite my lip and moan softly. She comes over and lays on the bed next to me, still clothed in the 'dress' with Jim Morrison's face. Looking at me with eyes wide and pupils dilated, Eden strokes the inside of my thigh with the tips of her fingers.

"I love being fully clothed and having you naked. Gets me so turned on." She says, touching herself between her legs. "I'm getting so wet already. My panties are getting soaked."

I open my mouth and she rubs her fingers that she touched herself with across my tongue. Tasting her juices I get even more aroused. Her juices taste sweet, reminding me of fresh berries just plucked from the bush. Maybe raspberries. "What do you want me to do, mistress?" I say.

Eden puts her hand on my inner thigh again. "Spread your legs a little bit more. I'm gonna cane you on the inside of your thighs." She also moves my hand away from my erect member. "You can't touch yourself yet either. That comes later."

I take my hand away yet my prick still remains rock hard. Closing my eyes, Eden begins to smack the inside of my left thigh with the cane. I inhale sharply as it thwacks against my leg. The sting tingles up and down the inside of my leg and vibrates through my balls. My dick throbs with pain and pleasure. *Whack! Whack! Whack!* She doles out the punishment continuously and I just experience this sensation in its totality—in its sheer ecstasy. There's a fine line between pain and pleasure, and once you reach that threshold, it becomes euphoria. As Eden continues to go to work on me, the orgasmic waves flow like a cyclone through my body and I begin to shake from the pleasure. Pre-cum is at the tip of my cock as the heat builds.

Eden licks, bites my earlobe, and then whispers into my ear. "Thirty-three strikes per leg. That seems appropriate to me." She begins on the other thigh.

"Oh my god! YES! Fuck... Oh my god..." I moan as the intensity continues to build. To edge toward that climax and then back off for a moment just to build up to it again is pure magic. I lose track of all time and *become* the sensation. My identity completely dissolves in the experience and I find myself swimming in the cosmic orgasm. Beyond the stars; beyond all Dimensions; beyond time; beyond Enlightenment. Suddenly I'm nobody—no one and nothing—and all I feel is bliss stretching to the edges of infinity. The tantric ecstasy which leads to immortality. Whatever I AM merging with the All and the Nothing.

"Thirty-one." *Whack!* "Thirty-two." *Whack!* "Thirty-three." *Whack!* "There that should do it." Eden giggles and rubs in the bruises on my inner thighs. At first I don't open my eyes. I'm too deep in this meditative trance—feeling all and nothing simultaneously. The tingles run up and down my body like tiny ants marching under my skin. My body spasms with a full-body orgasm, but I don't ejaculate. Then I finally open my eyes and look into Eden's bright blue irises; like glaciers falling into the ocean. "Are you okay?" She asks, looking down at me with a playful smile.

"Oh... yeaaaaah..." I draw out the words in a long moan. "That was—oh my god—I don't even know. I, like, went somewhere else but felt everything too. It was amazing."

"Subspace."

"Huh?"

"That's where you went. To Subspace."

"What's that?" I ask.

"It's actually a state of transcendence that many submissives enter during BDSM play," she replies. "It's a wonderful experience—which from the look on your face you have come to know."

"Transcendence..." I ponder this for a moment. "That's definitely the best way to describe it."

Eden pulls her dress off over her head. She's not wearing a bra underneath. I stare, taking all of her in. Her breasts are cute and perky; no more than a handful with nice little pink nipples. She sits next me me, naked except for a pair of pink panties. I look down between her legs. The shape of her venus mound is very pleasing to my eyes. She lays back against the pillows and says, "Suck on my nipples."

I lean over and oblige. Sucking for a moment and then flicking her erect nipple with the tip of my tongue, she moans the most beautiful moan I've ever heard. The sound is like the sigh of the Universe coming into manifestation. As I lick and suck and tease, Eden slides her hand into her panties and begins to massage her clitoris. "Oh my fucking god! You're getting me so wet! Don't stop, keep sucking on my titties. That's perfect. Uhhhh..." She closes her eyes and her cheeks turn red. I slide two fingers into her mouth and she licks and sucks on them which renews my erection. Tangibly I can feel the energy building in her body towards an orgasm. As I flick her nipple really fast with the tip of my tongue, her body shudders hard and she cries out loudly. I feel the orgasm shoot through the air as an electromagnetic wave. "Oh, Terry," she says, panting heavily. "I've never cum so hard in my life."

"Does that mean you're done?" I ask.

"Fuck no! You kidding me? I like to cum at least three times in a row." As Eden says this she strips off her panties which are now soaked and smelling of her sweet cunt. I stare at her bare sex as she spreads her legs. She's shaved with a little stubble around her labia. Her vagina is puffy and cute, wet with her own lubrication. I want to be inside of her so fucking bad. "Go down on me before I fuck you!" Eden commands and grabs me by the hair, pushing my face down between her legs. I'm more than happy to comply. I lap her labia greedily and then slide my tongue inside, exploring. As I taste all of her, drinking her vaginal secretions and then flick her clit with my tongue, I squeeze my cock which is now burning hot and ready for penetration.

Eden grabs the back of my head and pushes my mouth hard against her pussy almost to the point I can't breath. She's a screamer, moaning in shrieks of ecstasy. "Just like that. Yeah, baby. Make me cum again! I'm gonna squirt in your mouth." I start licking faster and sucking deeply on her clitoris. Her breathing quickens and moans start to build. "Oh my god! Oh my god! Oh my gaaaaaahhhd!" Eden shrieks a final time and I feel a gush of liquid rush into my mouth. I swallow.

"Get on your fucking back!" She commands me. Getting up off her back, she throws me down roughly to the bed. My cock sticks up straight into the air like a cell tower. Straddling me, Eden guides my cock into her wet cunt. Now it's my turn to cry out with pleasure. She slides all the way down on my shaft and grinds her clitoris against my pelvic bone. I'm so deep inside her that I can feel her cervix with the tip of my dick. She puts her palms against my chest and begins to ride up and down and then moves her hips forward and back; moving her spine like a snake. Our moans merge together in a collective symphony of musical orgiastic eternity. I lay my head back, close my eyes, and melt into her.

When I finally open my eyes, Eden still riding me, I'm shocked to see a liquid-like light flowing in tendrils from her solar plexus. It's color is not fixed, it shifts back and forth from red to pink. "Oh my god!" I exclaim. Eden stops her movement but keeps me inside her. I can't seem to get the words out. "You... you... you." I stammer. "You're one of..."

"What? What? What is it?" She looks down and her eyes go wide. "Wait... You can see—" But before she can finish the question, my own Soulmind bursts out of my chest like a spear. It pierces through her red energy, goes through her heart, and exits through her back. My energy, weaving together with hers now, loops up and over her head and meets back at the heart with a jolt of energy; making the shape of an ankh around her body. "Oh my god..." Eden says as our auras expand to fill the entire room; white, red, and pink energy braids around us like dancing nebulas dissolving. "I understand now," she continues, starting to ride my cock again. "This is why I was drawn to you. We both—"

"Have this energy." I finish her sentence for her. "This is so fucking intense. I've never felt this much energy."

"Me either," Eden agrees, starting to moan again. We start building to another climax. "Let me know when you're gonna cum. I want to swallow you."

I nod and close my eyes again. Even with my eyes closed the colors are fantastic. Closed eye visuals like taking a heavy dose of mushrooms. Patterns and Sacred Geometry spiral and vibrate on the backs of my eyelids. Time means nothing. This—like dreaming—is True Time. I don't know how long we are merged in this eternal now, melting into each other. It feels like a moment. It feels infinite.

Then my eyes burst open. "I'm gonna cum!"

Eden slides me out of herself and immediately puts my cock in her mouth, licking it and sliding it deep into the back of her throat. My whole body throbs with the orgasm. White light mixed with Eden's red and pink bursts out the top of my head and rains sparkles down through my skull. I feel the pulse in my perineum and a wave of semen gushes into her throat. She moans with her lips around the base of my cock and swallows, pulling the stream of cum out of the tip of my penis. The combination of the orgasm and our Soulminds merging creates a transcendent experience that words are not sufficient to describe. All my muscles collapse on the bed as sweat glistens on my naked body. The word *liberating* doesn't even come close to describing what I just experienced. I guess there's no use in trying to put it into words. Just to lay here, my body pressed against Eden, bathing in the afterglow, is enough.

The light of our Soulminds still shimmers in the air of the room. Eden licks my shaft from the balls all the way to the tip then flops down on the bed beside me; her back towards me. I slide my hand over her heart-shaped ass. "I want you to fuck me from behind as we rest," she says, eyes closed and waiting for me to penetrate her again. I scoot up behind her as the big spoon. My cock is still hard and eager. I enter her deeply as I slip my hands under her armpits and hold on to her shoulders to help me thrust.

Sliding in and out of Eden's juicy pussy, I feel her wetness soak my balls until I'm too tired to thrust anymore. And we both fall asleep into Dreamsphere, I still inside of her.

THREE

Rob's intuition had been correct about the possibility of Maya returning to his house to hide out. Currently Maya and her three companions were congregated in Rob's vacated bedroom, not really sure yet how to proceed. Tick, the fat one, was being lazy and just laying on the bed like a blob. Trick was over by the window doing bicep curls with fifty pound weights. Tock was sitting on the floor cross-legged with his back against the end of the bed. Maya sat in silence in the desk chair in front of Rob's computer. With eyes completely pitch black, it was difficult to tell if she was looking at anything in particular, or just staring off into space.

"What's the next move, boss?" Tock asked, looking up at Maya expectantly.

She shook her head. "That's what I'm trying to figure out."

"Let me at this little runt," Trick said, never stopping his flow of pumping iron. "I'll crush his fucking skull like a fucking tomato!"

"Yeah," Tock agreed. "I have the powerful need to peel some skin off and wear it over my face. Let me chop his dick off and make a hat out of it!"

Maya put her hand up for silence. "All in good time, my vicious friends. We must proceed with caution. You can't just storm his house without some planning first. This Terry is more powerful than you might think."

"How powerful can a measly little rat-faced human be?" Trick asked, not believing Maya's warning. "I could just rip his scrawny arms and legs out of their sockets and fucking *FUCK* him till he's dead!" His eyes bulged and all the veins in his neck and arms popped out spastically like a meth-head about to eat someone's face.

Maya shot Trick a soul-curdling stare. "Just shut the fuck up so I can think! We have to at least take a day or so to come up with a strategy. He most likely will not be alone either, so you'll have to contend with more that one human that has supernatural powers."

"Yeah," Tock interjected. "But there's no way that *their* supernatural powers are any match for *our* supernatural powers. We're the most super Supers in all the Spiralverse! No positive evolution is match for our destruction!"

"All you do is talk shit," Maya kicked Tock in the shin to shut him up. "Yes, I'm aware your history speaks for itself. That's why it took the combined power of all members of the Order of the Transcendent to lock you away in the Cube. I'm not doubting your abilities by any means. There just always seems to be something protecting him. The Order... or the Octobers..." She fell silent again.

Tick finally spoke up from his nest on the bed. "He'll probably be expecting us to strike again as soon as possible, so it might be best to wait for two or three days and then attack his house at night when he's least expecting it. That might give us an advantage and the element of surprise."

"Well, that's the first good idea I've heard out of any of you," Maya said. "Remember, you can't just kill him. He has to be alive when you extract a piece of his Soulmind to bring back to me. This is the integral part of my plan to destroy this Dimension. Fuck their ascension, let's wipe them all out."

"How are we supposed to hold on to part of his Soulmind?" Tock asked.

Maya held out her hand and a black cube materialized in her palm. It was the size of a Rubik's Cube and looked like a small replica of the Containment Cube that Trick, Tock, and Tick were imprisoned in. "This cube," she explained. "You will take this cube, and when you extract the piece of Terry's Soulmind, the cube will suck it inside and it will be trapped. I'm the only one who will be able to take it out and use it."

"I don't know if I can wait that long!" Trick growled. "I need some murdering right now! Or I'm gonna go crazy!"

Maya thought about this, her finger tapping her chin. "Hmm. Maybe I can think of something we can do to help satiate your blood lust."

* * *

The window that had been ripped in the fabric between the Dark Tethers and the Hollow Dimension was still wide open. All of the specters from the little village had travelled through the rift into the city. They were all now wandering through the streets of Chicago looking for desirable hosts to possess. There were hundreds of specters that found their way through the rift, but there were almost three million people living in the city of Chicago. For the specters to possess hundreds of people in a city of millions was dangerous, yes, but not an immediate threat. It would take days—maybe weeks—before the impact would become clear, spreading out like ripples in a pond.

The most desirable candidates for possession were people who were already susceptible to the darkness and very dense; at a low vibration. People that were just on the very brink of insanity, or already fallen over the edge. A specter could only possess one person directly, but by committing an atrocity on another who wasn't possessed, they could transmit the possession on to others through trauma. This way the darkness could spread like a virus on a wave of mutilation, cruelty, and horror. Inner cities were already places of immense atrocities and brutalities carried out under cover of night, or hidden by abandoned dilapidated buildings. Not to mention the savage unspeakable things that also take place in the high floors of skyscrapers—demons in business suits hiding their inhumanity within the safety of ivory towers.

So as the first few hundred people's souls were laid claim to by the ghostly specters, no one really took notice. In the city wickedness and corruption are business as usual.

FOUR

Terry woke up without being able to remember whether or not he had dreamed. His body was still pressed up against Eden's porcelain nakedness, skin on skin. He was no longer erect, of course, but his flaccid penis was touching the pink perfection of her vulva. Eden began to stir awake as well. There was still an orgasmic charge of electricity lingering in the air around them. Eden rolled over to face her new lover. She smiled, staring into Terry's deep clock-like eyes, and then kissed him lovingly on the lips.

"Hey, you." Eden whispered, breaking the silence.

"Hey, beautiful," Terry replied.

"That was so wonderful. My whole body is still buzzing."

Terry brushed Eden's hair out of her face and tucked it behind her ear so he could gaze into her big blue eyes. "I'm so happy that our Soulminds brought us together," Terry said, and for the first time in a very long while he wasn't thinking about Jessica and how much he missed her.

"Me too!" Eden agreed. "When am I gonna see you again?"

"I don't know... Tomorrow?"

Eden's smile grew wider, her white teeth sparkling. "I'd like that. I know we are going to have so much fun being lovers and playing together. You do want to be part of my polyamorous family, right?"

"Of course," Terry said. "As long as you want to be part of mine. I already have a couple lovers of my own."

"Of course I want to be part of yours. What we're creating is so beautiful and special."

"It definitely is," he agreed. "Speaking of which, I have to go in a few minutes. A couple of friends are staying at my house and they'll probably be back and wanting to get in. They don't have keys, so... But I want to lay with you and talk for a bit before I leave."

Eden held Terry's hand and squeezed it. Then she brought it up to her lips and kissed his palm and his fingertips. "Pretty Terry..." She said dreamily, her pupils huge like she had taken a dose of MDMA.

"When did you become aware your Soulmind was active?" Terry asked.

"It was about a couple years ago. Why? Are you pretty new to it also?"

"Yeah, I just became aware of mine this year. Do you have an October too?"

"A what?" Eden asked as she put Terry's hand against her cheek.

"Nevermind... What about Dimensional Travel? Have you been experiencing that at all?" Terry wanted to know how versed she was in her Soulmind abilities and if she could teach him anything.

"Hmm," she thought about this for a moment. "Not physically, no. Just Astral Travel."

"Astral Travel? That's like Astral Projecting, right? I've heard of that but don't know much about it."

"It's when you travel to other realms using your Astral Body but not your physical body. Your physical body stays here and you return to it when you're finished with your journey to wherever." Eden responded. "I could teach you if you want."

"I'd love that! That would be awesome!" Terry said, excited to be able to learn another Soulmind ability. He leaned toward Eden and started kissing her, their lips dancing again. Their tongues found their way to meet and each tasted the sweetness of the other. Terry could feel himself getting hard again, and he pulled away suddenly. "Oh, man! I better get going before I get too turned on again."

"Yeah," Eden giggled in response. "I might have to take advantage of you again and then you'll never leave. I'd have to tie you up and make you my slave." She winked at him. "You'd like that wouldn't you, you pervert?"

"Don't threaten me with a good time," Terry said as he finished pulling his pants back on. As he stood up he became a little dizzy from the endorphins still swimming through his brain like sperms trying to race to be the first to fertilize the egg.

"Are you okay?" Eden asked, pulling her Jim Morrison dress over her head but not bothering to put her panties back on.

"Yeah, I'm good. Just a lot of feel-good chemicals flooding my receptors."

"You can never have too many of those," she said. Her face was still flushed from all the sex they just had. "Come, I'll walk you to the door."

Holding hands, they went back up through the kitchen and the living room. The couch was empty and the TV was off now; Kat had gone. Terry hoped he might get to see him again—he was cute.

"Tomorrow?" Eden said as she opened the door. It was still daylight outside.

"Tomorrow," Terry confirmed.

She leaned in to kiss him. Lingering there, wet lips pressed firmly together, they felt their auras merge again. When they finally pulled apart, it was reluctantly. Eden smiled shyly at Terry as he was about to depart. "I love you..."

Terry completely relaxed and felt the strong connection between their hearts. "I love you," he said back to her. He gave a little wave as he stepped back onto the stoop. "Till tomorrow."

Eden smiled and closed the door.

When Terry got back to his house he was expecting to see Rob and Mothman waiting on the porch for him, but they weren't. He unlocked the door and entered the house. They weren't on the porch because they were already inside; sitting on the couch watching TV. Remius was curled up in Rob's lap getting petted. Terry glanced at the TV; they were watching *The Butterfly Effect*.

"Oh hey, Terry." Mothman greeted Terry as he walked in. "You ever seen this movie?" He pointed to the TV. "It's fucking crazy..."

"Hey, guys," Terry said. "How did you get in? I wasn't here to open the door for you."

Rob looked up at Terry. "Remius let us in when we got here after school."

Terry raised an eyebrow. "Remius let you in?" He laughed incredulously. "He doesn't even have thumbs! How could he have opened... You know what, forget it." Terry sat down on the floor with his back against the couch, joining his friends to watch the movie.

"So something really fucking weird happened today." Mothman said to Terry. "Our parents showed up at school looking for us. They were just waiting there to confront us when we were done with our classes for the day."

"Both of you guys?" Terry asked. "Both of your guys's moms and dads?"

"Yeah," Rob nodded in agreement.

"So what happened?" Terry wanted to know.

"It was weird," Mothman continued. "They looked really pissed off at first, but then when we got closer to them, all four of them got this really blank look on their face like they forgot why they were there."

"Huh... That's bizarre. Then what happened? Obviously they didn't drag you home since you're here."

"That's just it," Rob interjected, picking up the story. "I totally thought they were gonna force us to come home with them and ask me all these questions about where I had been."

"But they didn't?"

"No, they didn't. We told them that we wanted to stay at your house for a while and weren't ready to come home. They said: 'Okay, whatever you want.' Just like that, it was easy. We both noticed that our Soulminds were spiraling lightly out of our chests. Maybe that energy influenced them to agree to what we wanted."

Mothman nodded in agreement.

"That's exactly what happened," Remius finally spoke up. "Your Soulminds were working for you, exerting psychic influence over your parents."

"Yeah, what the cat said." Mothman chimed in.

"Well, that's actually a relief," Terry added. "Now we don't have to worry about either of your parents making problems for us. You can stay here as long as you want."

Rob looked back at the movie playing on the TV. "Holy shit!" He exclaimed. On the screen was the image of a baby in utero wrapping the umbilical cord around its own neck, choking itself to death.

Terry chuckled. "This is the Director's Cut isn't it? You guys haven't seen this?"

"Uh-uh." Mothman shook his head, eyes wide and staring at the screen.

"We found this in your collection," Rob said. "What a crazy-ass movie. Really good though."

The movie ended and Mothman shut off the TV as the credits began to roll. Remius jumped down off of Rob's lap to the floor next to Terry. "So you fuck that bitch you've been texting?" The cat asked.

Terry looked at the October with a shocked expression on his face. "How…?" Terry didn't finish the question.

"Oh, give me a little credit," Remius responded. "Cats are psychic; don't you remember?"

"Huh, that's right. I totally forgot about that," Terry gave up trying to keep the secret. "I guess I can't hide anything from you, can I?"

"Nope. Nothing."

"So are you gonna ask me if I activated her Soulmind by having sex with her?" Terry wondered.

"Don't need to," Remius replied. "I already know that she's awake and her Soulmind has been online. Don't worry, Terry, it's all part of the plan." The cat winked at Terry with a smile on his whiskers.

"What plan?" Terry suddenly raised his voice. He wasn't angry though. "Who has a plan? You? When are you gonna share this fucking plan with me? Instead of leaving me to stumble around in the dark? I feel like there's a lot you're not telling me, and I don't like that."

"All in good time," Remius said and then glanced up at Mothman and Rob who were still sitting on the couch. They had been intently watching the October's conversation with Terry. "Now all three of you boys need to get off your lazy asses and listen to good ol' Remius here. It's about time for some more training. It's important for you three to know how to combine your energy for a greater impact. Especially if and when Maya regroups and decides to bring a more calculated attack."

Terry, Mothman, and Rob all looked at each other.

"Who's Maya?" Mothman asked.

Rob rolled his eyes and then took the initiative to answer the question. "Maya is from the Dimension of the Dark Tethers. She's very powerful, and she used her charms to seduce me. I was weak to her, especially since she wore all *Black*. How could I resist? Anyway, forget about that. She needs a piece of Terry's Soulmind to bring some kind of total destruction to the Hollow Dimension—this world."

"Why doesn't she just attack Terry herself and get it?" Mothman asked.

Rob shook his head. "There's this group of pan-dimensional women called The Order of the Transcendent who kind of like police her if she gets too close to Terry... That's why she got me to help her."

"And you're not under her spell anymore?" Mothman wanted to know.

Rob shook his head once more.

Remius finally spoke up again. "It's most likely that she will find some other entity, or entities, to help her with her second attempt on Terry. And this time we won't have the luxury of Maya underestimating you. Now she knows the true nature of the power that she's up against. That's why it's so important for all of you to increase, expand, and know how to work together with your newfound abilities. Some of your Soulminds have only just recently come online and you won't be able to reach your full potential or utilize all of what you can do without someone like me to teach you the new ways to use this energy."

"Okay, yeah, yeah," Terry said, nodding his head. "This is good. I've actually been waiting for you to show me some more stuff. I didn't understand why you weren't."

"You can't rush these things," Remius said as an explanation. "Okay! Enough bullshit and chit-chat. Time for action! The three of you stand in a circle in the middle of the room facing each other."

Terry, Rob, and Mothman did as they were told. Standing on the rug between the couch and the TV, they made a circle with only a few inches between each other. Remius jumped back up on the couch so he was higher up to instruct them.

"Should we hold hands?" Mothman asked.

"What is this a fucking tea party with gay baby dolls being played with by a transvestite toddler?" Remius joked. Mothman didn't get the joke so Remius continued speaking. "No, no holding hands for this configuration. Put your hands in front of your heart, right above your solar plexus, with only your fingertips touching. Now close your eyes and imagine your Soulmind energy descending from the top of your head, ascending from your perineum, and meeting at your solar plexus. Use the consciousness of your hearts to move the energy. Now see this energy flowing out from your solar plexus towards the middle of the circle."

A sphere of light suddenly appeared above the crown of each of their heads. Terry's was white, Rob's was electric blue, and Mothman's was orange. As the light descended, it illuminated each chakra going down to the heart and then the solar plexus. Conversely their chakras illuminated coming up from the base as well. Their Soulminds converged at each of their solar plexuses at the same moment and the light began to flow outward in streams and spirals.

"Breathe!" Remius commanded. "Long, deep yogic breaths. Sync your energy with the movements of your breath. With your eyes still closed, visualize all three of your Soulminds joining together in the middle of the circle creating a sphere of light which is a combination and exponential increase of your threefold sacred grid pattern."

The white, the blue, and the orange Soulminds continued to flow out of their chests. In an instant they collided in the center of the circle and immediately a semi-translucent sphere popped out about a foot in diameter. Their energies continued to fill up the sphere like a multi-colored water balloon. Inside this new sphere the colors of white, blue, and orange danced together like a living entity made of aurora borealis. The colors didn't mix, they just swirled around each other getting brighter and brighter.

"Open your eyes," Remius said now that the sphere had come to its brightest intensity.

The three boys all opened their eyes, actually beholding the physical creation of what they had visualized. "Holy shit!" Mothman exclaimed in disbelief. "Is that real?"

The light of the sphere shimmered and shone into their eyes. It also pulsed slightly, vibrating and humming with a frequency elevated beyond anything they had ever experienced.

"Oh, it's real," Remius answered. "And you three created this. Manifested this. And you can use this culmination of energy for creation, destruction, protection, or anything you so choose. That's the beauty of having free will. But for whatever you choose, you have to be ready to accept the consequences. Unless of course you're exempt from the rules." The October chuckled at this. Suddenly the lights in the living room and kitchen began to flicker. The sphere also began to gyrate and pulsate unstably. The orange light within the sphere threatened to take over the other colors and explode out from the rim. The lights flickered again, making little clicking noises.

"What's happening?" Mothman yelled.

"It's you!" Remius said forcefully. "You're overloading the system. Get your Soulmind under control. You're making it unstable." The cat stood up on all fours on the couch, his tail stood straight up and puffed out.

"Mothman, stop!" Terry yelled at his friend. He tried to will the energy back to equilibrium himself, but without the cooperation of his friends he was unable to override what was happening. The perfect sphere had now begun to start warping into other shapes. Mothman's eyes rolled up into the back of his sockets and then suddenly all of the lights on the ground floor of the house shattered with a loud popping sound. The energy sphere collapsed and each Soulmind flowed back into its respective body. Mothman fell unconscious to the floor like a rag doll dropped by a child who had become bored with it.

Remius hopped down from the couch and went over to Mothman's unconscious body. The cat began licking the boy's forehead, the area between his eyebrows. Rob and Terry slumped down on the couch, utterly drained and exhausted. "That was so fucking intense," Terry said, taking long deep breaths. Rob nodded in agreement.

"You guys will get the hang of this and perfect it sooner than you realize," Remius assured them. "Mothman here is just new to this whole game. He just doesn't know how to keep his energy under control. Come to think of it, that hasn't been one of his strong points in life. You know what I mean, Terry."

Terry blushed and looked away from Rob who was staring at him. "Yeah," Rob said after a moment of thinking. "You never did tell me how Mothman came to have a Soulmind; you just said it was a long story. He didn't have one before."

"Uhhh..." Terry couldn't avoid the question anymore. "We kind of, uh, fucked. And when someone with a Soulmind does that with someone who doesn't, it activates *their* Soulmind. So, yeah, that's how it happened. I didn't know that that was going to happen before we did it."

Rob burst out laughing. He found the whole situation hysterical. "So that explains what you and Remius were talking about earlier about that girl you're seeing and whether you activated her. I didn't know what the hell you guys were on about earlier. I'm not really surprised about you and Mothman, though. Remember when we would have sleepovers at my house and all circle jerk in my basement? How come nobody got 'activated' during those times?"

"Cause there was no penetration involved." Terry replied. "Right, Remius?"

"That's usually the rule," Remius answered. "Sometimes a woman can activate another woman but that's a little bit more difficult. She would have to have a really strong Soulmind. In that case the penetration is more energetic and not physical."

"I get it," Terry said. "I think."

"So if I have sex with a girl who doesn't have a Soulmind already, then I'll 'activate' her? Is that right?" Rob asked.

Terry laughed. "Who's gonna have sex with you, Rob?"

"Dick!" Rob punched Terry in the shoulder.

Mothman started snoring lightly as he was sprawled out on the floor. Remius jumped back up on the couch between Terry and Rob. "Be careful with all the glass from the shattered light bulbs. We'll have to clean that up when you guys get some strength back. You three produced a lot of energy. That's really promising, you should be excited about this."

"Oh we are!" Terry assured the October. "Right, Rob?" Rob nodded in agreement and then Terry continued. "I feel more adventures coming."

"Your intuition is correct," Remius said, putting his paw on Terry's leg. "The more you guys advance, the more accelerated everything will become. And, needless to say, more will be expected of you. It's good to have fun, but know that you will come face to face with stranger and stranger worlds. Sometimes you'll be in very dangerous situations."

Terry's face got serious. "Understood. You ready for this stuff, Rob?"

"Man, I went through a lot you weren't even there for. It's Mothman I'm worried about not rising to meet *us*."

"I think that's enough training for one day." Remius smiled at his young students. "Who's hungry?"

FIVE

"Yeah, boss, who can we bring the murdering on?" Trick asked Maya, almost foaming at the mouth like a rabid dog.

"That's pretty obvious," Maya replied. "The easiest thing would be to terrorize and kill Rob's parents. You don't even have to leave the house."

"Fucking right!" Tock exclaimed. He was still sitting on the floor at Maya's feet. "Why didn't I think of that?"

"It would be easy and fun for you guys since they can't see you," she continued. "Neither Rob's mother or father have a Soulmind so we're invisible to them. You could, you know, chase her around the kitchen with a butcher knife. She'll think her house is haunted by a poltergeist or something."

"Fuck yeah!" Trick was so pleased at the prospect of having his bloodlust fulfilled that he was practically cumming in his pants. "Let's go fuck this cunt to death with a butcher knife! When can we do this, boss? I'm ready! I'm ready! Let me at her!" He dropped the weights he was using to do bicep curls and rubbed his crotch, turned on by the thought of the kill.

"Just go do it now," Maya answered a little absentmindedly. "It's not like we have anything better to do right now. The bitch is probably downstairs in the kitchen cooking like a good suburban housewife."

Tock stood up as Tick scooted off of the bed. "Are you coming with us, boss?" Tock asked.

Maya shook her head. "No, you three go have fun. I'll be here planning the best way for you to attack Terry's house."

"Let's go boys!" Trick yelled, pumping his fist up and down as his eyes bulged from his head. "We're gonna fuck this fat slut to death! Death! Death!" He kept chanting as they left the room and descended the stairs toward the kitchen.

Maya had been right; Rob's mother was in the kitchen finishing up a pie and about to put it in the oven. She was a chubby mom in her mid-forties, wearing a dress with a floral pattern on it. Her apron was green and said 'kiss the chef' on the front. Since Trick, Tock, and Tick were from another Dimension, they couldn't touch a non-activated human directly. However, they could touch and manipulate inanimate objects. All three of them shared a look and a chuckle as they thought about how much this bitch was going to scream.

Rob's mother opened the oven and slid the pie in to cook. "Should we smash her head in the oven door? Cook her fucking brains?" Tock asked, laughing hysterically like a *Looney Toons* character that just smoked crack.

"Nah," Trick answered. "It would be over too quickly that way. Let's terrorize this ugly broad."

The mother closed the oven and humming to herself went over to the door of the refrigerator. There was a white dry erase board held to the refrigerator door with magnets. She picked up the marker and started writing items she needed to get at the grocery store.

"Watch this," Tock said to his brothers. With lightning speed Tock whipped open one of the drawers and grabbed all the forks in one handful. Before the mother had time to react, Tock was chucking them at her like throwing knives. Screaming at the top of her lungs, the mother's back met the wall behind her as she retreated. Forks stuck in the wall inches from her head. Another fork lodged into her hand that she had raised to block herself from the onslaught. Two more managed to bury themselves in her belly and breast. Blood gushed from her hand and the places in her torso that the forks now stuck out of.

Trick, Tock, and Tick laughed and gave each other high fives. "Who's there?" The mother screamed. She pulled the forks from her flesh, wincing in pain. "Am I being haunted? What do you want, demon?" More screaming erupted from her but she was too much in shock to move much from where she had leaned up against the wall.

Now each of the three grabbed a knife from the butcher block. What Rob's mother saw were three knives with minds of their own floating out of the the block and advancing toward her like sharp birds flying through the air ready to attack. Her eyes widened and she screamed bloody murder. As she tried to run for the exit into her living room and then the front door, Trick ran around and cut her off from any attempt to escape. She was now surrounded by three butcher knives floating in the air like puppets with no strings attached. There was nowhere for her to run; she knew she was fucked. The mother began to cry and plead for her life.

"Don't you love it when they beg?" Tick said, drooling and sweating the excitement from his pores. "Gets me so hot."

"Oh yeah, fuck yeah," Trick agreed. Rob's mother was now on the ground trying to curl into a ball and make herself as small as possible. "I can even feel my nipples excreting!"

Then Tock spoke as they all hovered over her, knives pointing down and at the ready. "Sometimes I wish we could bathe in this moment right before the kill forever. Their fear is so delicious. Fuck it! Let's rape this old cunt with steel! Make her feel the cuts and slices of our jagged knife cocks!"

Then the knives came down at once, stabbing and goring the woman. They avoided her vital spots at first as not to kill her too quickly and miss the full enjoyment. The knives gored her in her love-handles, her legs, and her arms, slicing her extremities to ribbons. The mother screamed in a steady unrelenting stream as her blood splashed and flew all over the kitchen, and pooled in great puddles of shiny red around her blubbery body. Yellow fat and bile oozed from the wounds in her stomach. Her screams slowly began to get quieter as shock began to take hold.

"Quick!" Tock yelled at Trick. "Fuck her to death before she goes unconscious and can't feel it anymore." After all the stabbing, the woman was now sprawled out on the tile floor on her back, soaked in blood. Trick raised his butcher knife—which was now dripping and slippery—and swung it down hard, burying it up to the hilt in the woman's old wrinkly pussy. She screamed one final time and then laid motionless, stained red and almost unrecognizably mutilated.

Trick stood up, leaving the knife in the dead woman's vagina. His hard cock was making a tent under his pants. Breathing heavily he wiped the sweat from his brow like he just had an intense session with a whore who was very well-versed at her craft. "I think I just came," Trick panted. A wet circle stained the fabric of his pants right at the tip of his dick.

Trick, Tock, and Tick all took a deep breath and then howled loudly as if they were wolves under a full moon. Tock hopped up and sat on the counter by the stove, still admiring their handiwork. Tick went over and opened the refrigerator. "What kind of shit do these people keep in this box?" He rummaged around inside and pulled out an open carton of milk. "Some white juice from the animal's member that hangs between their legs. Make it look like she got soaked with animal jism!" Tick poured the milk all over the woman's body, the white liquid splashing and mixing in swirls with the thickening red.

Trick picked up one of the knives from the floor of carnage and slid it into the woman's mouth and down her esophagus like she had decided to deep throat the blade. The third knife he stabbed directly into her heart which had already ceased to beat.

Tock swung his legs off the edge of the counter, knocking his heels into the cabinet below. "Wait till this bitch's husband gets home and sees this! He's gonna shit himself! Then we get to do him too! Double our fun! Double our pleasure!"

There was the sound of a key being turned in the lock of the front door. "Speak of the Devil," Tick said. "What perfect timing—for a killing!"

They waited in anticipation for the husband's reaction to seeing the scene of horror that they had created like a Jackson Pollock painting all over the kitchen floor. The front door swung open and an older man entered the house. He was wearing a gray business suit and his short brown hair was thinning on the top. "Margaret! I'm home!" He yelled for his wife as he put his briefcase down on the couch in the living room. "Margaret," he said again, loosening his tie. "Are you in the kitchen? I smell a pie! I hope it's one of your delicious apple crumbles."

The husband approached the kitchen and Trick, Tock, and Tick waited in hushed silence for the first critic of their art project. As the man approached the threshold of the kitchen, he caught his first glimpse of the scene. "Oh my god! Holy Jesus! Margaret! Margaret!" Even in his shock, the man reached for the cordless phone on the counter to call the police. Tock was quicker by far though. Intercepting the man's reach, Tock grabbed the phone instead and hurled it at the man's face. It hit him dead-center, breaking his nose and unleashing a torrent of blood like Niagara Falls. The husband cried out in pain, but his foot slid in the blood below and he came crashing to the floor on his back. All the wind was knocked out of him and he started wheezing to catch is breath. Trying to get back up he only managed to slip and slide in the blood, guts, and bile that was soaking his suit now.

"How should we do this one?" Tick asked as they circled around their new victim who was unable to see his attackers.

"I know," Trick said as he walked over to the refrigerator. He grabbed it with his immense strength of ten Arnold Schwarzeneggers and pulled it down, letting it fall on the man trying desperately to stand up. It made contact and crushed the husband's pelvis, shattering it into a million tiny bone fragments. He screamed out loud and his legs ceased their movements. "Let's watch him struggle for a little bit," Trick suggested.

They all stood around gawking with stupid smiles on their faces as the man attempted uselessly to push the huge appliance off of himself. He wheezed and whimpered, straining his bloody face as he pushed the side of the fridge with all his might. After a few attempts he gave up and started screaming for help. He was covered in his wife's blood and he was spitting the blood that was dripping into his mouth from his broken nose. "Help! Somebody help!" He gurgled through the blood and phlegm.

"Should we silence his crying baby ass?" Tock asked. Trick nodded to him and Tock took the initiative to take the hot pie out of the oven.

The man stared in disbelief as the oven opened itself and the pie hovered its way out into the open air of the kitchen. The air around the oven waved and rippled with the heat.

"Drop it. Just drop it on his face," Trick suggested.

Tock dropped the steaming pie directly onto the man's face like he was a clown at the circus, except this pie was burning hot. The husband tried to scream but his mouth was full of pie burning is tongue and lips. He could feel the heat searing his skin and boiling his eyeballs. After knocking the pie off of his face, the husband realized he couldn't see and he had third degree burns on his face.

"Kill him! Let's kill him!" Tick snickered. "Ooo, ooo! Let me do it! Let me do it!" He jumped up and down clapping his hands excitedly, his fat jiggling around his midsection.

Trick gestured in acquiescence. "Be my guest," he said. "Make him taste his wife's cunt." Trick winked at Tick who understood what to do. He leaned down and pulled the knife from the wife's snatch. Then without warning he rained stabs into the man's face like a hailstorm turned violent. Tick screamed and cursed in delight as he gored the husband's face into a blob of brains, blood, and bone. When it was done he dropped the knife and had to catch his breath from the exertion.

"Fuckin' a! What a rush!" Tick stood up and wiped the sweat from his flabby brow. The three took several moments to admire the messy carnage on the floor. When they were satisfied with absorbing the totality of their work, they decided to go back upstairs to see how Maya was doing.

"Well, that was fun." Tock said as he closed the oven and turned it off. He followed the other two up the stairs back to Rob's bedroom.

Maya was still sitting in the chair by Rob's desk. "You guys done already?" She asked.

"Yeah, buddy! And it was fan-fucking-tastic!" Trick said and went back by the window where the weights were. He picked one up to continue working out his biceps. "What now, boss?"

SIX

The next day Terry went back over to Eden's apartment like he promised. His whole body was tingling with excitement and anticipation of their play date. What the details of their meeting would be was a mystery to Terry, but he had full trust in his mistress. After the experience with himself, Rob, and Mothman the previous day, he knew how powerful he was and could be. In the act of being a submissive, there was immense strength in giving up power—or more accurately, *lending* power to the partner. The dynamic of dominant and submissive was an intense sharing of control and let-go; but also protection and a compassionate guidance into a certain experience.

As he made the drive over to Eden's place, Terry thought about Rob and Mothman who had again decided to attend school that morning. He shook his head, confounded why they would still go to that oppressive institution. *They're not yet fully deprogrammed*, he thought to himself. *But if they continue to stay with me and Remius, it's only a matter of time until they come out of that conditioning and collective hypnosis.*

Terry parked without any problems and ran up to knock on Eden's door. Before his knuckles even touched the wood, the door was swung open enthusiastically and there was Eden as beautiful and radiant as before. She was wearing nothing but black lingerie.

"Damn, girl!" Terry said as he was pulled inside by the waist of his pants. Eden kissed him steamily as she slammed the door behind them. Terry noticed that there was no Kat here today; they were alone together.

Eden squeezed Terry's ass and smiled an inch from the lips she had just been kissing. "I got some fun stuff planned for us today, sexy boy!" She led him out to the backyard and then down to the basement. Terry stared at her round ass the whole way.

"What do you have planned for us today, my mistress?" Terry asked, closing the door as they entered the dungeon play area.

"This," Eden said as she slid her hands across the table with the restraints. She smiled wickedly. "Tell me, Terry, have you ever been flogged?"

"No, uh, I don't think so," he confessed. "But I'm open to it." Terry looked over and this was the first time he noticed several whips, floggers, and riding crops hanging by pegs on the wall.

Eden chose one with several leather strips on the end. It looked like a big tassel. "This," Eden explained. "Is a Cat-o'-nine-tails. This one is leather, but historically these whips were made out of rope and generally used at sea to flog offenders and troublemakers aboard ships." She gave Terry a sly smile. "Are you a troublemaker, Terry? Do you need to be punished?"

Terry giggled. "Yes, Mistress Eden. I'm always making trouble, disturbing the peace, and I never stop rocking the boat."

"I thought so," Eden replied, assuming the role and setting the scene. "Strip, you fucking disrupter! Your body is forfeit and now belongs to me! Take it all off, I want to see your vulnerable flesh."

Terry silently and subserviently removed every piece of clothing and stood before his mistress naked and exposed. It was a bit chilly in the basement and he instinctively put his hands over his manhood which was shrinking in the cold air.

"Move those hands, wretch!" Eden commanded. "I want to get a good look at every inch of your perverted meat." Terry moved his hands from in front of himself. His mistress approached him slowly, looking at his cock ravenously. She used the flogger to play a little with his dick and balls. "Do you want me to give you the honor of torturing you? I don't know if you're worthy, scum."

"Yes," Terry whispered.

"What was that? I can't fucking hear you!"

"Yes!" Terry raised his voice louder. "Yes, mistress. Do me the honor of punishment."

"I don't believe it," she said, feigning disinterest. "Beg me."

"I beg you! Please, mistress! I'm not worthy of your attention. I worship you! Beat me, fuck me, kill me!"

Eden smiled at this display, leaned in to Terry's chest and bit down hard on his nipple.

"Ow! Fuck!" Terry yelped in pain.

Eden slapped him across the left cheek, leaving a red mark and his eyes watering. "Silence, you cryptorchid secretion! Now get on the fucking table! On your stomach!"

Terry crawled onto the table without so much as a protest. The wrist and ankle cuffs were made of leather and lined with wool. Eden fastened them to Terry's ankles and wrists so he was fully restrained, unable to escape even if he wanted to.

Eden went out of character for a second to ask Terry, "What's the safe word?"

Terry thought back to what he had read about BDSM scene play. "*Red*, right?"

"Very good," she said then slipped back into her dominant role. "Now shut the fuck up and get what's coming to you!" Terry was tensing up his body and his back in anticipation for the impact from the whip. Eden came out of her character again and placed a hand tenderly on his back. "Relax, honey, just relax. It's better if you don't tense up. Breathe normally, and breathe out when the whip makes contact. Okay?"

"Okay," Terry said quietly.

Eden swung the whip and with a *crack* it made contact with Terry's back between his shoulder blades. He exhaled the air from his lungs and felt the stinging on his tender flesh.

Crack! Two lashes.

Crack! Three lashes.

Crack! Four lashes

The skin of Terry's back was red and the bruises were beginning to raise to the surface. He felt the pain—the sting—but it was mixing and pushing towards a feeling of euphoria. His head swam and he lost grip on his own identity in the midst of these new sensations.

"It's hard not to feel anything in your life," Eden said. Her voice was different; not the play-dominant voice but it was firm. "To have so much anger, rage, and hatred that you can't connect to anyone except for your own demons..." Terry's eyes were closed and Eden's voice came to him through that darkness, as if from very far away. "So you come to me to feel some kind of connection."

Crack! Five lashes.

Crack! Six lashes.

"Do you feel something now, you little faggot?" She continued her monologue as she beat him. "You psychotic-pervert-killer. To feel unloved and unlovable..."

Crack! Seven lashes. Now Terry was starting to hit his pain threshold and began approaching the border of subspace—that place of transcendence.

Eden began to sob quietly, admiring the red streaks on her submissive's flesh. *Crack!* Eight lashes. She raised her voice, getting more intense. "Such a greedy cunt! So cold and alone that all you cry and beg for is to fuck and be fucked! To be filled by something! Anything!"

Crack! The ninth lash sent Terry over the edge into subspace where he was swimming in the black void. His naked body was suspended, floating, and he could see nothing. Suddenly a huge sphere of white light exploded in front of Terry and he had to shield his eyes from the brightness. As the intensity dimmed, he could make out the form of a giant goddess within the light. She wore a long flowing white dress and a white turban on her head.

The goddess spoke and her voice reverberated like a gong inside Terry's skull. "She is the Perfect Forever! And you are the Steward of Time!"

As quickly as the vision had come, it vanished. Terry was pulled back into his body and was reunited with all the sensations coursing through it. He breathed, filling his lungs up with rich oxygen. Eden was rubbing the bruises on Terry's back with a touch only a lover could deliver. Nine lashes was the extent of his flogging for the day. There was pain but also pleasure coursing through his skin, blood, and brain chemistry. Eden slowly released Terry from his bonds. They were silent, yet connected deeply within that silence. Terry slowly sat up to pull himself off the table, his consciousness re-grounding itself into his physical body. He looked at Eden for the first time since before they started the scene. Her cheeks were still wet with tears. Terry reached out to her face and wiped them with his thumb. She smiled, her eyes glistening.

"Come, darling." Eden helped Terry off the table and brought him over to one of the couches by the bar. There was a blanket. She picked it up and wrapped it around his shoulders. They both sank into the couch and held each other tightly but compassionately. Closing their eyes, Eden and Terry felt each other's heartbeat and listened to their breathing—both energies synchronizing. "I love you, Terry," Eden whispered, eyes still closed. "Could you ever really love me?"

Terry didn't even have to think about it, he knew how he felt in his heart. "Of course, Eden. I love you unconditionally."

Eden smiled and fresh tears rolled down her cheeks as they both sank into the warmth of their aftercare.

SEVEN
FROM THE MIND OF TERRY BROSWALD:

Perfect Forever

Fall onto and into me
As my body escapes into whatever is left of my soul.
I have become nothing,
And in the process lost everything.
As I whip tentacles of liquid nitrogen

in a circle around my consciousness,
I realize what I need is the blankets of whatever came before.
But I've always seemed to lose whatever
could have been beautiful.
Then I open my eyes onto the
landscape of bizarre concordances
that only record my life
Thus far.
But now I know how it continues.
Because I finally understand how it began.
But for now I am still yours.
Still born and in your arms I wait.
I wait till I can finally show you how
I'm becoming everything.
For you and for me I know light and shadow
can be still as the dawn
As time drips my mind from the land I decided not to visit.
Snap off what hasn't happened yet
And create your own forever.

EIGHT

Terry returned to his house that evening after his day with Eden. They had laid on that couch holding each other for a long while after their scene was over. For Terry it was incredibly peaceful just laying in her arms; almost like being back in the comfort of the womb. Eden felt seen, held, and loved as well. They were both riding high on a wave of well-being and unconditional acceptance. Several times they were so relaxed that they slept for brief stretches of time, their heads pressed together. When Terry awoke, again he couldn't remember having dreamt at all.

On the drive home, in spite of the elation of his newfound connection with Eden, Terry's thoughts found their way to the image of Jessica. The vision entering his third eye started out blurry and then began to take on substance. An overwhelming feeling of sorrow gripped his body at seeing her face—even if it was in his mind. Terry's heart felt like it was being stabbed over and over but refused to die. Tears stung his eyes as the sobs emerged from deep in his lungs. As the vision became clearer, he could see Jessica was sitting on the ground meditatively in a cross-legged posture. Her eyes were closed. Terry couldn't make out the surroundings, it looked like paint running on a soaked canvas. And what was she wearing? Her clothes looked strange, like something from a Renaissance Faire.

"Where are you?" He silently vibrated the question inside his head.

Surprisingly Jessica's eyes fluttered open and she looked with a soft gaze into the distance. "Terry?"

The moment after his name was spoken, Terry was jolted out of his vision by a loud car horn beeping at him from the car behind his. He was stopped at a light that had recently turned green and the drivers behind were getting impatient. Stepping on the gas pedal, Terry grounded himself and returned to the present moment. He turned the corner onto the street his house was on. Having memories of Jessica bubble back up caused his heart to ache with a pain he didn't know how to remedy. *Maybe she's actually dead*, Terry thought. *And the only way for me to be reunited with her is to die myself.*

He tried to shake this notion but it lingered somewhere in his subconscious. Night was descending as Terry let himself in through the front door. He needed the support of his friends and lovers now more than ever. Rob was sitting on the couch scrolling through something on his phone; Remius curled up next to him.

Terry looked around. "Where's Mothman?" He asked.

Rob looked up and put his phone down. "He went upstairs to take a nap in the guest bedroom. He seemed real wiped out from that thing we did yesterday."

Terry plopped his body down on the couch with a long sigh. Scratching Remius's furry head, he continued the conversation. "Have you been having any dreams at all lately, Rob? When I've been waking up these days I can't seem to remember any dreams at all..."

"Yeah, actually I have," Rob conceded. "Last night I had this weird fucking dream about Arash. He was chasing me with some kind of chainsaw trying to kill me. Speaking of which, where is that guy anyway?"

Terry shrugged his shoulders and stared off into the space in front of him. "I miss my dreams. They were fun and sometimes even helped me figure stuff out. Even the ones that were downright nightmares."

"Maybe you've forgotten how," Remius spoke without lifting his head or opening his eyes.

"The fuck does that mean?" Terry asked emphatically. "Always with your goddamn riddles. How can someone *forget* how to dream? And isn't it your job to keep my mind active with dreams? I seem to remember you telling me that was your fucking job."

Remius snorted and gave a little chuckle, opening his eyes slightly. "You just want me to do everything *for* you, don't you? How are you supposed to learn *anything* if I spoon feed you *everything*?"

Terry didn't say anything but he could feel his face get hot and his heart still aching. Rob got up off the couch to fill up a glass of water at the kitchen sink. "I had a vision of Jessica today," Terry whispered to Remius so Rob couldn't hear. "I know you know something you're not telling me, you pussy!" His voice was low but desperate.

Remius raised his head and his green feline eyes pierced Terry to the point it made him uncomfortable. "What makes you think I know anything?"

Terry shrugged. "I dunno," he said, giving up on his forcefulness. "I figured you know everything about the other Dimensions and, like, you know, what this is all about. What the point of it all is."

Remius scoffed. "Get your head out of your ass, Terry. Come back to reality. I'm not *privy* to all information. Unfortunately I have not been granted access to the Akashic Records... At least as of yet."

"Uhhh, Terry?" It was Rob's voice coming from the kitchen. He was staring out of the window above the sink into the backyard.

"Yeah?" Terry asked, looking over to where Rob was standing.

"Who the fuck are these three guys lurking in your backyard? I have a bad feeling about this," Rob said, backing away from the window.

Terry bolted off the couch and ran over to Rob. He followed Rob's gaze through the window. There were Trick, Tock, and Tick standing in a circle off in the distance several yards away from the house. They spoke in hushed whispers to each other.

"Who the fuck?" Terry squinted, trying to make out their features in the dark outside.

"What is it?" Remius asked, now up on his feet.

"It's these three fucking guys," Terry answered. "It looks like one is tall and super muscular. There's one real skinny with long hair. And the third is, like, really fat."

"Oh, no," Remius said in response.

Rob and Terry exchanged a glance of worry. "Oh, no? What is that supposed to mean?" Rob asked.

The cat trotted over and jumped up onto the kitchen counter. "Those three are supposed to be locked up forever in the Containment Cube in the Dark Tethers. This has Maya written all over it." Remius anxiously swished his tail back and forth. "Rob, quick, go wake up Mothman. We're gonna need him if we have a chance to defend ourselves."

"Fuck," Rob said under his breath as he ran up the stairs to wake his friend.

The panic started to take over Terry and he began to tremble. The white light of his Soulmind was already emanating from his chest. As he felt the coming threat, the handle of Terry's machete popped out of his solar plexus. He pulled it out of his chest; the blade was long and intensely bright—made out of the energy of his Soulmind.

Suddenly Trick's face turned and stared directly into Terry's eyes with the most intense level of hate capable of being contained within a single entity.

"Are you ready for this battle?" Remius asked Terry, deadly serious.

"No," Terry whimpered, still staring wide-eyed out the window. He backed away even more.

Trick bolted with a crack, almost at the speed of sound, and dove through the kitchen window, shattering it into pieces. A shower of glass and wood poured into the sink as Trick fell over it onto the floor. He got to his feet just as Mothman and Rob made it back down the stairs.

"Surprise, faggot!" Trick yelled, his eyes delirious.

"Terry, get behind us!" Rob yelled. His longbow was already out and at the ready, strung with an arrow made of the blue energy of his Soulmind. Terry scrambled to get behind them, between his friends and the front door. He had the urge for a second to make a break for it, but knew he couldn't leave his friends to fight off three maniacs by themselves.

Mothman had a weapon now too. It looked like the handle of a bowie knife and the blade was the orange light of his Soulmind. He brandished it in front of himself awkwardly.

"Well, isn't this a pretty fucking picture?" Trick said. Tock was now crawling through the broken window followed by Tick who was almost too fat to fit through. Remius hissed at the three, his fur and tail puffing out. Trick grabbed a plate that was on the island in front of him and chucked it at the October. The plate narrowly missed, shattering next to the cat's paws.

"We just want Terry," Trick continued. "Give him up and we'll spare your pathetic lives."

"Fucking never!" Rob screamed. "I already betrayed him once, I won't do it again!"

Trick shook his head and clicked his tongue. "We don't even need all of him. Just a part of him. You can spare just that little piece. Isn't that right, boys?" Tock and Tick nodded agreement from behind their leader.

"I'm aware of that," Rob said and let his arrow fly. It struck Trick in the left pec below his collar bone. Blood spurted from the wound.

"You motherfucker," Trick looked shocked and tried to pull the arrow from his flesh, but he was unable to grip it. His hand kept going straight through the blue energy each time he tried. Screaming in frustration, Trick brought his fists down onto the island in front of him, splitting the marble countertop into two pieces like a sacrificial altar cracking in half. "Enough fucking around! You're dead!"

As Trick approached Rob and Mothman, he smacked Remius off the counter with the back of his hand. The cat meowed in protest as he fell to the floor. Trick held out his hands as he came closer and closer. Rob recognized the black ropes that were now growing from his attacker's palms.

"Fuck. No. Terry! Now, the grid formation!" Rob yelled for Terry's help but was cut off when the ropes of the Dark Tethers shot out of Trick's palms and wrapped themselves like tentacles around his throat. Rob dropped his bow to the floor and began to scratch and claw at the dense black energy ropes that were now choking him. Mothman made an attempt to cut the ropes constricting his friend's throat, but Tock attacked him. He shoved Mothman back forcefully and then kicked him in the chest. Mothman stumbled and fell on his back in front of the couch in the living room. His blade skidded out of his hand and across the floor. Tock pounced onto Mothman's stomach and began to choke the life from him, crushing his windpipe.

Terry felt paralyzed. He was frozen, unable to make a move to help his friends. Then Remius's voice pulled him from his paralytic fear. "Terry!" Remius screamed from the place he had been thrown. "Remember everything I've taught you! Don't give up now when you've come so far!"

Terry looked around him and it was as if time had entered into slow motion. Both his friends were being choked to death, but it almost looked like a still picture; a couple frames of pure agony captured on celluloid. He had to make a move. Terry screamed and time returned to normal speed. He projected a protective sphere of light around his whole body, still holding his machete at his side. Without skipping a beat, Terry sent an electromagnetic pulse out in every direction from the sphere.

The pulse went right through Rob and Mothman but violently collided with Trick, Tock, and Tick, throwing them off their feet and through the air. Tock was thrown over the couch and back against the glass doors behind them. Trick was hurled through the air across the island he had cracked in half and fell heavily to the floor on the other side. The black ropes disappeared back into his hands. Tick was thrown back on his ass against the kitchen counter behind him, completely splintering it into fragments.

Trick, Tock, and Tick laid stunned where they had fallen. "Quick," Terry yelled to his friends and Remius. "Get inside the sphere!" Taking advantage of the moment, Rob and Mothman scrambled to their feet. They ran over to Terry and slipped inside the protection of his force field. Remius ran over, trailing behind, and joined them inside. All three boys faced each other in a circle like when Remius had taught them the formation. The cat sat in the middle of their circle, looking up.

Terry dropped his machete and it disappeared into thin air. Instinctively Rob, Mothman, and Terry raised their hands in front of their hearts, fingertips touching. They closed their eyes and focused on visualizing the sphere of light. The Soulmind energy of all three spiraled from their chests and began converging in the middle, over Remius's head. Suddenly Terry gasped and he felt like he was being possessed by the presence of a powerful entity.

"Terry, what is it?" Remius asked, concerned.

With his eyes still closed, Terry's brow started to quiver. "I feel... Jessica." His eyes shot open and he began to speak with Jessica's voice overlapping his own. "Oh, Mother Gaia! I call upon the Elementals of the Earth to ground this energy and guide us into our full power! The Spirits of the trees, and the rocks, and the animals assist us in creating a stable projection of Soul-casting!"

The sphere of Soulmind light was gaining intensity as the three colors of their energies mixed within. This time it didn't pulse, it maintained its integrity. By this point Trick, Tock, and Tick were getting back onto their feet and readying themselves for the next attack.

"You think you're safe in there with your little rainbow beach ball?" Trick laughed and mocked them with his words. "Combining your weak small penis energies. That's pathetic—cute actually. But six can play at that game!" Trick whistled to his two comrades and jerked his head toward the three boys inside their force field. Before Terry could finish his spell or cast the energy, they were surrounded by Trick, Tock, and Tick. The brothers from the Dark Tethers circled the protective bubble with their arms down at their sides and palms facing in toward Terry, Rob, and Mothman.

"Shoot it out!" Mothman yelled. "We're surrounded!" He pulsed the sphere of energy and beams of light shot out of it and through the force field. Trick, Tock, and Tick each were struck by one of these beams of energy. Each current of Soulmind energy gave them an electric shock, but unfortunately didn't do any real damage.

"That tickled," Tock said. The three dark brothers laughed as they produced more black ropes from their palms. They wrapped them around the circumference of the protective shield, covering the whole surface making it look like a black egg. Terry could hear them laughing from outside of the barrier of darkness. The three boys and Remius could only see through the darkness by the light coming from their Soulminds and the sphere of energy still swirling between them.

"Now what do we do?" Rob sounded panicked.

Terry screamed and pulsed the energy of the ball like a flash bomb. It exploded and hit the inside of the black ropes surrounding them but couldn't break through. The light shrank back into the sphere; white, orange, and blue swirling like a violent storm inside the globe. "What now, Remius? How do we get out of this one?" Terry asked. Mothman was shaking with fear; a wet stain dripped through his pants.

From inside their containment, they suddenly heard a loud sound of a door being swung open with force and hitting the wall on the inside of the house. Terry's head jerked to try to hear what was happening on the other side of the black ropes. Remius pricked up his ears. "I think some help has arrived," the cat said.

"Who the fuck is this bitch?" Trick said and spun around as the front door was thrown open as if with a battering ram. Stepping into the house was Eden. She held a six foot long steel metal spear by her side. The shaft of the spear was carved with Celtic symbols and the blade at the tip was the bright pink and red of her Soulmind. Eden's aura was burning intensely around her body like the flame of a candle.

"*Who the fuck is this bitch?*" Eden spit the words back at Trick. "Who the fuck are you? You look like an unstable meth head who got ass fucked one two many times in prison."

Trick, Tock, and Tick looked at each other. A woman with a huge spear was a little more than they had been expecting. The black ropes that they had produced and wrapped Terry's force field in stayed solid even without being attached to each of their hands anymore.

"What's going on out there?" Terry yelled from inside the black egg. "Eden, is that you?"

"Yeah, Terry, it's me!" Eden yelled back.

Trick lunged at Eden, wanting to make an attempt to disarm her of the menacing spear. He was too slow. Eden's response was instantaneous. She swung the spear down hard; it made contact with Trick on his right side and sliced his arm off at the elbow.

Trick screamed in pain as blood poured out from where the lower half of his arm used to be. "You fucking cunt! You fucking bitch beast!" He yelled at her as his eyes strained and bugged out of their sockets. Even through the pain Trick managed to grab his severed arm and take a couple retreating steps. Eden swung the spear in front of her as a warning.

"Tock, get her!" Trick commanded his brother. Tock shook his head, his eyes wide and staring at the spear tip a couple feet from where he stood. Tick was already running away. He made it through the kitchen and was scrambling his fat ass back out the window. "Tick, get your fat ass back here, you fucking coward."

"Fuck this crazy pink-haired bitch!" Tick yelled back at them as he fell out of the window into the backyard and scrambled to his feet. He made a mad dash away from the house.

Trick's wound was leaking profusely, forming a red puddle on the floor. "You gonna make a move, or what?" Eden taunted Tock and Trick who still stood around the force field enveloped by the ropes of Dark Tethers.

Trick backed up a few more steps. "Fuck you, whore." He shook his severed arm at Eden threateningly but comically. "This isn't over! Next time I'm gonna enjoy raping you to death! C'mon, Tock." They both retreated through the kitchen, jumped out the window, and ran after Tick into the darkness.

Eden touched the black ropes around Terry's electromagnetic shield with the tip of her spear and they instantly fell away, disappearing as they hit the ground. Terry was shocked but glad to see her. Rob and Mothman just stared with their mouths hanging open. The force field flickered and disappeared. Then the three boys let their Soulminds dissipate and return to their bodies.

"Would you mind pointing that thing away from us?" Rob asked Eden, looking at her huge intimidating spear.

"Oh, sorry," she said. Letting go of the spear it turned to red and pink energy that returned to her solar plexus. Her bright aura dimmed and faded as well. Terry ran over and embraced his lover tightly.

"Holy shit, am I glad to see you, Eden," Terry said, kissing her on the cheek and then on the lips.

"This is your girlfriend?" Mothman asked.

Terry and Eden turned back to Rob, Mothman, and Remius. "Yeah," Terry replied. "Eden, this is Rob and Mothman. Guys, this is Eden."

"Nice to meet you boys," Eden smiled.

"Damn, girl, you fine," Mothman said, eyeing her up and down.

Eden coughed into her fist. "It looks like you spilled some water on the crotch of your pants there."

Mothman blushed and tried to cover the wet pee with his hands. "That's nothing," he said.

"All you three have Soulminds?" Eden asked.

"Evidently," Rob said.

"How the fuck did you find us?" Terry asked. "I didn't think you even knew where I lived."

"I don't know," Eden answered. "I had this vision—this premonition—of you being attacked by three figures. Then I just followed my Soulmind. It showed me the way here and I trusted it. Took me a while to get here on the train, but I knew I had to come somehow."

"That's fucking crazy," Terry responded. "I don't know what would have happened if you hadn't shown up. They had us trapped. I mean, you saw."

Eden nodded.

"That's the most heavy-duty Soulmind weapon that I've seen in my time," Remius finally spoke up.

Eden looked down at the October and pointed. "Did—did that cat just talk?"

"I did indeed," Remius smiled at Eden's reaction.

"This just gets fucking weirder and stranger," Eden said. "But to tell the truth, one day I just saw the spear in my mind's eye and the energy of my Soulmind materialized it in my hand."

"That's pretty impressive," Remius admitted.

Terry held Eden's hand and squeezed it. "Stay with me tonight?" He said.

Eden's facial expression softened with compassion. "Of course, my love. I'll stay."

NINE

Trick, Tock, and Tick returned in failure to Rob's house in order to report back to their master. Trick was the first to enter Rob's room, carrying his severed arm which was already shriveling and turning gray. He was followed closely by Tick and Tock who kept their eyes cast down toward the floor in embarrassment.

Maya was still sitting in the same spot she was when they left on their Soulmind retrieval mission. "What the fresh hell is this?" Maya exclaimed when she saw the state of them. "Please tell me you got what you were sent for and didn't get seriously wounded for nothing." She eyed them judgmentally and with much disappointment, already knowing the gist of what they were about to tell her.

"The human was more formidable than we anticipated," Trick said, trying to justify why they had returned empty-handed. "This little fuckwad had two companions with him who also had the power. Oh yeah, he had an October too—a witch's familiar. And some little cunt with pink hair showed up just when we were about to win. We had them wrapped up in the Tethers and about to extract what we came for. This bitch had this huge spear thing. Chopped my fucking arm off, boss!"

Maya sighed and rubbed her forehead. "A girl with a spear, eh? I wonder who she is... I'd do this myself if I could, but I have to rely on idiots," she said, exasperated. "Come here." She motioned for Trick to approach her. He hesitated but then slowly closed the gap between them. Maya grabbed his severed limb and threw it into the corner of the room.

"Hey! I wanted to reattach that to my fucking elbow!" Trick yelled angrily.

"Shut up, you fucking moron!" Maya squeezed Trick's arm above where his elbow abruptly ended. The black ropes of the Dark Tethers began to grow out of Trick's stump. The dark energy tentacles morphed and mutated, forming themselves into the shape of the rest of his arm. As the black ropes solidified, they suddenly transformed into what looked like a mechanical arm made of red and blue wires; the skeleton and structure of the arm was shiny titanium. "There," Maya said as she let go of his arm. "Now you're part robot. It suits you."

"Thanks," Trick said as he flexed the fingers of his new hand. "I can crush some fucking skulls with this!" He brought his fist down on the desk behind Maya, splintering a huge hole through the weak wood.

"Be careful with that thing," Maya said, pushing Trick's arm away from her. "Go do some more bicep curls or something."

"Sorry, boss." He returned to his spot by the window to test the strength of his new bio-mechanical arm. Tock sat back down on the floor and Tick took the bed again.

Maya was thinking again; she needed a new plan. "Obviously what I've been trying to do isn't working. There has to be another way. There has to be. I just can't see it." She closed her black eyes and tried to call on all the shadowy spirits of the Dark Tethers to give her a vision of an alternate tactic which could work. "Show me another way," Maya whispered. "Show me the way."

* * *

Terry woke up the next morning feeling frustrated again that he couldn't remember having had any dreams. He wanted some more nighttime adventures, not just the ones occupying his waking hours. "Hey, babe, did you have any dreams last night?" Terry asked without opening his eyes. There was no answer to his question. "That was a seriously wild night. I really thought that was it, that I was gonna die. Thank the fucking gods that you showed up, Eden. How do you feel after all that?" Silence. "Babe?" Terry rolled over and opened his eyes to find the other half of his bed was empty. "Eden?" He looked around his room but she wasn't there either.

Terry went downstairs to find that Rob and Mothman had cleaned up the rubble as best they could and were now using duct tape and cardboard to cover the broken window. Remius was sitting on the counter that was still intact.

"Thanks, you guys," Terry said. They acknowledged him as he entered the kitchen. "You guys seen Eden this morning?"

"I think she left early," Rob answered. "I didn't actually see her go, but I heard someone leaving through the front door about five or six this morning." He shrugged and continued to put strips of duct tape along the edges of the cardboard.

"Why would she leave like that?" Terry wondered and looked at Remius who hadn't said a word; he still didn't say a word. Terry flipped open his cell phone and dialed Eden's number. It rang and rang and rang. There was a click and then, *"Hey, this is Eden. Leave a message."* Beep.

"Hey, Eden, this is Terry. I wasn't expecting you to leave so suddenly. Where did you have to go in such a hurry? When can I see you again? Call me back when you get this." Terry hung up the phone and returned it to his pocket.

Mothman and Rob finished taping up the window and then abruptly went to the fridge to rummage for something to eat. "You want some waffles?" Rob asked.

"Oh, hell yeah!" Mothman replied. "And what the hell is this—vegan sausages?"

"Those are actually pretty good," Terry said. "Cook some up, I'm starving. Are you guys gonna go to school today?"

Rob and Mothman exchanged a look and then started laughing hysterically. "That prison for brainwashing? Fuck that shit. You were right, Terry. Go back to some boring ass high school after what we just went through?"

"I knew you guys would see that eventually. You've really changed and matured—even in just a few days," Terry said.

"Remember when I was saying that to you?" Mothman asked.

"Oh, yeah," Terry agreed. "You were saying that to me weren't you, before I activated you?"

Mothman nodded. He opened the package of vegan sausages and threw them in a pan on the stove.

"You're very quiet over there," Terry indicated Remius. "Did Eden tell *you* where she was going or why?"

"How should I know where your girlfriend is?" Remius answered with a question of his own.

Terry sucked in air through his teeth and wagged a finger at the cat. "You're a cheeky bastard. Sometimes I don't know when to believe you or not."

Remius winked a green eye at Terry. "Have I ever steered you wrong before? Have I not taught you many wonderful things, and helped you out of tight and dangerous situations? Not by saving your ass, but helping to empower you to save yourself."

Terry sighed. "Yeah, you're right. I guess I don't have any reason to distrust you. Thank you for being here. I know I don't say that enough." He scratched under the cat's furry chin and then petted his head down to his back. Remius closed his eyes and purred against Terry's hand.

Rob set the plates out on the table and threw a couple waffles on each. Mothman threw a vegan sausage that landed in front of Remius on the counter. Remius sniffed at it and wrinkled his nose. "What is this bullshit?" He said and nudged it with his paw. The sausage rolled off the counter and plopped to the floor.

Terry grabbed a can of tuna from the refrigerator and peeled the top off with the metal tab. He set the can of fish in front of Remius. "Now that's more like it," the cat said contentedly and put his nose down into the can to nibble his food.

Rob, Mothman, and Terry sat down to eat their breakfast as well. "Should we be worried that those three guys are gonna come back and attack us again?" Mothman asked, taking a bite of waffle.

Remius answered, "They wouldn't be that stupid to strike again so soon. Seeing as how much you three put up a fight—and Eden with her spear." He lapped up more tuna into his mouth.

"And what about Maya?" Terry asked.

"Knowing her, she'll be pissed that they couldn't bring back part of your Soulmind, Terry." Rob responded. "But it won't be long till she comes up with a new plan."

Mothman spoke through a mouth full of food. "So are we just supposed to wait around here until they come to get you again? Or are we gonna do something ourselves? Maybe go after them before they come after us again."

All three looked to Remius for an answer.

"Lay low for now," the October assured them. "Practice what I showed you and harness your collective energies to get stronger and more powerful. Then the next course of action will reveal itself."

Eden never returned Terry's phone call, and she didn't answer when he tried to call her several more times. The next day he decided to just drive over to her apartment to see if she was there and just avoiding him. When Terry knocked on the door Kat answered. He was wearing only a long silky red robe with pictures of Chinese dragons on it.

"Hey, Kat," Terry said. "I don't know if you remember me. We met the other day when I was here seeing Eden. Is she here?"

Kat ran his fingers through his hair and tucked a few strands behind his ear. "No, she isn't," Kat answered, shaking his head. "I haven't seen her in a couple days."

"Oh," Terry said, disappointed. "If you see her will you ask her to give me a call."

"I will," Kat replied. He stood there for a moment checking Terry out. "Do you, uh, want to come in?" Kat smiled shyly.

Terry knew exactly what that invitation meant. "Oh, thanks. Not today, I'm not really in the mood. But... next time?"

"Okay," Kat smiled and bit his lip. "I'll hold you to that." Without warning he suddenly leaned forward and planted a kiss directly on Terry's lips. After the initial surprise, he leaned in and kissed Kat back. Then Terry pulled away after a few seconds.

"Do you know anywhere that Eden might be, or might be hanging out at? Some place I could check around for her?" Terry was desperate.

Kat thought about that briefly then said, "You could try The Leather Rose. That's an S&M club downtown. She sometimes likes to go to that spot. You could ask around for her there. Other than that, I don't know."

"Thanks," Terry said as he turned to leave.

"Hey," Kat yelled after him. "Come back and see me, cutie!" He winked at Terry and blew him a kiss before closing the door.

Over the next few days Terry kept calling Eden's cell phone with no luck. Even the times he showed up at her apartment again there was no answer at the door at all. Terry even checked in at The Leather Rose. There were a few leather daddies and a dominatrix or two, but none of them had seen or heard from Eden. *Where the fuck was she? Why had she abandoned him?* This was starting to feel more and more like a repeat of Jessica and Terry didn't like it one bit. The sadness he felt at having Eden's love and then it being ripped away from him quickly turned to anger.

A couple more days dragged by in her absence. Yes, Terry had his friends Rob and Mothman to keep him company, but it wasn't the same as having Eden. Sometimes Rob and Mothman would go out riding their bikes or to the pool hall to play and leave Terry by himself. He had Remius's company and support, but the October didn't seem to be that particularly sympathetic to Terry's pain.

A week went by and after seven days it seemed pretty obvious that Eden's disappearance was more permanent than Terry was hoping it would be. He felt the abandonment tearing at his heart, leaving him with a lingering pain in his chest. Rob and Mothman were out at the pool hall trying to pick up girls. Terry hadn't wanted to go with them; he was too consumed by the thoughts of Jessica's abandonment and now Eden's as well. His plan was to watch a movie to get his mind off of things, but he just wasn't in the mood for anything.

Remius yawned, laying next to Terry on the couch. Terry bit at his nail anxiously as he stared off into space. "Remius, why would she leave me? Why would she fucking leave me? Especially after she said she loved me." The tears welled up in his eyes.

"Maybe there's some lesson here that's important for you to learn," Remius said.

Terry started sobbing. "What? What fucking lesson?" He choked the words out through snot and tears. "The lesson that everyone I love is gonna fucking leave me? Abandon me? Traumatize me?"

Remius kneaded his paws on Terry's leg. "Maybe what you need to learn is to not be so attached. This wouldn't be so painful if you weren't so attached to these girls. You need to find a strong center within yourself. Love yourself even when you're alone. When you make your center someone else—Jessica or Eden—it throws you off balance, you forget yourself."

"I don't know how to do that," Terry whined. "I need their love to hold me up. I feel lost without it. I thought Eden would help me heal from losing Jessica, but this has all just made it worse. And I still want to be with Jessica too."

"That's your problem right there," Remius said, trying not to be too harsh. "Your motivation is for the women, or to gain love. Find the strength within you to do all things because it's naturally from and for yourself. You are your own foundation, your own authority. The Soulmind is to empower you, to be more yourself and become your highest individuality."

"Yeah, yeah," Terry waved away Remius words. "I know all that bullshit. That's not what I want to hear right now."

"I'm not here to tell you what you want to hear, but what you need to hear."

Suddenly Terry's phone rang and he answered it instantly. "Eden?" Terry said, holding his breath.

A man's voice spoke on the other end of the phone. "No. This is Dr. Tim."

"Oh," Terry said and sank into the couch discouraged. "What?"

"Well," Dr. Tim continued. "I haven't heard from you in a while and you haven't been back for any appointments. Are you okay? I'm concerned about you."

"Are you now?" Terry said sarcastically. A wicked look suddenly came into his eyes.

"Yes, I am. Can you come in for a session? I'd like to speak with you."

Terry choked on the maniacal laughter that started to bubble up in his throat. "Are you in your office right now?"

Remius gave Terry a stern look and shook his head. Terry put his finger up to his lips to keep the cat quiet.

"Yes, as a matter of fact, I am," Dr. Tim answered.

"Okay, I'm coming over to see you." Terry hung up the phone.

"Terry, no!" Remius intuited what Terry had in mind for the psychiatrist.

"Don't you fucking dare try to stop me," Terry said as he stood up off the couch. "I don't always have to listen to what you fucking tell me!" He grabbed his van keys and headed for the door. "And don't you try to follow me."

Remius kept quiet and stayed put, his whiskers twitching his disapproval.

Terry sped the whole way to Dr. Tim's office. Rage gripped him and all he could see was red. He parked, went inside, and caught the elevator up to Tim's floor. There was no one in the waiting area. Terry went straight into Tim's office and slammed the door behind him. Dr. Tim sat in a leather back chair going through some notes on a yellow pad. He looked up from his reading at Terry who had an expression of pure hatred painted on his face.

"Terry. That was fast. Come, relax, sit down," Dr. Tim motioned toward the therapy couch.

"No," Terry said and continued to stand in an aggressive stance.

"Excuse me?" Tim put the yellow pad down on the desk that was next to him.

"You know what's wrong with your profession?" Terry asked rhetorically. "Psychology and psychiatry have never helped even one person! All you do is drug people up and dumb them down, keeping them oblivious to their true nature and their true power! Self-realization doesn't come in a fucking pill bottle!"

"You—" Tim started but was cut off.

"Shut the fuck, bitch! I'm not finished. Out of all professions, the suicide rate among psychologists and psychiatrists is higher than any other line of work. I wonder why? The answers that people need can't be found in the insanity of the mind. Cause the mind is the sickness itself! You have to go beyond the mind—I'm still getting there. But that's something you can never fucking grasp." Terry took a breath. "You have to connect the mind to the soul to transcend the mind."

"You're manic," Dr. Tim responded. "You're not making sense. Let me call—"

"NO!" Terry lunged forward and pressed his thumb against Tim's forehead right between his eyebrows. The skin of Tim's head that was being touched by Terry began to turn red and let off steam from an intense heat concentrated on the pad of Terry's thumb. Dr. Tim yelled out in pain. "I now open your First Eye," Terry continued. "Which gives you the gift of uninhibited sight."

Terry pulled his hand away and the spot on Tim's forehead burned red-hot. He stared at Terry and began to see things as they truly were. He could see Terry's aura flashing white and wafting off of his body like flames. The white light of his Soul-mind also began to spiral out of his solar plexus. Tim's mouth hung open in disbelief, his eyes wide with shock.

"What is this?" The doctor screamed. "Who are you?"

Terry scoffed. "I'm the one you wish you'd never met!" The hilt of the machete popped out of the white current at Terry's solar plexus. He ripped it out, the blade of energy blazing brilliantly. Tim stuttered and sputtered but couldn't manage to get any words out. Terry pointed the machete at Tim's throat. "You're a professional bullshitter. You don't care about any of your patients. You get paid an obscene fortune to listen to their full of shit sob stories and then ask them how those things make them feel. Then you go home at night to your rich suburban house, your good little wife, and maybe a couple kids who will grow up to be complete douche bags. Those people you see are human beings, not just numbers in your check book. But I'm wasting my breath on you. Your days of being a windbag are over."

Terry decided to get it over with and not draw the one-sided discussion out any longer. Psychoanalysts always think they know everything; they're all unteachable and Terry knew this now as an infallible truth. Without hesitation he stabbed Dr. Tim through the heart all the way to the hilt of the machete. His eyes expressed the utter shock of the day not going at all the way he'd planned in his schedule. Dr. Tim's own death was not something he had put down on the calendar for the day. The final breath left his body and he died, blood pouring and squirting out of his chest like a broken water pump. Terry pulled the Soulmind blade from the body of Dr. Tim, and just for good measure, chopped his head off as well.

TEN
FROM THE MIND OF TERRY BROSWALD:

Finding Eden

I have forgotten how to dream
I have forgotten how to cry

However, this is my world, Forever
I have created it
And I can destroy it.
I have discovered
And I have lost.
Without Forever is something I will have to live in.
Eden has brought me into the lush landscape
Then spit me out like a fish without its bones.

You are Still and Perfect
You are Still and Forever

But I know now that underneath everything in the dirt
Is the Sun.
And beneath every dead shell is a spirit,
Wafting somewhere on the breeze as one consciousness.
And I still have to find it.
Always Chasing Amy.
It wasn't all in vain,
All withered like a weed without a gardener.
It wasn't all useless,
As I am laying here in invisible arms.

Touchness

Touchless

Toothless and decaying in the Garden
of Eden.
You are beautiful,
Not forever on this Earth,
But forever inside me.
Teach me your sins so that I can make them my own.

I shall walk,
In the Shadow,
In the Light of Inspiration Knowing.
You have dragged me here,
Kicking,
Screaming,
Hiding my Face,
Then Accepting.

Timecode my life.

Do I start at Zero or at One?
Eden is like a sky captured in time-lapse:
Wispy, white perfection slipping away on a blue darkening.
How did I find it in this wasteland
of ever-present float nothingness?
I did,
No Timecode inside that spectrum of solace.
No Burn-In with me without a shadow of space.
I did not have a Screener to show me
how this was going to turn out.

This is life,
Without metaphor, without fancy meaningless words.
Life.

To live in the present,
To aspire for the sky and the blue darkening into
something amazing,
Is Enough for me.
I'll gladly look for Eden for the rest of my life.

What shape do you hold?

The paper I am writing this poem on is wet and stained with my tears. I scream a primal scream as I crumple up the poem in a ball and hurl it across my bedroom. "Eden, where are you? Jessica, where are you?" I scream to the nothingness. "Fuck this! Fuck it all! What's the meaning of any of this?"

I grab a sharpie marker that's on my desk and triangulate my throat, putting the three dots in a triangle around my Adam's apple. Hopefully this will work this time. Light projects from each of the dots to form the triangular screen in front of me. "Show me Eden!" I command it. The triangle flickers and crackles. "I said, show me Eden!" I yell again. The static appears inside the triangle like a bad TV. "Fuck it," I say, giving up and letting it disappear back into my throat. "What's the point of life anyway?" I choke out the question through a sob.

Who am I? What am I? Am I fucking evil? I can't seem to find the purpose in any of this. I'm a fucking murderer, that much is for certain. Two people have been murdered by my hand—four if you count the two others that I killed and then brought back to life. Can I live with what I've done?

"Jessica, I'm coming..." I whisper to the silence and run out of my bedroom and down the stairs. Remius sits on the counter, very alert and attentive. I shoot him a dirty look. "Don't try to stop me. Just fuck off!"

The October watches me but makes no move and doesn't say a word. So I rush out the front door and take off running down the street. In a few minutes I make it to the bridge over the freeway—the one where Jessica chose to disappear from this Dimension. The sides of the bridge are made of stone and the ledge on top is only three or four inches thick. Tears still pouring down my cheeks, I make the commitment to leave this world. Without giving myself time to rethink what I'm doing, I climb up and stand on the ledge of the bridge. I wobble off balance for a moment, and then I jump.

BOOK THREE

The Tethered Toys Come Out to Play

"Whatever is rejected from the Self, appears in the world as an Event."

- Carl Jung

PART 9

Switchback

"If you want to become mature, you have to become a very very skillful murderer. Unless you kill a few persons you will never become mature. You have to kill your parents, you have to kill your teachers, you have to kill your leaders. They are all clamoring inside you, and they don't allow you to become a grown-up person—they go on keeping you childish. They make you a dependent, they don't allow you independence."

- OSHO, *Maturity*

ELEVEN

Jim Barcelona was the CEO of a very successful Chicago-based news broadcast corporation. Every morning he would ride the Metra train to Union Station with his leather briefcase and wearing a freshly dry-cleaned black suit. Jim was in his early forties and considered himself on the young side to have amassed the wealth that he had. He kept himself in good shape, going to the gym everyday. And he kept himself well groomed; his hair closely cropped and his auburn beard full but controlled. Jim was a handsome man by anyone's standards. As he watched the landscape pass by outside the train window, he drummed his fingers on the surface of his briefcase absentmindedly. The rich CEO was blissfully unaware of the specter which sat on the seat next to him. This ghostly entity sniffed at the man's energy, sensing the dark shadow within.

It was cold in downtown Chicago when Jim departed the train, and there was a light dusting of snow on the sidewalk. The specter followed close behind as Jim took in the brisk air of the city. His destination was Tribune Tower where he had been working virtually all of his adult life. Jim's breath puffed from his mouth in warm white vapor. The specter hovered close to his back sniffing deeply, enjoying the scent of the *sinister* that lurked below his well-kept demeanor.

Jim Barcelona approached the entrance to Tribune Tower. Some strange feeling made him stop abruptly. As he did so the specter following him closely slipped into him, taking possession. Jim felt a chill and shook it off as the winter wind. Walking inside, he waved to the receptionist and security guards as he did everyday, making his way to the elevators. He hit the up arrow and with a *ding* the elevator doors slid open. The ascension of the elevator was all the way to the thirty-sixth floor where his office was.

"Good morning, Susan," Jim said and smiled at the woman who sat at the main desk as he exited the elevator.

"Good morning, Jim," Susan replied. "Do you need anything, sir? Coffee?"

"I'm okay, Susan. I'll page you if I need anything." Jim gave Susan a thumbs-up and continued to his office. The interior of his large top floor CEO office was just as one would suspect. The carpet was dark maroon, and the walls were cherry wood paneling. There were bookshelves, sculptures, and modern art on the walls. A huge desk resided in front of the back wall which wasn't a wall at all—three floor-to-ceiling windows that looked down on Chicago.

Jim closed his door and sat behind his desk. He felt strange—like he was slightly drunk but with a fire of power growing inside. Raising his hand in front of his eyes, Jim could *see* the strength pulsing in his veins and muscles like a river. He swiveled in his chair and looked out of his thirty-sixth floor window at the skyline. As Jim surveyed what he now perceived as all part of his domain, he felt like he was king of the city—fuck that, king of the *world*.

"I'm fucking rich and powerful!" He pontificated to the empty room. "Millions of people watch what I tell them to watch. They think what I tell them to think. And they pay me to do it." Thinking about this absurdity, Jim laughed at the irony of his position. He could feel heat building up in his loins.

Pressing the intercom button on the phone, he spoke to Susan at the front desk. "Susan?"

"Yes, sir?" She replied.

"Can you send in my secretary?"

"Right away, sir."

Jim let go of the button and anticipated the presence of a woman who was his subservient. He rubbed his crotch through his $5,000 suit pants, already feeling the blood warming and swelling his member.

His secretary, Wendy, entered the office.

"Close the door behind you," Jim commanded. Wendy obeyed without saying a word. She was petite, skinny, and blonde; and was wearing a gray dress skirt that ended at her knees and a blue long-sleeve button-up shirt. The shirt was tight enough to show off her breasts which she always kept in a push-up bra. "Come," Jim said and motioned with his fingers for her to approach his desk.

As Wendy stepped up to the front of Jim's desk, he slowly stood from his chair. She suddenly looked nervous, but also silently knew what was expected of her. Looking down she saw the bulge in Jim's pants and also the fire burning behind his eyes. He circled around the desk and approached her from behind. Wendy was quiet and didn't move. Her ass was a nice shape that filled out her skirt.

"Now, don't make a sound. No matter what I do to you," Jim whispered, getting close enough to Wendy's ear that he could lick it. "Or I will kill you. And I will get away with it. Have no doubt about that."

Without warning Jim grabbed Wendy by the hair and slammed her face down onto the top of the desk. She wanted to cry out but bit her tongue as blood began to gush from her nose. Jim ran his hand down her neck and her spine all the way to her waist. Wendy stayed bent over, making no move to resist. Then Jim pulled her skirt up, revealing her ass and the black panties that she was wearing. He pulled down the panties and exposed the pretty slit of her cunt to the air. Her sex was pink and meaty between her legs. Jim slid two fingers inside and was surprised to find that she was already lubricating. Wendy tried to stifle a moan, making it as quiet as she could.

He pulled his fingers out of her and licked them. Then Jim slowly unbuckled his belt and unzipped his fly. He was fully erect now and his cock throbbed to be inside the whore he had bleeding on his desk. Wendy knew what was coming next; her pussy was ready for his cock. Instead of penetrating her wet cunt, Jim suddenly, violently entered her asshole with no lube to wet the friction. It took all she could not to cry out. The secretary bit her lip and groaned as the thick cock stretched out her sensitive tight orifice. The friction of the entrance had ripped her and now a small amount of blood seeped from the rim of her anus. With the presence of the blood creating a bit of lubrication, Jim thrusted in and out of her, his hands gripping the sides of her thin waist. Each time he thrusted, he went the whole length of his cock deep inside of her; his balls smacking Wendy's outer labia each time.

Jim's eyes shot open and they had gone completely white—no pupil and no iris. He roared like a demon. Fire leaked from his nostrils and through his teeth out of the corners of his mouth. At this point Wendy was almost losing consciousness, separated from what was happening to her body. The red-hot dick pulsed inside her rectum and she could feel the tingling of him building to an ejaculation. The specter possessing Jim's body now replicated itself and hitched a ride on the semen that was being ejaculated into his secretary's orifice. He moaned as six loads were pumped from his cock into her tight sexy ass. When Jim was done busting his nut, he stayed inside Wendy for a few seconds, all of him up to the base of his penis. Then he pulled out, a small amount of semen dripped down Wendy's leg as her dilated hole shrank back to its original size. She breathed heavily onto the desk, her breath spreading the pool of blood.

From behind she could hear Jim zipping up his pants and buckling his belt again. He slicked his hair back with his hand, making sure it was in its proper place. Wendy timidly pulled her panties back up and her skirt back down over her raw ass. There was a tissue box on the desk. She grabbed a few to wipe her bloody nose. Pushing the wad of tissues to her nose with her right hand, Wendy's wedding ring glinted in the light streaming through the window.

"Now you must carry this entity with you," Jim commanded her. His eyes were still completely white. "Hold it inside you like a disease. And pass it to your husband and your children. This is your task and you will obey."

"I will," Wendy said succinctly and with conviction. She threw the bloody tissues in the wastebasket and left the office the way she had come.

As Jim sat back down behind the huge oak desk, his eyes returned to normal.

TWELVE

As Terry fell toward the the speeding traffic below him he thought, *This is it, I'm really gonna die this time.* As death became more of a certainty, his fall seemed to slow to a speed almost imperceptible. He thought his life would flash before his eyes, but it didn't. When he was about halfway to the street below, he heard a familiar voice coming from above.

"Terry?" It was a woman's voice calling out for him.

Eden? At the moment Terry realized it was Eden's voice, his fall was halted and he floated midway between the bridge above and the street below. A shining sphere of light popped out from Terry's heart and enclosed his whole body. And within that, around his whole body head to foot, a star tetrahedron formed from the energy of his Soulmind. Terry looked up and a familiar face with a pink head of hair peeked over the side of the bridge.

"Ah! Terry! What in the actual fuck?" Eden exclaimed at seeing Terry suspended in midair above the cars moving at high speeds. "You weren't trying to kill yourself, were you?"

Terry struggled to move, but it was like he was in zero gravity with nothing to push off of. "Actually, as a matter of fact, I was," Terry admitted.

"You stupid fuck!" Eden shook her head. "I should have known you'd try something like this."

"What's that supposed to mean?" Terry yelled up at her. "Wait till I get up there, I'll kick your ass for leaving!"

"I'm sorry! I'll explain everything." Eden looked genuinely remorseful. "Just get back up here."

"How?" Terry asked, struggling again to move himself and the star tetrahedron around his body.

Eden shrugged. "I don't know. Just visualize yourself floating up and then back over onto the bridge."

Terry closed his eyes and focused on visualizing the movement. He felt his body ascending and opened his eyes. "Holy shit! It's working!" Terry's head was up now, his body vertical, and the star tetrahedron was carrying him like a vehicle up toward the bridge above. Floating slowly, his head and shoulders cleared the ledge. Eden watched him nervously as he levitated up and over the side of the bridge then brought himself down to land softly on the sidewalk in front of her. The sphere of light and star tetrahedron disappeared into Terry's body again. Eden hugged Terry so tight he almost couldn't breathe.

"Oh my god," she said, breathing a sigh of relief. "I thought I'd lost you for good."

"What the fuck you mean?" Terry asked, not hugging Eden back as she squeezed him. "I thought I'd lost *you* for good."

Eden took her arms from around Terry and looked at him with tears in her eyes. "I know. I'm so sorry," she admitted. "It wasn't my idea. I swear to God."

Terry furrowed his brow. "What are you talking about? Not your idea? Who's idea was it then?"

She hesitated for a moment as if not sure if she should answer. Then finally she said, "It was Remius. He woke me up when you were sleeping and told me to leave and stay away for at least a week. Something about you learning not to be so attached…"

Terry's mouth hung open in disbelief. "I can't believe it! That asshole! I'm totally gonna kill him!" He started to stomp off back toward his house.

"Terry, wait!" Eden ran after him. "I didn't want to do it. He insisted."

"I'm a fucking idiot," Terry huffed under his breath. "That furry bastard is manipulating me."

"I gotta admit," Eden continued. "I don't really understand what's going on with you guys—you, your friends, and that cat. I've only just recently come into your life."

"Yeah, well, welcome to the party." Terry gave Eden a sardonic smile. He fell silent for a minute then asked, "Where were you anyway?"

"I was staying at my friend's club in Boystown."

"Hmm, Kat told me to check around at Leather Rose but he didn't mention a club in Boystown."

"Yeah," Eden said in response. "I've never taken him to the one in Boystown."

Terry picked up his pace, creating a gap between him and Eden. She had to jog to catch back up with him. "That fucking cat better have a good explanation for all this bullshit," Terry grumbled quietly.

"If I had known you were gonna try to kill yourself..." Eden started.

Terry stopped and turned around to look her in the eye. "You'd what? You would have told Remius *no*? Told him that you weren't going to pretend like you'd ghosted me?"

"Fuck, Terry, I'm so so sorry. It's not everyday that I talk to a magical fucking talking cat. You know how hard it is to say no to something that a magical creature tells you to do? It'd be like getting a mission from a leprechaun or a fairy and then saying: *nah, I'm too busy to retrieve that magical golden coin from Medusa's lair.* I don't know, it's like he had this sort of psychic ability to persuade me against my own intuition."

Terry laughed flatly and then sighed. "Yeah, I know. I can't blame you, I guess. But just remember from now on that you don't have to do everything he says. It took me a while to get to that point myself. Even though he can be annoying sometimes."

Eden trailed behind him as they reached the house. Terry threw the front door open and went to confront Remius. The October was sitting on the counter where Terry had left him. Eden closed the front door and followed Terry into the kitchen.

"Hey, you're alive! I knew you'd make it," Remius said, smiling his ambiguous smile.

Terry exploded. "Suck my asshole, you felonious feline fuckface!" He jabbed his finger at the cat as he yelled.

Remius laughed heartily. "That's funny. I haven't heard that one before. That was some good alliteration."

"How can you be laughing about this?" Terry continued, exasperated. "Eden told me everything. How long have you been manipulating me? I almost fucking died. And it's *your* fault!"

Remius suddenly got serious. "Did I push you off that bridge? Or did you choose to go there of your own volition and jump?"

Terry couldn't find a response to that. "I...I...I...Fuck you, bitch!"

"That's the best you got?"

"I hate you," Terry responded.

"That's fair," Remius admitted. "I did set some events into motion, I won't lie to you. Tell me, how did you survive? Something changed within you, didn't it?"

Terry hesitated for a moment. Now, for the first time, actually feeling how his energy had changed. He felt transformed, but he didn't know how. Terry felt lighter, elevated. "Yeah," he said slowly. "I halted in midair somehow. Halfway between the bridge and the highway below. Some kind of energy sphere appeared around my body—and a three-dimensional Star of David. Or something."

"I needed a catalyst to help you activate your Merkabah since you weren't getting it on your own," Remius said.

"My what?"

"Your Merkabah. It's the human lightbody. And it's not three-dimensional, it's Pan-Dimensional."

Eden just stood there silently, listening to the conversation between Terry and the October. She could understand some of what they were talking about, but most was a mystery to her.

Terry sighed, obviously exhausted from being so angry. "You could have just told me about this Merkabah or whatever. And helped me activate it."

Remius shook his head. "I couldn't. You needed to discover it on your own." The cat smiled. "Now you've escaped death a few times. Doesn't that make you feel powerful?"

Terry shrugged his shoulders resignedly. "I don't know. Now I have mixed feelings about this. For some reason I'm not able to stay mad at you for very long. In a way that's just as infuriating."

Remius grinned a fang-filled smile. "You know you love me. There are times to hate the Master and there are times to love the Master. I'm not here to make you like me. I'm here in order to give you an experience of your Soul and help you to grow spiritually and dimensionally."

Terry went into the living room and flopped his body on the couch like dead weight. Eden sat down next to him and snuggled up to him, wrapping him in her arms. "All your stupid 'lessons' are taking a toll on me. What's the point of teaching me all this stuff if I end up dead anyway?"

"You ever consider the possibility that you can't die?"

Terry stared at the cat with a blank expression on his face. "No."

Remius licked his paw and then continued. "Well, at least we were able to activate your Merkabah. I'll be teaching you the meditation so you know how to rotate it and program it. As far as learning to not be so attached... I guess we're gonna have to work on that one a little bit more."

Terry threw a pillow from the couch at Remius. The cat continued to groom himself as the pillow narrowly missed his furry body by a few inches.

THIRTEEN

Arash Khan awoke in a fancy bedroom. He was disoriented, confused, and had no idea where he was. The bed he woke up in was huge with a canopy over his head. The drapes were white and beautiful; the sheets were silk. As Arash looked around the room, he thought it looked like something that would be in a palace in India. There were Persian rugs on the floor and a sheepskin in one corner. The wooden bookshelf was filled with large rare books; most written by hand. There was an altar in the East corner with large crystals, burning incense, and a large statue of Ganesh. The paintings on the walls were of other Indian deities. Light streamed in from one large window.

Am I dreaming? Arash thought to himself. He yawned and stretched his arms above his head, extending his spine. Throwing the silk sheets off of his body, Arash stood up and walked to the window. There seemed to be no way to open it, but it looked down on a gorgeous view of a large garden with a pond in the center. Arash turned around to look for a door. There was one on the wall opposite the bed. He assumed it led out somewhere.

He went over and tried the doorknob. It was locked, of course. How could he have thought it would be easy for him to just walk out of here? Wherever *here* was. Arash tried to remember the events that preceded waking up in this strange room. The memories seemed to be fuzzy. They were only coming to him in bits and pictures. *That's right*, he thought. *The Public Works building. That's how this all started. Fuck, that* was *my idea, wasn't it?*

"Think, dammit!" He said out loud. Arash closed his eyes and racked his brain, trying to shake loose a sense of how he got here. There was a vision that appeared in his mind's eye. The vision was of a steak on a plate. There was a chicken fetus on top of it and was oozing with egg yolk and blood. Then another flash of an image entered Arash's mind: Rob and himself in a cage. It changed suddenly and his vision was himself being thrown violently onto a table by many women. Then he heard in his memory a female voice saying, *"He is to be trained."*

Arash was abruptly pulled out of his remembrance by a knocking at the door and then it opening. He looked up from where he was sitting on the edge of the bed. Walking into the room was the woman with the puffy blue hair like a lion's mane. She wore a white cotton dress which made her aura shine radiantly. Arash backed away nervously.

"It's okay. I'm not here to hurt you," the woman assured him. "My name is Leeah. I am the high priestess of the Order of the Transcendent. The Mahan Tantric. May I sit down?"

Arash swallowed hard and didn't say anything. Leeah sat down next to him on the bed. Arash eyed her anxiously, tensely. "I'm sorry if we scared you before," Leeah continued. "But we had to be sure, you see. To make sure you were the right one." She paused and looked around the room. "I hope you find the accommodations up to your standards."

"Yeah," Arash said slowly. "This is very nice. The garden outside is beautiful... But I don't appreciate being locked in a room, no matter how nice it is. Makes me feel like a prisoner."

"I assure you, you're not a prisoner," she tried to convince him. "That was just a precaution. We couldn't have you trying to run away before we could explain how special you are."

"What are you talking about?" Arash asked skeptically. "I'm not special."

"You see, at any one time there can only be one living Mahan Tantric—the high priestess of our Order. And before the Mahan Tantric chooses to leave this incarnation, they must choose a successor to transfer the position to after their soul leaves for a higher plane."

"What are you saying?"

"What I'm saying, Lord Khan, is that I want to mentor you to take my place as Mahan Tantric. This is my last incarnation on this plane of reality and I will be ascending to a realm beyond this level," Leeah explained.

"And what if I refuse?" Arash asked.

"Trust me, you don't want to choose that option."

"So, I pretty much don't have a choice."

"You have free will, don't get me wrong. You always have the choice. I'm just telling you the right choice. Because if you pick the wrong choice... Well, let's just say you wouldn't want to surrender to fate instead of your higher destiny." Leeah smiled at him with a meditative depth in her gaze.

Arash understood what she was trying to tell him. "I get it," he said. "And what's with that 'Lord Khan' business?"

"You are a powerful god, my Lord. You just aren't aware of the depth of your strength yet. As you will be my disciple—my devotee—our Transference may be, shall we say, so powerful it will be apocalyptic. This is your destiny."

"Okay, Leeah, high priestess of the Order. I will be your disciple," Arash agreed. "I don't know if this is all a dream. But if it is, might as well dream the best dream I can."

"That's the spirit," Leeah laughed and the blue mane around her head shook with the movement.

"Is this still the Public Works building?" Arash asked, looking out the window to the garden below.

"Same space, different Dimension," Leeah replied. "So even if you decide you want to try to escape, you won't be able to Travel back to the Hollow Dimension unless I teach you how to shift yourself between the different levels of reality."

"Oh, okay." Arash was slowly accepting this new fantastical situation he found himself in. "I gotta admit this is a pretty nice place. The grounds are gorgeous. I hope you let me enjoy them. And inside this room at least is like a temple. It's like the Taj Mahal or something."

"All in good time you will be shown the whole Palace Temple and taught our ways. I'm glad the accommodations are pleasing to you." Leeah smiled warmly again and lightly laid her hand on Arash's back to show that she meant him only kindness.

"So when are we to get started with me becoming the next Mahan Tantric or whatever?"

"All in good time, my Lord. You don't want to rush into something of this magnitude so quickly. You must be prepped and initiated into our Order. Are you hungry?"

"Yeah, actually."

"Come," Leeah said, standing up and offering her hand. "I'll show you the grounds and then the feast to celebrate!"

FOURTEEN
FROM THE MIND OF TERRY BROSWALD:

I wake up in my own bed, the light of morning streaming in through the window. The cool air of my room is chilly on my naked skin. Eden and I had a night of passionate lovemaking. Needless to say, I was ravenous for her after the week of separation. Turning over under the covers, I expect to see the smooth skin of her body laying next to me. To my surprise and dismay I find that I'm alone again. I sit, bolting upright in the bed. "What the fuck? She left me again!" I scream to the empty room.

Why am I getting a feeling that I'm completely alone in this house? I can't feel the presence of Mothman, or Rob, or even Remius. Getting out of bed, I pull on a pair of boxers and a t-shirt. "Remius! Remius!" I yell toward my open bedroom door. There's no answer from the rest of the house. Peeking out of my room, I glance across the landing at the top of the stairs toward the closed doors of my parents' bedroom. The window perpendicular to their room is cracked open and a cold winter breeze blows the curtains like a attention-seeking ghost. Shivering, I go and slide the window shut, trapping the cold outside where it belongs.

I note that the guest room is empty; no sign of Mothman or Rob. Then I look down into the living room from the top of the stairs. "Remius?" I call out again. He's not on the couch. Or anywhere I can see for that matter. So I descend the stairs feeling strange; like this is my house and *not* my house. It's surreal somehow; like I shifted timelines and didn't know it.

What I see when I get to the kitchen forces me to stop in my tracks and assess whether I'm hallucinating—or maybe I died in my sleep. My parents are there! Mom is busy-bodying around the kitchen cooking with a smile on her face and she's humming some indecipherable tune. My father is sitting at the kitchen table reading a newspaper. My mouth is suddenly dry and I take a couple swallows trying to bring the saliva back so I can manage to formulate some words to say to these two whom I thought were dead and gone.

"Oh, Terry, good morning!" Mom says with a huge grin. I have never seen her this happy—or smiling for that matter. She's mixing batter in a bowl. "I'm making you a special breakfast. Chocolate chip pancakes, bacon, and grapefruit! I know it's your favorite. Nothing is too good for my favorite son!" Mom starts spooning the batter out onto the frying pan.

I cough and clear my throat. "Mom?" I manage to say. "Are...are you feeling all right? Have you been eating more Vicodin than usual?"

My mother laughs at the joke which isn't really a joke. "Oh, silly," she says. "You're so funny. Always joking around. I've never felt better!"

I glance over and my dad looks at me over the top of his newspaper. "Hey, son! Come sit over here with your old dad." Reluctantly I go over and sit down across the table from him. He continues, "You know, I don't tell you enough just how proud I am of you. How much I love you, Terry. You're a special kid and both your mom and I are so lucky that you're our son."

I almost choke on nothing. "What the FUCK is going on here? Are you two on drugs? This has gotta be hell... It's gotta be." I shake my head violently to try to rid myself of this insane vision. When I open my eyes, they are still there grinning at me. "Aren't you two dead?" I ask, not really expecting to get any answer. "Am I dead too and now we're trapped here together forever?" All the blood drains from my face at this prospect and I swallow hard, trying to get rid of the knot in my throat.

My mother and father laugh good-naturedly as if that's supposed to answer my questions. Mom puts a plate down in front of me with a stack of *twenty fucking pancakes*. The stack reaches taller than my head. She puts another plate down next to me that's covered with what looks like at least five pounds of bacon. And then finally the grapefruit—and I should have expected that it is the size of my whole head.

"Don't you miss us, sweetie?" Mom asks me after putting the giant grapefruit down.

I scoff. "Miss you? Miss you? You never fucking cooked me breakfast like this. Dad, you never sat down with me man to man to have a conversation with me like I was your equal. What is this bullshit?"

My dad smiles without his eyes. "But, son, we're here now."

"Are you really?" I ask.

My mother shakes her head. "No, not really."

"I should have known," I say to myself. "Since I hadn't been dreaming at all, the feel of a dream isn't as familiar to me anymore. But that's what this is, isn't it?"

"But don't you want us back?" It is my mom's voice but it sounds distant and echoey, like she's underwater.

Before I can answer the question, the giant grapefruit opens up like a mouth full of rabid teeth, lunges at me, and devours my face.

FIFTEEN

Terry's whole body jerked, bringing his consciousness back to the waking world. It took him a few minutes to adjust back to reality from the weird dream about his parents.

"You okay, babe?" Eden asked. She was laying naked next to Terry in bed. "Bad dream?" Eden yawned and stretched her arms above her head, cracking her back as she did so.

Terry turned over and was elated to see that Eden was actually still there next to him like she was when they fell asleep cuddling against each other. She smiled at him, eyes wide and as blue as a clear sky. "Yeah," Terry said. "Weird fucking dream about my parents. My mom was cooking for me, making me chocolate chip pancakes and bacon. And my dad was at the kitchen table reading a newspaper. Strange. My mom never cooked me breakfast. In reality she always seemed to be pilled-out and basically catatonic in front of the television. And I've *never* seen my dad read a newspaper... Then this giant grapefruit ate my face and I woke up."

Eden gave him a weird look and cracked up. "Pfff! A grapefruit ate your face? Now that is fucking wacky. Speaking of your parents though, where are they? Come to think of it, I haven't seen them at all. Or heard you talk about them for that matter."

"They're...umm," Terry started. "They're dead. They're not here anymore."

Eden looked confused. "Okay... So, they're gone or are they dead?"

"Both," Terry answered.

"What?"

Terry shook his head and rubbed the sleep out of his eyes. "It's a long story. Let's just say they're out of the picture. Gone for good... I think."

"Did you kill them?" Eden asked without any judgment in her voice.

Terry was shocked. "NO! Of course I didn't kill them!"

Eden shrugged. "Chill out. I was just asking." She leaned over and started making out with Terry. Kissing his lips then slipping her tongue into his mouth. After a couple strokes of the tongue, Terry pulled away.

"I'm gonna go brush my teeth," he said. "I'll be right back."

"Okay. I'll be waiting." Eden slid her hand down her abdomen to between her legs and started rubbing her clit as Terry got out of bed to go to the bathroom. He passed by the guest room which was next to his bedroom and perpendicular to the bathroom. The door was open and Terry could see Rob and Mothman asleep in the bed together.

Terry shook his head and chuckled. "Lazy faggots." He went into the bathroom, and without closing the door, brushed his teeth and took a piss. Terry returned to the room where Eden was playing with her nipple with one hand and her clitoris with the other. He was getting hard watching her touch herself.

"Come here," Eden commanded. "Quickie? Let's cum together."

Terry was already naked and semi-erect. She didn't have to ask him twice. He crawled under the covers next to her. Eden grabbed Terry's hand and slid his fingers inside her then she started stroking him to a full erection. They moaned and kissed using their tongues as they jerked each other off. Terry fingered her hard, hitting the g-spot as she yelped with pleasure. He pulled his fingers out and rubbed her clit with the tip of his penis. The wetness of Eden's pussy flowed over the head of Terry's cock and down his shaft. As he rubbed her clit with his thumb, Terry slid his hard dick into her tight cunt. As he thrust deep inside her, he could feel the orgasm building rapidly.

Eden threw the covers off of them so that their naked bodies were exposed to the cool air of the room. They were both on their sides, thrusting their pelvises together, moans steadily increasing in volume. Rainbow colors danced in their auras and mingled together like a convergence of star systems. Eden intercepted Terry's hand that was on her clitoris and took over, rubbing herself vigorously. "Ah! Ah! Ah!" Her cries of pleasure built in pitch louder and louder. "Are you gonna cum soon? Cause I'm almost there!"

"Yeah," Terry said, breathing heavily. "Oh, fuck! Oh my god, it feels so good inside you!"

"I want you to cum on my stomach," Eden said, her face red from getting fucked so hard. "Fucking bust your load all over me, baby!"

Terry pulled out suddenly and Eden rolled over onto her back, squeezing her tits and playing with her little pink nipples. "Oh my god!" Terry moaned and a stream of ejaculate shot out into her navel. A few more pumps of jiz streaked Eden's sternum and across her breasts. She screamed with ecstasy and then her whole body collapsed on the bed, totally relaxed.

"Fuck, I came so hard," Eden said with a satisfied smile. She played with Terry's still-erect cock. There was a sudden din of laughter behind them. Terry craned his neck to look and there was Rob and Mothman standing in the doorway watching the sex show. Mothman was holding a Hi8 camera and was still filming the erotic scene in front of him.

"What the fuck, you guys!" Terry yelled and threw a pillow at Mothman. It hit him in the head and bounced off. "Fuck off!"

"Okay, okay," Mothman said, turning the camera off. "Nice work, bro, tappin' that ass!" Mothman gave Terry a wink and a thumb's up as he and Rob left the room, closing the door behind them.

Terry flopped back down on his back on the bed. They both started laughing at the absurdity of the situation. "Those guys," Terry said.

"They could watch next time," Eden suggested. "Or join in. I wouldn't mind."

"Really? That might be fun. You'd be up for that?"

She nodded. "Yeah, definitely I'm up for it! We're polyamorous, remember? And I can tell one of those two is your lover also. I picked up that vibe." Eden winked at Terry.

"Really?" Terry asked. "You could pick that up just from our energy? Okay, then tell me which one of those two is my lover."

Eden felt out the energy for a moment. "The one who was holding the video camera. What's his name?"

"Mothman."

"Yeah, that one!"

Terry was dumbfounded.

"Am I right?" Eden asked, excited.

"Yeah, actually you are. How the fuck...did you know that?" He asked, surprised.

Eden shrugged her shoulders. "I just have a knack for feeling out these things. I can feel the connection if two people have shared energy like that. I'm sure you could be able to intuit that as well if you developed that skill."

"Yeah," Terry said as if far away in thought. "Maybe that's another Soulmind power I haven't unlocked yet..." He turned his head and Eden was smiling devilishly at him. "What? What is it?" He said.

She giggled. "You want to clean up your mess?" Eden indicated the semen all over her torso.

Terry leaned over. "You're a naughty girl," he said as he leaned down to lick his own fluid off of her belly and tits.

"That's so hot, babe." She said as his tongue licked all over her body. "You have no idea how much that turns me on!"

Terry slurped the cum out of Eden's navel. She cracked up and playfully pushed his head away. "Hey, Eden?" He said.

"Yeah?"

"You remember before when I asked you if you'd physically traveled to any other Dimensions?" Terry asked. Eden nodded and he continued, "You said you hadn't, but you *had* Astral Traveled. Astral Projected or whatever... Would you show me? I want to learn how!"

"Okay. Here, you lay on your back on the bed. I'll stand on the floor so I can watch and guide you." She slid her legs off the side of the bed and stood up beside it facing Terry. "Close your eyes." Terry closed his eyes. He saw spinning patterns behind his eyelids; Metatron's Cube and the Flower of Life. "Now visualize, if you would," Eden continued, "a rope dropping down from the ceiling. The end reaches just above your sternum, close enough that you can grab it."

Terry projected the rope from his third eye and saw the end hovering just above his chest. "I see it," he said. "It's there."

"Good. You have a very vivid imagination and ability to visualize. That's going to serve you very well," Eden said, excited. "Now, your Astral Body is one of your energy or light bodies. What you want to do is pull the arms of your Astral Body out of your physical arms and grab hold of the rope."

Terry focused on what he was supposed to do. He could feel his consciousness pressing to break free of his physical form. Suddenly after a moment of intense concentration, a pair of semi-translucent arms pulled from his flesh. Waving his Astral hands in front of his face, Terry could visually see them in his mind's eye. Then he grasped the end of the rope hanging from the ceiling. "I did it!" He exclaimed. "I have the rope! Now what?"

"Pull yourself out of your body." Eden was watching him and could actually see all of this visually because that was one of the abilities her Soulmind gave her. She could see the rope and the arms of Terry's Astral Body trying to pull itself free of the physical. He struggled with the rope; his Astral Body seemed like it didn't want to detach from its abode with the physical dwelling.

Terry pulled and pulled, trying to get a higher grasp on the rope. Then he projected the word *release* across his third eye and suddenly he was loose. He climbed hand over hand and pulled his whole Astral Body from his physical body. His consciousness was separated now. There was a silver cord coming out of the chest of his Astral Body and stretched to connect to the heart within his unconscious physical form. Terry looked at Eden who stared back at him, seeing everything. He was hovering above his body, holding on to the rope. "Holy shit!" Terry said, looking down at his new form and the body below him. "I look like a fucking ghost. Now what do we do?"

With a gasp Eden pulled her Astral Body out and her physical body dropped limply to the floor. She hovered, feet above the ground and same silver cord attaching her consciousness to the physical form. "Had no idea that you could do this, did you?" Eden smiled. Terry shook his semi-transparent head. "Let's go!"

She grabbed Terry's Astral hand and they flew up towards the ceiling. They passed right through the solid matter and up and out of the roof of the house. The two lovers paused for a moment as they hovered above Terry's house, gazing in awe at this perspective of the neighborhood. "This is amazing!" Terry said, almost overwhelmed by the experience.

"Isn't it?" Eden agreed. "Haven't you always wanted to be able to fly? Maybe sometimes you have in your dreams. This is real, and you can go anywhere, explore anything, without restrictions. Like an angelic being."

Terry looked down on the houses, the street, and the sidewalks. There was a light dusting of snow making everything shimmer with a brilliant white gleam. In his Astral Body, he couldn't feel the cold at all. "I can fly," he said, barely able to contain his enthusiasm. "I can fucking fly!"

Eden squeezed his hand. "You want to go higher, love?"

"We can?" Terry asked.

"You ain't seen nothing yet!" Eden took control and guided them up higher into the sky. As they ascended, Terry's house got smaller and smaller. His whole suburb got smaller and smaller. At one point, just before they reached the clouds, they could see the entire city of Chicago in the distance. The skyscrapers were shimmering like diamonds, a giant metal toy created as a child's playground. Terry pointed at it in the distance, a smile of delight on his face. Then they flew through the clouds. They climbed up, up, up. A huge commercial jet careened past them as they gained altitude. Ascending through every layer of the atmosphere, Illinois was now a tiny patch far below.

"Are we going to be able to get back?" Terry asked, getting a little nervous going this far above the Earth. The stars were above, the clouds below.

"Trust me," Eden assured him. "Haven't you ever wanted to be an astronaut?"

"Yes, actually I did."

"Well, now's your chance!"

Terry and Eden finally broke through Earth's atmosphere and they both looked back in wonder at the blue planet below them. "It's so fucking beautiful," Terry said, Astral tears coming to his eyes. "That's our home! It's a miracle. I never really appreciated our Mother very much before. I took for granted how nature takes care of us and how magical our planet actually is."

"I know, right?" Eden agreed. "From this perspective our Earth is heaven. I don't understand why so many people want to turn it into hell…"

Then Terry looked up and all around at the sparkling stars and the vast voidness and darkness of space. It was so enormous. He wondered how many lifetimes it would take for him to explore all of it—every planet, every star system. "Where are we going?" He asked.

Eden pointed away from the Earth—the finger pointing at the Moon. "We go to Luna!"

"To the Moon! We are real astronauts!"

Eden smiled as they began to fly again. "We're psychonauts."

"What's that?" Terry asked.

"We explore all realms of consciousness and the Soul. We are mystics. Welcome to Mystery School!" Eden winked at Terry as they flew closer and closer toward the Moon.

"What's that?" Terry asked. They stopped halfway between the Earth and the Moon.

"What? What is it?" Eden looked around, scanning space and the stars.

"Down there, toward the Earth." Terry pointed.

"I don't see anything," Eden admitted. "Wait... What is that?" There was a small dot coming through the Earth's atmosphere and getting larger, as if it was propelling toward them.

"Maybe a rocket?" Terry said. "NASA could be launching something today."

Eden squinted as the object grew larger and larger as it came closer. Now they could make out that it was red in color and was being propelled by some kind of rocket thrusters. Whatever it was broke through the Earth's atmosphere and approached them at speed. The object zoomed past Eden and Terry and off into deep space. They only managed to get a blurry glimpse of it and then all they could see were the flames from its thrusters as it disappeared toward the sea of stars.

Eden looked at Terry with her mouth hanging open. "Was that a fucking van?"

Terry burst out laughing. "That's totally what it looked like. A red conversion van or something. With rocket thrusters attached to the back."

Eden couldn't contain herself and fell into a fit of laughter at the ridiculousness of what they had just witnessed. "Oh my god," she said, catching her breath from laughing so hard. "You never know the crazy stuff that you're gonna see out here."

"I can see that," Terry agreed. "A fucking van flying off into the depths of space. You don't see that every day. I'm definitely gonna wonder about that now."

"Some mysteries don't ever get solved," Eden said, looking off into the distance where the van had flown away. "We just have to appreciate the craziness of Existence and try not to think about it too much." She laughed again. "If I tried to figure out all the things that I've seen and experienced, I'd go totally nutty."

They began flying again, making their way toward the Moon. Terry was excited. This was even beyond some of the journeys he'd taken into the Dreamsphere. Hand in Astral hand they touched down on the surface of the Moon. The landscape was barren, gray, and rocky. Everything was completely still and silent. There were large craters and mountainous areas in the distance.

Terry began bouncing up and down from the ground into the air like an astronaut. "This is one small step for man," he joked, imitating a radio voice. "But it's one giant leap for a woman!" Terry laughed.

"Hey! You dick!" Eden said, pretending to be offended, but smiling nonetheless. The silver cords attached to their heart centers still trailed them, out into space and back down toward the Earth where they came from.

Terry looked around in every direction. "Where's that stupid American flag the guys who landed here set up?" He asked.

Eden shrugged. "I don't know actually. I've Astral Traveled up here several times and have never seen a flag anywhere."

"Strange... What's that?" Terry pointed off into the distance at a smooth black object.

"What?" Eden followed where he was pointing with her gaze. "The Black Pyramid?"

"There's a fucking pyramid on the Moon?"

"Yeah," she answered. "It's completely smooth on all sides. Come, I'll show you."

They went over to the pyramid, traveling with a mixture of walking and floating. When they were a few feet away from it they both stopped to admire the structure. The Black Pyramid was about the size of a house and there were no visible entrances on any of the sides. The black stone it was constructed from was completely smooth. "You don't think it's weird that there's a pyramid on the Moon?" Terry said.

"I don't know," Eden replied honestly. "I hadn't really thought about it that much."

"Hadn't thought about it that much?" Terry scoffed. "I'd be obsessing over this all the time! You never thought to mention to me that there's a *Black fucking Pyramid* on the surface of the Moon?"

"What do you mean? You think that would be something I would just bring up randomly in a conversation? 'Oh, hey, by the way, there's this pyramid on the Moon. Seems like something we should explore.' How would that *ever* come up organically in a discussion?"

"Okay, okay, I see your point," Terry conceded the issue and turned his attention back to the structure in front of them. "You ever been inside this thing?"

"Of course I went inside. I was curious about it too. It's just some weird room in there; seems totally useless."

"But no Moon men?" Terry asked with a serious face. "Never seen any Moon men in there? Or on the surface here?"

"Really? Moon men? Seriously?" Eden said sarcastically. When she realized Terry wasn't joking she answered, "No, I haven't ever seen any *Moon men*."

"Okay, I was just checking. Don't act like it's such a crazy question given the scope of all the different Dimensions we have access to with our Soulminds." He winked at Eden and floated through the side of the pyramid and into the chamber within.

"Hey, wait for me!" She called after him and slipped through the black stone herself. Inside it was pitch dark and neither one of them could see anything at all. "Terry, are you there?" Eden called out into the void.

"Yeah, I'm here," Terry answered. "Hold on, let me try this... Let there be light!"

Suddenly the inner chamber of the pyramid was illuminated by the light of four lit flames. The room was a cube and there was one torch mounted on each of the walls. Terry looked around at the space they were in. Each wall was covered with a plethora of strange hieroglyphics. The floor was checkered black and white like a chess board. And the ceiling was covered with some sort of black foam that Terry couldn't identify. In the exact center of the chamber was an empty sarcophagus. The stone lid was off and leaning against the side at an angle. Terry walked over and peeked inside. Eden watched him curiously. The space in the sarcophagus was large enough for a man to lay down comfortably. There was also some sort of black sand lining the bottom.

"Whoa," Terry exclaimed. "This place is just... *Wow!*"

"It is something, isn't it?"

"Do you feel that?" He asked, grabbing Eden's hand and pulling her closer to the side of the stone sarcophagus. "The energy around this is much stronger. There's some sort of pulse coming off of that sand in the bottom there. And can you hear that tone, that vibration?"

Eden stood there quietly and tried to feel what Terry was describing. Suddenly she felt the pulse like a heartbeat coming from inside the sarcophagus and stretching around it in an auric sphere. Then she heard it—a low vibrational tone of *aaaauuuhhhhh* buzzing the entire chamber. Eden could feel the tone resonating in her chest. When she opened her eyes Terry was climbing into the sarcophagus and laid on his back staring up at the ceiling.

"I feel it," she said, grasping the edge of the stone. "This is some powerful energy in here. Be careful in that thing, you don't know what it was designed for."

"Don't worry, my love. We're together. Don't be afraid." Terry felt a cyclone force of spiraling energy originate in his chest. It burst out of his solar plexus in bright showers of white light. As he stared at the ceiling, it dissolved and the vastness of space could be seen beyond it. Terry watched as if it was an IMAX movie at the planetarium. Galaxies, stars, nebulas, and black holes raced across the blackness of space. It was like he was watching Creation taking place at rapid speed. Stars exploded, planets were born, and whole solar systems were sucked into black holes and reincarnated on the other side of the fabric of space. He just stared in awe, feeling as if he was made of these celestial bodies, dying and being reborn on a cosmic scale. Then all the heavenly bodies of light converged, making a shining spiral stretching up into infinity. All of a sudden Terry felt like he was being pulled from below, that he was going to be sucked through the bottom of the sarcophagus and into an unknown realm. "Eden!" Terry yelled, unable to pull himself free of the force sucking him down. "I'm being pulled! It's trying to take me somewhere!"

"Don't let it take you!" Eden yelled back, panic in her voice. "You don't know if you'd be able to come back out again!"

"Help!" Terry managed to squeak out in spite of the tremendous force dragging him. Instinctively Eden reached down and grabbed his hand, trying to pull him out and free of the current. Her pink and red Soulmind immediately came to her aid, spiraling out of her chest and connecting to Terry's, pulling him up. With the combined power connected through Tantric embrace, the powerful grip pulling Terry down loosened and was severed. He was pulled up and out over the side of the sarcophagus. They embraced, both auras becoming one electromagnetic dance of white, red, and pink.

"I thought I was going to lose you there for a second. You'd be taken somewhere where I couldn't follow," Eden said with relief.

"I love you so much," Terry said, Astral forms hugging each other tightly. "Thanks for pulling me out."

"Of course, babe," Eden reassured him that she always had his back in dangerous situations. "Let's go."

Terry agreed and hand in hand they slid back through the wall of the pyramid out to the surface of the Moon. They danced, hand in hand, bouncing high into the air off of the ground. Spinning and flipping together, they were two psychonauts performing an Astral Tango of Souls. They both laughed with euphoric ecstasy, elated to be connecting with each other in this strange and transcendent way.

As they spun, silver cords trailing in a spiral around them, Terry and Eden floated farther and farther away from the Moon and back towards the blue planet they had come from. In a cosmic lovers' embrace, they streaked through the void, stars twinkling in the distance. Careening on a collision course toward Earth, the two felt again as if they melted into each other, becoming one entity—more powerful than the sum of their parts.

Finally they broke through the upper atmosphere. Through the clouds the continents of North and South America could be seen; small at first then rapidly becoming larger. Down through the clouds, then the outline of the shape of Illinois came into view below them. Terry didn't know if they were moving at the speed of sound, or the speed of light, but within seconds there was the whole of Chicago and surrounding suburbs, then just his town growing quickly in their vision. As the roof of Terry's house appeared below them, their descent slowed immediately and they halted, hovering above the house.

"That was some ride!" Terry said, trying to catch his consciousness up with the whole trip.

"You like it?" Eden smiled at her lover. "It's fun, right?"

"That was insanely cool!"

They floated slowly through the roof and back into Terry's bedroom. As they both came through the ceiling, they looked down at their unconscious physical bodies—Terry's on the bed and Eden's on the floor. The silver cords pulled at them and they re-entered their naked physical forms. Both of them gasped, drinking in oxygen as their Astral Bodies merged again with their flesh and bone.

Eden stood up from the floor and flopped down next to Terry on the bed. He sat up, smiled at her, and flexed his arms and hands to see if he had full control over his physicality again. "That was amazing, Eden!" Terry said, grinning at her. "Let's do it again!"

SIXTEEN

As Wendy, Jim Barcelona's secretary, drove home to her house in Wheaton, she felt the presence of the entity inside her. She was now host to a Dark Passenger. The specter had taken control of Wendy's body and mind. She was still conscious, but her shadow had been awakened and was now the dominant force within her. Wendy's eyes were bloodshot and the corners of her mouth twitched with the strain of her nervous system. She knew she had to pass on the sickness to her husband and sons. There was a limited amount of specters and this was the only way to create a pandemic of possession.

Wendy pulled into her garage when she arrived home to her expensive home in Wheaton. Her husband, Ted, was waiting to greet her as she entered. He was in his early forties, tall, with short brown hair, and a clean shaven face. Ted was also in decent shape since he watched what he ate and got sufficient exercise. These were things that Wendy insisted upon if he wanted to continue having sex with her. She smiled and kissed her husband on the lips as she came into the kitchen. The lights were low and it was already dark outside.

"Hey, honey," Ted said. "How was work?"

"It was fine," Wendy replied. She looked at the kitchen and the dining room table which was set for two. Ted had cooked dinner; salmon and greens with glasses of red wine. "What's all this? You made dinner?"

"Yes, dear," Ted answered. "Thought I'd do somethings special for my beautiful wife." He smiled and kissed her again.

"The twins are in bed?" She said.

"Yes, they're fast asleep."

"Good," Wendy said and gave Ted a seductive smile. "Then we can have some fun." She pushed her body against his, Ted's buttocks pressing against the kitchen counter. Wendy ravenously began making out with her husband. She was all tongues and saliva. Ted met her enthusiasm with the same vigor. She bit his lip, drawing blood.

"Ow!" Ted pulled his face away and put his finger to his lip. When he pulled it away there was blood on his fingertip. "Jeez, babe. You're kinky tonight."

She laughed wickedly. "I know you like it."

"I won't say I dislike it," Ted admitted. "Kinda turns me on actually." He started making out with her again and slid his hands down to fondle her ass. Wendy grinded her crotch against him as he unzipped her skirt and pulled it all the way down. She kicked it away across the floor. As Ted worked to pull her panties off too, Wendy's pussy was already dripping with desire. In a second her panties were gone and across the floor as well. She moaned loudly as he fingered her hard against her g-spot.

"Oh my god! I'm so wet!" Wendy groaned with ecstasy and a torrent of vaginal secretion squirted out of her all over Ted's hand. She could feel him hard now against her through his pants. Ted unzipped himself with one hand, freeing his throbbing cock from the fabric over it. He stroked himself as he continued fingering his wife. "Suck my clit!"

"What was that?" Ted asked. He was too busy rubbing one out on himself.

Wendy pulled his hair and licked the side of his face. She nibbled on his earlobe and then whispered in his ear, "Suck my fucking clit."

Before he had time to acquiesce or refuse, she pushed him down by the top of his head and smashed his face in between her legs. Ted sucked on his wife's clitoris and flicked his tongue in and out of her cunt. Her juices flowed into his mouth and down his chin like honey. He could barely breath from how hard she was pressing him into her crotch. Wendy's head tilted back and as she closed her eyes, the long and loud moan escaping from her lips became a low growl. When her eyes opened again they were pure white, and her teeth grew into sharp points. Green mucus coated her teeth and dripped from her lips.

She roared and smoke came from her nostrils and mouth. "I'm gonna cum in your fucking mouth, you worthless piece of slave shit!" There was a mixture of a roar and loud yelp of pleasure as the orgasm tore through her body with electric tremors. As she did so, the specter possessing her duplicated itself and entered into the fluid excreting from her pussy. At the exact moment of orgasm, she squirted a large amount of cunt juice into her husband's mouth and down his throat. Ted choked but managed to swallow all of the fluid his wife ejaculated into his facial orifice. Before he could do anything, Wendy grabbed a fork from the counter in front of her and stabbed it into her husband's head. He fell in a heap on the floor, unconscious but not dead, his erection still pulsing between his legs. One squirt of ejaculate escaped from the tip of his cock.

Wendy's face was still demonic—eyes white and teeth pointed. She grabbed a wooden spoon from one of the drawers and headed for the room where her twin boys slept. They had just turned twelve and their mother still spanked them when they misbehaved. She had been raised that way and had no remorse bringing the spoon down on a child's tender flesh, even if they screamed and begged for her to stop.

Wendy had her work shirt on but was still naked from the waist down. The green mucus oozed from the corners of her mouth and wet excretion dripped down the inside of her thighs. She sort of stumbled drunkenly as she climbed the stairs toward her boys' bedroom, wooden spoon gripped in her right hand. Snarling and baring her teeth, Wendy approached the door. As she opened the door slowly, it creaked and light dripped in from the hallway. Her sons, Will and Ted Junior, slept in two twin beds, headboards against the left wall of the room. She slowly walked closer to the first bed, a guttural sound escaping from deep in her throat. Will's eyes fluttered open as his mother stood over him with the spoon raised.

The child screamed at seeing the sight of his mother: white vicious eyes, mouth and chin covered in green slime, and her dripping cunt exposed. Hearing his brother scream, Ted Junior also woke up and started screaming. "Mommy? No!" Will screamed and tried to crawl out of his bed to safety. Wendy was too quick. She grabbed the boy by the back of his neck and pinned him to the bed so he couldn't get away. Will squirmed and kicked his legs to no avail.

Ted Junior was about to bolt and make a run for it when his mother pointed the wooden spoon at him and bared her teeth. The boy froze and pissed himself, a wet puddle spreading out and soaking the bed under him. "Don't you fucking make a move, you little turd!" Wendy shrieked at him in a raspy demonic voice.

All Ted Junior could do was watch in horror as his mother pulled his brother's pajama pants down, exposing the smooth curve of his white ass. *Whack!* Will screamed in pain as the first blow was dealt to his sensitive butt cheek. A red mark was already puckering up. Wendy kept the hits coming again and again and again. Her son sobbed as his ass became red and raw, blood even coming to the surface in some places where the wooden spoon had broken the skin. "No, mommy, please!" Will begged, now in excruciating pain. "What did I do for you to punish me?"

Wendy laughed, spraying green mucus on Will's back. "You were born, you little fucking waste of womb space. You piece of shit uterus destroyer!" She said, flipping him over so she could hover above his face. The boy closed his eyes and tried to cover his face as tears kept streaming down his cheeks. Wendy moved his arms and pinned them down by his sides. Then she hissed with her mouth open an inch from her son's face. The green mucus from her throat sprayed into Will's mouth, nose, and eyes. The fluid carried another duplicate of the specter inside it, infecting the boy as well. The ghost-like entity had replicated itself and jumped from Jim Barcelona, to Wendy, to her husband Ted, then to her son Will. The only one left in the house to infect was Ted Junior, who was currently trembling and trying to hide under his comforter.

Wendy left Will, who was now possessed, semi-conscious, and half-delirious with pain. She went over to Ted Junior's bed and threw the covers off and choked him so he couldn't squirm away. Raising the spoon, Wendy relished the terror on her son's face and then smacked the kitchen utensil across his cheek. The child cried out in pain and begged for mercy. "No! Mommy, no! I'm sorry! I didn't do it!"

Whack! Whack! Whack! Whack! She alternated cheeks, raining blows down across Ted Junior's face. He sputtered and coughed blood from his mouth. "You worthless piece of fetus shit!" Wendy shrieked, spitting mucus onto the boy's face. "I squirted you out, I should try to fucking shove you back inside, you little faggot! You're probably sucking your brother's dick every night and fucking each other. But you like that, you sick little fallopian shit. You're not even worth an egg sac!" Now she was close to Ted Junior's open mouth and expelling green mucus like a momma bird puking down her offspring's throat. He gagged and choked, trying to spit out the bile, but it was too late. The last possession in the house was complete. The boy's eyes rolled up in his head and he fell unconscious for a good night's sleep soaking in his own piss.

Wendy chuckled to herself, satisfied that she had accomplished what her boss, Jim Barcelona, had charged her with. She was still wet, and as she stumbled out of the twins' bedroom, she fingered her pussy, ready for another full body orgasm. Wendy's—and also the specter's—new violence fetish had been satiated for now.

***

Maya, as well as Trick, Tock, and Tick, had just been killing time in Rob's house. Or maybe time was killing them. Either way, Trick, Tock, and Tick were getting bored and antsy. They could only go so long without killing or bringing down some destruction. Maya was staring off into space, waiting for a vision.

Trick had given up doing his bicep curls for a while and was now sitting in the corner of the room. "Boss," he whined. "It's been days of nothing. We need to fucking break shit! Why are we waiting? We could attack that little fruitcake Terry again!"

Maya held up her hand to silence him. "Shut the fuck up! I'm getting a vision. Some guidance for what we should do next." An image started to take shape in her mind's eye. It looked like a boy around the same age as Terry. The boy was sitting, but the area around him was blurry in Maya's vision. "I see a boy," she said with her eyes closed. "He has black hair, a teenager's mustache, and tan skin. He looks Indian."

"A fucking featherhead is going to find a solution to our problem?" Tock asked.

"You're a fucking imbecile," Maya smacked Tock on the back of the head and then went back to focusing on her vision. "A fucking Indian—from *India*! You know, *dots not feathers*, you morons! Wait... The image is becoming clearer. He's sitting on a really fancy bed with a canopy and the room he's in is very chic. Fancy rugs, book shelf, statues and pictures of gods."

Maya focused on the Indian boy, trying desperately to decipher what the message of this vision was and how it could help them. Then she heard a voice in her head—it was a woman's voice and it said, *"Wait for him. He will come to your aid and carry the solution to your predicament."*

She opened her eyes and Trick, Tock, and Tick were staring at her expectantly. "We have to be patient," Maya said.

The three guys threw their hands up and sighed irritatedly. "How much more patient can we be?" Trick said as his face twitched. "It's been fucking days! Days! Might as well be a penis-sucking eternity when we can't go chop people into tiny bits."

"Chill the fuck out!" Maya ordered and they all hushed into silence, their protests crushed by their boss's intensity. "This boy is the answer. He will come here to find us, I'm sure of it. And it will be soon. I can't tell you exactly when, but it will be soon."

"Ahh! Goddamnit!" Trick yelled, his testosterone coursing through his blood like a river about to burst through a dam. "I can't take it anymore! We need to be out there destroying whole window-licking governments, splintering them into a million tiny worm fragments. Let us do something, boss, or our dicks won't go down! We need to fuck monkeys, crush skulls, and fucking cut open the stretch marks of society!"

"Okay! Enough!" Maya rubbed her eyelids as if she had a migraine. "You guys can be so annoying, you know that? Fine, just go out and fuck up the neighborhood. I don't care. Just do that to keep yourselves busy. And when I cross paths with this boy, we'll meet up again and continue our mission."

"How will you find us, boss?" Tock asked.

Maya scoffed at him. "Wherever there's destruction and chaos, that's where I'll find you."

SEVENTEEN
FROM THE MIND OF TERRY BROSWALD:

I find myself awake and alone in bed again. As I feel the energy, the familiarness of the surreality of the dream world becomes apparent. It feels good to be having dreams again, even though that first one with my parents was very strange and disconcerting. Is this one going to be a repeat of that? I really hope not. Already dressed, I get out of bed and walk to my bedroom door. There's a distinct sound of birds chirping as if they are inside the house. I discover that that's because the window in between mine and my parent's room is open again. The cold winter breeze blows the curtains as if some specter is trying to gain entrance into my sanctuary. I close the window and then go downstairs.

There they are again—my mom puttering around the kitchen cooking and my dad at the table reading a newspaper. *Seriously, what the fuck is this?*

"You guys are here again? Invading my dreams," I say as I approach them.

My mom looks hurt as she tosses a handful of bacon in the frying pan. "I don't know what this is about a dream," she says. "But we're your parents and we love you. We don't invade, or whatever it is you said."

I scoff at that. "Since when do you love me? You never gave a fuck before. Come to think of it, you never even showed an interest in my existence."

"Now how can you say that to your mother?" Dad says as he folds the newspaper and puts it down on the table. "She's cooking you your favorite breakfast: chocolate chip pancakes, grapefruit—"

"And bacon." I cut him off and finish the sentence. "Yeah, I know... Actually, fuck it. I'll play along." These two act nothing like my real parents did, so why not just play with them like they're different people? Maybe they are my *ideal* parents that I never had. So I sit down across the table from my dream dad.

"How's school been going?" Dad asks me.

"You know what, Dad, actually I've decided to drop out and pursue my own studies independently. How about that?" I say.

He smiles at me and replies, "That's great, son! I like your initiative. Taking control of your own life and learning the things you actually want to learn. That's enviable."

My mouth hangs open in disbelief. My real dad would never have been so agreeable. The voice of my non-dream dad's response rings in my head: *What do you mean you're dropping out? You're a worthless piece of shit! If you don't study in school and get good grades so you can get a decent job, you'll be out on the street. The way you're going, you'll end up a drug addict bum!*

I shiver and shake the thought from my mind. My mom comes over and sets a plate with twenty pancakes stacked on it in front of me. She smothers it with maple syrup and also puts the heaping plate of bacon next to it. Mom smiles down at me and puts her hand on my shoulder. It's creepily cold. "I know you miss us," she says. I don't respond so she continues. "You can bring us back, you know. We can be a family again. Everything can go back to normal. Back to the way it was."

In my mind I see the image of my real mom laying on the couch like a zombie watching *Dr. Phil*. She's high off her ass on pills. She mumbles at me, *Bring me my fucking Vicodin.*

I snap back to the moment and look up into my mother's smiling face. She looks like a mannequin with its smile painted on. I clear my throat. "What do you mean, bring you back?"

"Oh, you're smarter than that, son," Dad responds from across the table. "Your power. You can use it to bring us back to when before this all started. You can make this your reality, and all the rest will become the dream."

I don't know what to say to this. The thought and prospect of this strikes me as very strange and starts my mind down a rabbit hole of questioning whether what I think is my waking reality is really a dream, and this—what I'm experiencing now—is the real world. I shake my head again as if to fling the thought out of my mind. *Okay, Terry, take a breath.* I can't start thinking like that. I can't start questioning my own intuition, that would end up very bad.

Suddenly the house shakes and there is a loud thumping from outside. There's another thump and the house tremors again as if Godzilla is walking through my neighborhood. "What the fuck was that? An earthquake?" I ask to no one in particular. The violent shaking of the house had knocked over my large stack of pancakes and the other plates had fallen from their places and shattered on the wood floor.

"Was that you, honey?" My mom asks. "You're using your power to solidify us and bring our family back together! I knew you would come around!"

"No, no I'm not!" I spit out, looking around at the wreckage on the floor.

Mom looks disappointed at my answer. "But, sweetie, you must. You know it's the right thing to do. Forget all this Soulmind garbage and Dimension nonsense. Here is where you belong."

"What did you just say?" I ask, not sure if I heard all that correctly.

"What?" My mom plays dumb.

"Forget it," I say and get up out of my chair, leaving my two faux parents to see if I can find the cause of the house shaking. As I make my way to the front door, I start to see a large shape through the windows. Opening the front door, I rush out onto the porch. To my utter amazement, I see Sul—the dragon from Meddia! His huge green body is laying half on my front lawn and half out into the street. He smiles cheekily at me as if there's an inside joke that I'm not getting. "What the fuck are *you* doing here in my goddamn dream?" I yell, totally in shock that the ruler of the Octobers would visit me in my dreams. Standing on the porch, I raise my arms in a gesture that begs for answers.

Sul laughs a deep bellowing laugh. "You're funny. You crack me up, you know that?" The dragon says. Then he suddenly gets serious. "Don't put everything you've learned and worked for in jeopardy. If you choose to revert back, all your progress will be lost. You choose to exit now, all unsaved changes will be lost."

I shake my head in confusion. "What is it with you creatures speaking in riddles all the time? I don't know what you're getting at! Speak in fucking English!"

Sul sighs and flicks his tongue out against his sharp teeth. "Do you want to evolve?" He asks.

"Of course," I reply.

"You're an integral piece in the evolution of your planet. More than you can even realize at this point. Trust in your own authority and your own intuition above all else. You know deep down what is your true path. That path has chosen you. Either come into your higher destiny or be a victim of your fate."

"I feel like I've heard that somewhere before," I say, but I can't place exactly where I heard that or who said it to me.

"As your guardians, we can only guide you; show you the path. But it's you who must choose with your free will to walk that path," Sul admits. I can feel the deep compassion in this creature. He is giving me a charge but also trying to protect me—maybe even from myself. "You know what you must do, don't you?"

"I think I do now. They almost tempted me to question the quest and call it quits. Sometimes your mind tries to trick you into taking the easy way out," I say, breaking the spell my fake parents were trying to cast on me.

"To evolve you must move past them. If you allow them to dictate your actions—to have them clamoring in your mind whenever you make a decision—is to stay infantile, dependent. To truly ascend to the next level, you must cut all the tethers," Sul continues as he stands up onto all fours and swishes his tail from side to side like he's trying to swat away dream flies. He starts walking away and then stops for a moment. "Oh yeah, I almost forgot," Sul adds. "Don't be so hard on Remius. He's doing his best with you."

The dragon starts walking, stomping away and I go to follow him. As I step off the first step of the front porch, the ground shakes violently from the dragon's footsteps. I am knocked off balance, my foot slips out from under me, and I fall forward. Before I have time to break my fall, my head collides with the sidewalk and—

I wake up in my bed. Sweating and panting, I touch my body to make sure I'm really out of the Dreamsphere. Eden is already out of bed getting dressed. Now I *know* that I'm back in the waking world. Sitting up in the bed I ask, "You going somewhere?"

Eden comes over and kisses me on the lips. "I gotta go back to my apartment and take care of some stuff today." She replies.

"When can I see you again?" I ask.

"Don't worry," Eden reassures me since she did disappear for a whole week once already. "I'll be back later today or tomorrow."

She kisses me again. "Okay, babe. See you later," I say.

"I'll text you later," Eden adds as she grabs the rest of her things and leaves the room. I yawn and stretch, slowly waking up out of that strange dream. That was the second night I dreamt about my parents being alive. And then there was the dragon this time. I wonder what it means.

I'm naked as I slip out of bed and pick up a pair of boxers off the floor. I pull them on and a t-shirt as well. Remius taught me the meditation for the Merkabah yesterday. That's the meditation to activate and spin the living human lightbody. I decide to try it again right now. This is as good of a time as any. So I close my bedroom door so I won't be disturbed if Rob and Mothman decide to wake up and do stuff. I sit down on the floor, legs crossed and my back against the bed.

The Merkabah is a star tetrahedron that surrounds the whole body. It looks like a three-dimensional Star of David. The upper tetrahedron is the Sun Tetrahedron, and the lower tetrahedron is the Earth Tetrahedron. Closing my eyes I start the yogic breathing and visualization; I breathe in to fill the Sun Tetrahedron with bright white light, and exhale to bring the light into the Earth Tetrahedron. The breathing and visualizing are accompanied by different mudras. At the end of the exhale I hold my breath, focus my eyes up and in toward the third eye point and pulse the triangle in the middle of my chest down to the point of the Earth Tetrahedron. This action sends all negativity into the Earth.

The second part of the meditation is creating a sphere of light behind the navel. It's white light at first and grows with the breath. It expands until it gets to it's full size which is about one hand length in front of the navel and behind the navel. At this point the color changes from white to gold. I exhale out of my mouth and an energy sphere grows from the surface of the gold one and encloses my whole body. Taking a few breaths to stabilize this sphere, I focus on the energy coming from the two poles: through the top of my head and up from my perineum, and they meet at my navel point. Now I move the golden sphere from my navel and up to my heart center. Breathing deeply, I sink into the meditation and feel this new state of consciousness, which is a knowingness and experience of being connected to all life everywhere.

The third part of the meditation is to spin the Merkabah field so it can start working and programming itself. For a second I can't remember what Remius said to do at this point. I'm pretty sure that I need to rotate one tetrahedron to the left and one tetrahedron to the right. There's a specific ratio though. What was it? Fuck, I can't remember exactly what it is.

What I do remember is before I spin them, I do this one other thing. So I inhale deeply and blow out through my mouth; as I do, I visualize a large disc of energy expanding from an origin point at my root chakra—or perineum. *Or maybe I'm supposed to spin them first. Shit, I hope I'm doing this right.* I know that the tetrahedrons are supposed to spin at nine-tenths the speed of light. So I send the Sun Tetrahedron spinning off to the left, counterclockwise around my body; and I send the Earth Tetrahedron off to the right, clockwise around my body.

Something's not right. The energy is off in some way. I don't know how but it feels unstable. So I open my eyes for the possibility I might be able to see what's wrong. There's a bright white sphere of light around my body; it's shining and shimmering, spinning, but it's wobbling. *Oh, no.* Now I look around the room and it's tilting and warping like it's about to be sucked into a black hole. I try desperately to stabilize my Merkabah field but it's too late. My bedroom suddenly gets sucked away, the colors spiraling into a tiny point as if flushed down a drain.

Then new surroundings take shape around me. I'm standing upright now in a forest of redwood trees. What I see is not completely in focus, it's sort of blurry and washed out like I'm here and not here at the same time. My lightbody is still shining and wobbling, as if at any moment it could collapse, taking me into oblivion. There's an energy pulling my Merkabah deeper into the forest and I follow it to a circular clearing carpeted with green grass. There's someone meditating in the center of the grassy circle. I approach with caution.

As I get closer to the meditator, I start to recognize the form. The familiar long black hair, fair skin, and thin body. For a second I can't speak from the shock of seeing her again, then I yell out, "Jessica!"

Jessica's violet eyes slowly flutter open. At first it doesn't seem like she recognizes me inside the rotating ball of light, then finally recognition flashes across her face. "Terry!" Jessica exclaims. "I knew you were supposed to visit me today. Purely by accident of course."

"What do you mean?" I ask, confused.

"Your light field," Jessica points toward my wobbling Merkabah. "It's unstable. That's how you were able to travel here. Because your Merkabah is rotating incorrectly. I should have known it would take you a few tries to get the hang of it."

I'm dumbfounded. "How do you know about the Merkabah?" I ask.

"I've been learning the Craft from two wonderful people here," Jessica returns.

I look around at the surroundings; the trees that are still blurry to my vision. "Where exactly is *here*?"

"There's not much I can tell you at this moment. We don't have much time."

I scoff at this, not wanting to believe that I only have moments with the woman I love. "Come back with me, baby," I beg her.

Jessica shakes her head sadly. "I can't go with you... Not yet. You're here now because I need to give you a spell."

"A spell?" I say. "What kind of spell?"

She speaks slowly and deliberately. "This," she says. "Remember this: *What's done is done, until it is undone.*"

I repeat the spell back to her once. "*What's done is done, until it is undone.* What's that supposed to mean?"

Jessica stands up slowly to face me. We're only a few feet away from each other. I desperately want to hug her and kiss her. "We're almost out of time. You'll know when to use it." She holds her hands up in front of her chest, palms on either side of her heart. The purple tendrils of her Soulmind start to emanate from her solar plexus and create a sacred geometric figure between her hands. The shape is Metatron's Cube.

"What are you doing?" I ask, suddenly feeling fatigued and drained of energy.

She doesn't answer. Instead she says, "Through the Metatron Stargate I align you!" Jessica yells and suddenly shoots her hands out toward me. The Metatron's Cube made of her Soulmind spins and flies through the air. It collides with the white light of my Merkabah field, spitting off purple sparks through the circumference of the sphere. The geometric figure penetrates the sphere and then through my body, coming out my back in tendrils of purple light energy. Suddenly I feel my Sun Tetrahedron and Earth Tetrahedron lock together into a solid star tetrahedron and then I am pulled back through time and space. The image of Jessica gets smaller and smaller and disappears into darkness.

I am finally spat back out onto the floor of my bedroom like existential puke. After falling hard onto my back, I just lay there trying to catch my breath, the exhaustion laying claim to my body. The light of my Merkabah field flickers like a bad lightbulb and then goes out. "Fuck me, that was insane. At least I got to see Jessica again though." Even as I say this, the feeling of separation from her I had been trying to let go of now intensifies tenfold.

EIGHTEEN

It had been several days since Arash had begun training with the Order of the Transcendent to become the next Mahan Tantric. To his surprise, he found that he was able to slip into the role of disciple very easily. Arash Khan was beginning to feel like he'd been born for this work. At this moment he was walking through the rose garden reflecting on the past few days he'd spent at the Palace Temple. He wore all white; a long tunic and loose flowing pants. All his garments were made of pure organic cotton. The roses he now gazed upon, the Palace Temple—which did resemble the Taj Mahal from the outside, and all of the teachings he was receiving from the thirteen members of the Order were all things that had contributed to his sense of royalty. Arash had been utterly changed in a short period of time. He now carried himself upright, his head high, with the aura of a Prince of High Divinity. The memories of his previous life in the Hollow Dimension were now distant and hazy, almost completely disappeared, like a dream several minutes after awakening.

Leeah had been teaching the young *Lord Khan* all about the Spiralverse and the Dimensions within it. They were also beginning to teach him how to use his Soulmind to navigate through those Dimensions, Space, and Time. Arash still had a lot to learn, he couldn't become a master in only three days. The preliminaries of 'transforming his substance'—as Leeah called it—consisted of hours of the members of the Order chanting in a circle with Arash in the center. This process was to purify his energy and transform his body on a cellular level. Literally and totally, he was no more the Arash he once was.

As he was lost in thought amidst the roses, Arash failed to notice the presence of Rahjiah coming to meet him. Right as she approached, he finally registered that someone was there and looked in her direction.

Rahjiah bowed formally to him and said, "Your presence is requested in the Grand Hall, my Lord."

Arash bowed to her, acknowledging the Divinity in her as well. "As you wish," he replied.

Without another word spoken, Rahjiah turned back toward the Palace Temple with Arash following close behind her. Both of their white clothes blew around them in the breeze like ripples in the ocean of infinity. As they reached the large ornate door that was the entrance back into the Palace, Arash asked, "So, what is our main lesson for today?"

"You are to have another Auric Activation," Rahjiah replied, holding the door open for Arash to walk through. "We will be chanting to infrastructure this new program into your aura for specific powers you will be able to wield."

They walked in silence side by side into the Grand Hall. The other members of the Order were already configured in a circle and waiting for their forthcoming Mahan Tantric to take his place as the center. The Grand Hall resembled a huge ballroom. Sometimes there was a large round table with chairs around it in the room, but today it was empty, making room for the ritual about to be performed. High overhead was a crystal chandelier which hung from the ceiling.

The circle parted to allow Arash entrance to the inner energy of the circle, and then Rahjiah took her spot in the circumference as well. They all wore white; it was a sea of white. Their collective auras shone brightly like a trillion facets of a diamond. Closing their eyes, they all assumed prayer pose with their palms together in front of their hearts. All their voices were one chorus, completely in sync, chanting the mantra to connect to the Infinite Creative Consciousness: "*Ong Namo Guru Dev Namo...*" All members of the Order and Arash chanted this three times to set the energy.

They took a long deep breath and held a few moments of silence before beginning the main mantra for the Activation. The voices of all around the circle began to ring out as one instrument chanting, "*Ek Ong Kar, Sat Gur Prasad, Sat Gur Prasad, Ek Ong Kar...*" Now Arash was the only one who wasn't chanting. He stood in the center, eyes closed and arms at his side. He just soaked in the energy flowing toward him. The energy of Arash's yellow Soulmind expanded into his aura and began rippling with waves of electromagnetic energy. The white light energy of the collective aura of the Order flowed like a river into Arash's aura; charging it, feeding it, transforming it.

The Order of the Transcendent continued chanting the mantra over and over without missing a beat, in perfect time and with perfect reverence. Arash started to feel incredibly high, the vibration of his energetic frequency elevating beyond anything he had ever experienced before. He almost felt like he was leaving his body, merging with the sea of light, floating toward the ascended dreaming-land beyond this world.

"*Ek Ong Kar, Sat Gur Prasad, Sat Gur Prasad, Ek Ong Kar...*"

As the women of the Order continued their chanting unabated, the force of the energy pulled Arash off his feet into the air. He was now floating several inches above the floor. Behind his closed eyes, white light and every color spiraled around him. A pyramid of pure energy collided with his body from behind, and as it pushed through him, it morphed into a bright red oscillating Flower of Life which rotated off into the distance, bouncing around Arash's consciousness. His body continued to elevate through the space of the Grand Hall up toward the chandelier hanging from the ceiling. As the white energy from the Order fed into Arash's aura, it grew larger and larger, almost to the point that it filled the entire room.

"*Ek Ong Kar, Sat Gur Prasad, Sat Gur Prasad, Ek Ong Kar...*"

The crystal chandelier was coming closer and closer, till Arash was only inches away from it and he opened his eyes. Startled, he cried out softly and put his hands in front of his face to try to shield himself from the impact. Instead of colliding with it, the chandelier shook violently then imploded, collapsing in on itself and forming a black hole. Arash could see shimmering stars and planets on the other side of the black hole. And before he had a chance to react, he was sucked through into deep space...

"*Ek Ong Kar, Sat Gur Prasad, Sat Gur Prasad, Ek Ong Kar...*"

Arash could still hear the mantra being chanted as a distant echo, as if it was a lingering memory from a past lifetime. He was now floating in deep space—or he *was* deep space. Finding himself still aware of his surroundings, but not seeming to have a body, was a little disorienting at first. He was pure awareness in space. The planet Saturn was in his immediate vicinity and billions of stars shone an unfathomable distance away. Arash studied the rings of Saturn with his consciousness. There was a vibration—a hum—being emitted from them. They sang! They had a song. Arash felt as if he was melting into that song, and he was vibrating at the same frequency as the beautiful sound sung by those rings. The mantra being chanted for him by the Order entered his consciousness again; just an echo but there pulling him. The song of the mantra merged with the song of Saturn's Rings, and Arash found himself in a state of ecstasy and bliss he himself had never even dared to dream of.

Arash Khan wanted this moment to be his Eternity. He had surrendered into the ecstasy of the formless, and now that he had a taste of that, didn't wish to return to the world of form. Alas, he knew that he had to return. His work was not yet complete in that world. And as his thoughts turned to this truth, he could even feel the energy of the Order of the Transcendent pulling him back—and back to his body.

Before he was ready, Arash was pulled back through the black hole into the space of the Grand Hall. He gasped the oxygen into his lungs as the chandelier resumed its form above him. Still floating high in the air above the circle of women, their chanting penetrated him in perfect harmony.

"*Ek Ong Kar, Sat Gur Prasad, Sat Gur Prasad, Ek Ong Kar...*"

Their voices pulled him slowly back down through the air as if he was weightless on a cloud. Arash could still feel the sense of bliss he had touched near Saturn's Rings. His aura now actually was filling the entire space of the room. The yellow of his Soulmind and the white of the women's auras danced like psychedelic aurora borealis. As soon as Arash's feet touched down on the floor again, his eyes closed and the chanting ceased abruptly. The silence that followed was the loudest silence Arash had ever heard.

Suddenly he felt an intense heat climb up his spine and enter his brain in a shower of radiant golden light. The feeling was overwhelming. Arash's eyelids fluttered, his eyes rolled up, and just as his legs were about to give from under him, Leeah rushed forward to catch him as his body went limp. As she held Arash up from under his arms, she gave a silent signal to Rahjiah who left quickly and came back with a glass of water. Arash slowly came back into his body as Rahjiah put the glass up to his lips. "Drink," she said. "It will help bring your strength back."

Arash opened his eyes and acknowledged Rahjiah with a silent gaze. She tilted the glass against his lips and he drank gratefully. Once the water was finished, he was able to stand on his own. Leeah let go of her support on Arash's body, then she snapped her fingers and pointed. Without a word, the rest of the Order, all except Rahjiah and Leeah, bowed toward the center of the circle and then exited the room in a wave of white.

"How are you feeling?" Leeah asked.

Arash looked at her, shaky but able to hold his own. "I'm a little spaced-out, but other than that I feel... amazing, actually." He went over what he had just experienced in his mind and body, but had no words sufficient enough to describe what had taken place.

"Come, Lord Khan," Rahjiah took his arm and started leading him toward the door. "We'll go sit in the Rose Garden for a few minutes and then introduce you to your next lesson."

"What, there's more?" Arash joked. "That wasn't the core lesson for the day? Give me some time to integrate?"

Rahjiah smiled as they walked back out onto the grounds and toward the Rose Garden, leaving Leeah behind in the Grand Hall. "As the Mahan Tantric you must be prepared for many different tasks given in a single day. This is a great responsibility. You won't just be able to do one thing and then rest for the remainder of the day."

They sat down on a marble bench in the center of the Rose Garden. The rose bushes were in full bloom. They were all luscious and many different shades populated the garden; red roses, white roses, yellow roses, orange roses, green roses, blue roses, multicolored roses, and even black roses. "It's so beautiful here..." Arash murmured as he admired the landscape. "I never want to leave this place."

Rahjiah smiled with compassionate eyes. "It has its charm, doesn't it?" She looked at the beautiful blooms all around her and continued, "However, a Mahan Tantric's work is never done. Yes, you will spend a great deal of time here at the Palace Temple, but you will also be called to do many things throughout the Spiralverse. It is actually the highest position one can hold on Earth. You're very honored." Rahjiah put her arm around Arash's shoulders and then rubbed his back affectionately, the way a close friend would.

After a long moment of silence Arash asked, "Why me? Why now?"

Rahjiah shrugged. "I'm not entirely sure. The Spiralverse is very mysterious that way. Synchronizing events at just the right time. Your Soulmind had just recently become active and it drew you to the Public Works Building—you facilitated that whole adventure if I'm not mistaken. The position chose *you*. And we in the Order knew that Leeah has been thinking about leaving this incarnation for the higher planes. So we needed someone worthy to transfer the position to. You're a very powerful being."

"I am?"

"Yes, you are. And you have the pure potential and ability to stay in your neutral power and transcend beyond the duality."

Arash didn't bother to ask what that meant. He had already gotten a taste of it today when he became pure awareness in the presence of Saturn's Rings. "So what's this next lesson? I think I'm ready to give it a shot."

Rahjiah smiled and nodded. They stood up and walked deeper into the gardens. "Have you come in contact with your Soulmind weapon yet?" Rahjiah asked.

Arash shook his head. "What's that?"

"Everyone with a Soulmind has one that is unique to them," Rahjiah explained. "Part of the weapon is solid—the part you can hold on to—and the dangerous part is made from your Soulmind light. It is an energy weapon, originating from within you."

"What if I don't have one?" Arash asked.

"You do," Rahjiah assured him. "If you have a Soulmind, then you have a Soulmind weapon... Ah, here we are."

Arash looked up. They were standing on the outside of a ten-foot tall hedge carved into a circle. In front of them was the only gap in the hedge circle, which made room for a tall gate which was the only entrance inside. The area within the circle was empty and carpeted with soft green grass. There was enough room inside to run around without feeling crowded. "What's this?" Arash asked.

"This," Rahjiah answered, opening the gate and taking him inside, "is one of our Arenas." She closed the gate behind them. Arash craned his neck to stare toward the top of the hedge wall. It looked much taller from the inside.

Rahjiah stood in front of the gate, guarding the exit, and motioned for Arash to stand in the middle of the grass. He swallowed hard. "Why do I get the feeling I'm gonna have to fight something?" He asked with a sinking feeling in his stomach.

"You have very strong intuition, my Lord." Rahjiah responded. "You must do battle with the scourge from the Dark Tethers."

Arash started to get really nervous now but didn't want to show how scared he actually was. "I've never fought before," he squeaked. "I've never even been in a fight in my life."

"Just trust yourself and it will come naturally." Rahjiah started spinning her hands around each other, trails of blue light following her every move like erotic pixies. Then she started conjuring the spirit. "I split the temporary rift to the density of Dark Tethers," she incanted. A split began to open up in the air several feet in front of where Arash was standing. "Bring forth a specter of immense wickedness and trickery. I pull you one and one has been pulled!" Rahjiah made a fist with her right hand and pulled it back through the air. A dark shadowy shape emerged from the rift she had ripped in the fabric of Dimensions. Once it popped out, the split closed itself behind the specter.

The creature looked around, sniffing the air. It was a being of almost pure darkness; a shadow made flesh. But it wasn't even flesh since its form was semi-transparent. The creature was only about three feet tall and was squat, hunched over. To Arash it looked like the ghost of an evil leprechaun. "What the fuck is *that*?" He yelled in surprise at seeing this creature. The cry had drawn the specter's attention and it swiveled its head toward Arash and sniffed the air again.

"It's one type of specter from the Dimension of Dark Tethers," Rahjiah answered. "Destroy it!"

The specter made a lunge at Arash who narrowly dodged it and ran to the other side of the circle. "Destroy it? How the fuck am I supposed to do that?" At this point the danger of the situation had kicked on his adrenaline, which in turn was stirring up his energy. Arash's yellow aura blazed around him and tendrils of light began to spin out of his solar plexus. The creature made another attack and Arash avoided it by inches. He stumbled, almost tripping over his own feet as he tried to put distance between himself and that *thing*.

Then he felt something strange in his chest and all of a sudden a large bulky object popped out of his solar plexus. Arash looked down and it seemed huge to him. The thing was red and had two handles, one vertical at the base and one horizontal over the top. He grasped the vertical handle and pulled the weapon free from his chest. Now Arash could see what his Soulmind weapon resembled—a chainsaw. The long flat blade of the weapon was made of the yellow energy of his Soulmind. There were yellow spikes that spun like vortexes around the edge of the blade. However, there was no whirring sound like from a physical chainsaw.

Arash looked over at Rahjiah who still stood in front of the gate. "A chainsaw? Really?" He said, a little flabbergasted.

Rahjiah chuckled and shrugged her shoulders. The whole business with his Soulmind weapon emerging had temporarily distracted him, which gave a moment's advantage to the specter. It jumped into the air and swiped down at Arash with a black clawed hand. Arash lurched to the side and the specter smacked into the side of the hedge and bounced off of it a little disoriented. *This creature must be more dense than I thought*, Arash said to himself. *It's not like a ghost that can pass through solid matter.*

As the creature steadied and shook itself off, Arash took the time to ground himself in a fighting stance and brandished his weapon in front of him, right hand on the horizontal handle and left on the vertical. He sliced the blade down in front of him, lunging forward a bit and threatening the specter. Now the creature wasn't as quick to attack; it had to be more on the defensive at this point. Arash was more confident now that he had a way to defend himself, and his intuition was starting to kick in. He began to chase the creature around the Arena. It was a fast and spry little bastard, and it could jump incredibly high like a jackrabbit.

Arash started to get fatigued. He was wasting energy running after the specter; it was an inefficient tactic. So he stood in the center of the grass to catch his breath, and he swung the chainsaw around himself to keep the creature from making any sudden moves. He had to get it to stand still for more than one second at a time if he was going to kill it. Once he had this in his mind, Arash's Soulmind took over and did his bidding without even being asked. Tendrils of yellow energy braided together and grew from the top of his aura. The yellow rope of energy extended like a long arm and grabbed for the specter that was bouncing around the perimeter. It was fast—almost *too* fast. However, Arash had an advantage of being able to anticipate where the specter was going to bounce to next. He shot the braid of energy out a little ways in front of the creature and before it could change its trajectory, it had jumped into the stream of Arash's Soulmind.

The creature squirmed and wriggled as the tendrils of light constricted around it like vicious vines. It let out a shriek and continued to struggle in vain. The braid of Soulmind light, which was arcing over Arash's head, moved to bring the creature within reach of his blade. Without hesitation he sliced the specter in half. It's legs fell to the ground, kicking involuntarily and oozing black bile. He let the tendrils of light drop the other half as well. The creatures arms clawed at the ground as it shrieked and oozed from its upper half. After a few moments of struggling against its own death, it finally laid still.

Now Rahjiah spoke. "Back from whence it came!" She said and snapped her fingers. The rift opened back up momentarily and sucked both pieces of the specter back into the bowels of Dark Tethers. Then the rift sealed itself up as if nothing ever happened. Arash dropped his chainsaw to the ground. It changed into yellow energy and returned into his solar plexus. His aura also flickered and went back to being invisible. "Well done!" Rahjiah said with a huge grin on her face. "I didn't doubt you for a second!" She opened the gate again and Arash walked toward her to leave the Arena.

"That wasn't too hard," Arash said, putting a brave face on the insanity of the battle he just had to fight.

Rahjiah put her hand on his back and led him out of the Arena back into the gardens. "Well," she said. "We wouldn't want to start you off with something you couldn't handle."

"Yeah, totally. Right." Arash agreed, but he could still feel the sweat dripping down his face.

NINETEEN

Terry was still laying on his floor catching his breath from being spat back out into his bedroom. There was a knock at his door and then Mothman's voice from the other side. "Yo, Terry, you gotta come see this. Some crazy shit is going down! They're talking about it on the local news," he said, and then opened the door without asking if he could come in. Mothman looked down at Terry who was still only wearing a t-shirt and boxers. "Didn't feel like getting dressed today?" He joked. "What the fuck have you been doing up here all day?"

Terry slowly sat up and then stood up, feeling a bit wobbly. "Shut up, you dick," he said by way of reply. "I'll have you know I've been doing very important work. I was... meditating." He nodded and smoothed out his t-shirt.

Mothman laughed. "You do that with your left hand or your right hand?"

As Terry followed him out of the bedroom, he responded by saying, "Actually, I do that with both hands, thank you very much."

"I bet you do," Mothman busted out laughing again. They went into the living room where Rob was watching the TV intently. Remius was by his side on the couch. Mothman sat down and Terry sat next to him.

"So what's going on?" Terry asked. Rob was staring with an intense look on his face; jaw clenched and lips pursed. The volume on the TV was turned down low, but the image being broadcast was a reporter explaining what happened with destroyed houses in the background. The houses he could see in the frame had shattered windows, busted down doors, and one with its whole roof caved in.

"It's Rob's neighborhood," Mothman explained. "The reporter was saying that there's been a string of break-ins and destruction of property. He was also hinting that there might be people dead as well, but they're hesitant to report that right now. There's no suspects and no leads. And the people they've talked to that haven't had their houses fucked up say that they didn't see anything."

"It's them," Rob finally said. Terry and Mothman looked over at him, surprised that he spoke all of a sudden.

"Who?" Terry asked.

Rob clenched his jaw again. "Those three guys. The weird ones. The ones who attacked us trying to get at you, Terry."

They all thought about this. It made sense. If no one reported seeing anything, that would explain it. Rob continued, "They're getting bored, it looks like. Which tells me it's only a matter of time before they attack us again. I was hoping Maya and those three would get discouraged from trying to steal that part of your Soulmind and just give up and go back to Dark Tethers... Guess we wouldn't be so lucky." Rob looked anxious. He knew all those families in his neighborhood and the thought of those three terrorizing—and even killing them—turned his stomach.

"Okay, no more fucking around," Remius chimed in. "This is getting serious so it's about time Terry sets up a Protective Shield around this house that would ward off anything that might try to harm us."

"Do you want us to help?" Mothman asked.

Remius shook his head. "No, Terry can do it. You guys stay down here and keep watch. If you see anything suspicious or anyone tries to break in again, yell up for us and get your weapons ready... Terry, let's go up to your room and take care of this."

"Okay," Rob said. "We'll be here if you need anything. Holding down the fort." He gave a weak laugh and then fell silent.

Terry stood up and faced Mothman and Rob. "It is very important to protect this place. This is our Home Base. We need somewhere to be safe. We can't always be running and hiding."

Mothman nodded in recognition and solidarity. Remius jumped down off the couch and pranced over toward the stairs. Terry followed. As they walked up the stairs Remius said, "You fucked up the Merkabah meditation, didn't you?"

"What?" Terry said, surprised. "How did you know?"

"Psychic, remember?"

"Oh, yeah," Terry replied. "I don't know why I keep asking when I should know that."

"Where did you go?" Remius asked as they got to Terry's bedroom and closed the door.

"Wherever I went, I saw Jessica in a clearing in some forest."

"Well, that only happened because you rotated the Sun and Earth tetrahedrons *separately*. Luckily, whatever she did to you locked them back in place and sent you back here. You won't be able to do that again."

Terry was secretly disappointed by this. He wanted to be able to go visit Jessica again; now he knew that he couldn't. "So, wait, what exactly did I do wrong?"

Remius continued, "You forgot what I taught you. There are actually three *sets* of tetrahedrons around your body. That means three separate star tetrahedrons. One that rotates to the left, one that rotates to the right, and one that is stationary. Don't feel bad, you're not the only one who's made this mistake. And also the most important thing is to anchor the Merkabah field to your heart. Always to your heart."

"I think I got it," Terry said, hoping that he actually did get it and could remember the next time he tried to do the meditation by himself. "So how am I supposed to set up this Protective Shield?"

"You're going to do the Merkabah meditation and create a second one that you will program and anchor around the entire house," the October explained. "So, as you do the meditation and visualize your personal Merkabah, you also visualize the same thing happening to the surrogate Merkabah around this house. Sit down on the floor, your back against the bed, and close your eyes." Terry did as he was told. Remius sat down in front of him and continued, "Feel your prana tube that goes from your perineum up to the top of your head. Now set up one for the surrogate Merkabah. You'll want it to run through the center of the house, from the roof down to the foundation. Before we start, remember the most important thing. Connect to your heart, and feel this love for all life dancing through your aura."

Then Remius took Terry through the first part of the meditation; the yogic breathing, light going into the Sun Tetrahedron and then the Earth Tetrahedron, the mudras, and pulsing the triangle down to the tip of the Earth Tetrahedron. As Terry did all of this psychically, Remius was able to see it all visually. The cat could always see the energy of the human lightbody, and now Terry had that ability as well.

"The next part is to re-create spherical breathing. Visualize or sense the prana tube running through your body," Remius continued guiding the meditation. This second part of the meditation involved Terry creating a sphere of white light behind his navel. It started out the size of a grapefruit, and as he continued his yogic breathing, it grew to its full size which was one hand length in front of the navel and one hand length behind the navel. Continuing the breath, he changed the color from white to gold. On Remius's instruction, he blew out through his mouth. The golden sphere bulged to expand and then grew to encompass his whole body in a huge sphere of gold light. The small sphere was still contained within the large sphere. "This sphere is still unstable," Remius explained. "The next three breaths are to stabilize it."

Terry took the next three breaths and stabilized the sphere. The next instruction, which he carried out, was first to feel unconditional love in his heart. Then he moved the meeting point of the prana tube at his navel, as well as the small sphere, up to his chakra of Christ Consciousness, which is about two finger widths above the bottom of the sternum. The large sphere also moved up along with the smaller one. A wave of bliss washed over Terry and he just breathed from this new state of consciousness. He felt like he was surrounded by the presence of God, swimming in the oneness of the cosmic ocean.

Terry also remembered to visualize every step of the meditation in the surrogate Merkabah around his house as well. "Now as you sink into this new state of consciousness and breathe," the October continued. "Relax your hands into your lap, palms facing up, with the left on top of the right... Become aware of your entire star tetrahedron—all three of them. And as you inhale, say to yourself *equal speed.* One spins to the left, one to the right, and one stays stationary. Blow the breath out through your lips and they take off spinning. On the next inhale say to yourself, *34/21.* That's the ratio of the spinning of the two tetrahedrons. Exhale through the 'o' of your lips... They move from one-third the speed of light to two-thirds the speed of light. As this happens, the flat disk shoots out from the base of your spine fifty-five feet in diameter." Remius watched as Terry shot the disk out and its shape joined with the large sphere resembled a flying saucer around his body. It was slowly wobbling, still unstable. The next breath was to stabilize it. "Inhale and say to yourself, *nine-tenths the speed of light.*"

The speed of the rotation increased to nine-tenths the speed of light and stabilized Terry's Merkabah as well as the surrogate one around his house. Remius finished instructing him by saying, "This is the last breath. Make a small hole in your lips and blow out with pressure. You'll feel the speed take off. Blow out with force... You have just created the stable, living Merkabah field. Take a few minutes to relax and meditate... And program the surrogate Merkabah around the house with the instructions of protection. Just follow your intuition."

Terry breathed long and deep yogic breaths as he used his heart to send the instructions to the surrogate Merkabah. He meditated there for several minutes basking in the experience of unconditional love. Surprisingly, Terry even felt like Jessica was right there connected to him even though she was physically on a different plane of existence.

Terry lost track of how long he sat there meditating. It was like he was a dew drop that melted into the ocean. Or he was the dew drop and the ocean had melted into him. Night was descending outside and the pregnant clouds began to give birth to fat snowflakes. As the white began to thicken and pour down on the houses and streets below, Terry was jarred out of his trance by the sound of his cell phone ringing. He opened his eyes and saw the phone laying by a pile of clothes on the floor. Grabbing it, he looked at the caller ID. It was Eden. He quickly flipped it open and said, "Hey, you."

"Hey, babe," Eden replied on the other end of the line. "I know it's late. I just wanted to call so you didn't think I ditched you again."

"It's okay," Terry said. "I actually lost track of time anyway." As he said this, he realized Remius wasn't sitting on the floor in front of him anymore. Swiveling his head around to look behind him, Terry saw the cat curled up and sleeping at the end of his bed.

"Terry? Are you still there?" Eden's voice said after a few moments of silence.

"Oh, yeah, sorry. I was just looking for Remius. When are you going to be home?"

"Later," Eden answered. "Probably in a few hours."

"Okay, babe." Terry yawned and realized how exhausted he was from the day. "I've been working with a lot of intense energy today. So I think I'm gonna crash out here pretty soon. Just let yourself in when you get here and come snuggle with me in bed." He smiled, anticipating Eden's body against his as it would be when they cuddled under the covers.

"Okay, cutie! Love you!"

"Love you, sexy!"

Click. Terry hung up and threw his phone back on the pile of clothes. He could still see his own Merkabah spinning around his body. Terry decided to make it invisible, but could still feel it active around himself. The prana tube that he had set up through the center of the house shone brightly with white light. Looking out his window, he could also see the huge sphere of golden light shining around the entire house, as well as the new tetrahedrons spinning at nine-tenths the speed of light.

Terry felt satisfied and pleased that he got it right this time. He barely made it into bed and under the covers before sleep took him over.

TWENTY

FROM THE MIND OF TERRY BROSWALD:

I wake up in the dream again. I'm in my own bed like before, alone. This being the third time I've woken up in my own bed in the Dreamsphere, I can now feel the subtle vibration of this particular dream. I sigh. "This same fucking dream again?" I say out loud. "I'm beginning to get bored of this."

Dragging myself out of the bed, I walk out of the room, and sure enough the window in front of my parents' bedroom is open again. I shiver as the cold breeze blows the curtains like a ghost chained to the wall. Closing the window, I think back to what the dragon had said to me the last time I experienced this repeat dream. *What was it that he said? Do you want to evolve?* What could that possibly mean?

I groan at the prospect of having to go interact with my faux parents again. They are even more annoying than my real parents were. Fuck it, I wish I could just wake up and forego this whole ordeal. I chuckle to myself at that; ironic that I went for a period where I wasn't dreaming and practically begged to be let back into the Dreamsphere in my sleep. And now that I'm back to dreaming every night, I'm wanting to get back out. What a riddle; a puzzle; a conundrum.

So I descend the stairs to meet the parents for the third night in a row. There they are in the kitchen, just the same as they were the other two times. My mother is frying up the pancakes and bacon. My dad is sitting at the table reading a newspaper.

Mom greets me as I enter the kitchen. She rushes over, kisses me on the forehead, and says, "Darling, good morning! I'm making your favorite. How many pancakes do you want? Twenty? Thirty?"

I almost choke on my own saliva. "I'm not really hungry," I say.

"But, sweetheart," my mom coos back at me. "You must eat something. You're a growing boy. Some bacon? A grapefruit? I know what you like."

I wave her away and she goes back to cooking. As I approach my dad sitting at the table, I try to study the newspaper in his hands. Unable to decipher anything printed on it I ask, "Anything interesting in the news, Dad?"

He looks up at me, almost surprised that I am addressing him. "Oh, nothing much of consequence," he says, folds the newspaper and sets it down on the table. "You know, just politics. You know, weather. You know, sports. Something about an earthquake..." He trails off.

"God," I groan. "You two are even more annoying than my real parents."

"But, honey, we are your real parents," my mother says in a wounded voice as she brings over a plate of chocolate chip pancakes to the table. She sets the plate down and goes back to the stove to pile up a plate of bacon.

"How's school, son?" My dad asks.

Suddenly I feel the irritation start boiling into anger. *"How's school? How's school?* I don't want to fucking talk about school!" I smack the stack of pancakes and they go flying across the room. "I don't want your fucking pancakes!" My mother is now standing in front of me with a plate heaping with bacon. I smack that out of her hand as well. "Fuck your bacon! And fuck this shit!"

I grab my mother roughly by her hair and drag her over to the kitchen counter where the butcher block is. She screams and tries to pull away but my grip on a handful of her hair is too strong. Without time to think or hesitate, I pull one of the butcher knives out and stab my mother repeatedly in the chest. Her screams become shrieks as blood gushes like a geyser out of the myriad of stab wounds now open in her flesh. As I continue stabbing her upper chest and neck, her apron becomes soaked in red. Her screaming and struggling suddenly cease. My mother's last exhale escapes from her body as I drop her carcass to the floor.

I look over toward the kitchen table. My father is standing now, staring at me, but says nothing and makes no sudden moves. So without warning I lunge at him, knife raised, and bury it up to the handle in his right eye. Without having any time to react before death, he falls back over his chair and crashes hard to the ground, blood spurting from his penetrated eye socket. The look of shock is permanently frozen on his face.

I stare down at the bodies of my dead parents bleeding out on the wooden floor. Surprisingly a feeling of relief washes over me in an awesome wave. *It's over; it's done,* I think. There is only stillness in the air, and silence. I would have thought that I would have woken back up at this point, but I guess not. "Dragon? Remius? Anybody?" I call out to the empty house. "I'm ready to wake up now." Nothing happens.

I survey the carnage again. Wasn't this it? Didn't I solve the puzzle, the riddle, or whatever? *Oh, wait.* Flashing back to that day when I first discovered my parents' dead bodies, I could see in my mind where they were and the way they were configured. They weren't in the kitchen. *This isn't it. This is all wrong.*

With a nagging paranoid tug at the back of my brain that I might very well get trapped in this dream, I grab my dad's body by the wrists and start dragging him toward the stairs. With struggle and persistence, I finally am able to get the body up the stairs and into the bedroom that my parents used to share. I dump his bleeding carcass on the floor by the bed and then go to get my mother—she won't be as heavy. More easily than the first body, I am able to bring my mother's gored flesh up the stairs and dump her on their marital bed. With a crunch, I pull the knife from my dad's skull and place it on the nightstand.

Looking at the scene I realize this still isn't right. *How were they when I first saw them dead?* The blood puddles keep fanning out, soaking the white carpet and the bed. I go to work stripping them both naked. First I strip my dad down to his cock and balls. Then I strip my mom to her bare ass and hairy cunt. As I throw the clothes in the corner of the room I try to remember what the last thing was that I was missing... It's their genitals.

I bring my hand up over my nose; the stench of death is beginning to overwhelm my sense of smell. Grabbing the knife from the nightstand, and trying to breathe through my mouth as much as possible, I go to work sawing off my father's dick and balls. I circle my fingers around the base of the penis and the ballsack. As I stretch it away from the body, I press the knife against the flesh right under the pubic hair. Then I cut it like a side of beef. The knife is sharp and it slices through the soft tissue like butter. A river and more of blood gushes and soaks my hands as I pull the entire sex organ free from the body. Playing with the gooey, flaccid dick, I mutilate it beyond recognition—pulling the testicles out and ripping the dick in half down the middle of the urethra. I disgustedly throw the bloody mass down next to my father's body. Now it's my mother's turn to get the treatment.

I go over to my mother's naked body that's stained red and riddled with holes from my knife. Wrinkling my nose at the stench, I look at her old cunt—all wrinkles and hairy roast beef. *Let's get this over with.* So I use the butcher knife to cut an incision a couple inches below her belly button. I toss the knife aside back on the nightstand and then slide my hand into her abdomen. Almost gagging, I feel around for her uterus, follow the fallopian tubes, and then finally finding her ovaries, I rip them out—both of them. My hands and arms are covered in blood, bile, and bodily fluids. I drop the ovaries down next to my mom's body on the bed. Actually, it's not just my arms that are covered in red and muck, I realize my *whole body* is soaked in the shit.

The scene looks about right—just how I remember it from that day I discovered it. Now I'm ready to fucking wake up. I look around the room and listen to the silence. *Nothing.* I'm still here. Wiping the sweat from my brow, I only manage to smear blood over my face. Then I suddenly hear a voice echoing through space as if from some distant place.

"*Terry! Wake up.*"

It's a girl's voice. I'm trying to place it. She speaks again.

"*Wake up, Terry!*"

I realize it's Eden, and when I do, my consciousness is pulled from sleep; finally releasing me from the dream.

TWENTY-ONE

Terry awoke to Eden standing over him, shaking him awake. The room was dark, but he could still make out her pink hair in the low light. Remius was gone from the end of the bed and the door was open. "Thank god you woke up," Eden whispered, kissing him with relief. "I thought you weren't going to. It took several minutes of shaking you for you to wake."

"What time is it?" Terry whispered back.

"It's a little bit after midnight. Come on, get dressed. We gotta go." Her voice was urgent.

"Where are we going?" Terry asked, still not fully awake yet. Eden handed him jeans and a sweatshirt as he slowly pulled himself out of bed.

"Okay," Eden explained, still whispering. "I wasn't really taking care of stuff at my apartment today. I was discussing your situation with the friend of mine that owns that club—you know, the one I told you about. Anyway, I heard about those break-ins in Rob's neighborhood also. Most likely those three that attacked you that night I showed up to help you. It's only a matter of time before they come back here again, stronger and more ready for us. But they only want you, so if you're not here, they won't have a reason to attack Rob and Mothman—hopefully. So we think it's best that you—*we*—hide out in another Dimension for a while until we can figure out the best course of action to take next. Hopefully that'll send what's her name—Maya—on a wild goose-chase to find you and they'll be off track for a while... I don't know, that's the best plan I got. We can't tell anyone, not even Remius. For our safety, no one can know where we are. Except for my friend Darren who owns the club."

Terry was all dressed and ready to go. "If you think it's best, then I trust you... Where is Remius anyway?" He asked as he grabbed a winter coat from the closet. The snow was still coming down hard outside his window.

"He's downstairs sleeping on the couch," Eden replied.

"And my bedroom door was open when you got here?"

"Yeah... Why?"

"Huh... Nothing, nevermind," Terry said, having a thought and then letting it go. "Should we leave?"

Without answering, Eden turned and quietly left the room. Terry followed close behind her. *Why is it so cold out here?* Terry thought. Then he noticed the window next to his parents bedroom was open again, a chilling breeze flowing into the house. Terry tiptoed over to close and lock it. *That's fucking weird*, he said to himself. *So is this the dream or was the dream what I just came from?* He shook the thought from his head. *Come on, Terry, you don't have time to go down that rabbit hole right now.*

He followed close after Eden, tiptoeing down the stairs, careful not to wake Remius or Terry's two human friends. They exited through the front door, closed it as quietly as possible, and locked it behind them. "Give me your keys," Eden said, holding out her hand. She was wearing a pair of knit gloves with the fingers cut off. "I know where the place is so I'm driving."

Terry handed over the van keys. The night was dark and the snow was thick. Their breath hung in the air like clouds of smog. The powder crunched under their boots. Eden got into the driver's seat and Terry took his place as the passenger. She started the car and pulled away from the house, the beams from the headlights illuminating the large white flakes pouring through the air. "What day is it anyway?" Terry asked, staring out the window at the white landscape.

"Actually," Eden answered as if she was far away herself. "It's Christmas Eve."

"Huh..." Terry thought about this, remembering Christmas Eve just one year before. There had been a tree up in his living room, presents under it. He had been eager to go to sleep early that night so he could wake up early to eat eggs Benedict and open gifts with his parents. He guessed that there were some days that he didn't despise them. Remembering this, he didn't feel any type of way about it. Terry didn't feel sad at the loss of this holiday and the loss of his parents. There was only a deep acceptance and neutrality toward this change. Then he asked, "Are you sure this club'll be open? It being Christmas Eve and all?"

Eden looked over at Terry and smiled. "Trust me, they'll be open." She took Terry's left hand in her right and laced her fingers through his. As they squeezed their warm hands together tightly, they drove on toward Chicago and Boystown.

"*Angelfuck?*" Terry stood looking up at the pink lighted neon sign above a black door. The sign spelled out one word in all lowercase letters—*angelfuck*.

Eden laughed. "Yep, that's the name. Kinda catchy, don't ya think?"

"How do they get away with having a name like that displayed right on a public street?" Terry asked.

Eden shrugged. "Doesn't seem like many people even notice it. Except, of course, for the people in the know. Which now includes you and me. Come on, let's go." She opened the black door. Behind it was a narrow staircase that led down to a second door which was pink.

"So why is this club open on Christmas Eve?" Terry asked as they went down toward the pink door.

She looked back over her shoulder and replied, "Let's just say they have a Christmas *fetish*."

Terry didn't know what that was supposed to mean, but he would soon find out. Eden opened the door and led him into the bowels of *angelfuck*. What was beyond that door was a scene unlike anything Terry had ever witnessed before. He had never even been to a nightclub in his life—let alone one where people played out their *Christmas Fetish*. Surprisingly there were no bouncers at the door screening people who came in. Terry's jaw hung open as he took in the sights. The room was huge like the room of a warehouse, and there were two floors. The ground floor was basically a giant dance floor. The lighting was very dark and most of the luminescence came from strobe lights and multi-colored lasers flashing through the space. The second floor was like a balcony halfway between the floor and the roof. It was open with a railing so that people up there could look down on the dance floor below. Electronic dance music blared through giant speakers; it was being played by a DJ dressed in an elf costume made of leather. The stage he spun from was all the way on the other side of the room, farthest from the entrance.

The strangest part of the whole thing was the people and their costumes. There was imagery from Santa and his elves—even some people dressed up as horny reindeer with huge cocks. There were elevated platforms around the dance floor with cages on top. Inside those cages were dancers dressed in sexy Christmas outfits. One girl was basically naked, but she had pointed ears like an elf and scattered at her feet were unwrapped presents. The contents of those gifts were an assortment of sex toys. Another dancer was dressed as Mrs. Claus. She had on the red fuzzy dress with white around the edges, but she was naked underneath—her shaved pussy exposed beneath the skirt as she danced. On the shaved skin above her vaginal lips was tattooed a bow as if tied on top of a present.

There were a lot of girls wearing strap-ons as part of their ensemble. And some of the guys were wearing huge fake tits, bouncing around under long beards. Terry could see that there were real orgies going on as well. People on the dance floor were actually fucking. One guy dressed like Rudolph had his dick hanging out of his reindeer onesie and was getting sucked off by a guy dressed like Jesus with a crown of thorns on his head. Now Terry noticed that there were actually a lot of people dressed in different iterations of Jesus. He also saw a few *Wise Men* and maybe one or two Marys and Josephs. One corner of the room caught his attention where one guy who looked like Jesus was tied to a Saint Andrew's Cross. He was naked and had a crown of thorns that wrapped around a pair of horns that seemed to grow out of his forehead. There was a woman standing in front of him wearing a white dress and head covering—possibly could have been dressed like Virgin Mary. She was playing with the Jesus's cock and balls with a riding crop.

"There's Jesuses being molested in here," Terry said after he'd taken in the whole scene. "I ain't never seen that shit before!"

They both laughed and Eden took Terry's hand. "Would you rather it be *baby* Jesus being molested?" She winked at him.

"Now that's just... *wrong*."

"Come, my love." Eden started leading Terry through the crowd and throng of erotic energy. All of the sexual ecstasy was entering his energy field and making him feel orgasmic. It was more than a pleasant feeling. They made their way through the humans that were dancing, and fucking, and cosplaying; and the ones cumming into subspace and back. She looked back at Terry and said, "Darren's office is in the back there. Past the stage."

They got through the crowd without being pulled into an orgy. Darren's office was indeed past the stage and also hidden behind a curtain. Eden looked around to make sure no one was following them. Satisfied, she swept the curtain aside and they went in and through the door beyond.

"Ah, Eden, I've been expecting you," Darren said from behind his desk. The room was huge to be an office. It was more like a lounge with a desk to take care of the business stuff of the club. The lighting in the office was low and ambient, almost as dark as the rest of the club. The carpet was dark blue, and several red couches were placed around a table on which stood a few half drunk glasses of champagne. The bottle was there too, empty. There was also a bookshelf against one wall with lots of occult looking books on it.

Darren stood up from his desk when Eden and Terry entered the room. He was a tall black man, over six feet. His long dreadlocks came all the way down to his waist. Darren was muscular, Terry could see from the tone of his arms, chest, and abdomen. Over his upper body he was wearing only a leather vest which was open in the front. His pants were black bondage pants with straps and metal buckles hanging off of them. In comic contrast to the rest of his outfit, he wore a red Santa hat on his head. "Welcome to my lair," Darren said as he came over to greet them.

Terry shook his hand and noticed a long scar on the man's face, starting above his left eyebrow and going all the way down his cheek. "It's nice to meet you," Terry said.

"Likewise," Darren replied. "Any friend of Eden is a friend of mine." Eden embraced her friend and kissed him on the lips. This wasn't a surprise to Terry since they were polyamorous, and he didn't feel uncomfortable about it either. "So, Terry, do you like my club?" Darren asked, smiling a very white grin.

Terry nodded. "It's fantastic! I love it actually. *Angelfuck*, that's a great name."

"I'm glad you approve," Darren replied. "And I hope you both have more time to explore it once the danger has passed for you. Eden has told me all about you. You're a very powerful individual, I must admit. I felt it right away when you entered the room."

"So you must have a Soulmind, too," Terry said, stating the obvious.

"Guilty as charged. Now, if I'm correct and we're all in agreement, you want to hide out in another Dimension. And I can help you out here on my end while you're there; I'll do what I can. Eden has briefed me on all of it. The three thugs from Dark Tethers, etcetera. Anyway, I guard the portal to the Kingdom of the Stone Queen."

"The Stone Queen's Kingdom?" Terry asked, raising his eyebrows.

"Yes. Here." Darren went over to the bookshelf and slid it to the side. There was a small door about three feet high behind it. "Behind this door is the portal."

Terry laughed. "Did you steal that from *Being John Malkovich*?"

Darren laughed at the joke and said, "You're funny, Terry. I like you."

"What's *Being John Malkovich*?" Eden asked.

"Nevermind," Darren replied. "That's not important. What's important right now, I think, is you two knowing if you'll be able to get back when the time comes. Don't worry, you will."

"Okay, good. That's good," Eden said, squeezing Terry's arm. They were both in agreement on this decision.

"What are we gonna experience in there?" Terry wanted to know.

"I can't tell you much," Darren answered. "Only that it's... strange."

"Oh, yeah, strange. That's very specific," Terry said sarcastically.

"Are you ready for this next adventure, my love?" Eden asked, now taking hold of his hand again.

Terry smiled and kissed her. "I'm ready. And I'm glad it's you that I'm going on this journey with."

"Okay, you lovebirds," Darren said as he opened the tiny door. Behind it was the portal, a spiral vortex of blue energy. "The gate is all yours, my darlings." He stepped out of the way to let them enter.

Eden went first, getting down on her hands and knees. She crawled forward and slipped in, disappearing into the blue beyond. Terry was right behind her and was sucked into the vortex quickly. Out of the Hollow Dimension into the Kingdom of the Stone Queen. What surprises would they find there and what new lessons would they learn about themselves? Only Timestrus knew.

Darren closed the small door after them and then slid the bookshelf back into its place.

PART 10

Transcending the Schism of Duality

*"Every weakness in your mind is because
you are not in touch with your neutral mind.
Neutral mind is when you are not bound down
by the negative force or the positive force. Then
YOU are the force. Then that's God. Look, if you
are looking for God, there's no such thing... But
when you become a neutral person—in the
negative/positive vibrations you remain neutral,
when the pair of opposites do not affect you and
higher altitude is received of that of Infinity, and
the personality becomes so dominant and so radiant,
the person can understand that within all, all is...
all becomes one, that's God. Not what you think God is."*

- Yogi Bhajan

TWENTY-TWO
FROM THE MIND OF ARASH KHAN:

I am meditating in my chambers, in lotus pose, and on the sheepskin put here for that purpose. As I squeeze *root lock*—the muscles of the rectum, sex organs, and navel—I feel the heat of my Kundalini tingle at the base of my spine and then begin its ascent. The energy climbs my spine like two snakes weaving back and forth, creating a DNA strand which ascends through every chakra and meets to illuminate the crown chakra at the top of my head. When it reaches that point, I see in my third eye a huge lotus blossom blooming out of my seventh chakra. As it opens, a ball of light pops out and hovers above the lotus. This ball of energy vibrates and then rains golden light down on the lotus and into my brain, illuminating every cell within. I sit with no thoughts, just holding this feeling, so high—the highest I've ever felt. This high transcends all highs. And I feel like I'm floating above the sheepskin, weightless.

After a while of melting into this blissful emptiness, I hear a knock at my chamber door. Opening my eyes, I ground myself back into my physical body. "Yes?" I say, not getting up from my lotus position.

"Lord Khan, it's Leeah. May I have a word?" She says from the other side of the door.

"Enter," I reply.

Leeah enters my room gracefully. She's wearing a one-piece white jumpsuit with a sash tied around her waist. The legs of the jumpsuit are poofy like genie pants, and her blue hair puffs out around her head like a lion that decided to turn punk. She comes over and sits down on the floor in front of me. "What's going on?" I ask her. "Is everything okay?"

I sense that it's difficult for Leeah to tell me what it is she intends to tell me. For a moment she doesn't speak, and I have a tough time reading the expression on her face. "This is not an easy thing for me to tell you," she begins. "But I think you're now ready to know the nature of what exactly is happening here."

I'm confused by Leeah's statement. "What do you mean? Is there something happening here that I'm not aware of?"

"Yes," Leeah admits. "Everything is *not* okay. I'm sorry to say that our Order has been fractured. We've been divided over what our function must be going forward. If you feel misled, I am sorry, that was never my intention. However, this fact of our division is one of the sole reasons why it was so important to bring you here and initiate you as the next Mahan Tantric. You must be the bridge between our two sides, working in both polarities and neither simultaneously. There had been a perfect split in our Order—six for one side and six for the other. I was able to keep myself neutral for a while, but I failed. I chose a side, and in so doing, tipped the balance and I became polarized—which is not really allowed when one is the Mahan Tantric. But I guess I've always been a rebel in some ways."

"So what are you saying?" I ask. Admittedly I'm a bit lost.

"This is a pivotal time for the Evolution of Consciousness on planet Earth. Honestly, destruction can be a powerful catalyst for the Awakening. This is what the split was over. Half of our Order sided with using this method to aid in the Evolutionary process. Granted this way is more risky, but it's gets faster results. However, there is a slight chance that it could destroy the entire planet. In my opinion—and the opinion of the other six on this side—this is an acceptable risk. And if the planet is destroyed, fuck it, I'll be on to my next incarnation anyway. I know that sounds harsh, but that's how I feel. Rahjiah, and the five others with her, feel the opposite. They don't want any destruction. They are for a gradual shift into the next Level with the least amount of death and catastrophes. They think *that* way will be less traumatic for humanity. But I say, how long is a *gradual* shift going to take? We've already been doing this for *so* long and Humanity refuses to get into gear."

I take a couple minutes to process this information and integrate it into my consciousness. "I think I understand where you're coming from. And where Rahjiah is coming from as well. Are you going to ask me to choose a side? Cause to be honest, I don't really feel comfortable taking sides. I prefer to be on my own side."

"That's actually exactly what I want," Leeah agrees. "For you to not choose one, but to bridge both. So, what I'm proposing is that you don't have to join my side, but you can help us."

"Okay," I reply. "I think I can do that." This sounds like a reasonable request to me. I'm supposed to hold the totality of the Order of the Transcendent within my own aura, so to play both sides of the split seems more in alignment with the position I'm being groomed for than to pick one side over the other.

Leeah stands up and extends her hand toward me. "Come with me," she says. I take her hand and she helps me to my feet. We leave my chambers and Leeah leads me down the hall to a large wooden door which is the entrance to the Library. Leeah and I enter and I shut the door behind us. The Library is huge and has two floors of bookshelves. On the first floor there is a large open area in the middle of the bookshelves with pillows on the floor for sitting and reading. The six women Leeah had described, who are on the side of destruction, are sitting on the pillows and stare at us expectantly as we walk in.

"Goddesses," Leeah addresses the group. "Lord Khan, the next Mahan Tantric, has agreed to assist us in our cause." All the women clap their hands together in a prayer pose, expressing gratitude toward me. Leeah turns to me now and continues, "Now certain things are complicated since we are restricted in ways because of the rules of our Order. Restricted in ways that you are not, since you are still only an initiate and are therefore not yet bound by our laws. So... to fill you in briefly on certain things you may not be aware of; your friend Terry is pivotal in all this. We are still not exactly sure why, but that's irrelevant at this point. There's a female entity named Maya who comes from the Dimension of the Dark Tethers, and she is trying to get a piece of Terry's Soulmind so she can use it to dissolve the barrier between the Hollow Dimension and Dark Tethers. And in doing this, she hopes to be able to destroy the Hollow Dimension for good—assumedly making it an extension of her Dimension. We've been ordered to keep Maya from coming anywhere near Terry, she can't even get close enough to touch him. We *have* to do this because it's one of our laws that we keep order between the Dimensions. Rahjiah is the one who's been keeping a close eye on Maya and generally 'policing' her when she gets out of line. Rahjiah wants a slow, nice, gradual shift you see."

"So what does this have to do with me?" I ask, interjecting into Leeah's long speech.

"I'm getting to that," Leeah returns. "The way things are set up and how powerful our Order is to keep tabs on entities like Maya upsetting the balance, makes it so that she could *never* achieve her mission. She will never be able to get close enough to Terry to extract a piece of his Soulmind. And even her little thug henchmen Trick, Tock, and Tick aren't any match for Terry. Especially since he's been getting increasingly powerful with his companions around and his October familiar mentoring him. So this is the task I'm giving you. Here."

Leeah leads me over to a tall vertical cabinet which is built into the side of one of the bookshelves. The door on the cabinet is locked but is mostly a glass window so I can see the two shelves inside. On the top shelf is a very old and rare looking book with a leather cover. I can't read the inscription on it—it's in some script I don't recognize. The bottom shelf contains two thin cylindrical glass containers. The cylinder on the left has purple energy dancing inside, and the one on the right has white energy dancing inside. "What are these?" I ask.

"Both of these cylinders contain a piece of a Soulmind," Leeah explains. "This left one is from an individual that you don't remember now. But this one on the right, is from Terry. We extracted it from him when he came here with you."

"And you want me to give this to Maya?" I ask, starting to finally catch on to at least a bit of what Leeah is getting at.

"You're a very perceptive young man, Lord Khan," Leeah says and puts her hand on my shoulder. "That's pretty much it, but not so directly. Rahjiah has been hyper vigilant since the split within our Order. And our laws prohibit me, or any of my goddesses, from just handing this over to Maya. And we can't just give the cylinder to you to take to Maya. No, that would be too suspicious. So what you must do is leave the Palace Temple, exit through the Public Works Building, and go find Maya who will be at your friend Rob's house. She's not able to enter here herself since Rahjiah has placed barriers to her energy. Use her thugs that she sprung from the Containment Cube in Dark Tethers. It must look like Trick, Tock, and Tick followed you here without your knowledge. They must break in and steal the cylinder with the piece of Terry's Soulmind. And they will return it to Maya. She will finally attain what she would never be able to attain any other way."

"The plan still seems kind of risky," I say nervously, not sure if I really want to get involved in this. But I've been initiated to be the next Mahan Tantric and these are the types of tough decisions I know I'll be forced to make on a daily basis. I'm just going to have to get used to it. "What if Rahjiah catches me? And then she'll know that it was you who told me to do this. And what if the consequences of taking these actions results in the complete destruction of the planet? I don't want Earth to be done for. What if me agreeing to this brings about the end of the world? The apocalypse? Armageddon?"

"That's only one possible outcome," Leeah assures me. "And if that's the consequence that ends up resulting from the choices we've made, life with still go on in the Spiralverse. It will be changed forever, yes, but Existence still persists in one form or another."

I think about this for a minute. This is a heavy task, and I can feel it in my aura. But deep down I know that I've already agreed. It's already done. So I look Leeah straight in the eyes and say, "I'll do it."

TWENTY-THREE
FROM THE MIND OF JESSICA THORN:

We are sitting in the Fairy Circle—the magical clearing in the forest. I'm here on the soft grass with Magda and Jay sitting across from me. They are smiling and Magda holds a ceramic jug filled with some kind of green liquid. Laying next to Jay is a large hand drum.

"So what is that stuff?" I ask, indicating the jug.

"It's called Soma," Jay answers.

"Soma is a plant teacher. It can give you visions and an experience of your soul," Magda continues. "The depths of your soul so deep you may even keep hidden from yourself."

I'm wary of this and a bit frightened. Everything they've taught me up to now has been pretty harmless; sigils, elemental magic, moon phases, magical combat, and working with herbs. We haven't gone very deep into the Shadow yet. They've only mentioned that briefly to me and I'm not sure if I'm ready to confront those aspects of myself. "I've never done any drugs in my life," I say nervously.

Magda smiles warmly and puts her hand on my knee to reassure me it's safe. "Even if you find yourself deep in the netherworlds, battling your Shadow, we'll be here watching over you. We can intervene in your trip somewhat if need be, but ultimately we want *you* to be in control of your vision quest. Even when you feel like you are completely out of control, that is the crucial time for you to learn that you are in control and you and only you create your reality."

I'm still nervous. Magda hands me the jug and I take a reluctant drink of the green liquid. The taste is repulsive. Trying not to gag, I force myself to swallow. My stomach gurgles in protest and I hand the jug back to Magda. She nods at me, takes the jug back, and takes a drink herself. Wiping her mouth, she hands the jug to Jay and he takes a drink as well. As he sets the jug aside, Jay picks up the drum and puts it in his lap.

"How long is this stuff supposed to take to kick in?" I ask.

"A little while," Jay responds. "Just let the plant teacher do its work. You'll be purging in no time."

"Purging?" I ask, since I have no idea what that means.

"Yes," Jay continues. "Your body will purge everything that is not serving you—physically, emotionally, psychically. So we start by just relaxing and meditating, honoring the plant that will teach us so much."

So I close my eyes and start to sink into meditation. Jay starts drumming out a steady beat and then begins chanting something in Gaelic that I can't understand. I zone into the drum and Jay's chanting, pulling me into a trance so deep that I have no more sense of time or space. After a while it seems like my heart and the drum are beating in perfect sync. Then without warning a fire starts to rage in my belly. Painful cramps and knots take possession of my lower abdomen. It feels like someone has carved up my guts with a butter knife. I groan and open my eyes. Everything around me is a blur. My body pitches forward and I let loose a torrent of puke into the grass. Doubled over, orange bile drips from my lips and down my chin. The first purge does nothing to alleviate the pain in my gut.

"I'm dying... I'm dying..." I groan, holding my belly.

Magda comes beside me and rubs my back comfortingly. "You're not dying," she whispers. "This is the first stage. Purge out what doesn't serve you."

I feel it grip me again, and leaning away from Magda, I let loose another spew. The bile burns as it gushes from my throat. I'm dizzy and the trees on the edge of the Fairy Circle spin around me on the outskirts of my vision. Looking over, I hear Magda puking now herself. Her purge isn't as much as mine and she sits back up, wiping her mouth with the back of her hand. I lurch over almost involuntarily and grab onto Magda's dress. The tears start to flow from my eyes. The dam has burst and I have no control over the pain that comes flooding out from my eyes and through my nose running with snot.

"What is it, dear?" Magda whispers. "You can tell me."

"My fucking parents..." I sob, almost choking on the mucus running down the back of my throat. "They're so fucking... fake!" My voice sounds foreign to my ears. It's a little girl's voice—an echo of the child I once was. "They're all fuckin'... going to church faggots," I continue babbling. "All Christian and Jesus and... all nonsense. They couldn't stand each other. So phony pretending to believe the Bible and... cocksuckers..." I trail off, staring into space for a minute. Then I look back up at Magda; her eyes are all compassion. "My mom was cheating... fucking around on my dad. She would go out... called it 'church hunting.' But I knew her all... sneaky... sneaking around. Cunt bitch... Fuck her..." I trail off again incoherently into mumbling.

Magda puts her thumb against my third eye and my body falls back onto the grass. When I hit the ground, I feel like I'm being pulled *through* it—into the dirt and towards the inner Earth. At first I'm in blackness and I can feel the cool damp dirt all around me. Then it disappears and I am plunging into an abyss. My descent is suddenly halted when my body slams into the bottom of an object that is hollow—a wooden coffin. Before I have a chance to try to climb out, a lid is slammed down on top of me and I hear the nails being hammered into the wood of the coffin. I try to scream but no sound escapes from my throat. *I'm in the nightmare*, I think to myself. As I feel the coffin with me inside being lowered into the Earth, I start scratching the inside of the lid. My nails splinter off and streaks of blood are left by my fingers on the wood.

Just as my body begins to panic and go into shock, I am no longer in the coffin. I've been pulled into a different scene. It seems that I'm hoisted up high and I'm in the most excruciating pain I've ever felt in my life. There's a crowd of people gathered below me—not directly below but a small distance away. Some people are weeping, especially one woman in the front. I look and there's a man hanging from a cross on my left and a man hanging from a cross on my right. *Now I understand.* There are thorns piercing into my skull. Blood runs down my forehead, occasionally blurring my vision. My hands and feet are nailed, and I can't pull myself up to get a breath, so I'm slowly suffocating. A storm is coming, I can see the thunderheads in the distance. A Roman soldier stands below me with a spear. He comes closer and stabs me violently in the left rib. I scream out to the heavens as a crack of thunder roars in the distance. Sobbing and sputtering I cry, "Lord! Why have you forsaken me?"

Then my body is ripped apart by an unknown force—limb from limb and torso truncated. Blood squirts out of my dismembered body and showers down on the Roman soldiers and the crowd behind them. My consciousness is pulled from the mutilated corpse and hoisted into the sky. As I'm enveloped by the whiteness of a cloud, the scene in my vision quest changes once again.

This time I'm in a male body again. I'm standing on a stage and addressing a large crowd of men in uniform. Seeing my fist raise into the air emphatically, I hear words uttered from my mouth in a harsh non-english language. It takes me a second to realize it's *German*. After I say a few more words, the crowd cheers loudly and raises their right hands in salute. I feel the weight of death around this incarnation, then I am pulled from this vision into another.

Entering another male body, I am naked in a dark room. I can see pentagrams painted on the walls. As I stand, I survey a vast orgy taking place in front of me. It's a blood orgy. The naked men and women use daggers to cut gashes in their flesh, and as they bleed, they become a mass of gyrating bodies and blood puddles smearing their titillated skin. Looking down, I see and feel a beautiful woman licking my erect penis. I raise my arms into the air and chant an incantation. Intense light shoots out of my body and through my hands, illuminating the room and the fornicating bodies therein. As the light passes through the energy of us all, we all cry out in the most transcendent cosmic orgasm. As we all orgasm at once, our collective consciousness merges with the supreme light of the Godhead.

Just as quickly as I feel the ecstasy, I am out of that scene and into the next. In this incarnation I am in a beautiful room in a palace. I am wearing a very royal dress of red and black. Somehow I know that in this lifetime I am a high priestess; a very highly regarded woman who shares deep spiritual experience and wisdom. In this vision, I am giving counsel to the King. When or where this is I'm not sure. But what is revealed to me, and especially what comes to me in the incarnation of the high priestess, is that I've been many things throughout time. I've been above and below, and everything in between. And what I see beyond a shadow of a doubt is that in many lifetimes I have chosen a spiritual path of Magick—and that path may very well be different in each lifetime. Maybe the spiritual path has chosen *me*.

Finally this last vision dissolves and I find myself alone, standing in the aisle of the church I used to attend—the one where Brother Evan used to be the pastor. The sanctuary is eerily quiet, and as I look up toward the pulpit, I am horrified by what I see in front of the stained glass window depicting the Virgin Mary praying. Erected in the middle of the platform is an upside down crucifix. There's a girl crucified on it, her hair falling below her head to touch the floor. The girl—is *me*! I stare at the dead body fixed on the torture instrument. At the top my feet are tied together so the body doesn't fall down the cross. The feet are on top of each other and nailed to the wood. Blood drips from the wound and down the legs of the body. Subsequently, the wrists of my body are also tied to the arms of the cross; and nails hammered all the way through my palms. There's blood seeping from the wounds and small puddles collecting on the floor underneath. The eyes of my dead body are covered with a black silk blindfold. And shoved in my open mouth are crumpled up pages from the Bible.

As I process the horrific image in front of me, I fall to my knees onto the red carpet of the aisle between both rows of pews. Staring in both awe and repulsion, I suddenly become aware of a strange feeling on my forehead. As I bring my hand up to my face, I feel what's there. Running my fingers over the skin near my hairline, I feel two sharp points. There are two small horns growing out of the front of my skull. I start to cry and pound the floor with my clenched fists. I don't know what the fuck any of this means. Growing up I learned to believe that everything has a meaning—a reason—and God always has a plan in every situation. But now, I don't know what I believe anymore—or if I even believe *anything*. Maybe that's what this is. Maybe it's teaching me to give up trying to understand everything, and that what I need to do is just embrace the absurdity of this new life that I now find myself in.

In this moment I'm helpless, there's nothing I can do. I have no control—no control over these visions. I can't get out and I can't go around. So I must go *through*. And in this instant I totally surrender, but it's doesn't feel like I consciously will it. Surrender *happens* to me. The person that I thought I was—this *Jessica Thorn*—all in one flash is destroyed. I don't know who I am anymore and that's okay. Feeling the horns on my forehead again and looking at my dead body crucified upside down on the cross, I realize that within me I am both Jesus and Lucifer; a dark sex magician and a royal high priestess; Hitler and the spiritual

Teacher. I am all and I am nothing. The eternal mystery of the Spiralverse is also the eternal mystery of myself. And in this moment, everything is as it is, and everything is Perfect.

To even the surprise of myself, I find myself laughing out loud. The impenetrable silence of the sanctuary is shattered by the sound. It's hilarious. The ridiculousness of it all. With this realization an immense peace and calm washes over me. Suddenly the stained glass window behind the crucifix shatters and a beam of bright purple light streams in, through the dead version of me, and illuminates me and bathes my whole body—baptizing me where I kneel. I close my eyes and feel the warmth of this light. Taking this light into my heart and into my Soulmind, it reverses direction, igniting all of my cells with luminescence. The purple light seeps through the pores of my skin and I feel my physical body expanding from within as if it's trying to stretch me into a larger form. I feel the bonds of my cells, my bones, and my ligaments start to tear apart but there is no pain. In an instant my physical form completely tears apart at the cellular level, exploding into pure consciousness and light.

I am naked, floating in the black void silence of space in a fetal position. Stars surround me as I float through the darkness. I feel like I'm back in the womb about to be born again—but I don't want to be. I want to stay here in the bosom of the Great Mother. The bliss of the connection to All is the only experience I feel. But this feeling is like I'm experiencing *all* experiences at once—all incarnations at once; on every planet and every Dimension. It's very difficult to describe. I know I'm not in a physical body, I just see myself that way.

As I float through the ecstasy of consciousness, I secretly hope that this is my Eternity. Maybe I've completed my mission and finally returned to the Cosmic Womb. However, no sooner than I think this, a shining white light appears before me in space. I open my eyes as the light dims to reveal a figure. I can feel the Goddess energy as I stare at the entity floating in front of me. She is tall—very tall—and wears a long green dress. She also has long red hair and very pale skin. This Goddess speaks in a voice that echoes through my consciousness.

"Jessica!" She speaks to me telepathically. "I am Maeve, a Goddess from the planet Tar. You must return to Earth. Your journey is not yet complete. Terry still needs you, and your part to play in this Cosmic Opera is more paramount than your scope of consciousness can currently conceive of."

The vibration of Love coming off of this entity—Maeve—is greater than anything that I've ever felt or experienced. I just want to stay in this energy forever. But she is right. "I know," I admit to the Goddess. "Even though it is almost irresistibly tempting to want to stay within this Oneness, I know I must return to Earth. I *choose* to return to Earth. I want to go back."

Maeve smiles. "There's my blossoming Goddess. You are very powerful. More powerful than you can even comprehend. Just remember that even when you are incarnated in a physical form, you are still inseparable from Source. You *are* Source. Your consciousness has expanded and you're beginning to realize who you really are. Practice this *Self-Remembering* while you are within the illusion of reality—this is your meditation: remembering yourself, *the I*, and the actions you take within the Creation."

"Thank you, Goddess," I say, knowing that I am about to leave her loving presence and return to my body on Earth. No further words are necessary, and Maeve reaches out to touch my forehead and I begin to feel the density of physicality again. In an instant the white light dissolves me yet again.

Coming back to consciousness, I awake lying on the ground in the Redwood Forest again. Slightly disoriented, I realize that I'm no longer inside the Fairy Circle and Magda and Jay are nowhere in sight. I stumble to my feet feeling dizzy. Finally I stabilize myself, leaning up against a tree. I can feel the aura of the tree—it's consciousness and its love entering me through my hand pressed against it. I look around. All of the trees are watching me, anticipating what I'm about to do. I'm having a difficult time intuiting which direction I need to go to get back to the cottage. So I just pick a direction and start walking at a brisk pace.

After what seems like a long while, the trees in front of me start to thin out. *That's odd; I don't think I'm going the right way.* Before I have a chance to decide to turn back, I step out of the tree line into a hilly field and I freeze. There are men there, several yards away. Three are on horseback and the forth is standing on the ground beside his horse. These men are not wearing the clothes of peasants. I don't think peasants could afford such beautiful horses. Their garb is more akin to noblemen. They've spotted me!

"It's the witch!" One of them yells in my direction.

I turn to run but it's too late. Two men are already upon me and grab me by the arms, restraining me as I try to tear myself loose of their grip. Unfortunately, they're much stronger than me and I can't think clear enough to conjure my Soulmind to come to my aid—especially with my hands restrained. These two men drag me kicking and screaming back over toward the horses and their other two companions. One of the other men jumps down from his horse and proceeds to tie my wrists with rope while the two holding me keep me from struggling. As I scream for help, they shove a piece of cloth in my mouth and tie another around to gag me.

One man gets on his horse and the other two help hoist me up on my stomach over the saddle. After I'm up there they tie my ankles as well so I can't kick and try to jump off the horse. They all mount their steeds again and the man behind me leans down and whispers viciously in my ear, "Now you're gonna burn, witch..." I feel his hot breath on the back of my neck as he says this. After he sits back up in the saddle, we begin to ride off away from the forest.

TWENTY-FOUR

The specters that had come through the rift from the Dark Tethers were busy doing their work to duplicate and spread. Many were still in the city doing their deeds to infect as many unsuspecting individuals as possible. Others had hitched rides in their hosts to the suburbs and were spreading the possession epidemic there. The twin boys that Wendy had infected had already carried their specters to school and passed on the possession to several other children. The phenomenon was growing exponentially and was not going completely unnoticed. However, most of the pre-possessed people who noticed strange behavior from others, would soon become victims of a violent act and in turn be the next hosts in the chain.

Simultaneously, while all of this taking of bodies was occurring, there was another group of several specters—maybe fifty or so—who chose, for reasons unknown, not to take possession of any human host. They weren't all together and had wandered away from each other; some into different parts of Chicago and others had found their way into the surrounding suburbs. These spectral entities had a keen sense of smell and could sense different types of energy signatures.

Since Terry had set up the surrogate Merkabah around his house for protection, that huge spike in energy had started to attract the attention of two different types of entities. The first was the specters. The ones without host bodies scattered around the city and the suburbs all at once picked up the signal given off by the frequency of the electromagnetic field of the Merkabah field. Wherever they were at that exact moment, they stopped in mid-float and sniffed the air. When they all knew the time-space coordinates for this high-vibrational phenomenon, they began to flow toward it like magnets.

* * *

Rob and Mothman awoke to find no sign of Terry or Eden anywhere in the house. They stood in Terry's empty bedroom looking for any clue as to where he might have gone. Nothing promising was turning up.

"Where do you think he could have gone?" Rob asked.

Mothman shrugged, honestly at a loss. "I have no fucking idea, man. But I can't feel him, which is the weird part. I usually can at least feel his energy to know he's around somewhere." He looked on Terry's desk and through his drawers for any note that might have been left for them to find. "Did you try calling his cell phone?"

Rob nodded. "Yeah, a couple of times when we were searching through the house. It just rang a bunch of times and sent me to voicemail."

"Try him again," Mothman insisted. "It's not like him to abandon us like this. Remius is still sleeping on the couch too. So it looks like him and his girlfriend just ran off in the middle of the night. Now why would they do that?"

Rob shook his head to indicate he didn't know and then dialed Terry's number again. After a few seconds they heard a faint ringing coming from inside the room somewhere. "Do you hear that?" Rob asked.

"Shhh," Mothman hushed and strained to hear where the ringing was coming from. He looked around the room and finally his eyes caught sight of a pile of clothes by the bed—a pair of jeans and some t-shirts. Mothman bent down and fished around inside the pile. "You gotta be fucking kidding me," he said as he pulled Terry's flip-phone out from the folds of the pants.

Rob shook his head again and put his own cell phone back into his pocket. "I can't believe he left his cell here," Rob admitted. "He must really not want to be found. Do you think he's in trouble?"

Mothman tossed the flip-phone back onto the pile of clothes. "I don't think he's in trouble yet... But he might be soon."

"Why do you say that?" Rob wondered.

"I'm not sure," Mothman replied. "It's just this feeling I got. Could be wrong though."

"What if those three weirdos come back?"

"They only want Terry. If he's not here then they won't bother. And besides," Mothman continued as he looked out the window at the golden sphere spinning around the house close to the speed of light. "We have this protection field thingie around the house now."

Rob looked out the window now also. The snow wasn't coming down anymore, but it was at least a couple feet deep. "Where would Terry and Eden go? Especially in this freezing weather... And it's Christmas Eve!"

"It's really Christmas Eve?" Mothman asked, raising an eyebrow. He had totally forgotten that Christmas was coming up.

"Yeah," Rob said, suddenly looking pouty. "I was hoping we'd all do something to celebrate. Eat some good food and, I don't know, have some drinks."

Mothman laughed at this thought. "What? You thought we were gonna have a party like a big happy family? Eat, drink, and be merry while our very existence is being threatened on multiple Dimensional levels?"

Rob looked hurt and disappointed. "Well... yeah," he managed to squeak out. He looked out the window again at the snow, suddenly feeling very melancholy. "I mean, it's not like we're gonna go home back to our parents. I don't even know if mine are still there considering the destruction Maya and those three weirdos did to my neighborhood."

There was silence for a moment. Despite his brashness, Mothman did empathize with Rob's feelings. After a moment of feeling the heaviness, he said, "Maybe Remius knows more than we do. It seems that he usually does." Mothman laughed to try to lighten the mood. "Let's go talk to that fuzzy guy."

Rob nodded in agreement as he tried to hold back the tears that were threatening to burst through the dam that he had been so stoically trying to keep together. Mothman left the room and went downstairs to find Remius who was sleeping on the couch. Rob followed after, taking the opportunity to wipe his eyes and regain his composure. When they got down to the living room, Remius was indeed curled in a black ball of fur on the couch. His tummy moved up and down with his quiet breath.

"Hey, fuzz ball," Mothman said, standing over the cat, Rob next to him.

Remius opened one eye and registered the two boys who dared awaken him from his feline slumber. "I do have a name you know," he retorted as he stretched his legs and yawned, mouth wide and tongue curled. "Terry's gone, isn't he?" The cat sat up and started grooming himself.

"How did you know?" Rob asked.

Remius eyed Rob, trying to decide if the boy was joking or not. "Is this kid for real?" Remius directed the question at Mothman. "I can feel that his energy is no longer here in the house."

Mothman turned to Rob and poked him in the arm excitedly. "See, I told you!" He exclaimed. "We can totally feel Terry. When he's here and when he's not."

Rob rubbed his arm where Mothman had poked him. "Then where is he, Remius?" He asked, hoping on the edge of hope that the cat could use his psychic powers to locate their friend.

Remius finished licking his paw and shook his head. "That, I'm sorry to say, I do not know. He's currently beyond my range of Sight."

"What about Eden?" Mothman wanted to know.

"Her as well," replied the cat.

Mothman clenched his fist. "I knew it. I fucking knew it. Why would they ditch us like that and not tell us where they were going? This is so fucking gay." Now he was grumbling, not speaking to anyone in particular. Mothman turned and walked away toward the front of the house, continuing his rant under his breath. "If he expects us to wait around for his fucking ass..." He trailed off.

Rob sat down next to Remius and put his chin in his hands. "Why me?" Rob asked. "Why did Maya choose me?"

Remius cocked his head to the side and said, "You're having one of *those* moments again?"

"I guess," Rob admitted. "I'm feeling kind of... I don't know."

The October rubbed up against Rob's leg and then laid down in his lap. "Considering all you've been through, you're handling things remarkably well. Not everyone can deal with their Soulmind being awake, much less handle their weapon and defend themselves against foes from other Dimensions." Remius purred, trying to reassure Rob that he was actually doing all right.

"Well, I don't feel like I'm handling it very well," Rob sighed.

"What the *fuck* are those?!" It was Mothman exclaiming as he stood by the front door and stared out the window. Rob's and Remius's heads went up to look in his direction. "Guys, get over here!" Without turning around, Mothman motioned for Remius and Rob to come over to the window. Remius jumped down off of Rob's lap and they both walked over to see what Mothman was yelling about. Rob froze when he saw what was coming over the snow toward the house.

Floating above the snow on the front lawn were about a dozen semi-translucent gray specters. Rob recognized them as the same ones that came out of the rift from the Dark Tethers when he escaped as well. He put his hand over his mouth, his eyes wide like flying saucers. The golden sphere of light from the surrogate Merkabah was still spinning strong, and when the specters approached it, they suddenly halted in mid-float. They couldn't cross the barrier; the protection protocol programmed into the lightbody wouldn't allow them to pass beyond it. The boys looked down the street. Coming from one direction was about twenty more specters, and from the other direction about twenty more.

Still staring out the window, Mothman addressed his friend. "Rob," he started. "Why do I get the feeling there's something you need to tell me?"

Rob felt his stomach sink all the way into his balls. "Ummm..." He tried to get the words out but his throat suddenly felt really dry. "These ghost-things are from the Dimension of

Dark Tethers. When I was able to come through back to Chicago—through the window that had been opened—these guys were kind of coming through too. From the other side."

Mothman now looked at Rob with an astonished look on his face. "And what, you just sort of forgot to mention this before? I'm sure that Terry and us two could have taken care of this shit before it got out of hand! Now look! We're fucked!"

"I was gonna tell you guys! I swear I was!" Rob insisted.

They stared out the window again. Remius hadn't said a word. Their looks of disbelief were so vivid on their faces that they could have been painted from a mile away. The specters were now stacking themselves on top of each other. They couldn't cross the barrier of the Merkabah, but they could surround it. And that was exactly what they were doing. Rob didn't know if it was an optical illusion, but it looked like the specters were multiplying as they covered the sphere of golden light with their gray bodies.

"Looks like we're gonna be here for a while," Remius finally said. "I wouldn't try crossing that if I were you. Even with a powerful Soulmind, that many specters, they'd find a way to overpower you and possess you. And if more than one enters your body, that's even worse."

"Fucking great!" Mothman threw up his arms in exasperation and went back over to the couch. Flopping down on the cushions, he said, "Thanks, Terry! You picked the best time to go AWOL. Fucking deserter. Leaving your friends to fend for themselves..." His grumbling trailed off again. Rob and Remius came over to join him on the couch.

"What are we going to do now?" Rob asked. "What are we to do waiting around for Terry to come back? Just sitting around in this house, we'll go nuts!"

"No you won't," Remius said, confident that this was true. "Because you're going to take this time to learn a lot more from me. If those things out there are any indication, you both are going to need to move up a lot more levels of skill before you're ready to handle what's coming."

* * *

Darren, the proprietor of the club *angelfuck*, sat at his desk and thought about his good friend Eden and his new friend Terry who had just embarked on a journey into the unknown realm of the Kingdom of the Stone Queen. Unknown for them; Darren had had quite a few adventures of his own in that Dimension. How could he not, being the guardian of the portal? The sun was just peeking up outside and all the partiers had left the club for whatever their chosen festivities for the Christmas Eve day would be. Darren very much enjoyed hosting the *Nights of Saturnalia* every December. It was the time at his club that he looked forward to the most out of the whole year. As a shaman and a practitioner of Magick who was always more in the realms of Gray than either of the two extremes of White and Black, he quite enjoyed nights of debauchery and erotic role-playing.

Even though he didn't believe in God, Darren nevertheless said a silent prayer for the safety of his two friends who were now on the other side of the portal behind the little door. He stood up and walked out of his office onto the dance floor of the club. The floor was a mess, but that was okay because he actually enjoyed cleaning up after his people. The disaster meant that they had had a splendid time at *angelfuck* and would continue to come again and again. Speaking of cumming, the floor was littered with used condoms and was sticky with an assortment of sexual fluids both male and female. There were also splashes of blood here and there from the rough body play. Strewn about, there was also confetti, Santa hats, and random pieces of costumes that had been ripped or discarded in the orgy.

Darren enjoyed the energy of the throngs of people who came through his establishment, but he also enjoyed the solitude in the morning when he was the only one left behind. He stood in the midst of the mess and soaked up the silence, meditating in the subtle pulse that still remained in the air, lingering from the sexual energy excreted by all the humans who had danced and gyrated in this room. As Darren communed with the emptiness, his thoughts went again to Eden and Terry. They were so young—Terry especially and Eden only a few years older than him. He remembered when he was that age and just becoming aware of his Soulmind and its strange powers. It seemed like a lifetime ago, and in some ways it was. Darren remembered his own October, Jade—his feline familiar. She was such a gorgeous creature, and now and again he really missed her. It had been two decades since he'd seen her. Once he had fully embraced his own power, Jade had to leave so that Darren could become the Master himself.

He knew that Terry was at a very delicate and pivotal time. It could be exciting, he remembered, sort of like a honeymoon period for the Awakening. How Terry chose to proceed from there and what he took away and put into practice from the teachings of his October, would shape his destiny totally. Darren wished all the best for him—and for Eden as well.

Without warning, he felt a presence break into his bubble of solitude. Darren looked up toward the entrance, where the energy was coming from. A smile pulled his lips as his eyes found a familiar furry face he hadn't seen in twenty years. "Jade!" He exclaimed as he felt the love well up in his heart for his first spiritual master. Kneeling down to greet the cat as she trotted over to him, Darren opened his arms.

"My favorite disciple," Jade said as she reached Darren's outstretched arms. As he petted her and rubbed her silky black fur, she purred against his touch. "I've missed you," she said.

"And I you, Jade," Darren replied, feeling the joy of the unexpected reunion. "This is a surprise," he said, looking into the cat's yellow eyes. "Did you come because of my friends? The two young Soulminds who went through the portal."

"Yes, I have actually," she answered, swishing her tail. "Their energy is very strong. Sul and the other dragons are stirring inside the Earth. There's a much bigger picture to this situation than you are aware of. And like it or not, you have a part to play in it."

"I've been pulled into the Soulmind game again," Darren laughed. "It's been a very very long time."

TWENTY-FIVE

The portal behind the Little Door spat Terry and Eden out into the middle of a field of wheat. They laid on their backs catching their breath from the inter-dimensional journey. Staring up at the tops of the golden stalks, they noticed that the sky was bright blue and clear. The sun was high in the sky and the air was warm—a startling change from the frigid winter of Chicago. Both Eden and Terry stripped off their winter coats; they wouldn't need them in this heat.

"This place doesn't seem too weird from first impression," Eden observed, sitting up.

"Yeah," Terry agreed. "I feel like we've been transported to summertime on a farm in Ohio." He laughed, sat up, and then stood up fully to get a lay of the land. "Come up and check this out, Eden. We're definitely on some sort of farm, but I don't think we're in the same time period that we came from." Reaching his hand down, he helped Eden to her feet.

The growth of wheat only came up to a little bit past their waists, so they had an unobstructed view of the rest of the farm. In one large pasture there were several cows grazing and mooing contentedly in the sun. In the center of the acreage was what looked to Terry to be a medieval farmhouse with a thatched roof. The frame of the house was wood, but the walls were made of stone so that it could survive harsh weather. Closer to the house was a fenced in pen with a few goats inside munching away on greens and vegetables. There was also quite a large garden growing flowers as well as an assortment of edible plants. Far beyond the house was a range of very tall mountains capped with white snow. In the other direction, away from the front of the farmhouse, was nothing but grassy hills until the eye couldn't see anything further.

"Should we go knock on the door of that house, or what?" Eden asked, unsure of what their next move should be.

Before Terry could reply, the door to the farmhouse flew open and an old man with a ancient-looking rifle raised from his shoulder came running out toward them. "Trying to steal my goats again, are ya?!" The old man yelled, trigger finger twitchy. This man was wearing suspenders with a faded blue shirt that had three buttons under the collar that were unbuttoned and tucked into his pants. He also had long white hair and beard, and—from the way his voice sounded—mostly likely no teeth.

Terry and Eden raised their hands in surrender, dropping their winter coats to the ground. "We're not here to steal your goats, I swear," Terry said earnestly. "Please don't shoot us!"

When the old farmer noticed their strange clothes, he lowered his gun, knowing that these two were indeed not the goat thieves. "Oi, I reckon you ain't," he said, calming down somewhat. "From the looks of yous, y'all must be travelers from that Hollow Dimension."

"You know about the Hollow Dimension?" Eden asked, lowering her hands.

"Aye, I do indeed. It's been a long while since the last one, but coming through the way you must have, you already know who I is referring to," the farmer said. Turning back toward the house, he motioned for them to follow. "Well, c'mon then. I e'spect you'll be wanting something to drink and some vittles for your stomachs."

Eden and Terry looked at each other then followed the old man inside. Closing the door behind them, the two traveling lovers looked around the interior of the farmhouse. It was only one story and the floor was dirt with several goat hides put down in certain areas. The largest area was dedicated to the kitchen. There were a couple wooden cabinets with counter space on top, and a few shelves mounted to the wall held ceramic plates. A stone fireplace was in the corner where all the cooking was done. And in the middle of the kitchen area was a medium sized wood table with four chairs set around it. The only other significant feature of the house was toward the back where there seemed to be two separate small rooms with only curtains over the entrances instead of doors.

"Welcome to my humble farm," the old man said, showing hospitality to his guests. He poured two mugs of fresh milk from a jug that was sitting on the table. "You may call me Mika'el.

Please, sit. Y'all make yourselves at home." Mika'el motioned to the chairs and slid the mugs in front of them. Terry and Eden sat down gratefully.

"Thank you very much, sir," Terry said and sipped from the mug. It was the freshest milk that he had ever tasted.

Mika'el laughed, his toothless gums showing behind his mustache and beard. "No need to be so formal. Just call me Mika'el. Or *El* for short... That's what my wife used to call me."

"Where is she today?" Eden asked, drinking her milk gratefully.

"Oh," Mika'el said looking softly off into space. "She passed away some time ago."

"I'm sorry," Eden responded.

Mika'el shook his head. "No. It's okay. I miss her sometimes, but to tell you the truth, I actually enjoy my solitude..." He went quiet for a minute and then continued. "We had two children, a boy and a girl. They slept in that other little room back there." Mika'el pointed with his thumb toward the back of the house where the two rooms were. "Them two is grown now and have lives of their own in the Village. So you're welcome to stay here and sleep in that room if you wish. Make yourself at home. The other Traveler... Darren, I think that was his name... He stayed in there too. Damn, that was over twenty years ago now."

"Darren!" Terry exclaimed, tapping Eden on the arm. "That's who you were referring to before, weren't you, Mika'el?" Mika'el nodded. Terry continued, "Tell us about your world, the Kingdom of the Stone Queen. And the Village that you mentioned too."

Mika'el walked over to the stone fireplace which was blazing with orange flames. There was a stone shelf above the fire which was used to bake and cook food. Sitting on this stone shelf was a large pot with some kind of soup bubbling inside. Mika'el stirred it with a wooden spoon and then began sharing his story. "When Darren came to our Dimension over twenty years ago, he saved us... for a while. The Stone Queen wasn't stone back then. She was flesh and blood like you and me. To this day no one knows her real name or where she came from. But she was the most powerful entity that we simple people had ever laid our eyes on. And she used her power and magic to enslave our people... We were only the Village back then."

"Where is this Village?" Eden asked. "We didn't see it when we were out in the wheat field."

"I'm the only one who lives on the outskirts of the Village," Mika'el answered. "And I like it that way. The Villagers leave me alone... Except recently when someone has been stealing my goats. Anyway, the Village is about five miles north of here. Surrounding our entire occupied region is a large mountain range—you two must have seen it coming in. No one as far as I know has been beyond those mountains. So if there's more to this land of ours, we can't even get there."

"So is the Village the only occupied town here?" Terry wanted to know.

Mika'el shook his head. "There's also the City. We have the Village and the City. These two are separated by a large forest. And as of now the Stone Queen doesn't allow anyone from either the Village or the City to cross over the forest at all. We are completely separate, in two different worlds. The Queen used slave labor from the Village to build her perfect City. She taught them how to build huge towers and how to create technology that none of us had even dreamed was possible. This technology was completely indistinguishable from magic. So she kept the Village in a state of pre-technology and a very archaic way of life. And on the other side of the forest is a City which is like a dream of the future."

"What does this all have to do with Darren?" Eden asked.

"I'm getting to that," Mika'el responded. "Darren is a very powerful being in his own right, and when he came here and saw how the Queen had enslaved us, he made it his mission to free our people. Darren challenged the Queen, and to my surprise, they were pretty evenly matched. They fought for days. Neither one able to get much of an upper hand on the other. Darren drove her into the forest for most of their battle so that there wouldn't be a lot of innocent people killed from the powerful energies that were clashing. He somehow managed to push the Queen back and back into a huge cave that was in the middle of the forest. But she was strong, and she had weakened him almost to the point of killing him. And when Darren was bleeding and exhausted, almost to the point of his body collapsing, in one final effort, he concentrated all of his energy into a singularity and exploded it into the Queen's body. The force of the blast turned her to stone, trapping her consciousness into a form which could not move. He left her there as a statue in the depths of the cave and he dragged himself back out, half-dead. Darren used so much of his Soulmind energy to trap the Queen in stone that he was never the same after that. That one single act significantly shortened his lifespan and, even though he is still powerful, his energy will never reach that level again."

"So he freed your people!" Terry said. "But you said he only saved you for a while... What did you mean by that? Did the Stone Queen escape?"

"Not exactly," Mika'el said in response. "We were freed for a while right after Darren trapped the Queen in stone. She couldn't do anything, she was completely imprisoned. So we weren't under her rule anymore and could actually travel back and forth between the Village and the City. And we came to enjoy both lifestyles—playing with flying cars and robotics, and going up to the top of huge buildings; and then going back to our simple life in the Village growing crops and trading. But remember the Stone Queen is powerful and very crafty. Her consciousness was still active inside the stone, and she was learning. She learned how to leave her stone prison in her Astral Body. In her Astral Form, she cannot influence the physical world directly, she can only observe on an energetic level. But, wicked Queen that she is, she found a loophole. On her Astral Travels in space, she found a way to hack into the Akashic Records, which is all the information of Existence in vibrational form. Hacking into them, she found that she could re-write them to her liking. So she went into the files from our Dimension and re-wrote all of our Soul Contracts to serve her and become her slaves again. Now she as the Stone Queen exists as an energy vampire and syphons the majority of the energy we create and also have in our bodies. We're basically a battery for her. As we get weaker, she gets stronger. Within our re-written Soul Contracts, it specifies that all work we do is slave labor to serve her energy. And even though the Queen cannot get out of her stone physically, all the energy she syphons from her slaves goes to strengthening her Astral Body. And what she's doing out in the cosmos with it is beyond us."

Terry and Eden exchanged a look of amazement. "That's fucking nuts," Eden said. "I don't even know what to say to that story. I've never heard anything like that. No wonder Darren just told us that it was 'strange' here and didn't want to go into explaining it."

Terry reached for Eden's hand which was resting on her upper thigh. He squeezed it and they smiled at each other in reassurance that everything was going to be fine and that they must be here now to accomplish something. Mika'el walked over and stirred the soup in the pot again. "The stew is done," he said, glancing back over to Eden and Terry. "It's beet stew with several other assorted root vegetables... Do you want some?"

"Yes, please," Eden and Terry both said at the same time. They were famished. Mika'el filled two bowls with the stew and placed them in front of his guests. Then he filled one for himself and took a seat across from them. They were all so hungry that they didn't mind the silence while they ate.

TWENTY-SIX

Arash woke himself up and snuck away in the middle of the night. Leeah had taught him how to access the gateway back into the Hollow Dimension, and how to get back into the Palace Temple from the other side. The gateway looked like a huge doorway in the stone wall. Where the door or passage should have been instead was a smooth black surface. Arash placed his hand vertically in the middle of this blackness. The area around his hand illuminated in a yellow glow, registering that he was indeed allowed access. As he turned his hand to the right ninety degrees, the black surface began to ripple and flow like waves on a pond. Arash withdrew his hand and immediately walked through the portal back into the Hollow Dimension—a place he hadn't been in a long while.

He came out in the stairwell of the Public Works building. As Arash descended the stairs to the ground floor, he could feel the chill of the night even before he emerged into the open air. After exiting the building, his teeth began to chatter and he wrapped his arms around his body to try to generate some heat against the frigid winter freeze. There were a bright moon and stars shining down from a cloudless sky. The snow crunched under his feet. Arash wanted to get this over with as quickly as possible so he could get back to where he preferred to be—the Palace Temple. Since he had done so much spiritual work in a short amount of time, the energy of the Hollow Dimension felt very dense, threatening to crush his higher vibration. Arash knew he wasn't for this human world anymore. He was still human himself, but he had become something more.

Arash hurried at a slow jog through the dark suburban streets in the direction of Rob's neighborhood. The houses and the streets of his old town were eerily dead and silent except for the occasional dog barking that heard his footsteps crunching the snow as he passed by its yard. He was all but frozen when he reached the street Rob's house was on, his body turning numb against the bite of the chill.

The front door was unlocked when he got there, so Arash just let himself in without knocking. He almost puked as the stench of death reached his nostrils. Dry heaving, he put his hand over his nose and mouth. When he approached the kitchen, Arash saw the destruction and the dead bodies of Rob's parents rotting on the floor in puddles of coagulated blood. *They must have been there for at least a week*, Arash thought. Flies buzzed and swarmed the dried blood and bodies like moochers at a wedding feast. Gingerly he stepped over the mess of death and continued further into the house.

Seeing no signs of anyone on the ground floor, Arash decided to go upstairs and check for who he was looking for in Rob's bedroom. Leeah had told him that Maya would definitely be here. Arash hoped that she hadn't left, because he would have no idea where else to look if she ended up not being here. As luck would have it, she *was* still here—waiting for him even if she didn't know that completely. Arash spotted her as he entered the darkness of what used to be Rob's bedroom. Maya was sitting in the desk chair, hunched over with her elbows on her thighs and head in her hands. She stood up suddenly as Arash entered the room.

"Who's there?" Maya asked in a strong voice.

Arash put up his hands to show he meant no harm. "I'm not here to hurt you," Arash insisted. "Are you Maya? I have a message for you."

Maya's totally black eyes needed no assistance to see perfectly in the gloom. Her night vision was immaculate; it had to be where she was from. So as she took in the image of Arash, she recognized him as the same boy from her vision and she relaxed, sitting back down in the chair. "I am Maya," she replied. "I had a vision of you. You were sitting on a fancy bed with a canopy, in a room filled with pictures and statues of Indian deities."

Arash nodded. "Yes. My name is Arash."

"Come, sit with me," Maya said and patted the bed next to her. "Do you have a creative solution to the difficulties I've been having trying to procure Terry's Soulmind?"

Arash went over and sat down on the edge of the bed. The look of Maya—her all-black eyes, her long hair, and black leotard—made him a little bit uneasy, but he made sure not to show any discomfiture. "I think I do," he answered.

"Well, then, spit it out, boy!" Maya was urgent, she had waited long enough and had too many failed attempts to dilly-dally any longer.

"What if I told you that there was a piece of Terry's Soulmind sitting in a jar, just waiting for you to claim it?"

"I'm listening."

"In the Palace Temple of the Order of the Transcendent, in the Library, inside a glass cabinet, is a cylinder filled with a dancing white light—which is the piece of Terry's Soulmind."

"That is intriguing. But if you've actually been with the Order, you know that there's no way I could get in there and steal it. They watch me too closely and have *binds* against my energy."

"That's why you send the three—Trick, Tock, and Tick, was it?" Arash looked around the room. "I didn't seem to see them downstairs. And they're not here with you."

Maya made a dismissive gesture with her hand. "Those idiots got impatient so they left to destroy the neighborhood and kill people for amusement. I swear, those three can't sit still for more than five minutes."

"So they're not with you anymore?" Arash asked. If this was the case, his whole mission coming here would be for nothing.

"Oh, no," Maya returned. "They are. I'll just have to go find them and tell them what to do and where to go. Shouldn't be too hard to track those three down—just go where the screaming can be heard." She laughed.

"Oh, good," Arash said and relaxed a bit. "I almost thought I had wasted my time coming here."

"No, you didn't," Maya assured him. "Thank you, Arash. I know I'm a heartless woman who's hell-bent on seeking destruction, but I actually do appreciate what you're doing. I know it's not easy for you to make a decision like this, especially because of who you are." Arash was silent and stared into her eyes, deep like ink wells. She continued, "It's okay, you don't have to say anything. I can feel your energy."

Maya gently took hold of the sides of Arash's head and pulled his forehead in toward her own till both of their skulls touched at the area of the third eye. She closed her eyes and so did Arash. Surprisingly, he did not feel uncomfortable anymore. He could see she was a divine expression of Source as well, just like he was. And they were reflections of each other. "Now psychically transfer where the location of the cylinder is with the Soul-mind," Maya whispered.

Arash visualized the Public Works building and then how to enter into the Palace Temple from there. Then he saw the Library and the cabinet with the two cylinders, one with white light and the other with purple light.

"The Divine within me recognizes the Divine within you," Arash said to Maya as he finished the transference of knowledge.

"And I, the same," Maya returned. Slowly and gently she kissed Arash on the lips. He knew that even in an entity such as Maya, there was still Love even if it was buried deep. After the kiss, she pulled away and bowed her head to him once more. "Now, go," she said. "Your work is done here."

Without another word, Arash got up and left the house that used to be Rob's. Now he didn't know what it was. Entering back into the chill of the night, he shook off the energy of death that he had encountered in the kitchen. As quickly as he could, Arash took off back toward the Public Works building, shivering as he went.

He made it without freezing to death and took the stairs in the creepy stairwell two at a time till he reached the top and the concrete wall. Thrusting his hand into the middle of the wall, the yellow glow circled his hand again. He turned his hand ninety degrees to the right and the black portal appeared, rippling before him. Gladly he walked through back into the Palace Temple. The black gateway smoothed out and solidified behind him. The halls of the Palace Temple were just as still and silent as they were when Arash had absconded from his quarters.

Quickly he went back to his room, closed the door softly, and wrapped himself in the blankets on his bed. His bones still ached from the cold winter of the Hollow Dimension. Only once he started to warm up and truly believe he was back in the Palace

Temple where he belonged, did he allow himself to fully relax and fall into a deep sleep.

JANUARY

ONE

Jessica Thorn was having no little difficulty breathing through the gag in her mouth and because of the constant bouncing against her diaphragm from the horse below her. From what she gathered, they were taking her to the nearest village to be executed as a witch. Jessica wasn't quite sure whether this was all part of her Soma trip or if it was actually real and the threat against her life direly imminent. Maybe she *was* actually going to die this time. These were the thoughts bouncing around her very confused head.

Jessica managed to turn her head to the side and get a glimpse of the village they were approaching. They trotted past a carved wooden sign which read: *Welcome to the Village of Thanatos.* The riders with their captive galloped into Thanatos and through the marketplace where the bystanders stared aghast at the sight of the *Witch from the Woods.* The villagers looked to Jessica like people who took the Renaissance Faire way too seriously. The man on the horse that Jessica was slung over spoke without looking down at her, "You see how they all despise you, witch?" He snarled. "They know you're disgusting and evil. Seduced by the Devil himself… Or maybe it was you who seduced *him*."

The four men halted their horses outside of a large ominous stone building. Jessica almost whimpered behind the cloth gag in her mouth, but she didn't want to give these men the satisfaction of seeing her fear. In front of the building was a hitching rail where they could tie up their horses. They all dismounted and proceeded to secure their horses to the rail. When the man on who's horse Jessica was still draped over was finished, he pulled her roughly off of the animal and slung her over his shoulder. She struggled uselessly as they all four entered the building.

They went into a main room on the ground floor which was dark and musty. The floors were wood, very old, and smelled like they were beginning to rot. There was also a jail cell in the corner for holding prisoners before a trial or execution. An older man snored in his chair behind a large oak desk. The man had a long bushy mustache and was wearing a uniform which looked almost military, like something that might have been worn during the Revolutionary War. He wore a long green coat which was buttoned all the way up to the collar with large gold buttons. The cuffs of the sleeves were extravagant and he wore white gloves over his hands.

"Chief Officer!" The man holding Jessica spoke loudly enough to startle the old man from his nap. The Chief Officer blinked sleepily and then stood up hastily, almost getting the sword at his hip caught in the chair he was sitting on.

"Nobleman Barnabas," the Officer said, addressing the one who spoke and saluting him briefly. "What brings you to my office?" He asked, attempting to hold back a yawn but failing.

"We've captured the witch from the forest," Barnabas replied, indicating Jessica by smacking her ass a couple times. She mumbled in protest.

"Oh my God," the Officer exclaimed. "That's her, innit? How'd ya find her? We usually cain't go past that enchanted circle the *Old Ones* put a spell on. Those two never come out far enough for us to catch *them*."

"Oddly enough," Barnabas continued. "She stumbled out of the forest just as we had stopped our horses for a rest. And I'll be damned if we were gonna let the little bitch get away."

"Well," said the Officer going over to the barred door of the holding cell and opening it. "Throw her in."

The only two things inside the jail cell were a small cot covered with straw and a bucket in the corner. Jessica kicked and struggled as Barnabas threw her down on the cot. The other three noblemen held her down so she couldn't try to squirm away, not that she could go very far being tied up. "Do you have the contraption?" Barnabas asked the Chief Officer.

The Officer nodded and retrieved a strange object from the bottom drawer of his desk. The *contraption* looked like a metal skull cap. The Officer came into the cell where the three noblemen were restraining Jessica and Barnabas was standing as witness. "Hold still!" The Officer commanded. "Don't fucking move or I'll run you through with my blade. Don't test me."

Jessica glared at the old man, but nevertheless ceased her struggling. The Officer slid the skull cap snugly over her head. It was tight and came all the way down to the bottom of her eyebrows, covering her entire forehead. He locked the straps of the contraption below Jessica's chin tightly enough that she wouldn't be able to wiggle it off.

"Now try to do your Devil magic through that," Barnabas taunted and slapped the side of her head. The metal was hard against her skin and rattled her brain inside her skull. Barnabas turned to the three noblemen he had come with on horseback and said, "You may go now."

The three men nodded and left the way they had come without as much as a word uttered. "Now we're going to cut your bonds and take the gag from your mouth," the Officer said. "But I swear, if you try *anything* or say *anything*, I will run you through with my blade." He took the sword from its sheath and pointed it at Jessica's throat while Barnabas pulled his knife from the scabbard at his waist. Jessica didn't make a sound but gave the Officer the most intense look that could have wilted a flower. "Don't look at me, witch!" He yelled. "Cast your gaze down with those evil eyes!"

Jessica looked down at the floor while Barnabas cut the bonds at her wrists and ankles. Then he pulled the gag from her mouth. She gulped the oxygen in deep lungfuls. Without any sudden movements, she sat up slowly on the cot and eyed the two men warily. Barnabas stood up and returned the knife to his waist. The Officer still had his blade at her throat and ready. "That bucket over there is for when you need to do your business," Barnabas indicated the rusty bucket in the corner. He wiped his hands on his trousers and left the cell. The Officer slowly backed out of the cell with sword still up then locked the door of the cage behind him.

"Enjoy your last days, witch," the Officer said as he sheathed his blade. "Because it won't be long till we burn that pretty flesh right off your bones."

Barnabas made a gesture with his hand for the Officer to come to him. "Let's talk business," he said as the Officer turned away from Jessica. "Not in front of *her*. Outside."

Both men gave Jessica one more look as she sat behind bars with her arms folded across her chest. Then they turned and exited the room, leaving her alone in the gloom. Jessica let herself fall back onto the straw cot and put her hands over her face. *How the fuck did this happen?* she thought to herself. *This morning I was safe in the Fairy Circle with Jay and Magda, and now I'm locked in a jail* cell. How much worse can it get? Is this really it, am I really gonna die this way?

Outside, standing by the one horse still tied to the hitching rail, Barnabas and the Officer spoke in hushed whispers. "So do you want me to torture her?" The Officer asked.

"No," Barnabas said, giving a wicked smile. "Leave her unspoiled... for me."

TWO

Rob, Mothman, and Remius were standing in a wide circle in the basement of Terry's house. It was an unfinished basement with a concrete floor and pillars holding up the foundation of the house. There were also random boxes in the corners of the room put there for storage. Remius had been attempting to teach the boys alternative ways of Soulmind combat that did not involve using their weapons. Apparently it was taking Mothman a little while to catch on.

"All right," Remius said with a sigh. "Mothman, concentrate your Soulmind into a ball of energy in your palm. Feel the heat and visualize it grow above your palm and between your fingers and thumb."

Mothman raised his hand in front of himself, palm facing up at chest level. He concentrated like a bodybuilder trying to lift an eight-hundred pound barbell. Visualizing an orange sphere of light, he tried to will his Soulmind into a ball in his hand. Mothman scrunched up his face, strained as his face turned red, and swore at himself as a small light began to flicker above his hand. "Oh!" He exclaimed. "I got it! I got it! I got it!" The orange sphere of energy grew slowly larger, spiraling tendrils of color like an electromagnetic storm. It stabilized at about the size of a baseball.

"Okay, you finally got it going," Remius remarked. "Now squeeze the sphere and make it shoot out of your hand into a thin blade. Lord knows your actual Soulmind weapon is so impotent that it couldn't even harm a loaf of bread." The October was referring to the small bowie knife which was Mothman's Soulmind weapon.

"Hey fuck you, cat!" Mothman spit back. "I can do this..." After a moment of concentration, he squeezed the ball of energy, but instead of extending into a blade, it just fizzled out in his fist. Mothman opened his empty hand. "Fuck!"

"You fail the class," Remius shot the insult like an arrow.

"Goddamnit!" Mothman cursed. "I swear I had it that time! What am I doing wrong?"

"Well, for starters you don't have that much sexual energy left to fuel it," Remius answered. Mothman stared at the cat with a dumbfounded expression. "Look," Remius continued. "It's all on account of you buggering Rob all night long and dissipating your fucking life force into his ass."

"Hey fuck you, asshole!" Rob yelled back at Remius's insult. "We don't do that!"

The October scoffed at the denial. "What, you don't think I know you two are a bunch of little queermos? Most likely tea-bagging each other and sixty-nining, deep throating each other's cocks till you cum with gay ecstasy drinking each other's semen... Faggot."

"Shut the fuck up, you cat fuck!" Mothman screamed, the words hit him deep. "Don't you fucking call me that! I swear I'll kill you!" His face was getting hot and red with boiling rage.

"What? Faggot?" Remius egged him on.

"I swear to God I'll chop you up and eat you!" Mothman retorted. Rob was just standing silently watching the cat and the human go at it.

Remius was silent for a moment. Then after the pause he said, "Faggot. Faggot. Faggot!"

"Aaaaaggghhhh!" Mothman screamed so loud it could have woken sleeping dragons in the bowels of the Earth. "Suck my fucking dick!" As he yelled, Mothman jutted his hands out in front of his chest as if throwing a basketball. Instantaneously an orange sphere of Soulmind energy ignited and was double the size of the one that he had had in one hand before. As his arms reached full extension from his body, darts of light shot out of the sphere straight at Remius. The cat's aura illuminated in each spot that a dart made contact with his electromagnetic field and was reflected harmlessly away. Mothman stared in awe at the uninjured October as he let his arms fall to his sides and the sphere vanished.

Remius smiled at the boys and swished his tail contentedly. "See! I knew you could do it," he said cheerily. "You just needed a little motivation, that's all."

Mothman shook his head. "You're such a fucking dick. You know that, right?"

"Shut up, you two!" Rob suddenly interjected, holding up his index finger in the air.

Mothman jerked his head to look at Rob. "What is it?"

"Shhh," Rob hushed his friend. "Do you hear that?"

They all fell silent and strained their ears to hear what it was Rob could possibly be talking about. After a minute or two of listening quietly, Mothman thought he could make out a *chop-chop-chop* sound like rotors—or propellors.

"We're not alone," Remius said forebodingly.

High above Terry's house was a black helicopter hovering in the sky. The two men sitting in the aircraft wore black suits and black sunglasses. Of course, they couldn't see the Merkabah or the specters around the house, but the high energy signature given off by all the entities in that small area showed up on their radar as a strange electromagnetic spike. The coordinates where the house was blipped on the small radar screen and spit out readings that looked like high math or a foreign language. After monitoring for several minutes, hovering in the same spot, the two suited men gave each other a nod without any exchange of words. The helicopter then peeled off and flew back toward the Chicago skyline.

"That was creepy," Rob said as they heard the sound of the helicopter fade away.

Remius now looked genuinely concerned, pensive. "If we end up attracting the attention of government agencies," the October said seriously, "we might have on our hands more than we bargained for."

THREE

Dawn was breaking and Maya stared out of Rob's bedroom window as the sun peeked over the horizon. She had decided to wait until the morning light to go and find Trick, Tock, and Tick for their new mission. What miracle had brought Arash to her? she thought. Just when her vision for changing the world had become all but hopeless. It seemed that the rising of the Dark was to become a reality after all. How long had she waited for this? To bring her realm to the Hollow Dimension which thought itself so high in the order of things. To knock the humans to their pompous knees and show them the horrors which they themselves had wrought. Then they would finally see that how much faith they put in their own power was an illusion all along.

Maya finally stood up from the desk chair where she had been sitting for days and went downstairs, stepped over the dead bodies and through the flies, then left through the front door. It was still early enough for the sidewalks and streets of the suburbs to be pretty much empty. The freeze of the air and the winter snow bit at her but she didn't feel it. Her breath puffed into the air like clouds of smoke. She could feel Trick, Tock, and Tick's energy right away and knew they were a couple blocks down and a few houses over. As she walked the streets, it was apparent that her three comrades had been busy. Almost every house she passed was destroyed in some way—windows shattered, roofs reduced to splinters, and front doors ripped off their hinges. Shaking her head, she chuckled to herself. These dimwitted humans had never even known what hit them until it was too late. Most likely the destruction would be contributed to some supernatural force like a poltergeist and they would send in a paranormal investigator to exorcise the demons. Little would they know that the ones who had haunted the houses were long gone.

When she arrived at the house that they were still having fun in, she could hear furniture breaking and lamps being shattered within. "Hey, idiots! You having fun in there?" Maya said as she entered through the broken front door. Trick and Tick were in the living room and still going at it. Trick held a floor lamp like a club and was using it to smash all the bookshelves in the room. Wooden splinters and book pages flew through the room. Tock was running around the house like he was on speed shattering all the windows. Tick had cut a hole in one of the arms of the couch and he was currently fucking it, his eyes rolling around his head and drool pouring from his open mouth. Maya looked down and saw a dead baby on the floor in a pool of blood with a pencil stabbed through its left eye. It had also been decapitated with a butter knife.

"You know you guys are are seriously fucked up, right?" Maya said and they all stopped what they were doing. They stared at her standing in the doorway, evidently surprised to see her. Tick pulled his fat dick out of the couch and started stroking it. "Put that thing away!" She snapped at him. "We have work to do."

Tick abruptly stopped jerking himself off, and as a stupid look came over his face, jiz squirted from the tip of his dick and became flaccid simultaneously. Tock walked in to join them, abandoning his joy-smashing of the windows in the rest of the house. "What is it, boss?" Tock asked. "Find a way to kill that Terry kid for good?"

Maya shook her head. "Something better," she replied. "I've received information that there's already a piece of Terry's Soulmind separated from his body and waiting for us to snatch it up."

"Why haven't you gone to get it already, boss?" Trick asked, dropping the floor lamp he was still holding.

"Unfortunately, it's in a place where I can't go," Maya admitted. "It's too risky for me to try. The Order of the Transcendent would know I was there the minute I entered their domain."

"So you need us to go and retrieve it for you," Tock said.

"Hey, you're not as dumb as you look," Maya returned. Tock grinned as if that was the highest compliment he ever received in his life. "Trick, come here." She made a motion with her finger for him to come closer.

"What?" Trick asked. He wasn't sure if she was planning to kiss him or punch him.

"I said come here, you numbskull!"

Trick hesitantly came a little closer to Maya, but not close enough. She rolled her eyes and sighed. Then without warning she reached out and grabbed Trick by the back of the neck and pulled him toward her until their foreheads were touching. Maya psychically transferred how to get to the Public Works building, how to enter the Palace Temple from there, and the coordinates of the Library and the cylinder therein which contained the piece of Terry's Soulmind. Trick received the Transmission loud and clear and knew exactly where to go and how to get there.

After the Transference ended, Maya pushed him away from her. "You got that? Where to go. What to do. And what you need to bring back to me."

Trick nodded. "Aye, aye, boss!" He was psyched and ready for the new task at hand.

"Wait till cover of nightfall," Maya instructed. "You'll be less likely to get caught. Once you have procured the package, come find me back at Rob's house. And be careful not to open it or break it. If you fuck this up for me, I swear I will kill every last one of you—and it will be in a way you won't enjoy."

"Awww, we have to wait all the way until nighttime?" Tock whined. "That's so fucking *long* from now! What are we supposed to do in the Greenwich mean time?"

Maya was about to go back to her base at Rob's house and leave the three to their own depraved devices. She turned back from the doorway and said, "I don't know. You all can just keep fucking that couch."

FOUR

Waking up the next morning in Mika'el's guest room was a bit disorienting for Terry and Eden. It took them a couple minutes to actually remember where they were. The room was very small with a tiny window which looked out onto the back fields. They had to squeeze together pretty tight on the cot that they were sleeping on, which they didn't mind particularly.

"How do you like waking up in a different world?" Eden asked Terry as she kissed him awake.

"Fantastical," he replied. "It's like something out of a dream. I feel like I've gone back in time somehow." As they kissed, Terry was pressed against her thigh.

"What's this?" Eden slipped her hand down and grasped his hard cock. Terry inhaled a sharp gasp of pleasure. "Is this a present for me?" She said as she stroked him up and down the whole length of his erection. Before Eden gave Terry a chance to answer, she pressed her lips against his and slid her tongue deep into his mouth. Her strokes became faster and Terry's whole body shuddered with ecstasy. He moaned against her mouth which was open and ravenously licking inside of his.

"Do you want me to fuck you like a lord fucks a peasant girl?" Terry said playfully.

Eden squeezed his cock hard and smiled, biting her bottom lip. "Mmmm, that sounds delicious," she whispered. "But Mika'el is right out there and we have nothing but a bit of curtain separating us."

"Since when have you been modest *ever* in your life?" Terry teased.

She pretended to be aghast and punched him in the arm playfully. Rolling over, Eden grinded her ass against Terry's rock-hard cock. It was throbbing and ready to be inside of her. Terry pulled her panties down off of her ass and she was already wet.

"Oh no, my lord. Please don't!" Eden played, taking on the role of the innocent peasant girl who was about to be taken advantage of by the lord who owned the land. Terry teased the tip of his prick between her moist pussy lips. "No, I beg you, my lord! I'm saving my virginity for my husband. He's a humble pig farmer."

Terry couldn't hold back his laugh at the idea of Eden ever being a virgin—or married to a pig farmer for that matter. "You know you want this fucking cock, wench!" Terry said, playing his part as well.

Eden turned her head to look over her shoulder and broke character by saying, "I don't think a lord would say that."

"Shut up, bitch, and take this dick!" Terry put his hand over Eden's mouth as he entered her hard and deep. Her lubrication seeped out around his shaft and dampened his balls. He thrusted in and out so deep that the tip of his cock touched her cervix. Eden moaned softly behind Terry's hand. He took his hand off of her mouth and moved it down to her slim waist so he had a grip for his deep thrusts. "I own this land and I own everyone on this land," he said, still in character.

"Oh God..." Eden let out a deep moan of pleasure. "That's so fucking hot, babe!"

Terry looked down and watched Eden's perky ass slap against his abdomen. "You like that don't ya, slut?"

"Yes! Oh, yes! Fuck me harder!" Eden exclaimed and Terry obliged. "I want you to fucking cum in me! Oh fuck, Terry, cum in my tight pussy!"

Terry slowed down, hesitating for a second. "Are you sure?"

Eden turned her head over her shoulder again as her breathing got heavier. "Just shut the fuck up and cum inside me!"

Hearing Eden say that sent Terry right over the edge and he couldn't hold his nut. Moaning with such orgasmic ecstasy, five separate spurts of semen shot out of his cock deep inside her. Still inside her, Terry held Eden tight and squeezed her small breasts as they caught their breath. "Oh my God! I came so fucking hard," Terry said breathily.

Eden licked her lips, her eyes still closed as she bathed in the sensation. "Mmmm... Oh fuck yeah. Me too, babe. I love feeling your hot jiz inside me." She grinded her ass against Terry's body and squeezed her pussy muscles around his cock before pulling him out and turning over to kiss him again.

After a few minutes of passionately kissing and touching each other, they got dressed and left the room to see what Mika'el was up to. When they met Mika'el in the kitchen, their faces were still flushed from their recent fuck session. Mika'el was cooking up some fresh eggs and there was a large bowl of freshly picked berries on the table.

Mika'el eyed the two lovers as they came in. "Eh, I e'spect you'll be wanting some breakfast after all that," he said.

Terry smiled, trying to hold back his laughter. "What do you mean?" He asked, knowing very well what Mika'el was referring to.

"I mean, it sounded like you two were having quite a time in there," Mika'el said, a smile toying at the corners of his mouth. "Maybe the 'wench' would like some berries." He pushed the bowl of berries toward Eden. "Maybe some cherries..."

Eden gave Terry a look and they both lost it, unable to contain their laughter. They were both rolling, laughing so hard they could barely breathe. It was contagious and Mika'el started to laugh along with them. After the hilarity had subsided, they all felt a great deal more comfortable with each other. Terry and Eden sat down at the table while Mika'el served them plates of eggs that had been cooked in the stone oven. They used wooden forks to eat the eggs and just helped themselves to the fresh berries. Everything was delicious.

Mika'el sat down across from them with his own plate of eggs. "You two going to see the Village today?" He asked.

"Yeah, actually. That's what we were planning on doing," Eden answered. "How did you know?"

"I just had a feelin' is all," Mika'el replied. "You can't be wearing those clothes, though. You'll stick out like a sore thumb. I have some clothes you can wear that'll help ya blend in better. And when you're ready to cross the forest and see the City, I have clothes fer that too."

"We can't just wear our normal clothes when we go to the City?" Terry asked.

"You'd think so, wouldn't ya?" Mika'el responded. "It's much more advanced than where you all come from. I know that's hard to believe till ya've seent it. Them folks is strange over there. I prefer my humble little *pig farm*." Mika'el winked at Eden and she blushed, diverting her eyes to her food. Terry didn't catch the joke.

"Is there anything else we need to know about the Village before we go?" Terry asked.

"Yes, now that you mention it," Mika'el said, getting up from the table. He rummaged around in a cupboard till he found what he was looking for. When he was back at the table, he slapped down a stack of what looked like paper bank notes. "Money," he said. "This is our currency. You'll be needing some."

Terry picked up one of the bills and inspected it. It almost looked like American money except for the woman's face in the center; underneath it read *The Queen*. Terry scoffed. "The Stone Queen has you guys put her face on the money?"

Mika'el sighed. "That's just how it is. All the money technically belongs to her and we're just *lent* it. Each note actually just represents a debt to be owed her. So the more money you have, the more debt—as in energy—that she gets to suck from you... Oh, but don't worry. You two aren't under the same Soul Contracts as we are. So those rules don't apply to you. It's *my* money. I'm just letting you use it while you're here."

Eden touched Terry's hand on the table. "Does that sound familiar to you, babe?" She said.

Terry looked confused. "What? About the money?"

Eden shook her head. "Nevermind. Doesn't matter anyway."

Mika'el grinned, showing his toothless gums. "Somefing tells me y'all are gonna be meeting her soon."

"Who?" Eden asked.

"The Queen, a'course!"

"What makes you say that?" Terry wondered.

Mika'el shrugged. "Like I say, it's just a feelin' I got."

Terry and Eden had been walking along the dirt road which led from Mika'el's farm to the Village for quite some time. It didn't feel like they had been walking that long since the food they had eaten gave them ample energy and they were enjoying the scenery of the beautiful countryside. The forest that separated the Village side from the City side ran parallel to the dirt road. However, they wanted to go experience the Village before crossing over to the other side. Besides, they'd have to come back to Mika'el's in order to get the clothes they needed to blend in with the people of the City.

"You look sexy in those tights, babe," Eden joked and spanked Terry's ass playfully.

"They're not tights," Terry insisted. "They're called stockings. Apparently this was common attire for men in the Medieval period." He was wearing a long brown tunic which was tied with a rope around his waist and green stockings underneath.

Eden giggled. "It's like you're wearing a dress with leggings. You'd make a cute girl."

Terry blushed but didn't argue with the statement. "Yeah, and what the fuck are you wearing?" He retorted. "It looks like you're wearing a blue bed sheet. And that thing on your head makes you look like a nun—or maybe an Amish bag lady." Terry laughed and poked her in the ribs.

Eden came close and rubbed her body against his. "Oh, come on. You know you like it," she teased. "The idea of you defiling a nun or a virginal Amish girl during Rumspringa."

Terry smiled and rolled his eyes. He pushed her away in mock protest. "Don't get me started," he said. "You'll get me all horny again and I'll have to take advantage of you right here in the middle of the road."

"Promise?" Eden pressed her hands over her dress and into her crotch. She gave a preformed moan.

"I've never met a girl who wanted to fuck as much as you," Terry commented.

"Are you complaining?"

"Definitely not," he answered quickly.

Eden giggled and said, "I'm a farm girl now. All the time I've spent milking goats has made me an expert at milking your cock."

"Oh my God, you're gonna get me hard again," Terry said and thought he could see something coming up in the distance. "Hey, I think we're almost there."

Eden dropped her sexy peasant girl act and squinted into the distance. "I think I see it!" She confirmed. "That's gotta be the Village. It didn't take us as long to walk as I thought it would."

They picked up their pace as the small buildings of the Village got larger as they approached. Most of the dwellings resembled Mika'el's farmhouse—walls made of stone and wood frames with a thatched roof. In the center of the Village was a marketplace bustling with the local inhabitants.

"This feels so weird," Terry said as they came closer to the marketplace.

"What does?" Eden asked.

"It's surreal, you know. Like we're in a dream of a time long past..." Terry trailed off as he became mesmerized by the activity of the market. There were many booths and stands which had been erected to sell various wares. Several vendors were selling food goods—fresh fruit and vegetables. Others sold butchered meat and the furs of the animals that they had slaughtered. Another person was selling pottery; another handmade clothing; and another arts and crafts. But Terry was instantly drawn to one booth where there was a man selling an assortment of blades and also crystals with the most luminous energy.

"Eden, look! Look!" Terry pointed at the booth with the blades and crystals. He pulled on the sleeve of her dress since she too was looking about in an awestruck fashion. The Villagers seemed to pay them no mind since both Eden and Terry were wearing the traditional garb of the time. The stream of people flowed around them like the current of a fast moving river. Everyone buying, selling, and trading. They exchanged money and goods like the economy was booming. "From the look of these people you'd never guess that they were slaves to the

Queen, would you?" Terry whispered to Eden as they made their way over to the weapons and gems booth.

Eden shook her head in agreement. "No, actually. I would never be able to tell if we didn't already know. Maybe they're happy in their enslavement. Lord knows people in our Dimension certainly are."

Terry looked at her. "I wasn't. You weren't."

"Yeah, but we're in the minority," Eden returned. "Neither of us fit into mainstream society."

"That's true," Terry agreed as he perused the variety of daggers and swords laid out on the table before him. The shiny crystals were arranged in the spaces between the weapons. Behind the table stood the vendor of the booth. He was a large man with a thick red beard. More blades hung in the booth behind him.

"Can I help you find something?" The vendor asked from behind the table.

Terry smiled at the man. "No, thanks. We're just browsing right now."

The red bearded man nodded. "Just let me know."

There were long blades, short blades, thick blades, thin blades, epic swords with two-handed hilts, and even intricate curved blades with rubies imbedded in the handle. Terry picked up a thin rapier that caught his eye. He removed the blade from its leather scabbard. The metal working was immaculate. The sword was smooth and sharp on both edges. There was a strip of brown leather wrapped around the hilt large enough to wrap the hand around. And right at the base of the blade were two silver metal snakes circling each other in a spiral. It reminded Terry of the tendrils of his Soulmind.

"This one is beautiful," he said in awe of the craftsmanship of the weapon.

Eden laughed. "Yeah, like you need that."

Terry ignored the remark. "I like it. The craftsmanship is just amazingly intricate." He turned to the vendor who was patiently watching them. "How much for this one?" Terry returned the blade to its scabbard.

"That one is fifty Queens," the red bearded man answered. "A nice piece, that one."

Terry dug around in his pocket for the money that Mika'el had given them. As he pulled the Queens from his pocket, he pointed at a particularly shiny amethyst on the table. The stone was multi-faceted and about the size of a Ping-Pong ball. "And for this amethyst here? I'll take both the rapier and the amethyst."

"That stone is twenty Queens. Beautiful shiny, that is," the man replied. "Seventy Queens all together, if you please."

Terry pulled out several bills from the stack and handed them to the vendor. "Thank you," he said as he picked up the amethyst.

"Thank you very much, sir. Appreciate your business. Enjoy the rapier and the stone, and come back to see me anytime," the vendor said as he counted the Queens and stuffed them into his pocket.

Terry fastened the rapier to the rope at his waist as they walked away from the booth. He handed Eden the amethyst. "And a beautiful stone for my beautiful lady," he said.

She smiled and blushed as she held the gem in her hand, feeling the pulse of its energy. "Thank you, babe," she said and gave Terry a kiss. "I love it! This is the most beautiful amethyst I've ever seen. It's so... radiant." Eden stared into the depths of the crystal.

"Don't stare into it too long," Terry joked. "You might get trapped inside it." He winked at her and she pushed him playfully.

"I'm kind of hungry," Eden said as she put the amethyst in her pocket and looked around at the other booths.

"I am kind of too," Terry agreed. "What about this fruit stand over here?"

The woman selling her goods at the stand had crates full of freshly picked fruit—oranges, apples, pears, grapefruit, berries. Eden and Terry both grabbed two pears each for themselves to snack on.

"That'll be two Queens," the woman at the stand said.

Terry handed her two bills and then took Eden's arm in his as they continued their exploration. They walked through the Village munching their pears, and admired the quaint little buildings and the folk who went about their business never giving the two strangers a second glance. Coming upon an establishment who's sign read *The Queen's Cave Tavern*, Terry turned to Eden and asked, "Do you want to get a drink?"

"Yeah, why not?" Eden replied. "This will definitely be an interesting story to tell when we get back to our world."

It was dark inside the tavern, but it was busy with customers. There were many wooden tables with scruffy guys sitting around them drinking beer from tall mugs. Terry and Eden approached the bar. There was an older man with unkempt long black hair and beard behind the bar wiping down mugs with a dirty cloth. The man eyed Terry as he got to the bar; he also looked Eden up and down, checking her out. "Oi, barkeep!" Terry greeted the bartender in a way he thought made him sound like a local. "Let's have a mug of ale for me and me lady."

The barkeep nodded and filled up two mugs with fresh ale. The foam bubbled and frothed over the rims like soap suds. "That'll be two Queens," the barkeep said. His voice was gravelly and he was missing more than a few teeth. Terry paid the man and they took their mugs of ale. They both sipped, foam sticking to their upper lips like a milk mustache.

"Damn, this is pretty good," Eden said, licking the foam from her lip.

"For real," Terry agreed.

They leaned with their backs against the bar and watched the lively scene going on in the tavern. One of the tables of men spontaneously burst into song. Several men drummed on the table while the others sang a song Terry had trouble making out. He caught little bits here and there. The song seemed to be about the *Wicked Queen* and a savior who would come and rescue them from her tyranny. At the end of the song they all started chanting, *"Fuck the Queen! Fuck that bitch! Fuck the Queen! Fuck that bitch!"*

Eden exchanged a knowing look with Terry. "They really hate the Queen," Eden commented.

"Well, duh," Terry responded. "She's enslaved them all for their psychic energy. I'm even surprised they even get to have this little bit of fun."

"Well, I mean," Eden started. "She's gotta at least let them do *something* for comfort. Even in ancient Egypt the Pharaohs would serve the slaves beer as payment for their labor. Actually, now that I remember correctly, they weren't slaves but free Egyptians that worked for the gods and beer was one way they were compensated. For a long time historians thought that the pyramids were built by slave labor, but now they've come to understand something different."

"Huh," Terry said, thinking about this. "You learn something new everyday." He took a big swig of ale. A tall man in his twenties came close to Terry and stared at him and Eden. This man was about a head taller than Terry and he was thin but muscular. Terry looked at the man incredulously and took a step away from him. "Can I help you?"

The tall man eyed Eden like she was a piece of meat. "Yeah," the man said, not looking at Terry but still at Eden. "How much for you's lady friend?"

"What?" Terry asked.

"How many Queens for your lady friend?" The man said this louder now and he was joined by three friends who came up behind him.

"Fuck off! I'm not for sale," Eden snapped. "And he's not my pimp. He's my husband."

Terry raised an eyebrow. "You heard the lady. Get the fuck out of here!"

The tall man shook his head. "He ain't your husband. You is lyin'. C'mon, let us just have fun with her for an hour. We'll even let you watch." The man grinned and licked his lips.

Before the tall man had time to react, Terry hit him across the face with the mug in his hand. The man spit blood on the floor and rage entered into his eyes like a bull about to gore a matador. "Oh, you're gonna fuckin' regret that!"

He pushed Terry against the bar hard enough to knock the wind out of him. Terry kicked at the man's legs and got a couple punches off on the guy's face. The punches were returned and Terry could feel his lip swelling up and the blood pouring from his nose.

"Hey! No fighting in my tavern! Take that shite outside!" The barkeep yelled as the fight intensified.

"Get the fuck off of him, asshole!" Eden screamed and tried to pull the tall man off of Terry but was no match for him strength-wise. The tall man's three friends weren't interfering yet and just watched. Instantly Eden's red and pink Soulmind blazed around her body. The long spear shot out of her solar plexus and she caught it before it sailed across the room. She didn't extend the energy of the blade—the men wouldn't have been able to see it anyway—so she just used it as a Bo Staff to whack people away and keep them at a distance.

Eden hit the tall man in the back of the head with the end of the Staff. He cried out and grasped the back of his head which was now split and bleeding. Taking advantage of the man's wound and temporary disorientation, Eden grabbed Terry's hand and pulled him toward the door. "Let's get out of here," she said.

"Where do you think you're going?" The tall man growled. The man and his three friends followed them just as they got to the door. Everyone in the tavern was now staring at them, eager to see a fight break out again. "You think you're getting away?" The tall man yelled. "We're gonna beat you till you're almost dead and we're still gonna fuck your lady while you watch and bleed to death!"

Terry and Eden stumbled onto the dirt road outside the tavern, their pursuers close behind. Eden stood ready with the Staff in front of her. Terry was also ready with his rapier out. Now as the four men circled them, more folks from the tavern came out to watch the fight. Night was falling, it was about dusk. The tall man had a sword which was now in his hand, and his three friends had smaller blades which they brandished as well.

Eden slammed the end of her Staff down on the ground which caused the earth to shake violently. The men from the tavern had to brace themselves to keep from falling over. "She's a Sorceress! Get her!" The tall man screamed as they advanced. The three friends sheathed their blades and closed in on Eden. They grabbed her Staff and attempted to wrestle it away from her grip. With the aid of her Soulmind, Eden's strength was increased and she kept the three men from pulling it out of her grasp.

Terry lunged at the tall man with his blade. The man blocked Terry's rapier with his heftier sword. As the two went at it sword-fighting, blow for blow and block for block, the three men managed to pull the Staff away from Eden. Once they did, it disappeared in their hands. They stared into the empty air where the Staff was a moment ago, dumbfounded. Then they all three tackled her to the ground and began tearing at her clothes. They ripped the top of her dress, exposing her breasts. She tried to kick them away, but they pinned her arms down to the ground and her legs just flailed in the air. "Terry! Help me!" She screamed.

"Fuck this!" Terry said. All in one movement, he sheathed his sword and stomped the ground. When his foot touched the ground, a electromagnetic pulse shot through the four men and the crowd watching. "I give the gift of Sight!" Terry yelled. As the energy touched all the Villagers in that area, they began to see the energy of Eden's Soulmind blazing around her. And they could see Terry's huge white aura. The hilt of his machete came out of his chest and he pulled the energy weapon from his body. The blade was blazing and shimmering like lightning. The tall man as well as the onlookers stared in awe. Taking advantage of the frozen dumbstruck look on the tall man's face, Terry lunged forward and sliced off the man's hand that was holding his sword. The hand and the blade fell to the ground and blood spurted from the stump. The man screamed and clutched the space where his hand used to be. He looked at Terry with terror in his eyes and then took off running down the street into the shadows.

Now Terry started chopping at the three men's backs who were still holding Eden down and attempting to rape her. They all screamed as gashes split open on their backs and gushed blood like water through a broken dam. They released Eden and ran in the direction that their friend had disappeared into. The onlookers stared wide-eyed and backed away with their hands raised. They pushed each other clamoring to get back inside the tavern. Soon Terry and Eden were alone on the dirt road outside the tavern.

Terry dropped his weapon and its energy disappeared back into his body. "Are you okay?" Terry said as he bent down to help Eden to her feet. She was crying and trying to pull the ripped part of her dress over her naked breasts. "Shh, baby. It's okay now." He whispered and hugged her close to his body. She weeped with her face pressed against his shoulder. "Here. Here," Terry said as he helped her stand on her own so he could remove his tunic to let her wear it. Eden held her hands over her face and her shoulders shuddered as the tears kept freely flowing down her flushed cheeks. Terry was wearing a white undershirt, so lending his tunic to Eden didn't leave him half naked. He slipped it over her head and she put her arms through the sleeves. She looked funny with the long brown tunic overtop of the blue bottom of her dress. Terry had removed the rope and re-tied it around his waist so he could leave his rapier fastened there and have both hands free to hold Eden as they followed the dirt road back to Mika'el's farm.

"I love you, Terry," Eden whispered in his ear and kissed his neck softly.

"And I love *you*, Eden."

FIVE

The first night in the jail cell Jessica slept fitfully, hoping that Jay and Magda might show up to rescue her. She had used the bucket to pee, and she puked in it a couple times—purge left over from the Soma still flowing through her veins. This morning the Chief Officer had left to go perform whatever other duties he had in the village of Thanatos. He had been replaced by a lesser guard who was charged with watching her and making sure she didn't try to escape. Not that she could even if she wanted to. The guard was sitting at the desk and a friend who had come to keep him company was sitting across from him. They played cards for some type of coinage. The playing cards were strange-looking and handmade; they were circular instead of rectangular.

The guard's friend was incredibly large and rotund. His head was bald, but his brown beard was long and unruly. He also had several gold teeth in his mouth, and his clothes were ratty in comparison to what the guard was wearing. They paid the girl in the cage no mind as they continued playing their game and drinking whiskey.

Jessica slouched on the cot, sulking with her arms crossed. She wracked her brain for an idea of how to get out of this situation. The metal contraption around her skull was significantly uncomfortable and impeded her thought process. It also completely restricted her ability to use any powers associated with her Soulmind. If she couldn't break her way out with Magick, then maybe there was a chance she could talk her way out.

She timidly approached the bars of her cell and looked at the men playing cards. They didn't even look over to acknowledge her presence. Jessica cleared her throat loudly. The two men turned their heads to stare at her. Without thinking she said, "I *demahnd* to see the king!" *Holy hell*, she thought. *Is being in Pangea changing my voice as well as everything else about me?*

Both men burst out laughing. "Eh, what the fuck is she on about?" The fat man asked. The guard shook his head. Then the fat man got up from his chair and approached Jessica behind the bars of the jail cell. "Oi! There's no fuckin' *king*," he said as he pressed his face close to the bars. Jessica backed up a few steps but could still smell the rancidness of his breath. The man's gold tooth looked dull in the dim light of the room. "There's no justice, sweetheart," he continued saying with a crazed look in his eyes. "Just *us*," he whispered menacingly.

Jessica looked confused. "No king? There must be..."

The fat man laughed in her face. "Eh, bring me that piss pot. Set it right there." Jessica didn't move. The man held the bars in his fists and shoved his face closer to intimidate her. "What did I say, witch? Right fuckin' now!"

Hesitantly Jessica pushed the bucket with her foot closer to the bars. With a swift kick the fat man knocked the bucket over and the contents splashed her feet and ankles. The stench of the piss-soaked puke was awful. Trying not to hurl again, she backed up and sat down on the cot. Obviously her *see the king* tactic wasn't going to work. The fat man laughed and taunted her as the puddle of puke and piss spread on the floor of the cell. Maybe she could convince them she wasn't a witch. What did she have to lose?

"I swear I'm not a witch," Jessica pleaded. "I beg you! I'm a believer in Jesus. A Christian like you two... maybe..."

The fat man spat at her through the bars. "Who da fuck is *Jeezus*? Oi, Thomas, have you ever heard of dis *Jee-zus*?"

The guard, Thomas, shook his head. "Never, Barty. Never heard the name a'fore."

"See, witch?" Barty taunted Jessica who had fallen silent again. "None of yer tricks will work on us. That's cause we're too smart." Barty tapped the side of his skull with his finger. "Yer dumb, girly. You know how I know? Cause you chose to be a bloody witch. And everyone knows... All witches burn." Barty walked back to his card game cackling and left Jessica to think about her fate as a cloud surrounded her with the stench of her own urine and vomit.

SIX

"These clothes are fucking bananas," Terry said after changing into the outfit Mika'el had given him to traipse around the City in. He looked at Eden who just shook her head in astonishment. She was wearing purple leggings under a skirt made of vinyl which was blue and looked like a cone that had the point at her waist and the base at her knees. The cropped shirt she wore was white and soft like a pad; the sleeves were short but like huge hoops. Terry cracked up looking at her. "You look like what eighties people thought the future would look like. *Back to the Future* style," he said.

"Look at yourself, smartass," she shot back.

Eden was right. Terry looked down at himself and his outfit was just as ridiculous. The pants he wore were basically parachute pants and bright pink. His shirt was green and skin-tight with short sleeves which were large rubber rings molded together. "I know," he admitted. "Whoever designed this was definitely on Wonderland drugs."

"I know they're strange," Mika'el said. They were all standing around the dining table. It was morning and Terry and Eden were getting ready to cross through the forest to see what the City had to offer.

"Are you sure you're okay from last night?" Terry asked Eden and lightly touched her arm.

She nodded and smiled warmly. "Yeah, I'm fine. Thanks to you, babe. I bounce back quick. Besides, it's not the first time a group of men tried to take advantage of me. I mean, you've seen that massive spear I have. Do you think a weapon like that would come out of a weak person?"

"No, definitely not," Terry said, glad that Eden didn't seem too shaken up by their violent encounter in the Village. "Those guys got their lesson learned permanently. Every time that tall man remembers he only has one hand, he'll think twice about fucking with a beautiful woman." He winked at Eden.

"Yeah, they can get pretty rowdy there in the Village sometimes," Mika'el commented. "Especially if those men have been drinking. That's why I prefer the peaceful solitude of my life here."

"Yeah, it is really nice here on your farm," Terry said.

"You need anymore Queens?" Mika'el asked.

Terry shook his head. "I think we're good. I still have a lot left from what you gave us yesterday. Only bought a couple things in the Village. The rapier was the big thing." He touched the hilt of his blade he had tied around his waist.

"I wouldn't bring that if I were you," Mika'el advised. "They ain't too keen on weapons in the City."

Terry untied the rope from his waist and laid it down with the sword on the table. "Okay, yeah. You take care of it for me," Terry said.

"Okay, come on. Y'all'er burning daylight," Mika'el said. "Better get hiking through the forest if ya wanna get to the City by midday."

Terry nodded and took Eden by the hand. They left through the front door and Mika'el waved as they walked off toward the dirt road and the border of the forest. In no time at all they arrived at the edge of the trees. Both hesitated for a moment before penetrating the border into the shade casted by the canopy above. "What did Mika'el say?" Terry asked. "Just go straight across? No turns?"

"You're too queer to go straight," Eden remarked. She raised her eyebrows and gave Terry a sexy smile.

"Fuck you," he returned.

Eden smiled wider. "You already did."

Terry laughed and they both walked into the forest.

They had been hiking through the trees for quite some time, but to Terry and Eden it felt like forever. "Does this seem like it's taking too long to get to the other side to you?" He asked. "I mean, it didn't seem this long walking to the Village on the dirt road."

Eden shrugged. "I don't know. It does feel like a while. At least there's still sunlight. I don't think I'd want to be in this forest at night... Hey, what's that?" She pointed off to their right and several yards away was the mouth of a cave the size of a large circular door. There was a rock face, and around the opening was overgrown with greenery.

"Holy shit," Terry said. "That's gotta be the Stone Queen's cave!"

"You want to go in and check it out?" Eden said, half joking.

"Uh-uh," Terry said, shaking his head. "Fuck that. We have no idea what's down there."

"Yeah, it's probably creepy as fuck," she said as they continued walking, leaving the cave behind them.

They pressed on in silence for some time more until Terry caught the sounds of something other than the forest and the animals therein. "Do you hear that?" He asked.

Eden stopped and listened. "Hmm?"

"It sounds like the noise of traffic!"

"Traffic?" Eden said. "Oh yeah... I hear it!"

"Let's go! We must be almost there!"

They picked up their pace and soon came to the end of the trees. Crossing over the tree line, Eden and Terry found themselves on a concrete sidewalk next to a paved street. Cars zoomed and honked in front of them. It looked like rush hour in Chicago. Terry looked up and in the air there were cars flying overhead. Terry couldn't believe it—there were cars on the ground and cars in the air. They looked at each other, both with their mouths hanging open in amazement. The buildings of the City before them were massive. They rose high into the sky like Towers of Babel. The sidewalk on the other side of the street was bustling with pedestrians going to and from wherever it was they went everyday. Some of the people were wearing clothes like Terry and Eden had on, and others were wearing attire which was less flamboyant, but nonetheless modern.

"This is incredible," Eden said, still staring up at the flying cars.

Terry looked down the sidewalk to his left and saw a man approaching them. His clothes weren't outlandish like the retro eighties garb they wore. The man was wearing business clothes; a white button-up shirt with a blue vest over it, and blue slacks with leather shoes. He also wore circular wire-rimmed spectacles and smoked a hand-rolled cigarette.

"Not from around here are you?" The man addressed the two lovers as they stood gaping at the urban landscape.

"How could you tell?" Terry asked, silently appraising the man as he approached.

The spectacled man laughed and took a drag of his cigarette. "I just saw you come out of the wood. And no one from our world can cross over that barrier between this City and the Village on the other side."

"Oh yeah," Terry said, feeling stupid. "Of course."

The man put his cigarette in his mouth and extended his hand to introduce himself. "I'm Nikola."

Terry shook the man's hand and so did Eden. "I'm Terry. And this is Eden," Terry said. "It's nice to meet you."

"It's very lovely to meet you both as well," Nikola responded. "I just came out for a short walk to get some air and have a smoke. Why don't you two come back with me to my lab. I'd love to show it to you. And from the look of you both, you'll need a guide to tell you what's where in the City."

Terry looked at Eden. "Sure, yeah. We'll come," Eden agreed.

"Marvelous! It's just down this way and across the street," Nikola said as he turned and began walking back the way he had come. Eden and Terry followed, excited to be shown around the City which to them was a glimpse of the potential of what the future could be.

As Nikola led the two Travelers back to his lab, Terry and Eden absorbed their new surroundings. Some things seemed very similar to their world, yet others were drastically different. For example, the cars driving on the road were not unlike the makes and varieties of the ones in the Hollow Dimension. There were taxis honking, and fancy cars, and old beaters weaving through lanes of traffic. However, the flying cars weaving between the buildings were utterly alien. They had no wheels, obviously, and the bottoms of the vehicles where smooth metal discs that by some technology allowed them to glide through the air. Also the architecture of the skyscrapers resembled the buildings of Chicago except that they seemed to tower much higher into the sky—miles even. They were like giant spears piercing the clouds.

"This place is wild," Eden commented as they crossed the street with a throng of other pedestrians.

"It's really something, isn't it?" Nikola said. "The beauty of our craftsmanship, architecture, technology, and ingenuity... It's a shame we're not free to really enjoy the fruits of our labor."

"Oh yeah," Terry said gloomily. "The Stone Queen."

They were on the sidewalk on the other side of the street now. Nikola stopped and looked at Terry, sizing him up. "You know about the Queen?" He inquired.

Terry and Eden had also stopped when Nikola did. The foot traffic flowed around them as if they were a large boulder in the middle of a stream. Terry nodded in affirmation. "Yes," he said. "Mika'el—"

Nikola suddenly laughed, cutting off Terry's comment and said, "Of course he did."

"You know Mika'el?" Eden asked.

Nikola pulled another rolled cigarette from a silver case and lit it. "Yes," he answered. "We were great friends actually. Intelligent man. We knew each other during the Golden Time right after Darren imprisoned the Queen in stone and before she grew powerful enough to enslave us and separate us down the middle again." He took a huge drag of his cigarette and puffed the smoke out in a large cloud. Strangely the smoke smelled sweet in the air. "Okay, enough chit-chat and dilly-dally. Let's get to my lab. It's that black ominous looking building one block up."

Nikola continued walking again; Terry and Eden followed close behind. There was a revolving glass door as the entrance to the building. It was locked until Nikola swiped a magnetic card so they could get in. Directly inside looked like the lobby of an office building. There was a man behind the reception desk. He was maybe in his thirties and wore a black suit. However, it wasn't a normal suit, it was shiny and looked like it was made of vinyl.

"Seyba!" Nikola greeted the man at the reception desk. "These are my new friends Eden and Terry. I'm going to show them around my lab."

Seyba signed them all in while the two newcomers said *heys* and *nice-to-meet-yous*. "Anytime, Nikola," Seyba said. "You know you're my favorite guy!"

"And you're not too bad yourself," Nikola said and they both laughed. "Thanks a lot, Seyba. Catch you later, homie."

The three of them left Seyba and walked to the elevators. "You talk like that?" Terry asked.

"Ehhh," Nikola said by way of response. "I like Seyba. And that's how the younger folk talk nowadays. I guess it's my way of relating... I don't know, it's fun." He hit the down arrow next to the elevator. It dinged and the doors slid open. They got in the elevator and Nikola continued talking as he pressed the button for *Lower Level 3*. "There are apartments on the upper floors. I live up there. And there are lab spaces and studios on the underground levels."

"These buildings are huge," Eden said. "Are there even enough people in the City to inhabit all of these skyscrapers?"

"You wouldn't believe it," Nikola responded. "But there are actually clone factories here that pump new people out like an assembly line."

"Are you a...?" Terry started to ask and then trailed off.

"Clone?" Nikola said, finishing Terry's question. "No. I'm flesh and blood natural, born from a woman's vagina the normal way. I would hate to be an engineered human. I mean, we're all technically slaves, but that's just a whole new level of subservience." He shuddered at the thought.

The elevator dinged again and the doors opened to a hallway that was completely white. Nikola led them down the hall and around the corner to a grey door which was the entrance to his lab space. He swiped his keycard again and opened the door. Turning on the lights as they entered the room, Nikola let Terry and Eden stare in wonderment for a moment. The room was large like the space inside a warehouse. And it was filled with contraptions, electric gizmos, chemistry experiments, and a half-built robot.

"So what are you—an inventor?" Terry asked, his estimation of Nikola rising several notches.

"No," Nikola said. "I'm a pediatric proctologist." He waited for the laugh at the joke but it seemed to have gone over his friends' heads. After a beat of silence, Eden laughed, finally getting the joke. Terry was a little slower on the uptake.

"That's a real thing?" Terry asked, totally serious.

"Of course not," Nikola said, laughing. "I was only making a joke. Yes, I'm an inventor. My official title is *Technician of High Technology*."

Terry and Eden walked through the lab admiring the technical wizardry. He walked over to the unfinished robot and touched the back of its metal head. "What's this? Is it working yet?" Terry asked.

Nikola strolled over to join him by the metal man. "No, not yet," Nikola answered. "Artificial Intelligence is really what I'm focused on developing right now. It's all loaded into the machine's artificial cranium. You see, we have a gigantic database of billions of terabytes of information all stored in a mechanical cloud that floats above the City. I connect the Artificially Intelligent being wirelessly to said database so that it has access to all information from all of time. I've got that part working..."

"But?" Eden said, joining in on their conversation.

"But," Nikola continued. "I can't seem to get it to access the information in any intelligent fashion. Can't make it connect dots or solve real time problems." He shrugged and sighed. "Oh well, I'll figure it out one way or the other. I'm determined."

"Seems like it," Terry commented.

"You know why I invited you to come here?" Nikola asked. Terry and Eden shook their heads. Nikola continued, "Because you two are special. I felt it right away in your energy—in your auras!"

"You know about auras?" Eden asked.

"Of course I know about auras," Nikola responded. "Someone who works with electricity must have knowledge of all of those subtle energies. You two are outlanders... and hopefully the ones we've been waiting for."

"Waiting for what?" Terry was confused now. "We just decided to come here on a whim. To hide from someone who's looking for me in the Hollow Dimension."

"Ah, yes, well that's how destiny works," Nikola said with a smile. "That's how the Spiralverse brought you here to free us once and for all from the Stone Queen's tyranny."

"Whoa, Nikola!" Terry said, shaking his head. "I think you got the wrong guy. I'm no savior. And besides, I don't want to go into that creepy-ass cave."

"Nevertheless, there *is* a prophecy," Nikola continued. "A prophecy of another Outlander coming to finish what the great Darren had begun—to free us for now and for always. All you would have to do would be to find a way to sever the connection her Astral Body has with her physical body of stone. Her stone form is the only thing grounding her into this physical realm and it is the means for her to syphon all of our energy... Who knows, that Outlander from the prophecy could be you, Terry. Or it could be you, Eden. All I know is I *feel* it in your aura."

"That's a lot of responsibility to put on us," Terry said. "I don't know exactly how I feel about that." Eden was quiet beside him.

"Oh, look at the time!" Nikola suddenly exclaimed. "The sun should be going down about now. Where *are* my manners? You must be exhausted from your hike through the forest. Come up and stay the night in my apartment. We'll eat some delicious food and have a good night's rest."

They followed Nikola back to the elevator to make the ascent to the upper floors where people lived. His apartment was on the three-hundred-thirty-third floor. "That's so high!" Terry exclaimed. "Does it take forever for the elevator to make it up there?"

Nikola winked at him and punched in the number for his floor on the elevator's keypad. "Just wait," he replied. "Do you feel that?"

Terry shook his head. "Feel what?"

"Exactly," Nikola said. "We're actually going so fast that it doesn't even feel like we're moving at all."

Eden snorted, trying hard not to laugh. Then Terry said, "What? That doesn't even make any sense. How does that work?"

Nikola just laughed, leaving the question unanswered. Before even a minute had passed, the elevator dinged again and the doors slid open. On the wall opposite the elevator, it said in big gold letters *Floor 333*. Terry was amazed. "It's almost like we teleported here. I can't believe how quick that was!" They all left the elevator. The halls up here were much nicer than the ones on the lower floors by the labs. The floor was carpeted and next to each apartment door was a soft yellow light. It almost looked like the hallways from a fancy hotel.

"My unit is just down the hall here," Nikola said, leading them past several doors. He used the same keycard to unlock his apartment as well. Inside looked like a really swanky loft apartment; something you might see in New York or LA. There were lots of whites and grays. One wall was floor to ceiling windows, but the view was just of the next building. It was all very open and spacious. There were long gray couches in the living room with a marble coffee table in front of them. There was a large TV mounted on the wall. There were also several green house plants that gave some color to the decor. The kitchen had an island with several stools arranged around it. And the second floor where Nikola's bed was was like a balcony, open to look down on the living room.

"Wow, this is really nice," Eden said.

"Well, there are some perks to being a smart slave," Nikola joked. "You two can sleep on the couch. Make yourselves at home. I made a big batch of chicken tikka masala earlier and there's enough left over for all of us. You want some?"

"Yes, please," both Terry and Eden answered. They were grateful to rest on the couch while Nikola went to reheat the pot on the stove that still contained the chicken tikka masala from lunch.

"I didn't realize how tired I am from that hike through the woods," Eden said as she snuggled against Terry while stretching out on the couch.

"Me too," Terry agreed.

Nikola came over and placed a folded map down on the marble table. "This is a map of all the districts in the City. I'm sure tomorrow you'll want to explore the sights and sounds of this fantastical place. There are things that can be fun here. It would be perfect if it wasn't so oppressive."

Terry sat up and unfolded the map. Completely open it was wider than the full width of his arm span. "Holy shit," he said. "This place is way bigger than I thought."

"Captains of Industry and Wizards of Technology helping to create a spectacle no one in the Spiralverse has ever seen before," Nikola said proudly. "You have the Factory District, the Industrial District, the Farm District, the Live and Work District, the Red Light District, the Casino District... and so on and on and on. Here's where we are in the Live and Work District." Nikola pointed to the area on the map. "Wherever you end up, just remember to come back here to find me."

"Seems easy enough," Terry said. "You know how to read a map don't you, Eden?"

She nodded. "I know how you are," Eden joked. "You could get lost in your own basement without a GPS." She laughed and tickled Terry playfully.

"Hey! You shut your whore mouth!" Terry said, tickling her back.

"You two talk to each other like that?" Nikola asked as he folded the map back up and placed it on the marble coffee table.

"Yeah, we're just joking around," Eden responded.

Nikola shrugged. "That's nice that you're so comfortable with each other," he said. "Who am I to judge... Tikka masala's almost ready," he continued, walking back over toward the stove. "Come, we'll sit at the island and eat."

"You look funny," Terry said to Eden.

"*You* look funny," she said back, wrinkling up her nose.

"Okay, babe," Terry said, slapping her on the thigh under her weird dress. "Let's go get some spicy Indian food. My favorite!"

* * *

Mothman was coming down the stairs after taking a shower. Rob was in the kitchen making something to eat and Mothman could smell it as he dried his hair with a white towel.

Coming into the kitchen Mothman asked, "What the hell are you making?" He draped the towel over his damp hair and watched Rob take a frozen dinner out of the microwave and start peeling off the plastic film.

Rob shrugged. "It's like salisbury steak and some veggies and mashed potatoes." He licked his fork after stirring the potatoes.

"Barf," Mothman commented. "Only old ladies eat salisbury steak. That's like some meals-on-wheels shit."

"Then what do you suggest?" Rob asked.

"Fucking pizza! Don't you want that greasy melted cheese and slimy pepperoni and maybe some cock sausages?" Mothman said, moaning and making a play like he was having an orgasm from eating pizza. He grabbed Rob by the waist and started dry humping him from behind. "Oh, Robert! Oh, Robert! Pizza gets me so horny!"

"Get off!" Rob said and pushed Mothman away.

Mothman laughed, "Oh, I *do* plan to get off."

Rob rolled his eyes as Mothman grabbed the cordless phone to order the pizza. "What about those things out there?" Rob asked, referring to the specters all around the surface of the Merkabah field.

"Pizza guy will be fine," Mothman said pretty confidently. "I think. Whatever! Fuck it! I want some goddamn pizza!" Mothman dialed the number for the pizza joint and put the phone up to his ear.

"By the way," Rob interjected. "Where's Remius? I haven't seen him in a little while."

"He's upstairs sleeping on Terry's bed," Mothman answered. "I think that fucking cat misses Terry. That's weird, isn't it? That's weird... Oh, hi. Yes, I'd like to place an order to be delivered," Mothman said into the phone and gave the name and address. "Let me get a extra-large cock lover's—I mean meat lover's pizza with extra jiz—I mean cheese." Mothman winked at Rob who just shook his head and rolled his eyes. "Yes, that's all," Mothman continued into the phone. "Forty-five minutes? Thanks." He hung up the phone.

"You got money for that?" Rob asked.

"Yeah, I found a wad of cash in that drawer over there," Mothman indicated one of the drawers by the sink. He looked over and noticed the TV was on and some Anime was playing. "What you been watching there, Rob?"

"It's *Cowboy Bebop*," Rob replied.

"Man, I haven't seen that show in *forever*!" Mothman said, walking over to the couch. "That's one of my favorites along with *Outlaw Star*. Cartoon Network had some good shit on back in the day..."

Rob dumped the frozen dinner in the trash can and went over to join Mothman on the couch.

About forty minutes later Mothman thought he heard a car pull up out front of the house. "Hey, Rob, that's gotta be the pizza guy," Mothman said and slapped Rob's leg as he got up to look out the front window. "Come on, loser," he yelled back at Rob. "Let's watch this."

Rob got up and joined Mothman at the front window. They could barely see through the dark gray bodies of the specters covering the entire surface of the Merkabah. But there was a car that had just pulled up and a pimply teenage boy got out carrying a large pizza box. "Do you think he's gonna make it? I don't think he's gonna make it," Rob said.

"Shut the fuck up! He'll make it," Mothman shot back.

They watched, almost holding their breath, as the pizza guy approached the threshold of the Merkabah field. Obviously, he couldn't see the specters or the Merkabah, but it seemed he was feeling some type of energy because he slowed down as he approached. The boy looked suddenly scared and hesitant to go any further.

Mothman grabbed Rob's shoulders and shook him. "He's stopping! He's stopping! Fuck, Rob, what if he bails? I want that fucking pizza!" Mothman yelled vehemently.

"Chill the fuck out, dude," Rob said, trying to pull away from Mothman's grip, but it was too strong and Mothman's fingers dug into his shoulders. "It's not the end of the world if you don't get your pizza."

"Yes it is, Rob! Yes it *iiiiiiiiiiissssssssss*!" He emphasized the last *is* and shook Rob even harder.

The pizza guy slowly came closer to the threshold. Right before he was about to walk through it, three specters jumped off of the surface of the Merkabah and latched themselves on the boy's head and shoulders.

"Oh, fuck! Oh my god!" Rob cried out, not wanting to watch anymore. "He's done for. There goes your pizza, Mothman!"

Mothman held his breath, hoping beyond hope there was some miracle to save his precious pizza as he squeezed Rob's shoulders even harder. Rob finally jerked away from the grip and pushed Mothman off of him. They both stared out the window. The pizza guy could clearly feel the specters on him and began to stumble backwards. As he fell back, the pizza went flying forward. As he watched, Mothman put his fist in his mouth and bit down from anticipation. The pizza box fell onto the ground just past the border on the inside of the Merkabah.

"Oh! Fuck me, that was a close one," Mothman said, allowing himself to breathe again. "I thought our food was a goner for sure."

Rob shook his head. "And you don't care about that poor pizza delivery guy? He's totally fucked now. Look at him."

The pizza boy was struggling now. Still stumbling backwards and trying to shake himself. He knew something was wrong and he was clearly terrified. Mothman and Rob watched as one by one each of the three specters on top of the boy entered into his body. "I don't envy him right now," Mothman commented.

Rob punched his friend in the arm. "Dude, you're a colossal dick! If you hadn't wanted to order a fucking pizza that guy wouldn't be possessed by three ghosts right now! This is your fault. You should feel ashamed. Really."

Mothman laughed. "You're not gonna say that when we're enjoying that pizza."

The pizza guy stood up, now possessed by all three specters. His eyes turned totally white and he growled through pointed teeth. "Holy hell," Rob said. "You see that?"

"That's fucking crazy!" Mothman stared in awe as the pizza guy, looking demon possessed, quickly got back into his car and drove away. Rob and Mothman exchanged a look with their mouths hanging open. "Hey, Rob. Go get that pizza." Mothman made a movement with his head indicating to go outside.

Rob shook his head. "Are you crazy? I'm not going out there. You're the retard who ordered it."

"Fine," Mothman said. He couldn't argue with logic. "But you owe me one for this."

"I don't owe you shit," Rob shot back.

Mothman opened the front door timidly and then ran as fast as he could. He grabbed the pizza box and darted back inside, closing and locking the door behind him. "Woohoo! Free pizza!" Mothman did a victory dance.

"You're unbelievable," Rob said as he walked back toward the kitchen.

Mothman opened the pizza box and started eating a slice as he followed his friend. Five minutes later they were both joking about the whole crazy experience as they enjoyed free pizza and watched *Cowboy Bebop*.

SEVEN

Terry and Eden had been having fun all morning exploring the sights and sounds of the City. They had slept well on Nikola's couch and after briefly having some tea together, Nikola sent them out with the map into the future. First thing they did was have a nice breakfast at a little cafe on the corner near Nikola's building. They enjoyed exotic pastries which had no equivalent back in their world. After which Terry and Eden continued their exploration, navigating the mile-high buildings, the traffic, pedestrians, and flying cars zipping around above them.

"What's that?" Terry said, looking down at the map then pointing across the street. "We must be in the Casino District." It was difficult to see what was in their immediate vicinity due to the high density of foot traffic. Terry had never seen so many people in his life—even in downtown Chicago. The throng of people was like a moving mosh pit carried downstream and upstream depending on where their jobs were in the City. Eden gazed across the street, and looming over them was a very large block-like building. Written on the side of said building in fancy script were the words *The Queen's Wild Orchid Palace*.

"The Queen's Wild Orchid Palace," Eden read out loud. "That must be the main attraction in this Casino District."

Terry nodded and confirmed where they were on the map. "You wanna go check it out?" He asked.

"Why not?" Eden replied. "Let's see how these City folk party it up!"

Terry pocketed the map as they crossed the street. A huge canopy of lights led up to the entrance of the casino which was made up of many swinging glass doors and they were all lined with bright carnival lights. The energy of the establishment was warm and inviting, almost like it was sucking them both inside. Once they were on the other side of the doors, they were hooked. There were so many dazzling neon lights it was almost overwhelming. It was like a circus and a casino fucked and *The Queen's Wild Orchid Palace* was the culmination of their endless orgasm. There were an array of slot machines which dinged and chimed as people put in Queen coins and pulled their levers. Other areas had craps tables, poker tables, roulette tables, and several other games neither Terry nor Eden recognized. All the men and women playing and frolicking in the casino were wearing outlandish clothes like the ones Mika'el had given the two Travelers. The ceiling towered high above them and there was a net stretched across the room several feet above the slot machines. This net was to catch the trapeze artists who were performing above them in the top half of the room.

"Holy fuck," Eden said, awestruck by the entire spectacle. "This totally looks like Vegas on acid!"

"I've never been," Terry remarked.

"Hmm, which?" Eden nudged him. "To Vegas or on acid?"

Terry laughed. "You're funny, you know that?" He looked around, a little overwhelmed by the multitude of all that was going on. "What should we do first?"

As if to answer his question, a female server approached them with something strange on a platter. "Welcome to *The Queen's Wild Orchid Palace*," the woman greeted them. "Would you care for a wild orchid?"

Both Terry and Eden studied the woman's appearance. Her hair was blue and she wore dark makeup around her eyes. She was barely wearing anything at all—just a strange silver bra on which the cups were cones that jutted out to sharp points in front of her nipples. And her thong was made of some sort of clear plastic; her shaved cunt could be seen quite clearly through it. In her hand was a round platter, and on top was a potted orchid plant. The plant had one long stem that came out of the dirt and curved over to the side. Several white orchids bloomed from this stem.

"You can eat those?" Eden asked.

"Certainly," the server answered. "It's our specialty here—our delicacy. It deeply enhances your experience of what we have to offer here—visually and sensually."

That definitely had Eden sold. "That sounds sexy," she said, plucking one of the orchids off the stem.

"It most certainly is," the server replied, a palpable sexual energy oozed off of her beautiful body.

Eden nudged Terry with her elbow, he almost seemed to be in a trance staring at the woman. "You alive?" Eden said to her lover. "Come on and eat one with me."

Terry shook the daze out of his head and plucked an orchid from the stem as well. They both put their flower in their mouth at the same time. As they chewed them, the taste was surprisingly sweet and a strange nectar excreted from the petals and coated their throats with its essence. Eden almost had a spontaneous orgasm as she swallowed the flower.

"Enjoy your stay at *The Queen's Wild Orchid Palace*. And don't forget to spend your Queens freely," the half-naked server smiled at them and continued on her way.

Terry turned to Eden and he noticed that her pupils were dramatically dilated. "So we only have Queen bills but no coins," he said. "Let's go cash in some of these bills for Queen coins so we can play the slots and whatever else requires coins. We'll keep a chunk of the bills because we don't want to run out of money completely. But I'm sure we'll win a bunch! I'm feeling lucky today. We'll buy a bunch of casino chips so we can play cards and craps too." They were both excited and Terry took Eden by the hand and they skipped over to where they could happily trade in their Queen bills for coins and chips.

After getting a bunch of coins and chips, Terry stuffed them in the pockets of his parachute pants. They both looked at each other and burst out laughing just at the ridiculousness of how they looked, and not to mention their swollen pupils. They started to see rainbow colors spinning off of all the bright multi-colored lights in the casino. Every sensation was intensely heightened. Terry waved his hand in front of his face and could see trails coming off of it as it moved through the air. "Do you feel funny, Eden?" Terry said, giggling.

Eden snorted and then laughed out loud. "Yeah. In all the best ways!" She said, totally excited and turned on. "Fuck that bitch who's after you, Terry. She'll never find us here!"

"Go see if there's any other cool rooms in this place," Terry said. "Then come find me, I'll be winning us some Queens at the slot machines."

"Slot machines?" Eden said, making fun of him. "That's kinda gay."

"Well, maybe I am *kinda gay*." Terry winked at her and went to go try his luck.

Eden turned and went to explore more of the casino. The adjoining room was gigantic. The first thing she saw when she walked in was a stunning fountain about half the length of a football field. The jets shot high into the air and would also oscillate. There were lights below lighting the streams of water that cycled between the colors. In Eden's altered state she could see auras coming off of the water and sacred geometrical patterns being shot into the air from the jet streams. She stared, mesmerized by the psychedelic sights.

On the other side of the fountain was a full sized carnival. There was a tall ferris wheel that lit up blue and green. The people riding as it turned made exclamations of joy and excitement. There was also a roller-coaster which had at least one loop and one corkscrew. Eden could also see a carousel populated with fantastical beasts for the casino-goers to ride on. Scattered in with the rides were booths with carnies who facilitated games to win prizes like giant stuffed dragons. She saw a young woman walking around with one that was almost as big as she was. The festive music was also lulling Eden into a blissful trance.

Dazed, she continued her walk around the fountain and toward this carnival. Everyone seemed to be having a stellar time with smiles and glazed-over looks in their eyes. When she got to the carnival, the roller-coaster towered high above her head and she stared as the car whooshed by on the track; passengers screaming with glee. The carousel was also larger than it looked from the other side of the fountain. Eden stared through it as it went round and round. The riders were all adults but they were laughing and having fun with total abandon as if they were children again. Suddenly Eden caught a glimpse of a break in the casino wall far in front of her, almost unnoticeable. Yet she was drawn to it. The wall was pink and there was a black curtain in the shape of a small doorway. It almost blended in with the wall because of the constantly changing lights.

She walked around the carousel, through the steady stream of people, toward this curtain. As she did so she felt oddly aroused. Her clitoris swelled between her legs and she could feel herself getting wet instantly. First checking around to make sure no one was watching her, and only after she was satisfied did she slip quietly through the curtain. On the other side of the black curtain was the biggest group sex party she had ever witnessed. She had found the *Orgy Room*. Eden put her hand between her legs as she watched the scene before her. There was guy-on-girl, guy-on-guy, girl-on-girl, and multiple groups of more than two people in the throws of orgasmic ecstasy. The moaning and sounds of sex echoed through the room like a cosmic vibration of oneness. The floor was checkered and the panels lit up in random patterns of colored light. There were projections of stars and nebulas dancing on the ceiling and walls. And the walls were made of erotic stone carvings like the Khajuraho Temple. Carved into the wall right below the ceiling were the words *Temple of Cosmic Fuck*.

Terry would love this, Eden thought to herself. She was tempted to just get naked right then and join the fun. By this point her hand was under her skirt and inside her leggings, fingers deep inside her dripping pussy. She caught sight of a really sexy girl covered in tattoos riding her lover reverse-cowgirl. Eden rubbed her clitoris vigorously as she watched the tattooed girl bounce up and down the full length of the man's hard cock. The girl's eyes were closed and her head tilted back as she screamed with pleasure. As she shuddered with a full-body orgasm, Eden came as well, her body spasming as her pussy squirted onto her hand and soaked her purple leggings. Eden's face was hot and flushed, her mouth hung open as she breathed heavily, and she noticed the girl she was watching had opened her eyes and was now staring directly at Eden. The tattooed girl smiled and Eden blushed even more at realizing she had been spotted. She pulled her hand out of her leggings and licked her own juices off her fingers. Just as the tattooed girl motioned for Eden to come join them, it was a moment too late. Eden had already slipped back out of the curtain and disappeared into the crowd of the carnival to go get Terry so she could bring him back with her to the *Temple of Cosmic Fuck.*

When she found Terry again, he was having so much fun pulling the lever of a slot machine. The coin tray was overflowing, the lights lit up, and a bell dinged as he won the jackpot again. "Eden! Look what I won for us!" Terry said as he scooped the Queen coins out into his cupped hands. There were so many they spilled out of his palms and scattered on the floor.

"That's so awesome, babe!" Eden said, smiling and genuinely excited. "Guess what I found?"

"What? What?" Terry said, excited as he shoveled all the coins he had won into the pockets of his pants. "You're wet." He licked his lips as he grabbed Eden's cunt through her drenched leggings.

Eden grabbed Terry's wrist and brought his hand up to her mouth. She sucked on his fingers sensually and Terry couldn't help getting hard in his parachute pants. "I found an orgy room!" She exclaimed, totally excited.

"What?" Terry couldn't believe his ears. "What are we waiting for?"

Eden squeezed his hard cock and then took his hand to show him the way to the Sex Temple. Terry was so taken by the huge fountain and the carnival beyond it that he almost forgot about the Orgy Room and wanted to ride the roller-coaster. He stared up at the monstrosity of engineering and was hypnotized by the blue lights and the car full of riders that zoomed by on the track. Eden pulled at his arm. "Don't you want to fuck with a bunch of people?" She said, trying to drag him on. "We're almost there. Just behind that curtain."

Terry looked at her with glazed eyes. "Oh yeah. I'm so up for this!"

Eden led her lover to the black curtain and they slipped inside unnoticed. The scene was just how she left it and just as intense. Terry stared at the pile of copulating bodies and his hand shot right to his crotch which was already becoming erect again. "I know, right?" Eden said. "Isn't this the most beautiful sight you've ever seen?"

Terry was already one step ahead of her and stripping off his clothes. First went his shirt then his pants; and he kicked his clothes into a pile against the wall. There were other piles of clothes against the wall as well. Terry's raging hard-on stuck out toward the orgy like a sexual compass. Eden quickly caught up by ripping off her own clothes and throwing them on top of Terry's. Now they were both completely naked and incredibly aroused. They found a space in the middle of the group so they could feel the energy of all the sex around them. Terry laid down on his back and Eden straddled him as they started to make out. She grinded her pussy lips up and down his shaft but didn't put him inside yet. Terry moaned as the lubrication from his lover's cunt slicked his cock. Eden licked and sucked on Terry's neck as she could feel his erection pulsing against her. He was in orgasmic heaven as he felt the sexual energy of everyone else in the room enter his aura. This was the most erotic scenario that he could have ever conceived of even in his wildest fantasies.

"I want to be inside you," Terry whispered breathily. Without stopping her nibbling of his neck, Eden reached down between her legs and slid him inside. He gasped, his cock bathing in the warm wet embrace of her cunt. She sat up and started riding him, slowly, sensually moving her hips forward and back. Terry reached up and cupped her tits in his palms, massaging them and rubbing her nipples. Eden stared down at Terry as she moved with every inch of him inside of her. Now the pupils of her eyes were so large that there were no more irises to be seen. The cycling colored lights from the floor illuminated her thin sexy body in blue, purple, red, orange, and then green. Her aura started to waft off of her like steam and then expanded to a field of dancing pink and red light. Terry felt like his Astral Body was being pulled out and he was suddenly diving into Eden's dilated pupils. He was in her mind, in her body, in her spirit as they merged in a snake rotation—a Red Tantric embrace where they melted into one and then into each other and then into one again.

Terry's Astral Body flowed out of Eden's eyes and back into his physical body again. He realized that a very attractive young man and young woman had come to him and were now licking and sucking on his nipples. The pleasure was almost too much for one body to bear and he felt that at any moment his whole body would rupture and his energy would go back into the endless cosmic orgasm. His aura was shining now too and growing as they both built to a climax. Eden's Soulmind was now emerging from her solar plexus and reaching for Terry's which was emerging from his chest as well. As the energies of their two Soulminds met, a surge of electromagnetic energy pulsed from their merged auras and rippled through the rest of the orgy all around them. Everyone in the room moaned in harmony and they all touched for a second the void of the Universe, the nothing and the everything—they touched God.

Terry opened his eyes and looked up at Eden who rode up and down on his cock which was aching for release. She took him all the way inside of her until her clitoris was pressed firmly against his pubic bone. As Eden rubbed her clit against her Forever lover, several men and women came to the edges of her skin. These were the sexiest men and women that Terry had ever seen. It looked like they had been drawn to Eden's energy. They worshipped her like a goddess and wished to pleasure her for eternity. They kissed her skin, licked her, touched her breasts, and brushed their lips sensually against her face and neck. Eden loved every minute of this whole experience and so did Terry. They never wanted it to end. They wanted to form a loop and stay in this ecstatic moment of bliss for all infinity.

"Are you gonna cum, baby?" Eden said, looking down at Terry as she pushed him deeper into her. Her admirers were against her, skin on skin, all fingers and tongues. Terry's two worshippers were also still licking his nipples and caressing his soft skin.

"Oh my fucking god, am I ever!" Terry said, barely able to get the words out he was breathing so heavily. The orgasm was building in his Soulmind and the energy felt like it was pushing at his skin from the inside, wanting to escape, wanting to burst him apart.

"Cum inside me," Eden moaned. "We'll rock all these people's worlds. As we cum together, we'll help them touch the outer reaches of the Spiralverse!"

To Terry that was the hottest thing anyone had ever said to him. On the threshold of the cosmic orgasm, he felt like he was almost ceasing to exist and just becoming the pure energy of ecstatic union. The naked men and women loving on them were getting more frenzied, anticipating the climax. "Oh my

God Fuck!" Terry screamed, his whole body shuddered under Eden.

"Yes, baby!" She said, riding him harder as she panted and moaned. Sweat glistened on her immaculate body. "Fucking cum, baby! Fucking give me your cum! I love you so much I want to be one with you Forever!"

At that moment, they simultaneously had the most stellar synchronized orgasm the Spiralverse had ever vibrated. Terry ejaculated an ocean deep inside Eden and she squirted a river onto his belly which flowed down and pooled under his ass and balls. The energy that shot through their auras lit up the whole room like a lightning flash. Every individual in that room became a screamer in that instant. In Terry's perception, that moment which was just a moment, slowed to a freeze-frame and lasted for all of Time. The rainbow of lights below them and the projections of nebulas above them fell away and became a real sea of stars. The orgasm which had blown through everyone's bodies dissolved their physical forms and Terry could see them all now as pure souls. They were all ultimately the same soul, made one in orgasmic bliss, and the illusion of separation only existed as a trick of space and time.

Terry gasped and just as quickly as the vision had gripped him, it evaporated. "Did you see that?" He asked Eden.

"Yes, my love," she answered quietly. "It felt like you and me were one for infinity. Throughout time. Beyond time." Eden collapsed onto Terry's chest, both of them heaving lungfuls of rich oxygen. He was still inside her and he flexed his cock playfully. Giggling, Eden returned the gesture and squeezed herself around his shaft. The naked men and women who were all around them came closer to kiss their glistening skin. Letting themselves be taken by the affection, Eden and Terry melted into the glowing bliss of the buzzing energy which was still humming with orgasmic electricity. How long they stayed like that, they couldn't be certain. They were so high that they felt like they had entered into a new state of consciousness. Even if they weren't moving themselves, they enjoyed the sensation of the lips and tongues on their warm skin. Couples and groups continued to have sex all around them and they came into closer proximity to the two Travelers, wanting to drink in their energy like living waters of the Kama Sutra. Eden loved feeling the skin on skin; asses and tits and cocks brushing all across her body. Occasionally some horny girl would rub her pussy on Eden's back or she would feel a wet tongue darting in and out of her asshole.

Hours passed like that—going back into a sexual frenzy thrusting with all cocks and wet cunts, then falling into relaxation, sometimes falling asleep for short periods of time. They all stretched over each other's naked bodies, never wanting to leave the *Temple of Cosmic Fuck*. In a daze, Eden and Terry finally pulled themselves to their feet. Dripping with sex fluids, they stepped carefully over the people still engaged in their orgiastic fuck-fest. After putting their clothes back on, they both slipped back out of the curtain together.

The bright lights seemed harsher now that they were back in the hustle and bustle of the carnival. A female server approached them with one of the trays holding an orchid plant. She was wearing the same outfit the first server had also been wearing. "Orchid?" The server asked, holding out the tray. Terry and Eden didn't have to be asked twice. Terry plucked one of the white orchids off its stem and chewed it with relish. He felt the oils of the flower amplifying his trip anew. Eden also took one and enjoyed the sweetness of it on her tongue.

Terry approached the server and kissed her on the mouth, slipping his tongue over hers. She leaned into him, holding the tray to the side so it didn't fall. As they passionately made out,

Terry slipped his hand into the girl's transparent plastic panties and began fingering her. She closed her eyes and started panting heavily. Terry turned his head and Eden's face was right there close to theirs. She kissed the server as well, swapping saliva and getting them both hot. "Rub my clit," the server whispered in Eden's ear. Terry pulled his fingers from the girl's pussy and allowed Eden access. She rubbed the server's swollen clitoris and worked her closer and closer to exploding. "You're so fucking hot," the girl said to Eden. "You're gonna make me cum." She gasped, sucking in air violently then moaned hard with her eyes clenched shut and mouth open wide. The girl came incredibly hard and Eden could feel the muscles of her pussy contract against her hand.

Terry was hard again as he watched his lover pleasure this sexy young woman. Eden turned to Terry and gave him a mischievous smile and a wink. He knew what she was scheming. Without warning they both pushed the server through the curtain and into the *Temple of Cosmic Fuck*. They laughed and hand in hand walked back toward the huge fountain.

"She's gonna have some fun in there," Terry said.

"I know! She looked like she needed a break from work," Eden commented and they both laughed again. They were feeling giddy and lucid from the second orchid they had just eaten. The rainbow lights were spiraling again and trails were dancing off anything that moved. They were in the dream again. And why not Dream to the fullest?

"Have you been upstairs yet?" Terry asked Eden.

"Upstairs?" She shook her head.

"Yeah," he replied, pointing ahead of them to the right of the fountain. There was a huge staircase leading up to an floor above them. The stairs were carpeted in red and the railings were pure gold. There were other casino-goers always walking back and forth between the sections of *The Queen's Wild Orchid Palace*. A young woman carrying a giant stuffed green dragon walked past them in the direction of the ferris wheel. "Hey," Terry said, touching the woman's arm. "What's upstairs?"

The young woman stopped but didn't seem like she registered that Eden and Terry were there at first. She stared off in the distance with dilated pupils as if in a deep trance; almost like she was sleepwalking. Terry waved his hand in front of the woman's face and she slowly turned to look at them. "Yes?" She said slowly.

"Do you know what's upstairs?" Terry asked his question again.

The woman smiled in slow-motion. "Beautiful," she said. "Yes, upstairs... That's the spa. It's just lovely. You should go try it. It's heavenly." The woman then walked away, continuing toward the ferris wheel. "Stay with me Forever and for always..." She said almost inaudibly as she disappeared into the crowd.

Terry and Eden had all but instantly forgotten that last statement the woman made as she walked away. They were too excited at the prospect of enjoying a relaxing spa after many hours of hot sex. Still holding hands, they took the stairs two at a time. At the top there was a receptionist behind a desk to greet them. He was a gorgeous man wearing nothing but a Speedo and a bow tie. His muscles were perfectly tanned and oiled, and his huge cock threatened to escape the sides of the tiny Speedo. The man's long brown hair cascaded luxuriously over his rippling shoulders. Eden was almost visibly drooling over this Adonis of a male specimen. Behind him on the wall in gold letters read *The Queen's Sensual Spa*.

"Welcome to *The Queen's Sensual Spa*," the Adonis greeted them. He stood up and handed them both a towel. "If you enter through the door to your right, you may enjoy any and all of our wonderful facilities. The Queen appreciates your business."

Eden and Terry giggled to each other as they walked through the door. "The Queen?" Terry said, unable to contain his amusement. "Who the fuck is that? Who the fuck cares about *her*?"

"I know, right?" Eden replied, brushing up against Terry's shoulder as they walked. Inside the Spa they luxuriated in the hot tub, then the sauna, and then the steam room. They were always surrounded by the most beautiful people. The whole place was like a wet dream for both of them; enhanced because they were both there, together experiencing a shared magnificent trance of epic proportions and tantalizing sensations.

As they sat together, naked in the cloud of steam, an older yet still attractive woman leaned closer to them and said, "Have you tried the Metaphysical Massage yet?"

The two lovers looked at each other, their minds blown by the sound of those two words together. "The what?" Eden asked, touching the inside of the woman's thigh.

"The Metaphysical Massage," the woman replied. She closed her legs and squeezed Eden's hand between her thighs. "When you go out of this room, it's the room right across the hall. That's where you can get them."

"Thanks for mentioning that. It sounds divine," Eden said as she leaned in to kiss the woman on the lips and stroke her vulva before standing up to take Terry by the hand and lead him to the Massage Parlor.

Once they were face down on the tables to get their Metaphysical Massage, their massage therapists entered. They were two identical female twin clones who wore matching skin-tight pink latex catsuits. They both had on purple gloves with spinning balls on the fingers which would materialize and dematerialize. These gloves allowed the massage therapist to massage a person's *entire being*—outside, inside, spirit, soul, mind, identity, and consciousness. As the masseuse moved her appearing and disappearing gloves over Eden's back, her skin pulled free of the muscle and hovered in the air, revealing swirling pink and red energy within. The masseuses went to work *inside* of Terry's and Eden's total being. It almost felt the same as they did when they were deep in the orgy, yet now their whole energy and consciousness was being massaged, manipulated, and rearranged.

All of their cells were being regenerated and reconfigured. Terry felt like he was made of stardust traveling through a conscious nebula. Every atom of his being blinked in and out of existence in a pattern of resurgence. As they were being massaged, Terry's white Soulmind energy oozed from inside him and reached across the gap between their tables to try and merge with Eden's. Her pink and red Soulmind reached across too as her body was being disassembled and her pieces moved around like a Rubik's Cube. Their energies touched each other like the hands of lovers timid to connect for the first time. But once they collided, they went through both energies like rainbow conveyor belts. For a time Terry was in Eden's body and Eden was in Terry's—identities completely dissolved into the void of silence.

After the indescribable experience of the Metaphysical Massage, the two lovers stumbled drunkenly back downstairs to be pulled like ones under a spell toward all the festivities once again. They rode the roller-coaster and the ferris wheel. They laughed as they scooped water from the fountain. Then they returned to their beginning to gamble the day away. Terry won some more at the slot machines and then decided he wanted to try his hand at playing craps. Eden stood behind him, watching him toss the dice. There were other players circling the table, yelling excitedly and making bets.

Suddenly Terry's head trip dulled a bit and he squinted against the harsh lighting of the room. He felt nauseous and held his gut. "Are you okay, baby?" Eden said, putting her hand on Terry's back.

Swallowing hard, Terry rubbed his eyes and could tangibly feel the energy being drained from his body and making him weaker. "No, I don't think so," he answered. "Do you feel sick, Eden? Weak, maybe?"

Eden now squinted against the harsh lights herself. "Actually, now that you mention it," she replied. "I do feel kinda sick and my body feels really heavy. We should get out of here, shouldn't we?" Eden suddenly looked very concerned.

"Eden! Terry!" It was an urgent familiar voice. They both looked to see who it was and before they were even aware he was there, Nikola was at their side trying to get their attention.

"Nikola?" Terry said, looking at the man as if he just emerged from a dream.

"Come on, we have to go!" Nikola said. He was very adamant about this as he motioned toward the glass doors which led outside. "I should have warned you about this place. When you didn't come back for three days, I had my suspicions that this was where you'd be."

"Three days?" Eden exclaimed in disbelief.

"You ate the orchids didn't you?" Nikola asked. When he didn't get a response, he said, "Shit, we got company. We better go."

Terry followed Nikola's eye line and saw three men in black suits and sunglasses quickly walking toward them. One of them spoke something inaudible into a walkie-talkie. Nikola pulled out a small remote from his pocket and pressed a button on it.

"What are you doing?" Terry asked.

"Improvising," Nikola said as a flying car came smashing through the glass doors. The glass shattered and the metal bent and broke off their hinges. The vehicle glided over and hovered by the three of them. Its doors opened like wings or doors of a DeLorean. All of the casino-goers stared in awe, locked in their trances. The three men in black suits picked up their pace and were almost close enough to reach out and grab Eden and Terry.

"You better get in fast!" Nikola yelled as he jumped in the driver's seat. Terry and Eden took the hint and scrambled as fast as they could through the passenger door. Nikola closed the car doors, quickly turned the vehicle around, and flew back through the destroyed entrance out into the City.

Once they were away from the influence of *The Queen's Wild Orchid Palace*, the two of them returned to their normal state, but still felt slightly weaker. "Who the fuck were those men in black suits?" Terry asked.

"Those are the Queen's Mind Controlled Agents. They're clones," Nikola answered. "You were still under the influence of the orchid but starting to wake up. They wanted to make sure that didn't happen."

"Yeah, what was with those orchids?" Eden wanted to know.

"Even though you're not from this world, and are exempt from the Soul Contracts that we are under, the fact is that once you ate the orchid flower, the Queen was able to syphon your energy." Nikola explained. "As long as you were in the casino and in the trance, she could keep sucking from you indefinitely."

"Holy shit, Eden," Terry said as he touched her arm. "That's what we were feeling right before Nikola came in to save us. That was the most horrible feeling."

Eden nodded her head in agreement.

"Those Mind Controlled Agents will still be coming after you since they now know that you're both Outlanders," Nikola informed them. "So I have to get you back to the edge of the forest. Once you're past the tree line, you'll be safe from anyone following you."

Terry looked down at his hands, they were shaking. The weakness from the energy drain was threatening to pull him into unconsciousness. He fought the feeling with all his will. "Now I know what you all have to go through every day," he said slowly. "With no choice and no hope of an alternative."

Nikola looked grim as he flew the car, weaving between buildings and heading toward the sidewalk that ran parallel to the forest. "You've felt it now," Nikola said. "Before you had nothing to compare it to... So you given any more thought to helping us out? Destroy the Stone Queen for now and for always."

Terry looked at Eden and held her hand. "We gotta try, don't we?" He asked. Eden nodded silently. "We can't just leave back to our world without at least attempting to liberate them. It wouldn't be right... Especially now that we've felt what they feel."

"Here we are," Nikola said. He hovered the flying car over the sidewalk and close to the edge of the forest. Before opening the passenger door, Nikola rummaged around under his seat and pulled out two headlamps and handed them to his new friends. "You're gonna need these in the dark cave."

They took the headlamps gratefully. "Thanks, Nikola," Eden said. "For everything. We'll come back and see you."

"Yes, we can't thank you enough," Terry agreed.

"Say *hey* to Mika'el for me," Nikola added. He opened the passenger door. "Now get going! I can see in my rearview mirror the Agents approaching in their own flying car!"

Without another word, Eden and Terry hopped out of the hovering vehicle and, as fast as they could, ran into the forest. Just as quickly, Nikola closed the passenger door and flew off into the distance with the Agents trailing behind him.

The two Travelers from the Hollow Dimension kept running until the City sidewalk was no longer visible to them past the tree line. Only then did they slow down to a normal walking pace. Terry stopped to catch his breath. Eden was attempting to regain her strength as well.

"That was so close," Terry said, now that they were finally out of harm's way. "I almost can't believe we actually got away. That casino really had us. Three days! Did that seem like three days to you?"

"No," Eden replied. "It seems like it was just a moment—just one blur of flashing colors bleeding into themselves."

"Do you really think we're any match for this Stone Queen? I mean, how hard could fighting a statue be?"

"I don't know," Eden admitted. "But like you said, we have to try, right? *Let my people go* and all that jazz..."

"Oh my god..." Terry put his hand to his forehead, suddenly feeling dizzy. "I'm so exhausted. How are we even gonna fight an inanimate object in this condition?"

"I feel like shit myself," Eden agreed. "Here, let me try something."

"Huh?" Terry said, standing back up after leaning over to catch his breath. Eden came close to her lover and embraced him tightly. Her breasts pressed against his chest, bringing the energy of their heartbeats together. They both closed their eyes and breathed in synchrony. From a centering at her heart, Eden drew down energy from the sun and up from the Earth. Both of their bodies started to glow as they were being recharged by the natural elements around them. Their auras converged and grew massively wide and tall enough to reach the tops of the trees. The power of nature and the power of solar was restoring them to their full strength once again.

Once it was over, they detached, and Terry felt totally clear and refreshed—so did Eden. "Feel better?" Eden asked, smiling at her lover.

"I feel a million times better," Terry said, dumbfounded. "How did you do that?"

Eden shrugged. "I don't know. I just tapped into the power of my heart and was able to draw energy from the natural elements around us."

"You *are* the Perfect Forever," Terry said, almost as if it was to himself.

"The what?"

"Oh, it was just something I heard in a vision... The *Perfect*. The *Forever*."

"What does that mean?" Eden asked.

Terry shook his head. "I don't know actually."

She laughed. "The *Forever*. That's funny. Especially since psychics have told me that this is to be my last lifetime."

"Psychics," Terry laughed. "What do they know?"

By the time they reached the mouth of the Queen's Cave, the sun was going down and it was getting dark quickly. They had their headlamps on and the light it casted illuminated a short distance in front of them. Stopping right at the entrance to the cave, they felt the chill of the wind on their skin and got goosebumps as they listened to the night sounds of the forest. The edges of the cave mouth were overgrown with vines that looked like they were trying to choke the rock to death.

"This place gives me the creeps," Terry said, shivering.

"Me too," Eden agreed. "Are you ready?"

"As ready as I'll ever be."

They stepped over the threshold and could feel the energy suddenly get dense once they were inside. They shined their headlamps around. The walls were damp and bats flew over their heads and out the cave mouth into the night. The passageway narrowed as they pushed deeper inside. Terry was in front, slowly proceeding with caution. Without warning he suddenly stopped.

"What is it?" Eden asked.

"There's a drop-off."

Eden peeked around Terry's shoulder and shined her light down. There was indeed a drop-off but it wasn't straight down. It was at an incline, like a slide. The stone floor leading down was smooth like it had been carved, and there were small straight grooves carved into the stone in a labyrinthine way. Water flowed down through these small channels like a labyrinth fountain. The channels were just big enough to fit fingers in.

"So, are you gonna go down or not?" Eden asked.

"Just give me a—"

Before Terry could finish his statement, Eden pushed him forward and his foot slipped on the wet stone. He fell onto his ass on the incline and began sliding down. Everything was wet and he couldn't grab onto anything to slow himself down. All he could do was brace himself as he slid the whole way down to the bottom. Eden sat down at the edge and then pushed herself off, sliding down after him.

When Eden reached the bottom of the slide, Terry was already standing, staring in awe at what he was witnessing before his eyes. They were standing on the rest of the labyrinthine fountain. The water that trickled down the incline joined a flat circular surface that was carved in the same pattern. The flat stone Terry and Eden were standing on was shaped more like a donut because the center of the circle was hollowed out for a pool of water. And in this pool of water stood the Stone Queen! Light poured up from the water below her, bathing her in a soft illumination. She looked like she had been petrified instantly. Her hands where up as if she were about to pounce and her face was drawn in a snarl. Her eyes were intense even in stone. Her hair was flowing up all around her head as if it had been frozen while floating in water. The dress that she had been wearing was now gray and stiff, but with folds looking masterfully carved as good as any statue by Michelangelo.

"Outlanders!" The Queen's voice bellowed and echoed off the walls of the cave. "You dare to come challenge the great Queen? I will have fun killing you!"

"Where is she? Is she everywhere?" Eden whispered to Terry. When he didn't answer, she illuminated her red and pink Soulmind all around her and in an instant had her spear in her hands, the tip blazing with energetic flames. Eden rushed at the statue and raised her spear over her head to strike. Before her weapon could make contact with the Stone, the Queen's Astral Body appeared in front of her. The Queen's form flickered and a dark gray shield of energy appeared around her as Eden's spear came down and was deflected by it. Quickly, she retreated a few steps and looked at Terry who also had his Soulmind weapon out now. "I thought Mika'el said that she couldn't affect the physical world," Eden commented.

"I guess she's gotten stronger than even he knew," Terry replied. Their eyes darted around the room as the Queen's Astral Form phase shifted in and out of their spectrum of vision. Now Terry ran around the stone circle trying to get a hit from his machete to connect with the Stone Queen's petrified form. Each time he went to make a strike, there was her Astral Form so quick she was already in front of him to block the attack with her dark electromagnetic shield.

"You puny humans are no match for me!" The Queen taunted. "I eat your energy for breakfast! Or don't you remember how I was draining you while you were having fun at my Palace?" She laughed at their pathetic efforts.

Even when Eden joined the attack and both her and Terry tried to get a hit on the statue at the same time, the Queen was too quick, and she had the ability to project multiple shields around the room simultaneously. So any joint effort that the two made together was blocked at the same time.

As Terry and Eden were getting tired out and irritated, that's when the Queen decided to go on the offensive. Running around and swinging his blade over and over had exhausted Terry and now his pace had considerably slowed. Eden was standing still with her spear in front of her, but she was unable to think of a new strategy that might break through the Queen's defenses.

"I have split this world in two," the Queen's voice echoed and bounced off the rock walls. "I have divided and conquered, fracturing all unity into an endless duality. Don't try to heal the split, it is useless. You'll only end up fragmenting yourselves."

"Where'd she go?" Terry panted. Eden shook her head. They couldn't see her Astral Form but they could hear her cackling at an almost deafening roar. Suddenly she became visible in front of them and shot spikes of gray energy out from her body. The attack was too quick and neither Eden nor Terry had time to block it. The spikes ripped through their tender flesh like razor blades. Their clothes were reduced to tatters and blood gushed from a plethora of cuts all up and down their bodies. Terry fell to his knees, almost dropping his machete in the process. Eden was still standing, but she was weak and could barely hold up the heft of her spear. Terry was on the brink of giving up hope. The thought flashed across his mind that this was how he was going to die—in a dark cave, at the foot of an idol of an wicked Queen.

"Submit!" The Queen bellowed. "You're no match for me even in my non-physical manifestation!" Her Astral Body flickered and appeared right in front of the statue of herself. After swirling her hands in front of her chest and then raising her arms out to the side, a sphere of dark energy grew out of her and surrounded her Astral Body and her physical body petrified in stone.

"She's blocking us at every turn!" Terry yelled to Eden. "How are we supposed to break through her defenses? I feel like my body is about to shatter!"

"What did Mika'el say about Darren concentrating his energy into a Singularity?" Eden asked, blood dripping profusely down her body.

"No, Eden! That's too dangerous," Terry warned. "You could die trying to do that!"

Eden looked over at her lover and smiled. "What was it you said, babe? I'm the *Perfect Forever*, remember. Charged by the power of the Earth and the Heavens. You just be ready to strike."

Before Terry could stop her, Eden concentrated all of the solar energy she had absorbed from the sun into a golden ball in her heart. Once it had reached critical mass, Eden expelled the solar energy from her heart in the densest beam of golden light straight at the Queen's Astral Form and the shield around her. As the beam of light pierced the dark energy shield, the Queen screamed in protest, but couldn't stop the chain reaction. Golden cracks fractured the gray sphere around the Queen and her stone body behind her. Light of the sun shot out from those cracks in blinding golden rays and all at once shattered the energy shield, leaving the Queen unprotected. After the shield was down, the beam continued its journey by spearing directly into the chest of the Queen's Astral Form.

"No human can defeat me!" She shrieked as she tried to hold the energy of the sun beam back from her body. The energy of shadows shot from her hands as she tried to deflect the beam, but it was too strong. The Queen's Astral hands began to shake and she knew she couldn't hold the beam for much longer. "Mark my words," the Queen warned. "I will return. And at that time you will regret meddling with me and wish you had left this world to rot..." She couldn't hold the beam any longer and was forced to drop her defenses, at which point the beam of golden light violently entered her Astral Body. The light took her over from the inside and in an instant her shadowy non-corporeal body exploded in a shower of golden orbs. The beam had disappeared also, but the cave chamber was illuminated by hundreds of tiny golden orbs hovering in the air around them.

Terry was ready to make his move, and ran forward to the edge of the stone right in front of the statue. He jumped high in the air, both hands on the hilt of his machete as he swung it down from above his head. As he came down, the Soulmind blade of his weapon sliced through the top of the scalp of the Stone Queen's statue. As Terry's body came back down through the air, assisted by gravity, his blade sliced through the whole statue, cutting it perfectly in half. His feet touched the ground again as the statue fell, split perfectly into two halves. And each half shattered into pieces as it crashed onto the floor on either side.

Terry just stood there, heaving lungfuls of air, amid the spheres of golden light and staring at the rubble of the Stone Queen's statue. *It's finished*, he thought. *For now and for always.* Terry's weapon disappeared back into his body as he dropped it from his hand and turned to see if Eden was okay. She was lying on the floor in spatters of her own blood. Her weapon had disappeared as well. Terry, concerned, now ran over to her and rolled her over onto her back.

"Please don't be dead. Please don't be dead," he prayed under his breath as he brushed Eden's hair out of her face. Her eyes were closed and her mouth was slack. Terry's heart was beating so hard he could feel it pounding against his ribcage. Eden suddenly coughed into Terry's face, blowing his hair with her breath. He sucked in a lungful of air not realizing that he had been holding his breath. "Oh my god, thank god you're alive!"

"I don't think God had anything to do with it," Eden mumbled. "Or, I don't know, maybe she did..."

Terry laughed. "I was so scared you'd killed yourself with that move."

"It would take more than that to fucking kill me," Eden responded. "I'm one tough bitch. You should know that by now."

Terry laughed again, almost crying with relief. "You are that," he agreed.

"Help me up," Eden said. "I'm a little weak, but I'm okay. You did great, love. Struck just at the right time. We're in sync." She winced and held her side.

"What is it? Where does it hurt?" Terry asked as he pulled her other arm around his shoulders to help her to her feet.

"It hurts everywhere," Eden admitted. "But my fucking ribs... Just bruised I hope. I don't think they're broken."

They walked, half supporting each other, back over to the inclined flat labyrinth fountain that led back up and out of the cave. "Those grooves that the water runs through are big enough for finger holds and toe holds," Terry said. "Are you strong enough to climb back up?"

"I'll manage," she said. "I'll have to. I'll be damned if I'm getting trapped down here... I'd become a fucking Stone Queen myself." She grinned at Terry and then winced again.

It was slow going, but they both managed to climb up the carved slope back to the tunnel that led to the mouth of the cave. The darkness of the night had descended on the forest once they got back out into the trees. Somehow during the fight and climb back up, they had both lost their headlamps, but they didn't care. The light of the stars and the moon were enough to light their way back to Mika'el's farm. And despite their wounds and diminished strength, their support and love for each other was enough to get them there.

PART 11

GOD: Generator, Organizer, Destroyer-Deliverer

*"Not by might nor by power,
but by My Spirit."*

- Zechariah 4:6

EIGHT

The day had arrived and the village of Thanatos was buzzing with excitement for the coming public execution—one of their favorite pastimes. They had set up the stake that Jessica was to be burned on in the middle of the Town Square. People were already gathering in anticipation of the main event. The execution instrument was a tall wooden plank with bundles of kindling all around the bottom. Right above the kindling, attached to the plank, was a small platform where the witch would stand as she was burned to death. Hanging down from the top of the plank were two ropes that would be used to tie her hands.

Understandably Jessica hadn't been sleeping very well in the musty jail cell, being that she was just waiting around until the people with the intention to kill her decided to do so. After running such a deficit of rest, this morning she slept feverishly, tossing and turning as her mind fed her nightmares of being tortured in a myriad of creative ways. She sweated and moaned on her cot within her unconsciousness.

The Chief Officer sat behind the desk and stared at the witch woman he had captive. Needless to say, he was creeped out by her and it would be a relief to him to have her dead and out of his office for good. This man's simple mind could not fathom the depths of power which was dormant within this young woman. That fact—even if unconsciously—terrified him. Hearing footsteps break the silence, the Chief Officer was pulled from his stream of thought and looked up to see Barnabas entering his doorway.

"Barnabas," the Chief Officer greeted the nobleman as he stood up from his chair out of respect. "Is everything ready for the Burn?"

"Yes, Chief Officer," Barnabas replied. He held in his hand two long poles that were attached to a collar. "Is the prisoner ready for her death?"

The Chief Officer looked over at Jessica who was still rolling and mumbling in her fitful slumber. "I'll wake her now, Sir."

"See that you do," Barnabas replied.

Quickly walking over to the cell, the Chief Officer yelled loud enough to wake even someone in the sleep of death. "Oi, witch! Wake up and face yer fate! Yer time is up and now you get to meet the Devil—yer God."

Jessica opened her eyes without a sound and stared silently at the Chief Officer who had woken her so rudely. Her icy gaze made him anxious and he looked away, not wanting to meet her eyes. Barnabas walked over with the poles and collar.

"We are going to take you to the Town Square for your reckoning," Barnabas said, addressing the prisoner. "Now don't try anything funny while we restrain you and bring you, or it will be even worse for you than it already is. Trust me."

"Don't look at me, witch!" The Chief Officer yelled at Jessica as he opened the cell door. "Cast yer eyes down or I'll cut them from yer skull!"

Jessica looked down at the floor as the two men entered the cell. What was the point of resisting? She was going to die anyway. Jessica had already surrendered to her own death which was quickly approaching. The outcome had preliminarily been decided for her, so she might as well have been already dead.

And she had become that—a *dead girl walking*. Barnabas held the poles as the Chief Officer fixed the collar around Jessica's neck. Then he tied her hands behind her back. Fighting was useless.

Each man holding a pole, they roughly pulled her to her feet as they controlled her by the neck. They dragged her from the cell and then turned her around so that they were pushing her from behind. "Walk, bitch!" Barnabas commanded and Jessica started to walk forward as they paraded her out of the door and into the sunlight beyond. She had spent almost three days in that dark room, and the brightness of the day was painful to her unadjusted eyes. Squinting, she stumbled forward as she was driven by the pressure on the spine at the base of her skull. Jessica almost chuckled to herself at the idea of this being a medieval version of a *perp walk*. Any humor in the situation quickly faded as village folk surrounded her as she was brought to the stake. Men and women—and even children—taunted her, spit on her, and occasionally would throw a rock that struck her hard and painfully.

"Witch!" One lady yelled as she spit in Jessica's face.

"Whore of Satan," a man taunted as he threw a stone which struck her chin, scraping it and drawing blood.

Bringing her head back up, she could now see the stake where she was to be burned alive. There was a sizable crowd anticipating the opportunity to satiate their blood lust. This was just as much a ritual for the people of Thanatos to purge the hatred in their hearts and to project all of the qualities they rejected in themselves on to Jessica—the witch who deserved to be despised.

"Burn the witch! Burn the witch! Burn the witch!" The crowd chanted as they pumped their fists in the air.

"Back up!" Barnabas yelled at the crowd as they approached the stake with the prisoner. There was a small wooden stepladder up against the side of the stake high enough for someone to stand and reach the ropes hanging from the top of the wood. However, Barnabas and the Chief Officer didn't let Jessica use this to step onto the platform, they swung the collar around so the poles were in the front and they lifted her by her neck into the air. She grimaced and tightened her neck muscles as they set her feet down onto the platform with her back against the stake. The Chief Officer climbed up on the stepladder to unhook the collar from her throat. Barnabas pulled it off of her and threw it to the side. Then the Chief Officer pulled Jessica's hands up behind her back and tied them to the ropes hanging from the top of the stake.

A man in the front of the crowd handed Barnabas a flaming torch as the Chief Officer got down from the stepladder and stood to the side. "What is the punishment for being in league with the Devil?" Barnabas asked the crowd.

"Death!" All the villagers chanted in unison.

"Is she guilty as sin?" Barnabas egged on the crowd.

"Yes!" The crowd yelled as one voice.

"And what should we do?" Barnabas asked finally.

"*Burn! Burn! Burn!*"

That was the only cue he needed to set the kindling ablaze. As the flames spread through the dry wood, Jessica didn't even pray for her life. She didn't even hear the yelling and taunting of the crowd. A peaceful silence had taken her over. It was strange in a way, that she felt like she was dead already. That she had already returned to the tranquil unity of all Existence. Jessica felt like she had in the church within her Soma vision. That Jessica Thorn was no more. She didn't know *who* she was, and she was okay with that. More than okay with that. She felt more totally herself than she had in her entire life, but who that *herself* was actually didn't matter at all.

The flames grew higher and she could feel the heat but there was no pain. The blaze was also heating the metal of the Contraption still strapped to her head. The pressure was felt deep in her skull. Then suddenly she looked out into the crowd and a few people in the front row parted, revealing two people behind them. These two individuals wore hooded cloaks and their heads were bowed down so Jessica couldn't see their faces. Then as they raised their heads, Jessica recognized them—Jay and Magda! She almost cried out for them, but Magda raised one finger to her lips and Jessica remained silent.

Even as the flames lapped around her, she found that her flesh wasn't melting off—she wasn't dying. The fire had become impotent as a way to kill her. When Jessica realized this, she knew that she wasn't going to die. And this realization struck her as an absurd thought—that she had surrendered herself to death, but now she was actually going to live. She raised her face to the sky, to the clouds and the blue above, and from deep within her soul came the laughter. They were strong belly laughs, an existential maniacal response to the darkest joke told by a cosmic jester. This was the laughter of pain and bliss; of madness and sanity.

Barnabas looked at the Chief Officer. "What's going on?" He asked. "She should be screaming. Not laughing!"

The Chief Officer shook his head in bewilderment. "Witches have never been able to avoid death when we've decided to kill them."

The two men stared, and as Jessica continued laughing, the flames began slowly shrinking until they had extinguished entirely, leaving only puffs of smoke rising from the charred bundles of wood.

"Goddamnit!" Barnabas yelled. "This is impossible!"

The crowd had fallen silent as they stared at the miracle before them. Then the fear set in. Terrified that the witch who had escaped death would curse them all, they turned tail and ran for their homes, scattering to all corners of the village. Jay and Magda also ran away with the crowd as to not be spotted and discovered before they could work whatever Magick they intended to. The town square was empty in less than a minute leaving only Barnabas, the Chief Officer, and Jessica hanging by her wrists but very much alive. She had stopped laughing and fell silent again.

"She's going to fucking die one way or another!" Barnabas shrieked. Addressing the Chief Officer, he said, "We'll do a hanging instead. Break her fucking neck. This... okay... We'll bring her back to the cell and get the gallows ready for the execution first thing tomorrow morning. Even if the villagers are too scared to come watch, we'll do it ourselves."

They let Jessica's arms down from the ropes, fastened the collar back on, and dragged her back to the cell which still stank of puke and piss.

NINE

The carnage had been so glorious, so absolute, so satisfying that Trick, Tock, and Tick found it difficult to pull themselves away from that and return to their original mission. However, Maya had been very clear on where they were supposed to go and what they were to retrieve; and besides, they owed her for breaking them out of the Containment Cube. They weren't about to forget that loyalty to just go rogue and have fun murdering housewives. Night had come quickly after they spent the remainder of the day breaking into the rest of the houses on the block to kill time—and whoever was unlucky enough to be in those houses.

Trick had led them to the correct spot and now they stood outside of the Public Works building, preparing to break into the Palace Temple of the Order of the Transcendent. They were unable to find an open entrance in the fence so they had to climb over. Trick and Tock had no issues at all, they shimmied up the chain-link effortlessly and hopped down on the other side. Since Tick was so fat, he was having significantly more difficulty pulling his body up. He was only up half-way and hyperventilating. Tock poked his belly through the chain-link fence.

"Come on you fat fuck, tub of lard, cum bucket," Tock taunted his companion. "Can't you even climb a fucking fence, you tubby bitch?"

"Shut the fuck up!" Tick wheezed. "I got this... When I get over there... I'm gonna fucking kill you..."

Trick was distracted, looking at the side of the Public Works Building darkened by the shadows of the night. "Just get over here," Trick said, not looking away from the building. "We don't have all night!" He went over the plan in his mind to make sure he knew exactly what to do so that they could get in and get out as quickly as possible. It took him a while, but Tick finally was able to drag his lard-filled ass to the top of the fence, after which he abruptly fell onto his back on the ground on the other side of the fence.

"My back ass!" Tick wheezed, barely able to breathe. Tock helped his compatriot to his feet, but was laughing and making fun of him the whole time he did.

"Are you two done fucking around fucking each other and ready to finish this?" Trick said, irritated that it was taking them so long to even get into the building.

"Yes, sir, Trick, sir, master," Tock giggled and gave him a Nazi salute. "Sieg Heil, you fuckface." Tock couldn't stop laughing like a deranged maniac.

Trick punched Tock in the side of the head and said, "Let's get the fuck going. We don't have time for your crackheadery."

Tock rubbed the side of his head as he and Tick trailed behind their leader as he went to the door leading to the Public Works Building stairwell. He brought his club-sized fist down on the door handle and it snapped off like it was a plastic toy. Sticking his hand in the doorknob hole, Trick flung the door open to reveal the dark dank stairwell within.

"He fucked that door up!" Tick said, cackling like a lunatic.

"Let's go, ladies," Trick said as he entered through the broken door followed by the other two. It took them much less time to climb the stairs than it did to climb the fence. When they reached the dead end at the top of the stairwell, Trick stared at the smooth black portal that was the entrance to the Palace Temple once unlocked. He punched the closed gateway hard enough for cracks to spread all through it like a spider web.

"How are we supposed to get through?" Tock asked. "You didn't think about this, did ya? Did ya?"

"Shut your fucking mouth before I shut it permanently," Trick said, using his hand to push Tock's face away from him. Then he opened his palm and let the black ropes of the Dark Tethers start dancing on its surface. Smashing his palm against the closed portal, in the middle of the cracks, allowed the black energy ropes to slither inside and work their magic. Green light began to shine from between the cracks, the portal was trying to fight back against the intrusion but ultimately failed. Finally the green illumination broke free and dispersed through the rigid black surface, destroying its particles at a molecular level. This artificially allowed the portal to appear, like ripples on the surface of a pond. However, since it was forced open, it was unstable and it flickered occasionally like static on a broken television.

"Let's go boys," Trick said. "And I don't want to have to tell you to shut your fucking mouths when we're on the other side. Let's get in and get out unnoticed."

Trick slipped through the broken portal followed by Tock and Tick. When they were on the other side, Trick put his finger up to his lips and then motioned for them to follow him down the hallway. It was dark and silent in the hallways of the Palace Temple. Arash and all the women of the Order had retired to their chambers for the night. The three trespassers tiptoed down the hallway toward the door to the Library. When they were outside the door, Trick stopped for a moment.

"Oh Lordy," Tock whispered. "I can't believe we broke into the Palace of the Order. We're so naughty! If they only knew it was us, they'd—"

"Shut up your fucking anus-face!" Trick said in a harsh whisper as he closed his hand over Tock's mouth. When he took his hand away, Tock didn't dare to speak again.

As quietly as possible, Trick opened the door to the Library. Even in the darkness, he could make out the layout of the room. The first thing he saw was the large open area in the middle of the room where the members of the Order could sit and read. And all surrounding this open area were the bookshelves stocked with every piece of writing imaginable. Tock pointed over to the side as they entered the room, and there was the glass case with the cylinders with the Soulminds. The light from the Soulmind energy shone brightly in the darkness. Trick nodded and they approached the case quietly.

He stood, staring through the glass, confused that there were two cylinders—one with a purple light dancing within and the other with white. "There's two..." Tock said in a low whisper.

"I can see that, you mo-tard," Trick shot back. "Which one are we supposed to bring back to Maya?"

Tock shrugged. "Don't ask the mo-tard... Besides, you're the one she gave all that info to. Don't act like I'm the stupid one when *you* should know this."

Trick didn't like not knowing what the plan was or what he was supposed to do. "Fuck it," he said finally. "Be ready to run. I'm gonna smash this glass and just take both of them. It'll be kinda loud so we're gonna have to be quick in getting the fuck out of here."

Trick punched the glass with his enormous fist, shattering the glass loudly in the silence of the Palace Temple. He grabbed one cylinder in each hand and then immediately ran for the door. Tock and Tick followed quickly behind him as he exited the Library and jetted down the hallway, making a break for the portal before it shorted out and collapsed into itself. They didn't have time to look back to see if anyone had heard the noise and was following them now. The portal was flickering even worse and Trick knew they only had moments to make it back through. He was the first to go back through. It was painful and he could feel an electric shock as he crossed to the other side. In a second Tock and Tick were back through, yelling out in pain from the mild electrocution.

Just a moment after they were all back through the portal, it ruptured, and where the rippled surface was turned back to a concrete wall riddled with cracks and fractures. "We did it! We did it!" Tock exclaimed, jumping up and down and dancing in victory. "The Order of the Transcendent can suck my swollen cock! They can fucking try to police these nuts!" He grabbed his crotch and spat on the wall.

"Do you still have them?" Tick asked. Trick opened his hands and showed that he still had both cylinders.

"Let's get these back to Maya," Trick said, starting to walk down the stairs. "You know how long she's been waiting for this. How long *we've* been waiting for this..."

Tock and Tick didn't quite understand what Trick meant by that, but they knew that an Event was about to take place that would alter the fabric of the Spiralverse forever. They followed their leader down the stairs and back out into the night air toward the fence where they had climbed over.

"Do we have to climb that again?" Tick moaned.

"You know what? Fuck this fence," Trick said. "Tock, hold these for a second." He handed the two cylinders to Tock who held them as if they were the most expensive china in the world. Trick grabbed the chain-link fence and tore it like it was a piece of paper. Bending the metal, be made a big enough tear for them to walk through. "Gimme those back now. I don't fucking trust you." He took the cylinders back from Tock and then they all slipped through the tear in the fence onto the suburban sidewalk again.

The audacity of hope, Maya thought to herself as she was waiting in Rob's bedroom. *Dare I hope that the three idiots can pull this off and I'll actually be able to manifest my ultimate plan?* Even though she was a creature of the Shadow, she still had the capacity for optimism and hope despite all odds. Why would the Powers—the *Shadow Forces*—have used Arash to bring her a Final Solution if it was all going to be a failure anyway? There would be no reasonable reason for that outcome. And through this logic, Maya was confident that Fate, or Destiny, or Whatever had smiled on her enough to reward her perseverance.

Trick, Tock, and Tick entered the room as she was immersed in the stream of thought she was reveling in. As Maya looked up at the three who stood before her, she smiled—which was something she didn't do very often. "Please tell me you got it," she said.

Trick stepped forward and opened his hands, revealing the two cylinders, one with purple and one with white. Maya clapped her hands together. "I can't believe you actually pulled it off!" She squealed. "I underestimated you, I have to admit... Well, I knew you could do it, just thought you'd have a bit more difficulty is all." She took both cylinders from Trick and studied them. "I only needed the white one, which is the piece of Terry's Soulmind. I don't know where this purple one is from though..." Maya opened one of the drawers in Rob's desk and stashed away the cylinder which contained the piece of Jessica's Soulmind. Then she held up the other cylinder; the light from the piece of Terry's Soulmind illuminated her face. Her completely black eyes were wide and drinking in the energy. She began to laugh softly—a victory laugh. Then the laugh grew louder, bellowing from her diaphragm and vocal cords. "This is it! Finally I have you, Terry!"

Maya cracked the glass cylinder in half and the Soulmind light floated into the air. Before it could fly away and disappear, she lunged her face forward and inhaled the energy into her nose and mouth. Trails of the light also swam into the ducts at the corners of her eyes. Trick, Tock, and Tick stared, hanging on every move that Maya made.

"I can feel him inside me," she breathed. "It's glorious!" Then she looked at her three servants from the Dark. "Are you ready for what comes next? Your petty little breaking and entering is nothing compared to the power we're about to unleash."

TEN

Club *angelfuck* transcended gender, race, sexual orientation, art, music, dance, fetish, Dimension, and spirituality. This was the purpose to why Darren had created it in the first place. It was a special space unlike any other, where anyone could come to connect with each other and whichever deity—or deities—they felt affinity with. Darren had never come across a safe place like that in all of his life, so he took it upon himself to build it.

It was early in the morning after another spectacular party. Darren laid on the couch in his office with Jade curled at his feet. It was comforting to have his October familiar back in his life after so long of an absence. Suddenly the cat opened her eyes and raised her head. "It's time," she said.

Darren was brought out of his reminiscing about the time when he was younger and creating *angelfuck* from pure passion and vision. "Time for what?" He asked, looking down at Jade between his legs.

The cat twitched her whiskers. "To bring Terry and Eden back from The Kingdom."

"Oh yeah?" Darren asked. "Already? And you mean the Kingdom of the Stone Queen... Why are you calling it just *The Kingdom*?"

"You'll find out when you get there," Jade answered. "You must be the one to go in and tell them they're needed urgently."

"Why? What do you sense?"

"Something wicked this way comes... A Force that will shake the foundations of the Hollow Dimension and the Spiralverse as we know it."

All of the blood drained from Darren's face and he went pale. "Oh no... So them hiding from the danger in the Kingdom of the Stone Queen was all for nothing?"

"I wouldn't say that," Jade responded. "Hurry! You must move quickly!" The cat jumped down from the couch and trotted over to the bookshelf which hid the Little Door. Darren pulled himself up off the couch and followed. Sliding the bookshelf aside and opening the Little Door behind it, he admired the portal of spinning blue energy which led to the Dimension which was now just called The Kingdom.

"Okay, Jade," he said, crouching down in front of the blue vortex. "You keep the portal open so we can get back quickly and safely."

"I'll be right here when you return," Jade said, smiling fondly at her friend.

Darren nodded, and without another word, dove through the portal to the land beyond.

The portal spat Darren out onto the spot in Mika'el's wheat field which was still flattened from when Eden and Terry came through. He stood up and used his hand to shield his eyes from the bright sunlight. Thinking he heard footsteps, he squinted into the distance toward the dirt road and the forest. There *was* someone walking from the dirt road toward the farm. The figure was still too far away for Darren to make them out.

"Darren?" The man in the distance spoke and waved. Darren was surprised at someone recognizing him and knowing his name. Then he remembered the voice and saw the fancy suit, suspenders, and spectacles as the man got closer.

"Nikola!" Darren exclaimed. He was so overwhelmed with joy to see his friend again from twenty years ago.

The two men ran toward each other, laughing with delight, and embraced. Nikola held Darren out at arms length to get a good look at him. "Wow! You're a real man now, Darren," Nikola said. "Last time I saw you, you were just a spindly youngster. How are you? It's great to see you again."

"I'm good. I'm good," Darren replied. "I've been busy running my club in the Hollow Dimension... How is it that you're on this side of the forest? I thought the Stone Queen had overcome my turning her to stone and enslaved you all again."

Nikola laughed with joy. "It's a miracle, Darren. They did it. Your friends really did it! I don't know how, but they found a way to sever the connection the Queen's Astral Body had with her petrified physical body. Her physical form petrified in the stone statue was the only thing grounding her to this physical Dimension and what she used to syphon our energy."

"Holy shit," Darren said, thinking about the impact of this. This was the reason Jade had referred to this Dimension now as just The Kingdom. "So the Queen is dead? I had no idea those two had it in them do something this huge!"

They started walking toward the farm house. "It's been a long time since I've seen my old friend Mika'el," Nikola commented. "And I have a feeling this is where Eden and Terry will be as well."

They knocked on the farmhouse door and a few moments later Mika'el answered. When he saw who was at his door, a wide toothless smile erupted on his face. "As I live and breathe!" Mika'el said, hugging the two men and then ushering them inside. "Come in! Come in! Welcome to the new Kingdom where free men and women can live and create without the oppression of a tyrant weighing down on us."

Terry and Eden were sitting at the table eating hot stew and regaining their strength. They were wearing their regular clothes from the Hollow Dimension. Both of them had also been washed and their wounds cleaned, but they were still covered in red cuts and scrapes which had begun to scab over. Curious to see who was at the door, they turned around in their chairs.

"Darren?" Eden exclaimed, surprised to see him. "And Nikola?"

"We arrived at about the same time," Nikola replied, patting Darren on the back.

"Wow, you two look like shit," Darren said, seeing the state of Eden's and Terry's wounds. "But I'm not surprised after hearing that you two took on the Stone Queen."

"Yeah," Terry said, looking at Eden. "I can't believe we actually did that. Can you, babe?"

Eden shook her head. "That was so insane. I can't even remember much of it now. It's all kind of a blur."

Nikola walked over to Mika'el and they started talking together quietly. Then Darren remembered why he had come here. "It's so amazing that these people and The Kingdom are now liberated..." He started, speaking to Terry and Eden.

"But?" Terry picked up the stream of thought. "I'm sensing a *but* here."

Darren sighed. "But... It's urgent that you come back with me now. I've been told that something wicked is on its way to Chicago."

"Something wicked?" Eden said, raising her eyebrows.

Terry looked at her and then back at Darren. "You mean Maya?"

Darren shrugged. "I don't really know. I'm sure Jade will tell you more once we get back."

"Jade?" Eden asked. "Who's Jade?"

"Jade's my October," Darren answered.

"She's back with you?" Eden asked. Darren had told her about his October, but she hadn't known her by name. "When did that happen?"

"She showed up right after you two left," Darren responded. "I'm sorry to rush you, but we gotta go."

Terry and Eden stood up from their chairs and pushed them back into the table. Nikola and Mika'el turned their attention back to their friends when they noticed the movement. "Leaving so soon?" Nikola asked.

"Yeah," Darren said. "Sorry to rush off like this, but there's stuff going on in the Hollow Dimension that demands our immediate attention."

Mika'el nodded. "We understand. That's the life of a pan-dimensional being... Come back and see us any time. You may be surprised how The Kingdom will change now that we ain't divided." He and Nikola walked over to the three Travelers from the Hollow Dimension and embraced them all in a group hug.

"Thank you so much for everything. Both of you," Eden said to Mika'el and Nikola.

"Yes," Terry agreed. "For everything. We can't thank you enough."

"Now get going," Nikola said, ushering them toward the door.

The two old friends Mika'el and Nikola watched from in front of the doorway as the Travelers walked back to the flat spot in the wheat field. They all stood in a circle facing each other. "How do we get back through the portal?" Terry asked.

Darren winked at him. "It's my secret little trick," he answered and raised his hand into the air. "We wish to return!"

After Darren made this command, a vortex of blue energy appeared above their heads and a silver rope descended toward them from the center. Before they initiated the return journey, they all turned and waved goodbye to the old farmer and the inventor who waved back to them from the farmhouse.

"Grab ahold," Darren said. They all grasped the rope at the same time and they were pulled up and through the spiraling blue vortex of energy. Once they were through, it disappeared, closing the portal behind them.

They were all ejected from the portal on the other side, through the Little Door and onto the floor. As they laid there, trying to recalibrate themselves to the Hollow Dimension, the furry face of Jade smiled down at them. "You made it," the cat said. "Feels like it was only a moment ago that you left."

Darren sat up on the carpet. "Eden. Terry. This is Jade, my October," he said, introducing them all.

Eden and Terry were sitting up now also, but they weren't quite ready to stand all the way onto their feet. "Oh, hey. Aren't you adorable," Terry said to the cat. "Do you know Remius?"

Jade winked at Terry in a strange feline way. "All us Octobers know each other," she answered.

"So what is this about something dangerous headed our way?" Eden asked, quick to get to the point.

"Ah, yes, that little inconvenience," Jade continued. "Maya has finally acquired what she was after... In spite of your little hide-and-seek routine."

Terry's jaw dropped. "How? I mean... There's no fucking way she..." Suddenly a memory flashed in his mind. It was back when they had all broken into the Public Works building. He remembered Leeah extracting a piece of his Soulmind and putting it into a glass cylinder. "Oh my god... Oh shit..." He couldn't believe it. "No matter what I did, she still would have gotten a piece of my Soulmind." Terry shook his head, frustrated.

Eden squeezed Terry's hand. "It's okay, babe. I don't know how she could have gotten the piece of you, but it wasn't your fault. You did everything you could."

"I know exactly how she got it. Well, not how she got it, but where it came from," Terry said. "I'm so stupid... Some weird lady with blue hair had a piece of my Soulmind that she trapped in a jar. Maya must have found out about it and was able to steal it." Eden looked confused. "It's a long story," Terry added. "Which obviously we don't have time for if Maya's on her way to Chicago. That's where I guarantee that she'll rip open the fabric between the Hollow Dimension and the Dark Tethers."

"Oh fuck," Eden said, putting her hand up to her mouth, her eyes wide. "We're so fucked... Are we fucked?"

"I don't know," Terry admitted. "I mean, we did destroy the Stone Queen and that took a lot of power." He thought for a second. "Okay, we might have a chance to stop Maya and those three weird fucking crackheads if we combine our power and efforts—me and you, and Darren, and Mothman and Rob."

"Do we have time to go back to your house and get them?" Eden asked. "Assuming that they're still there."

Darren cleared his throat. "I can help," he said. "What can I do?"

Terry reached into his winter coat pocket for the keys to his van. Luckily he and Eden remembered to bring their coats back with them through the portal. "Okay, Darren," Terry said, handing Darren the keys. "You go drive as fast as you can back to my house and pick up my friends Mothman and Rob—they have Soulminds too so they can help us fight Maya and whatever she summons from the Dark Tethers. My home address is programmed in the GPS that's in the glovebox."

Darren stood up and went to grab his coat which was draped over the arm of a couch. "I'm on it," he said. "You can count on me."

"Thanks," Terry responded. "When you get back into the city, just park it here by your club again so we know where it is when this is all over. Me and Eden will try to find Maya and intercept her before she can do any real damage... If we're lucky."

"Got it," Darren said, swinging the van keys around his finger. "You coming with me, Jade?"

"Of course," the October replied.

Before Eden or Terry could say anything more, Darren was out the door of the office, followed by the cat, and off to get Rob and Mothman. Eden stared at Terry in silence, not knowing what to say. A sense of dread was growing in the pit of her stomach. "Oh my god, Terry," she whispered. "Is this the end? The end of everything?"

"No," Terry shook his head. "There is no end and there is no beginning—just transitions."

"What's going to happen?"

"I'm not sure," Terry admitted reluctantly. "But you'll be safe to expect the worst... and then multiply it by a thousand."

Eden swallowed the lump in her throat. "Do we have a choice other than to go out there and face it?"

Terry shook his head. "None whatsoever."

ELEVEN

There was a hollow sense of the inevitability of death hovering around Jessica. It was night, but she couldn't sleep because she wasn't able to stop imagining how it would feel to be hung until her neck broke and she finally died choking. She had cycled through all the different emotions regarding her own death. At one point she had craved the sweet release of death. Then she just surrendered to the prospect, feeling neutral and not positive or negative toward it. Now another feeling was growing within her—the desire to live. Strange as this may have been to her, she felt a certain inevitability to this new perspective. That this whole ordeal was actually revealing to her that truly she wanted to live.

The Chief Officer had been charged with the duty of keeping an eye on her overnight in case she tried any *funny business*, as Barnabas had put it. He had tried to stay awake, but was now snoring in the chair behind his desk, drool dripping from the corner of his mouth. Feeling despondent, Jessica wished that there was some trick she could pull to help her escape this nightmare and return to the safety of Jay and Magda's cottage. *That's right, Jay and Magda,* she thought. That had been unmistakably them in the crowd while Barnabas had attempted to burn her to death. Why did they run away instead of coming to her rescue? Jessica wondered if there was a possibility that she had hallucinated them after all, and that they weren't actually there at all.

Dragging herself off the cot, she walked over to the bars of the cell and started banging her head against the metal. The Contraption on her head struck the bars with a loud clanging sound. The noise was interrupting the Chief Officer's sleep and he began to mumble and stir as he came back to consciousness. Jessica heard footsteps and suddenly Barnabas came through the door and into the room. He looked wild with the most intense rage burning behind his eyes.

"Wake up!" Barnabas yelled and pounded on the oak desk. The Chief Officer jerked awake and almost fell out of his chair from surprise.

"B-Barnabas," he stammered. "I had just rested my eyes for a second. I wasn't slacking in my duty, sir. I swears." The Chief Officer wiped the drool from his chin with the back of his hand.

"I couldn't sleep all night thinking about how this little bitch cheated our execution," Barnabas growled, glaring at Jessica who had stopped hitting her head against the bars of the cell. "It haunted me and haunted me. Then I realized that we need to teach her a lesson. Teach her some humility. Teach her to fear us."

"S-sir?" The Chief Officer said, not quite awake or understanding what exactly was happening.

Barnabas pointed at Jessica. "Go on. Open the cell. Get your sword ready in case she tries anything stupid."

"Yes Sir, Sir..." The Chief Officer fumbled with his keys, almost dropping them onto the floor.

"Some time tonight would be nice," Barnabas sighed.

Jessica retreated from the cell door as the two men approached her. She didn't know exactly what Barnabas had planned for her, but it felt like there was a rock in the pit of her stomach. The Chief Officer obediently unlocked the cell and Barnabas entered slowly, menacingly. He lunged forward unexpectedly and shoved Jessica with force enough to knock her down. She tripped on the cot behind her and fell back onto it.

"Please," Jessica begged, close to tears now. "You're already going to kill me. Isn't that enough? You don't have to—"

"Shut. The fuck. Up." Barnabas said slowly and deliberately. Jessica closed her mouth and didn't continue her sentence. He turned to the Chief Officer. "Get the fuck in here and point your sword at this little cunt's throat."

Without question, the Chief Officer did as he was told. The point of his blade pressed a light prick into the side of Jessica's neck. It broke the skin and a small trickle of blood dripped down to her collar bone. At this point her entire body was trembling. The panic had set in despite her efforts to resist it.

Barnabas leaned down over Jessica and pulled the skirts of her dress up to her waist, revealing a white pair of panties. Licking his lips, he rubbed his hand over her pussy mound. Jessica began to sob, choking on phlegm and snot. "Please. Please. Please..." Jessica pleaded.

"I thought I told you to shut the fuck up!" Barnabas yelled, and in one swift motion he tore Jessica's panties off and stuffed them into her mouth. At this point she clenched her eyes shut and tried to imagine that she was somewhere else—anywhere else.

Barnabas stared down at Jessica's bare cunt. The lips of her labia trembled with her sobs. He could feel his prick getting hard in his trousers. And as he started to open his pants, the Chief Officer interrupted him. "Uh, Barnabas... Do you really think you should be doing this? I mean, we is going to be hanging her in the morning anyway. That seems like punishment enough..."

"Did I ask for your fucking opinion?" Barnabas snapped at the Chief Officer, his trousers halfway down already. "Just shut your goddamn mouth and enjoy it." He pushed his pants all the way down to his ankles and his prick was at complete attention like a gay Navy man saluting a rainbow fuck-flag. Barnabas's eyes were delirious as he began stroking himself, the vein bulging from the underside of his shaft pulsed with desire. When he inserted his fingers into Jessica's tight slit, she was already wet even though she was trying to force herself not to be. It was an automatic physiological response. She sobbed harder, the tears running down the sides of her face and into her ears. As Barnabas slid his middle and ring finger in and out of her almost-virginal pussy, she groaned, the sound dampened by her own underwear in her mouth.

Jessica's eyes shot open and she cried out as she felt the nobleman enter her. His cock was thick and long; almost big enough to be painful inside her. She watched him on top of her. His eyes were closed as he thrust deep into her. It felt like the tip of his cock was punching her cervix like a boxer punching his opponent in the side of the head. Barnabas opened his eyes and stared down into Jessica's terrified ones. He had a glazed-over look and his pupils were larger than normal. "You know why I fucking hate you?" Barnabas said between moans. Jessica just stared at her assailant with wide eyes. "Because I fucking... want to be you..."

Jessica was so confused. Already with the fear and the large man raping her, the adrenaline was swimming through her bloodstream and she was having a difficult time processing what exactly was happening. In fact, her mind was threatening to dissociate from her body completely.

"Barnabas..." The Chief Officer began. "What are you saying? This is cra—"

Barnabas ignored him and continued speaking as he fucked Jessica hard. Her vaginal lubrication was frothing up around the base of his cock as he slid it all the way in to the base and then out again until he rubbed the tip against her clitoris. "I always wanted to have magic... To be special and to commune with nature... To run through the trees naked and to cast sorceries from the power of the Earth." Suddenly his expression became red with rage and he pounded his prick into her so forcefully that he knew he was hurting her now. A little bit of blood started to come from the friction of the movement. "I hate you! I hate you! I hate you!" He screamed, totally delirious now. "Why was

I never allowed to be one of you? Why was I born without Magick? You fucking whore!"

Jessica clenched her eyes shut so tight and let out a bloodcurdling scream in spite of the gag made of panties. Suddenly a bright purple light began to appear in the metal of the Contraption in the spot right in front of the area between her eyebrows. As this dot of light grew in intensity, the purple light of her Soulmind also started to emanate out from between the lips of her cunt and started traveling up Barnabas's cock and into his body. The expression on his face suddenly changed from hate to surprise. He couldn't see the light, but he could feel it entering into him through his penis. Now it was his turn to scream, and before he had a chance to pull out and run, the purple energy spread completely through the inside of his body and began to press on his skin from the inside. Purple illumination erupted from his screaming mouth, his eyes, his nose, his ears, and his asshole. In an instant, every cell ruptured and Barnabas's whole body exploded, showering Jessica and the Chief Officer with a wash of blood and guts.

In the same moment Barnabas exploded, the Contraption on Jessica's head split in half violently and fell to the floor smoldering as if it had been burned in a kiln. The Chief Officer, covered in blood and carnage, shat his pants and dropped his sword to the ground. And even before his blade stopped clattering, he had hightailed it out of the cell and out of the building.

Jessica's face was soaked with Barnabas's bodily fluids. Luckily it wasn't his semen all over her, she thought. Spitting her panties out of her mouth, she wiped the blood from her eyes so she could see. As she sat back up on the cot and pulled her dress down, she looked around at what she had done. The floor was an ocean of red goo and there were even entrails hanging and dripping from the ceiling. She could feel her stomach retching, and doubled over to hurl onto the floor. It was only a small amount of liquid that came up, since she hadn't been given any food for several days.

Dizzily, Jessica stumbled to her feet and putting one foot in front of the other, was finally on the other side of that hideous cell. She regained her balance in the dark and a glorious feeling of relief washed over her. After all of that—she didn't know what to call it—she was free; and she was never so grateful to be free as she was in that radiant moment—despite being covered in blood and exploded organs. Beyond the entrance to the building, she could see the light of the moon shining down on the sleeping village of Thanatos, and stepped outside to bathe in its glow.

As she made it onto the dirt in front of the building, breathing in the night air, there were two hooded figures waiting to greet her. Jessica stared, not quite ready to believe her eyes. "Magda? Jay?" She sputtered, spitting blood from her lips.

The two figures slowly took down there hoods and revealed that, in fact, it *was* Magda and Jay. They smiled at their young disciple, happy that she had made it through the ordeal alive. "You look like a murder scene," Magda said.

Jessica laughed, even against the horrific nature of the situation. "Yeah... well..." She began. "I guess, technically, it was a murder scene."

"First time you killed somebody," Jay commented. "Brutal."

"Why didn't you come to rescue me? I saw you out there in the crowd," Jessica wanted to know. She suddenly felt the exhaustion grip her body totally since the adrenaline from the situation had worn off considerably.

"We couldn't," Magda admitted. "We wanted to, dear. Trust me. You created and chose this experience to teach yourself something. And those sort of things we can't interfere with."

Jessica didn't say anything.

"I know that's not what you would want to hear right now," Jay said, genuine empathy in his voice. "Let's just go home. Get out of this hateful place."

Jessica looked up and realized there were two horses tied to the hitching rail that she didn't notice were there before. She sighed long and sorrowfully. "I do want to go home," she acknowledged. "I did learn a lot from everything that's happened... But I'm too exhausted and traumatized right now to think about any of that."

"Of course you are, dear." Magda said, walking over and putting her arm around Jessica's blood-soaked shoulders. Jay was already untying the horses so they could ride off into the darkness of the night. He silently mounted his steed and Magda helped Jessica get up onto the other one. Then Magda finally mounted behind Jessica. And without another word, they rode off toward the sanctuary of their forest home.

TWELVE

"I know what you did," Rahjiah said in an angry whisper, confronting Leeah. The two women were standing in the hallway by the destroyed portal.

"You can't prove anything!" Leeah shot back.

"I know I can't *prove* anything," Rahjiah admitted, frustrated. "But I know you had something to do with this. Waking up to find the two cylinders gone and the portal busted. This is suspicious, Leeah."

The voices down the hall woke Arash from his light sleep. He opened his eyes and tiptoed to his door to eavesdrop on their conversation. Slowly cracking open his door, Arash couldn't see where the two women were in the dark hallway, but he could hear them.

Leeah didn't comment on any of Rahjiah's accusations. "Well, it's going to take a few hours to get this portal up and running again," Rahjiah continued. "But then we all have to go to prevent this Event from occurring."

"No, we aren't," Leeah said decisively.

"Excuse me?" Rahjiah couldn't believe what she was hearing from the current Mahan Tantric of their Order.

"I said: *we aren't going to do anything.*" Leeah folded her arms across her chest.

Rahjiah laughed and put her hand up to her forehead. "I can't believe I'm hearing this. You're suggesting that we sit around here and *not do our job* while the Hollow Dimension gets attacked by the Dark Tethers?"

"That's exactly what I'm suggesting."

"Leeah, you're out of your mind," Rahjiah said, raising her voice and then bringing it back down to a whisper. "You're out of your mind... This is the whole purpose of why our Order exists."

"Well, maybe we need to start re-thinking our purpose," Leeah responded. "Maybe we need to take lesson from the Galactic Federation's book and start exercising the Law of Non-Interference. Sometimes it's better to practice discernment in each situation individually. I mean, sometimes maybe we should go intervene in certain situations, but other times we need to stand back and not monkey with Destiny."

"*Not monkey with Destiny?* Do you even hear yourself? The whole reason that the Galactic Federation created our Order was *because* they have to live by the Law of Non-Interference. They needed a group to get around that to keep things on track in the

Spiralverse. You're talking crazy. Do you *want* life as we know it to come to a screeching halt?"

"And how do you know if things are on track or they're off track?" Leeah asked incredulously. "Who put you in charge as judge and jury on what's best for all the Dimensions collectively, Rahjiah? To make any real progress always requires sacrifice. You seem more inclined to maintain the status quo than to help facilitate real evolution—physically, spiritually, or otherwise."

"Hah! The *status quo*? You can call it what you like, but we're here to keep the balance—"

"Fuck the balance!" Leeah interjected, cutting Rahjiah off in mid-sentence.

Rahjiah shook her head indignantly. "You're incorrigible, you know that? You'd rather see the Spiralverse in chaos then go help restore the Order. Tell me I'm wrong."

Leeah shrugged. "Maybe we need to see a little chaos to shake these beings out of complacency. What are a few deaths in the grand scheme of the Ascension Process?"

"Oh my god," Rahjiah couldn't believe her ears. "We're charged to *protect* all beings in all Dimensions. What you're saying is evil."

"Oh please, don't think so dualistically. And if that's evil… then I guess I'm a little bit evil."

"This is nuts," Rahjiah threw her hands up. "You're nuts."

Leeah ignored the judgment. "How long have we waited for humans to evolve? They're barely past the point of being apes. Some of them even act in ways lower than animals. Sometimes we have to *not-interfere* in order to *interfere*. Do you see what I'm saying?"

Rahjiah shook her head. "I'm not following you at all."

"I've seen a vision of a future that's possible," Leeah whispered in a way emphasizing the grandness of the idea. "A future where the Order of the Transcendent is no longer needed—it's no longer relevant. And frankly, that's the future I want to help create. Where all beings are free to govern themselves, and travel between all Dimensions, and interact with whatever types of beings that they can imagine. I know this: the Order will be irrelevant in the Future to come."

"What?" Rahjiah almost yelled this then lowered her voice again. "The Order will always be needed as long as beings exist. There must be rules and structure for things to run properly. We already have enough problems with the Dragons meddling—along with their *cat henchmen*—in the trajectory of the evolution of consciousness. Taking things to an accelerated timeline could prove dangerous. You know this! And what about Arash? You bring him here to train to be the next Mahan Tantric of our Order even though you think that we'll become irrelevant in the future? Come on, that's just cruel. He's still a child for god's sake."

"Arash has a Destiny far higher than our Order," Leeah responded. "You must know this by now. You don't feel it?"

Rahjiah gave an exasperated sigh. "I don't know... Yes... Maybe. Shit, I feel something special from him definitely. But it's cloudy, I don't know what it is yet. There's still pure potential. It could go anywhere."

"Exactly," Leeah agreed with Rahjiah on pretty much just this one thing in the whole conversation. "And that's what makes him have promise to transcend me—to be that much greater than me. Each Mahan Tantric should surpass the last in marvelous ways that their predecessors couldn't even dream of."

Arash was riveted to the conversation he was overhearing. As he listened, he didn't realize that he had been craning his neck farther and farther out into the hall. Now that his eyes were adjusting to the darkness, he could make out Leeah and Rahjiah's silhouettes off in the distance down the hallway. Fearing that he was about to be discovered listening in on their passionate dispute, Arash quickly retreated into his room, pulling the door closed behind him. The movement was just a little too forceful and the door made a creak and a click as it swung shut. Arash winced, knowing that the sound must have been heard by the two women arguing down the hall. Without waiting for anyone to come knocking, he just crawled back into bed and pretended he was sleeping.

Leeah had felt Arash's presence the entire time he was eavesdropping. The sound of his door closing was all the confirmation she needed. Rahjiah hadn't noticed since her emotions were so wrapped up in the conversation. But Leeah smiled, satisfied that *Lord Khan* had indeed heard all that he was meant to.

THIRTEEN

The sky over Chicago was already darkening with black storm clouds as Darren drove toward the suburbs and Terry's house there. Jade sat in the passenger's seat, staring straight ahead out of the windshield. They were both quiet as Darren drove, feeling the weight of the situation growing heavier. The air seemed to become denser by the minute, and there was an electric feel pulling at them as Maya's plan came closer and closer to fruition.

"Is there any chance of escaping from this?" Darren asked.

"If there is," Jade replied, "none of us will ever be the same again."

A shadow was cast over Darren's face and he gritted his teeth, hoping that his part to play in this madness didn't arrive too late. He stopped the car as they pulled up outside Terry's house. As he turned off the engine, Darren looked past Jade and out of the passenger side window. When he saw the Merkabah field covered in specters, he almost didn't know what he was looking at.

"What the fuck is that?" Darren asked, staring at the strange sight.

"Specters," Jade replied. "I should have known."

"How could you have possibly known about this?"

"Well, I sensed there were entities in the Hollow Dimension that didn't originate from here," Jade admitted. "I just wasn't sure what they were."

"Let's go," Darren said hastily as he got out of the car. "We don't have very much time. The Dark Storm is coming." He looked up at the sky which was covered in pregnant clouds; lightning was tracing across them horizontally. The day was almost as dark as night now and the flashes of lightning would occasionally light up the areas below. Cold winter wind whipped his dreadlocks around his face violently. Hugging his coat around his body, Darren waited while Jade leaped over his seat and followed him into the cold air. He closed the van door and they both approached the house. Before reaching the barrier covered in specters, Darren put his hands together in a triangle formation, jutted them out in front of his chest, and then pulled them apart. As he did this movement, the specters flew off of the Merkabah field and froze, hanging in midair, as if caught in a Stasis Field. The specters tried to wiggle and get free but they couldn't. Darren's energy was too strong for them to escape it.

"Nice work," Jade commented. Darren nodded and both him and the cat slipped through the golden sphere of the Merkabah without any resistance. They climbed the stairs onto the porch and banged loudly on the front door.

"Anyone home?" Darren yelled and looked into the window next to the door.

A moment later Rob answered the door, looking surprised that someone had made it through the electromagnetic shield. "You got through the Merkabah," Rob said to the strange man on the porch. He looked around and saw the specters frozen in the air. "What happened to those ghosts? They're not around the outside anymore."

"I took care of them," Darren said quickly. "Listen, we don't have much time. Terry sent me to fetch you and your friend."

"Terry's back?" Rob said, excited. "Come in, come in. It's fucking freezing out there and that wind is brutal." As he closed the door behind them, he noticed Jade trotting in behind Darren. "You've got an October too?"

"That I do. That I do," Darren responded distractedly. "Let's get your friend—"

"Mothman."

"Mothman," Darren repeated. "And we have to go quickly back downtown to help Terry head off whoever this Maya is. Apparently she finally got what she was after."

"Oh, fuck," Rob said, his face going pale. "She got a piece of Terry's Soulmind? How could she have…"

"That's what she was after?" Darren returned. "Then we're definitely more fucked than I thought. Hurry, let's get the fuck out of here."

"Mothman!" Rob yelled up the stairs. "Mothman! Get your faggot ass down here!"

As Mothman emerged at the top of the stairs, Remius hopped down from where he was sitting on the kitchen counter. He bounded over to where they were huddled by the door. Jade smiled and went to greet her old October friend. The two cats purred and rubbed against each other lovingly.

"What's going on?" Mothman asked once he was at the bottom of the stairs. "Who's this?"

"I'm Darren," Darren introduced himself. "Your friend Terry sent me to pick you guys up."

Rob turned to Mothman with a grave expression. "Maya's got a piece of Terry's Soulmind and now she's gonna unleash the Dark Tethers on downtown Chicago."

"Fuck me," Mothman said, shocked at how things had gone south so quickly. He pulled two winter coats out of the closet and handed one to Rob. "What are we waiting for then?"

"Remius, are you coming?" Rob asked, looking down at the two cats rubbing on each other.

"No," Remius replied. "Jade and I are going to stay here. This is a battle you all must fight for yourselves."

The October offered no further explanation so Darren, Rob, and Mothman were on their own to go back and find Terry. "I guess we're on our own," Rob said. He looked down at Remius again. "I guess we'll see you later—if we don't die, that is."

And with that, the three of them braved the chill and the wind of the coming storm. Piling into the van, they knew the fight had already begun.

* * *

The morning light now looked like night, darkened by Maya's Shadow-energy which was summoning the storm that would bring a reckoning to the Hollow Dimension. She stood in front of Trick, Tock, and Tick in Rob's old bedroom which hadn't been his for quite some time now. The Blackguard house had become a dwelling of Death, stinking of bodies and cloak-and-dagger madness.

"Ready yourselves for Matter-Relocation," Maya said to her three companions.

"Yes, boss!" All three replied in unison.

Maya opened her palms toward the floor and a black circle appeared under her feet. They also appeared under Trick, Tock, and Tick. Instantly the black tentacles from the Dark Tethers grew out of the circles below them and wrapped them up tightly like they were each in their own separate pod. One by one they exploded into a gray and black mist as they were transported to downtown Chicago.

The three Matter-Relocation pods re-materialized in Daley Plaza in front of the Picasso sculpture. The black tentacles unwrapped them and disappeared into the circles from which they had come. The clouds above this area were just beginning to become dense. The frigid wind whipped through Chicago's Loop like an ice dragon devouring all warmth in its path. Maya surveyed the scene in front of her. The chaos was tightening its grip on the people as well.

By this point, the specters had had quite a bit of time to spread their possession through the inhabitants of the city and even extended to the suburbs as well. Tens of thousands of people were now possessed completely by specters. The pedestrians running through the streets looked like violent mental patients who had escaped from a maximum security asylum. Men and women were assaulting each other—gouging eyes out, biting, devouring, tearing to shreds. Some were stabbing people to death and raping others—or raping the dead bodies which were strewn through the streets and the sidewalks.

Maya cackled loudly, ecstatic at finally being able to see her vision made manifest. Possessed drivers even careened down Randolph Street and Washington Street. They crashed into other cars, sometimes flipping over violently and rolling down the middle of the street. Others sped at one hundred miles an hour squashing pedestrians under their tires like bugs. It looked like a war zone—streets covered in shrapnel and dead bodies.

"This is more like it, boss!" Trick exclaimed excitedly, almost cumming in his pants.

"You approve?" Maya smiled wickedly.

"Fuck yeah!" Tock interjected. "Now we really get to FUCK SHIT UP! Let's go fuck this city a new asshole!"

* * *

It took Eden and Terry a little longer than they wanted to get moving. Once they were on the sidewalk outside *angelfuck*, they no longer had the option to ignore what was happening. The wind, the black clouds, and the cold all set an ominous tone for Maya's plan to tear apart the fabric between Dimensions. They stared as a woman with a hatchet ran past them in the middle of the street. She was chasing after a man who was screaming deliriously. A few seconds later, the woman overtook him, jumping on his back and tackling him to the ground. Then she proceeded to bury the hatchet over and over into the man's skull. Blood and brain matter gushed like a broken faucet all over the woman as she dealt the blows.

"What. The. Fuck..." Eden said as she stared at the brutal scene. "What are we supposed to do now?" She looked to Terry for answers.

"Fuck," he began his thought with an expletive. "Maya will definitely be downtown in the Loop. I can feel it." He looked up at the sky. "All the clouds are flowing in that direction."

"We're so far away from there," Eden said, exasperated. "You gave Darren your car! What are we supposed to do? Take the fucking bus? Hail a taxi?"

"Just calm down," Terry said, placing his hand on Eden's back between her shoulders. "It won't be long before they're back this way with Rob and Mothman. We'll catch a ride and we'll all go to the heart of this together."

Eden hugged the hood of her coat around her head to try to shut out some of the cold. They walked down the street toward Lake Shore Drive and Belmont Harbor. There was a bike path that ran along the lake and they walked over to it, staring over the harbor and out toward Lake Michigan. The waters were choppy and churning like the Kraken was about to emerge from below. The clouds above the lake were particularly black and billowy like smoke. Thunder cracked deafeningly loud and lightning shot down, striking the waves beneath.

"The whole city's gone crazy!" Eden yelled over the roar of the wind. She was referring to the madness of the pedestrians and drivers that could be seen in the near vicinity. Cars drove wildly down Lake Shore Drive. Some were crashing into each other and others struck parked cars at high speeds, sometimes jetting over them like a ramp and smashing down on the other side. Every person who could be seen outside on foot was trying to assault others in the most vicious ways.

"I hope Darren gets here soon," Terry said.

A red sports car suddenly came flying up onto the grass and across the bike path, striking the guardrail next to Eden and Terry. "Jesus Christ!" Eden cried. The piece of the guardrail that had been struck by the car groaned and collapsed as the car continued forward and fell into the water below. "Is that your van?" Eden pointed toward the oncoming traffic on Lake Shore Drive. A white minivan was upon them in seconds, rolling up onto the grass and came to a stop next to them. The side door slid open and Rob poked his head out.

"Get in!" Rob yelled. He didn't have to tell them twice. Terry and Eden jumped into the middle seat next to Rob and slid the door shut behind them. Darren hit the gas pedal and swerved back onto the road.

"How did you know how to find us?" Terry asked. "Especially since I told you to go back to the club and park the car."

"Yeah, that was a stupid idea," Darren commented.

"I picked up on your energy," Mothman said from the front passenger's seat. "I said we should just go scoop you up. Couldn't leave you out in this insanity without us."

"We think Maya's gone to the Loop to start summoning the Dark Tethers," Rob added.

"You figured that out too?" Eden asked.

"I kinda picked up on that," Terry continued. "It's what makes the most sense... What's with all these people killing each other and driving crazy?"

Rob looked hesitant, but he answered the question. "They're all possessed... By specters from the Dark Tethers. They came through the same rift that I came through..."

"What!" Terry yelled. "And you failed to fucking mention this to me?"

"I said that to him," Mothman added. "I did. I told him he should've."

"Can all you guys just shut the fuck up? I'm trying to drive," Darren said, swerving in and out of erratic traffic. "It's a little difficult when all the other drivers are possessed."

Suddenly a black SUV zoomed through the red light of the intersection on the street perpendicular. Darren slammed on his brakes to avoid a head-on collision. The whole van spun out like he was doing donuts, black tire marks screeching on the asphalt. Luckily they didn't hit any other cars as they came to a stop all the way on the sidewalk and knocking down a light post.

"Holy fuck! Are you guys alive?" Darren said, looking over his shoulder into the back seat. They all nodded, shaken up but okay. He hit the gas and skidded back onto the road, on track toward the Loop again.

As they drove, Terry closed his eyes and started doing the Merkabah meditation, setting up a surrogate one around the van. The star tetrahedrons and golden sphere of light popped out and enclosed the whole vehicle in its glow and protection.

"That's a good idea," Eden whispered to her lover and put her hand on his leg. Just as Terry had the Merkabah stable around the van, a small silver car appeared from their left to t-bone them hardcore. When the silver car struck the protective Merkabah shield, it exploded in metal shrapnel and fire balls.

"Oh my god! That was close!" Rob screamed, seeing the fire blaze out of his window.

The tires skidded on the wet street as they sped over Clark Street Bridge. There were cars crushed and upside down, cars in the river, and cars even split in half or wrapped around light poles. "We're almost there," Darren said.

Snow suddenly began to dump from the storm clouds hanging oppressively above Chicago. There was snow and lightning. This was a weather phenomenon that none of them had ever seen before in their lives. Daley Plaza was coming into view as Darren sped toward it, trying to avoid other vehicles and possessed pedestrians as best he could. When they got to the corner of Randolph and Washington, Darren slammed on the brakes again. Their vehicle smashed through one of the stone benches on the sidewalk and they came to a stop halfway into the fountain. Through the windshield they could see the figures of Maya, Trick, Tock, and Tick standing in the middle of the Plaza.

"We're not too late," Terry said, opening the van's side door. He and Eden hopped out followed by Rob. Mothman and Darren exited the vehicle as well. They all converged together and stared to see what Maya and her companions were about to do. Maya's black eyes caught their movement and she turned her attention to them.

"It's too late, Terry!" Maya yelled in their direction. "There's a part of you already inside me!"

"Is it just me or does that sound sexual?" Mothman commented out of the corner of his mouth.

"Shut the fuck up," Terry snapped. "This is not the time."

"Watch in horror!" Maya continued. "And feel your utter powerlessness!" She raised her hand and suddenly the whole ground began to shake like a violent earthquake. The street fractured, splitting the asphalt as cars and people running were swallowed into the gash. A gigantic black tentacle began to emerge from the gaping crack in the Earth. It whipped itself high into the air as if there was a giant octopus hiding under the foundations of the city.

"What *is that*?" Eden said as they all stared up at the massive black shape towering above them. The tentacle swung its whole weight into the building next to it, shattering all the windows and destroying the steel. Glass and metal rained down to the street below in a deafening roar.

The impending danger started to activate Terry and his friends' Soulminds. Their auras shone brightly in the shadows casted by the dense cloud cover. In seconds Terry had his machete in hand; Eden had her spear at the ready; Rob had his bow and arrows; Mothman had his small bowie knife; and Darren's Soulmind weapon was a huge broadsword, the blade bright yellow with the energy of his Soulmind.

"How are we going to fight *that*?" Rob yelled over the noise of the giant tentacle as it continued beating against the building.

"The only option it looks like we have is to kill Maya and her three henchmen," Terry yelled back. "I don't know if that'll send the Dark Tethers back into their separate Dimension, but we have to try!"

"Let's have some fun!" Trick yelled and took off running toward the street. He zig-zagged to the huge crack and jumped over it and disappeared on the other side of the giant tentacle.

Eden looked at Terry and then took off after Trick, spear heavy in her hands. "That fucker is mine!" She yelled as she went after in pursuit. Using the energy of her Soulmind, she was able to boost herself high enough to clear the fissure in the asphalt, and when she came down on the other side, Terry could no longer see her.

Taking the cue from their leader, Tock and Tick bolted also. Tock went quickly, light on his feet in one direction, and Tick took off waddling in the other.

"I got the skinny one!" Rob yelled and gave chase to Tock.

"The fat-ass is mine!" Mothman yelled back and went after Tick, who couldn't run nearly as fast as the other two.

With Trick, Tock, and Tick gone along with their pursuers, Terry and Darren were left staring at Maya, alone without her companions. "Should we attack?" Darren asked.

"Yeah, let's go!" As Terry and Darren started rushing toward Maya, the giant tentacle whipped around and dipped down toward Maya. And before the two of them could reach her, she jumped onto the tentacle, with arms and legs wrapped around its girth so she wouldn't fall off. After Maya was attached to the end, it raised high into the sky again. With the black tentacle's rider clutching it like a koala bear, it began traveling down the street like a black wave, extending the fracture in the process.

"I gotta go after her," Terry said.

"What should I do?" Darren asked, feeling at a loss.

"Just stand here and look pretty," Terry replied.

"What?"

"Nothing..." Terry looked around. "Just stay here, it'll be safer... relatively. And if you need protection, just get back into the van. The Merkabah will shield you. Just hold on to the keys for me."

"I wish I could be of more help..." Darren said, almost too quiet to hear over the wind.

Terry touched the side of his arm. "You've done more than enough already... Now I have to go."

Without another word, Terry took off at a sprint in the direction the tentacle was traveling. In seconds he was out of sight and Darren just stood there alone, feeling awkward surrounded by all the destruction.

After Eden had cleared the crack in the asphalt, she spotted Trick again as she pursued him. All the streets in the near vicinity to Daley Plaza were in the same state of chaos. Street lights and lamps shorted out and exploded as Eden ran by them. She also saw a car in the middle of the street upside down and spinning on its roof. Trick turned the corner and ran around the side of the Burnham Center building. Eden was quickly around the corner too and saw Trick stopped in front of a window that looked into the Jimmy John's on the first floor of the building. He turned his head, and when he saw her coming, he lunged forward and smashed through the window of the restaurant. The customers and employees inside were assaulting each other in a multiplicity of violent ways. Trick just ran through it and out the other door, going deeper into the building.

Eden jumped through the window soon after and had to duck to get out of the way of a man swinging a table at her head. All the customers were beating each other to a bloody pulp with the chairs and tables in the restaurant. It looked like a wrestling smackdown. A male employee wearing a Jimmy John's uniform was behind the counter choking his coworker to death by shoving a french baguette down his throat.

To prevent being brained by a chair or a table flying through the air, Eden swung her spear in a circle around herself as she made it to the door that Trick had escaped through. The blazing red and pink tip of her spear clipped a few people in their sides, gashing them open and spilling their entrails onto the floor. She made it to the door finally, almost slipping on the intestines that had gushed to the ground.

Knowing Trick had gone to the elevators, that's where Eden went. Just as she got there, the elevator doors were closing and she saw Trick stick his tongue out at her and wave. "Fuck," she said, too late to stop the doors from closing. Luckily there was a second elevator next to that one. Impatiently she watched the numbers light up above the elevator that Trick was riding up. She hit the up arrow next to the other one just as she saw the number stop at six. Quickly getting into the other elevator, she punched the floor number until the doors closed.

She jumped out on the sixth floor which was some sort of media arts academy, and school was in session. Running past the security guard who was stationed at a desk outside the elevators, she looked around for where Trick might have gone.

"What the *fuck*?" The security guard yelled as he stood up and got on his walkie-talkie to call for backup. "You can't be in here!" He yelled after Eden.

Suddenly she spotted Trick dancing around in the hallway in front of her. He made the *suck-it* sign with his hands against his crotch and then went into the nearest room to his right. As Eden got to the door which read *Screening Room*, she could hear screaming erupt as she went inside.

Film students who had been screening the movie *Casablanca* were now shrieking in terror, scrambling over the seats, and trying to make it to the door. Eden looked at the terrified students. "You can see him?" She asked. They didn't answer her, they just continued screaming and huddling together as far from the two intruders as possible.

"Fuck this fucking movie!" Trick yelled as he punched a hole in the screen and tore a piece out of the fabric.

"Go! Go! Go!" Eden yelled and made a gesture for the students to all run out the door. They hesitated at first and then almost trampling each other, dove for the exit.

Eden waved and jabbed her spear at Trick who put up his hands and wagged his tongue at her. She had him cornered in the room with no way out.

"You think you're so tough with that spear," Trick said, spitting toward Eden's face. "You can never fucking kill me. My legacy will live on."

"I took your arm already," Eden growled. "Now I'm going to take the rest of you!"

Trick laughed. "Fucking try it, whore!" Suddenly a black whip grew out of his hand and he swung it at Eden before she had a chance to react. It wrapped around her neck tightly and kept her at a distance where she was too far to stab Trick with her spear. "You're gonna die choking to death, cunt!" Trick continued his taunt. "But I'm sure that's one of your fetishes. You like that don't ya, bitch? I'll probably give you the best orgasm of your life—right before you die!"

Eden's feet were off the ground as she was hung by her neck and Trick shook her like a rag doll. Trying to swing her spear so that the tip would cut through the black whip, she missed the first time. The second attempt sliced through and she fell to the ground sputtering. The end wrapped around her throat fell off and melted into the floor. "Don't try it again!" Eden growled as she lunged at Trick who was still laughing at her.

The first two lunges with the spear were smacked away easily—too easily; as if Trick was just toying with her. Her rage built to a blaze and the fire of her aura licked around her like flames. Eden leaped up into the air unexpectedly, and holding the spear with two hands, before Trick had a chance to block it, she brought it down, piercing the weapon straight through his chest. Trick gasped, shocked by his sudden defeat. He looked down and blood started to gush from the wound. Eden had gotten him directly through the heart. Pulling the spear out, Trick fell to his knees, his hands going to his chest. The wound gushed and doused Eden in a shower of red.

"My legacy will live on forever..." Trick whispered as his dying breath escaped his lips and he fell flat on his face. The pool of blood soaked the carpet as *Casablanca* continued playing on the ripped projection screen.

The giant black tentacle with Maya riding on it was traveling north and already getting farther and farther away from Terry as he ran after it. His legs burned with lactic acid and he seemed to be making no gains in his pursuit of Maya. So he stopped to catch his breath. The freezing air burned as he gulped it into his lungs. Maybe he had stopped, but the mayhem continued all around him. Possessed drivers, not seeing where they were going, plummeted to their deaths into the deep fracture down the middle of the street. A woman not ten yards away from Terry smashed her son's face into the sidewalk. Her child was long dead but she still kept pulverizing his skull into a bloody pulp.

"Fuck this," Terry said and connected mentally to his Merkabah. The golden sphere illuminated around him, the star tetrahedrons spun so fast that they could only be seen as a blur, and then the disc of energy popped out from its anchor at Terry's perineum. After floating several feet into the air, he propelled himself forward, flying in his light body, again in pursuit of Maya. Since she was traveling directly north, Terry had a premonition that she was headed for the John Hancock building for a good view of the city and Lake Michigan.

As he flew across the bridge over the Chicago River, he noticed that the water level was almost up to the bottom of the bridge and spilled over its banks. The waves were violently churning like the water in a broken washing machine. Once Terry was over the bridge, a car flew through the air out of nowhere and collided with his electromagnetic shield. The Merkabah protected him and the car exploded into flames and metal. For a second Terry's view was obstructed by the fire and smoke. "Holy fuck!" He yelled, realizing that he could have almost died in that situation. Flying on, he broke through the smoke and was almost to the base of the John Hancock building.

Maya was a few minutes ahead of Terry and when she arrived at the John Hancock building herself, the tentacle grew high into the air and she rode it all the way to the top where it deposited her onto the roof. The two huge white antennas towered high above her as she gazed down at the churning waters of Lake Michigan. Snow continued to pour down from the clouds, thunder roared, and the cracks of lightning illuminated the whole scene like a slow strobe light much to Maya's delight. The tentacle she rode in on sank back down and disappeared into the Earth below.

She could see the whole city from her current vantage point. And as she raised her arms toward the sky, summoned many more giant black tentacles all around Chicago. "Come forth, my Dark Dominion! The Dark Tethers of the forever night!" She yelled against the wind, casting her spells into the storm. "Rupture the Hollow Dimension! And bring the whips—the Tentacles of Destruction to the human scourge!"

All around the city, new giant black tentacles erupted from the Earth, strangling the buildings above them. Skyscrapers were ripped from their foundations and toppled into other buildings and the streets below them. Other tentacles pierced up through the center of the towers and brought them down, exploding in ways that resembled a controlled demolition. Maya laughed maniacally at the sight of Chicago falling to its knees. Her cackles were carried far and wide on the wind like omens of doom.

Terry finally reached the base of the John Hancock building and could hear Maya's laughter booming from the roof. Then suddenly he heard a noise that was different—it wasn't laughter and it wasn't the roar of the wind. *Helicopters!* As Terry hovered over the fracture in the Earth, riding in his Merkabah, he looked up to see four black helicopters descending toward him. Why they had chosen to target him and not Maya was beyond Terry and he didn't exactly have time to think about it. All four helicopters shined their spotlights down on Terry. They were so bright that they almost blinded him. He put his hand up over his face to try to shield his eyes from the onslaught.

"Stop what you are doing and come quietly!" A voice boomed from a megaphone out of one of the helicopters. Terry put up his hand and swiped it through the air toward one of the helicopters. The energy shot through the air and hit the helicopter, spinning it out of control and then crashing into the building next to it. Fire, glass, and metal rained down to the sidewalk below like fireworks.

"Don't interfere!" Terry screamed. And before the helicopters could fly off, he swiped his hand toward the sky again and each helicopter exploded one by one like bombs detonated in midair. Fragments of shrapnel hurtled down toward Terry and were deflected once they came in contact with his electromagnetic shield.

High above, on the roof of the John Hancock building, Maya was reveling in her reign of terror as bolts of bluish-white lightning struck the antennas above her over and over again.

Mothman figured he had a pretty good chance at killing Tick since he was so slow and fat. That was a decent assessment since Tick hadn't gotten very far when Mothman caught up to him. Knowing that he was being followed, Tick spun around and took Mothman off guard, punching him in the stomach. Mothman sputtered and stumbled backwards, the wind knocked out of him.

"Hee hee!" Tick laughed, doing a little dance as his fat rolls jiggled.

"You fucking fat ass!" Mothman yelled and lunged for his opponent, tackling him onto his back. As he tried to stab down with his Soulmind bowie knife, Tick was quick at grabbing his wrist to block the attack. The chubby fucker was stronger than Mothman had anticipated. As they struggled, locked together, Mothman felt something hard poke him between his legs. "Eww! Are you hard?" He said, disgusted as he realized that it was Tick's cock pressing against him. Breaking free of the chubby whack job, Mothman backed away a couple steps. He watched in repulsion as Tick pulled his pants down to show his hard little prick poking out from under his fat rolls.

"Hoo hoo! Hee hee!" The fat one cackled deliriously as he started violently jerking himself off. "I'll cum on you to death!" He screamed. "I'll fucking fuck you to death till your head explodes with my SEMEN!"

Mothman didn't know whether to run or to try to kill him again. Part of him didn't even want to touch this disgusting creature. Before he could decide to make a move, streams of semen erupted from Tick's cock like the gush from a firehose. The spray covered Mothman's glasses and even got into his mouth. He sputtered, spitting the vile liquid out even as it kept coating his tongue. Then doubling over, he puked—it was completely white like the cum he was expelling. The stream finally stopped and dripped from the tip of Tick's dick.

"Agghh, this is bullshit!" Mothman cursed and dropped his bowie knife and it disappeared back into his aura. He thrust his hands out in front of his chest, and as he screamed, created the orange ball of energy between his palms. Darts of his Soulmind shot from the sphere toward Tick, who raised his arm in front of his body. Every orange dart was deflected by a dark shield which appeared in front of Tick's arm. "Seriously?" Mothman yelled, frustrated.

Being so fat made Tick slow to react and Mothman decided to take advantage of this fact. He charged toward his fat enemy with a battle cry let loose from his cum-soaked throat. Right before they collided, Mothman zagged to the side and swung around to Tick's back and jumped on him. He wrapped his legs around Tick's fat waist like he was getting a piggy-back ride. Stumbling around, Tick tried to knock Mothman off of him but was unable to. Mothman's bowie knife re-emerged from the

Soulmind spiral at his solar plexus, and in one movement pulled it from his chest and slit Tick's throat.

The obese creature choked and gagged, puking up red ooze. Mothman jumped off of his back and just watched as Tick tried to hold the geyser of blood back with his chubby hands. After a couple of minutes of struggling and gargling on his own blood, Tick fell over and laid still—just a puddle of dead fat in a pool of his own blood.

Mothman glanced back toward Daley Plaza, but everything was a blur through the darkness and snow. He wiped the semen off his face as he walked back the way he had come.

Rob was a couple blocks away, shooting Soulmind arrows at Tock as he gave chase. Luckily one of them found its mark, embedding itself in the back of Tock's left calf. This slowed him down as blood gushed from the wound. He grasped for the arrow but it was made of pure energy and his hand just passed right through it. Rob made up the distance between them as the wound slowly rendered Tock's leg useless. He finally collapsed under a streetlamp that flickered over them. Fallen with his back against the pole, Tock breathed heavily, worn out from the chase and his bleeding wound. He laughed as Rob raised his bow again, aiming it at Tock's chest.

"You're all just pawns," Tock chuckled, looking at Rob with those delirious eyes. "You're all just his puppets."

Rob let the tip of his arrow drop slightly. "Who's puppets?"

Tock just continued laughing in response. Then he said, "We're all just controlled—being manipulated. You, me, everyone—even Maya... And she doesn't even realize it."

Rob let loose an arrow and it pierced through Tock's chest. He coughed and spat blood out of his mouth. "Don't you try to play games with my head!" Rob shot back.

Tock grinned and his laugh got lower, menacing. "You're all so fucking naive. And you think you're smart—especially Terry, it seems. We're all just dominos that they set up, and now they're just watching them fall."

Rob didn't want to hear anymore. "I won't let you fuck with my mind! You're a liar!" Then he let loose another arrow. And another. And another. One arrow through each eye and one through the middle of his forehead. Tock sighed—the last breath—and died with his head falling back against the light post. Rob stared at the aftermath of what he had just done. Blood continued to pour from the now eyeless sockets and the point between his eyebrows. Red blood also dripped from between his lips, courtesy of the chest wound. Rob contemplated the last words of the dying man-thing. He wondered what the meaning of those cryptic statements could be—if they even had any at all, and weren't just the ravings of a deranged lunatic.

Lightning continued to strike the antennas that towered above Maya as she continued to break open the divide between the Hollow Dimension and the Dark Tethers. Waving her hands toward Lake Michigan like a cosmic conductor, she made the waters churn even more violently, provoking huge swells that threatened the shore. Maya raised her arms up to the lightning-filled sky and pulled the most enormous wave from the lake. Pulling it toward the shore, the wall of water fell onto the city, crashing into the nearest buildings and flooding the streets below.

Terry had already begun ascending when the ground below him became covered with water. After seeing the flood washing through the streets, he accelerated his ascent. Soon he was above the rim of the roof. He saw Maya, mad with power, standing behind the short rail around the edge of the roof. "It's too late to stop this!" Maya yelled at Terry who was floating in midair, surrounded by golden light, a yard or two from the rooftop. "Admit there's some part of you that wants this," she continued. "After all, it is *your* Soulmind that has created all this!"

"Only because you stole it from me!" Terry shot back. "I would never do something this destructive! Now you're going to give me back what's rightfully mine!"

Maya shook her head and laughed. "Never!" She made a *come-at-me* gesture with her hands. "You're gonna have to take it from me!"

"With pleasure," Terry said as he swooped down, landing a little way from Maya on the surface of the roof.

"Everyone wants the power to remake the world," Maya continued. "To remake the Spiralverse in their own image. To be the one that the *new myths* are written about."

"That's narcissistic psychobabble!" Terry yelled back. "I'd fucking murder a shrink for less than that!"

"Enough chatter," Maya said, growing a black whip from her hand. "If you won't join me in remaking the world, then you die! A part of you will always live on inside me."

"You don't have the vision to remake *anything*," Terry laughed. "Learn *your* world!"

Maya whipped her black rope at Terry repeatedly. Each time it was reflected off of his energy shield. "You've gotten stronger," she admitted. "That stupid *fur ball* has been teaching you new skills, I see."

Terry, with his machete out at the ready, lunged forward to attack Maya. She was too quick. Throwing her hands forward, more black ropes shot out and wrapped themselves completely around Terry's Merkabah field. It was like he was enclosed in a capsule, and he couldn't see anything because the shield was totally covered. He had to act quickly since he couldn't see what Maya was doing on the other side of the ropes obstructing his view. So Terry concentrated his Soulmind energy into a single point at his heart. Once it was so dense no more energy could enter, he exploded it out through his auric field as if detonating an atom bomb. The energy broke through the ropes surrounding him, shredding them like confetti. Now he could see Maya again in front of him, but the expulsion of that amount of energy left his shield temporarily down, and his machete flickered and disappeared from his hand.

"Now you're mine," Maya said as she charged. She managed to get her hands wrapped around Terry's throat and he got his around hers. They shoved each other at arms length, locked together in a Tantric Death Dance. Each of them wouldn't allow the other one to detach from the struggle, but they couldn't get enough of a grip around the other one's throat to do any real damage.

"Give me back what belongs to me!" Terry screamed in Maya's face. "My Soulmind is part of *my* energy, not yours!"

Thunder roared from the clouds not that far over their heads. The strike of lightning was instantaneous with the clap of the thunder. The bolts of bluish-white fire kept striking the antennas above the two locked together in battle. Snow continued to pour around them in thick sheets of white. Then bolts of lightning started to strike the roof in a circle around where Maya and Terry were still locked together.

"You're already inside me Terry," Maya said as she shoved him back toward the edge of the roof. "Why don't you just stick it in me? I know you want to fuck me. We could be merged for all eternity."

"Never!" Terry shot back. "I'd never want to be joined with you in an intimate way." His feet were about to trip over the rail around the edge of the roof, so he pushed back with all of his might. Maya skidded back in the snow. Her black eyes flashed at Terry as he stared into them, and he could feel her trying to pull his consciousness into her. "Give it back!" He screamed as he pushed his thumbs into the hollow spot at the base of Maya's throat. Opening his mouth wide, Terry started to inhale deeply. His white aura was now blazing around him again, growing wide and so high that it almost reached the clouds above. A spear of white light shot out of Terry's solar plexus and into Maya's chest, reaching in to grab her heart like a hand grips a breast. As he pulled with his energy, Maya gritted her teeth and furrowed her brow in an angry grimace. The Soulmind energy that she had ingested started to come up, leaking through her teeth, out of her nose, and out of her eyes.

"No!" Maya screamed, and when she opened her mouth, the piece of Terry's Soulmind escaped from her body and Terry inhaled it back into himself to join with his energy again. "You little shit!" Maya growled. "What is it that they say in your world? If I can't have you, no one can!"

She pushed Terry forward hard, his feet slipping on the wet snow on the surface of the roof. He couldn't get any traction and Maya just kept pushing him closer and closer toward the edge of the roof, never loosening her grip on his throat. The backs of Terry's ankles suddenly hit the edge of the rail behind him, and he tripped backwards. The weight of his body made him fall down, slipping in the snow. Then Terry plummeted down off the roof into the air, taking Maya down with him.

Five police cars with their sirens blaring and several SWAT vehicles converged on Daley Plaza while Darren was taking shelter in Terry's van. All the vehicles stopped abruptly wherever there was a flat area of the road or sidewalk, as they avoided the huge gash in the middle of the street. The police officers opened their car doors and crouched down behind them as they aimed their guns at the van which was still askew and halfway in the fountain. The SWAT guys piled out of their vehicles in full riot gear. "Get out of the vehicle and put your hands up!" One of the police officers commanded through a megaphone.

"Oh shit," Darren said to himself. "This isn't good. Why the fuck are they after me? I didn't do anything..." Slowly, as non-threateningly as possible, Darren opened the van door and got out with his hands raised. "Don't shoot! I'm unarmed!" He yelled at the uniformed men who were currently threatening his life.

"Is that him?" One of the officers said to his partner.

"It is," the partner responded.

"Open fire!" The first officer screamed into the megaphone.

"Oh fuck!" Darren said as every police officer and SWAT guy unloaded their weapons in his direction. He barely had time to expand his yellow Soulmind into a large sphere around his body. It took all of his strength to hold the field stable enough to keep the bullets from penetrating. The handguns and semi-automatic weapons were emptied straight into Darren's electromagnetic shield. Every bullet was halted in midair around the front of the yellow sphere. He had to clench his fists together tightly to maintain this stability until he heard the discharging of weapons slow and then stop. For a second he relaxed and all of the bullets fell to the ground. All of the militarized agents couldn't believe what they were witnessing. They stared in amazement.

"Singularity, don't fail me now," Darren whispered. He had no time to waste, so before the men could reload and start firing on him again, he condensed all his energy into a point of yellow light at his heart. When it reached critical mass in seconds, Darren screamed and lunged forward, throwing his arms out toward his attackers. The yellow energy of his Soulmind exploded violently, sending an energetic ripple out in front of him. The electromagnetic pulse ripped through the vehicles and sent them flying toward the buildings behind. They exploded against the glass and metal. The officers and SWAT guys were also violently thrown off their feet into the air. Some of them got crushed by their own vehicles. Others got ripped apart by the energy, their blood and internal organs mixing with the explosions of shrapnel tearing through the air around them.

Destroyed vehicles burned in the street and on the sidewalks amid the scatter of dead bodies. No one was going to get back up to resume fire on Darren. He fell to his knees, feeling the toll that the Singularity had again taken from him. "I guess there goes another ten years of my lifespan," he said, trying to pull himself back toward the van. Suddenly a flood of water from Lake Michigan flowed through the streets and into Daley Plaza like a dam had burst. It was about a foot deep and it was so cold that it felt like it was freezing Darren's legs as it rushed under him.

Terry continued to struggle with Maya as they fell through the air down the side of the John Hancock building toward their most certain deaths at the flooded street below. He kicked at her legs to try to push her away from him, but she was too locked on to him. The frigid air burned their skin as they plummeted, and the snow felt like razor blades slicing at them. Maya still had her hands around Terry's throat and she pulled herself closer to him. He tried to resist but couldn't, the fight was too difficult in their current circumstance. She had pulled herself so close to him that she moved and in a second had him in an embrace. Terry didn't know what to do, he felt helpless with her arms locked around him in a hug. If they were going to die anyway, he would want to die loving instead of hating. So he embraced her back. They hugged each other tight, their eyes closed and feeling the beat of each other's hearts. Terry could feel his energy returning to him.

Just as they were about to smash into the flooded street below—probably to be flattened like bugs and contract hypothermia as they died together—Terry's Merkabah popped back out around his body, stopping them in midair and saving them from a certain death. "Holy shit!" Terry said, laughing at the fact that he wasn't dead. He was still locked in an embrace with Maya. "We're alive! We're alive!" Letting go of his hold on the Merkabah field, it shook and they fell into the water below which was only a couple feet deep. Quickly they let go of each other and stood up. Maya stared at Terry with her all-black eyes and Terry stared back. When he realized again that he should probably kill her, she had already turned around and took off around the corner of the building. When Terry caught up to her, she had wrapped herself in a Matter-Relocation pod and in an instant vanished in a puff of black mist.

Maya reappeared back in Daley Plaza. Darren was still making his way back to the van and turned to watch as Maya became visible again. Without any hesitation, she ran back through the rift that the specters had come through. Once she was on the other side back in the Dark Tethers, she sealed up the rift behind her so no one else could come through.

Darren stared after her, and then he noticed that the dark clouds above were thinning out. All of the giant black tentacles that had been summoned sunk back into the Earth and disappeared. He squinted and saw a golden sphere of light floating through the buildings in the distance. It was Terry, flying back to meet everyone where they had dispersed. He touched down next to Darren and extended his hand to help him to his feet. "You look like you just got hit by a bus," Terry said.

"I kinda did," Darren replied. "Hey look." He pointed across the street. There was Eden approaching the fracture in the middle of the street. Again, she used the power of her Soulmind to propel herself over the crack to the other side. She trudged through the water back to her friend and lover.

"Oh, thank God you're both alive!" She said, embracing and kissing them both.

Then, emerging from opposite directions, were Mothman and Rob. "I knew we'd all be coming back here," Rob said as their group was reunited.

Terry looked up, the clouds were parting completely now, and the snow fall was slowing to a stop. The sky above wasn't exactly clear. It was streaked with an uncountable amount of chem-trails.

FROM THE MIND OF TERRY BROSWALD:

I stand amidst the rubble of Chicago and I wonder what the significance is of this whole battle. If there even is any. I look at the ruins of all the buildings and dead bodies scattered within them, and I imagine myself sitting on a stone throne in the middle of it all.

"I think I've watched *Akira* way too many times," I say.

My friends and lovers laugh, "You think you're Akira?" Eden asks.

I shrug. "Maybe... The Awakened One."

"Maybe you're Tetsuo," Rob says.

"Maybe I'm both," I respond.

"Or neither," Mothman shrugs. "I don't know what the fuck you guys are talking about."

"Huh..." I look around again at the destruction. Am I the villain in this story? Or am I the hero? Maybe ultimately these are both antiquated concepts—and I can't be put into a conceptual box. I am just me. And that's all I can be.

Avtar Simrit is a modern mystic and an artist. His writings and art are inspired by mystical inquiry as well as all inner and outer journeys. Avtar's main artistic mediums are the written word, Hip Hop music, and video. To check out his music and other work, visit the author's website: www.mc-pan.com.

CPSIA information can be obtained
at www.ICGtesting.com
Printed in the USA
LVHW020712151021
700519LV00002B/115